MW01673030

Lion Rampant

BERNARD SHRIMSLEY

MACMILLAN PUBLISHING COMPANY
New York

Copyright © 1984 by Bernard Shrimsley

All rights reserved. No part of this book may be reproduced or transmitted in any form or by any means, electronic or mechanical, including photocopying, recording or by any information storage and retrieval system, without permission in writing from the Publisher.

Macmillan Publishing Company
866 Third Avenue, New York, N.Y. 10022
Collier Macmillan Canada, Inc.

Library of Congress Cataloging in Publication Data

Shrimsley, Bernard, 1931–
Lion rampant.

1. Henry Frederick, Prince of Wales, 1594–1612—Fiction. 2. Great Britain—History—James I, 1603–1625—Fiction. I. Title.
PR6069.H7L5 1984 823′.914 84-12186
ISBN 0-02-610500-4

10 9 8 7 6 5 4 3 2 1

Designed by Jack Meserole

Printed in the United States of America

For Amanda, as promised.
And to Norma, for Amanda.

Acknowledgments

I AM particularly grateful to the editors of *The Political Works of James I* (Harvard), the *Calendars of State Papers, Venetian and Domestic* (Her Majesty's Stationery Office), *The Letters of John Chamberlain* (American Philosophical Society), *The Jacobean Commissions of Inquiry* (Navy Records Society, London), *Spain and the Jacobean Catholics* (Catholic Record Society, London), and *Shakespeare's England* (Oxford). I also found inspiring the scholarship of Professor David Harris Willson's *King James VI & I* (Cape), Dr. G.P.V. Akrigg's *Jacobean Pageant* (Hamish Hamilton), Archbishop David Mathew's *James I* (Eyre & Spottiswoode), Dr. Beatrice White's *Cast of Ravens* (Murray), Elizabeth Burton's *The Jacobeans at Home* (Secker), E.C. Wilson's *Prince Henry and English Literature* (Cornell University Press), and J.W. Williamson's *The Myth of the Conqueror* (AMS, New York).

This Prince would make
The world to shake

—JOHN DONNE,
on the Incomparable Prince Henry,
1612

Foreword

TODAY, his Highness lies forgotten in the vaults of Westminster Abbey, a few paces from where he would have been crowned Henry the Ninth. His presence is marked only by a bare name inscribed in the floor. You can hardly make it out in the shadow of monuments to others, which stand also as monuments to the fact that his father commanded none such for him. It is as though James the First was determined to wipe his son and heir from history.

All the men and women named in this novel are real: it is their accounts, and contemporary accounts of them, upon which I have drawn and which have led me to imagine this answer to the enigma of the sudden life and sudden death of Henry Frederick Stuart, tenth Prince of Wales.

[1]

Friday the Third of July, 1612

AS EVER on this day, Sirius the Dog Star, by far the brightest in the sky, was up before the sun. As ever, the world would now seem to bear the heat of both until the forty Dog Days had run their course. As ever, they would induce in that meantime a matching fever in the blood of men and of women. It was always a season to make the Devil at home, but this tenth summer of the English reign of James Stuart was the hottest in living memory.

At the height of the afternoon, in the quiet meadows on the Middlesex bank of the Thames, Frances Devereux (born Howard), the twenty-year-old wife of the Earl of Essex, sat in the shade of a willow tree and breathed deep the fragrance of the wild woodbine encircling its trunk. Honeysuckle was the emblem of affection and faithfulness: the Lord Chamberlain's well-favoured daughter was the creature of a court that trafficked in both and trusted in neither. Frances looked across the river toward the many-towered Palace of Richmond on the Surrey bank and watched a fine, auburn head bobbing between powerful arms as they drew closer. This was the match her mother dreamed of for the house of Howard: after the blood royal, the noblest family in the land. This was Henry Frederick Stuart, Prince of Wales and of Scotland, Duke of Cornwall and of Rothesay, Earl of Chester and of Carrick, Lord of the Isles, and Baron and Knight of Renfrew. This was the man who next would be King, and whose wife would next be Queen.

And why not Frances for that crown? After all, England had already seen three Howard queens. First, Anne Boleyn. Then Anne's cousin, Catherine Howard. Then, more fortunate than either consort (for she kept both her crown and a head to place it on), Anne's daughter, the sovereign Elizabeth herself. True, there was an obstacle in Frances's path. But, as Henry the Eighth had secured a nullity to marry each of his Howard brides, so a Howard bride would now secure a nullity to marry Henry the Ninth. The bishops would surely be doing no more than God's mercy by granting a divorce to this unfortunate countess who, in six years and six months of marriage to the hopeless Robert Devereux, had never once been his wife, nor he her husband. Frances's father put it most plainly when he told the Archbishop of Canterbury, "There is no ink in his pen." And from the King and Queen down to Kate Dandanell and Anne Jaconim, the maids who lavendered the immaculate sheets between which Frances lay naked with Robert, the whole court knew it. Because the match had been the King's own whim to reconcile rival houses, he felt much guilt that the son of Elizabeth's rampant Essex should prove dormant with the court's ripest beauty. And now, to stanch the pleading of the Howards, he had agreed that, since the poor Earl was still found wanting three years after the full age of eighteen, the bishops should right the matter. The case would come before them in the spring; until when, the Howards were keeping quiet about their plans for Frances's next husband, and the King was keeping quiet about his.

THE LONG MAN in the oak tree at the ridge topping the meadow slipped his rings from his fingers lest the sunlight catch them and give him away. Out of sight, his big bay munched at the carpet of clover that seemed barely to have diminished in the half-dozen times he had waited at this spot over the last month.

Always, the pattern was the same. From the late Master Falconer Aston's manor house that she had conveniently bought at Cranford le Mote, Frances would ride through the deer park with the pretty widow Turner, her mother's close friend and the repository of many secrets. In the lane that ran to the river, the girl would slip away while Anne Turner ambled off to find some shade for herself and the horses, and the poetry book she never opened. When an hour or so had gone by, Mrs. Turner would come back to wait for Frances, and they would return home to Cranford le Mote. Sometimes the girl would sing quietly as they went, and the man who watched from the ridge would note that also, to tell the patron who had placed him high in the Prince's service to observe and report.

FRANCES ran the tip of her tongue under her lip as Henry parted the reeds to wade the final yards to the bank. His fingers combed the Thames from his hair, clearing the proud forehead that enhanced his five-foot-eight-inch frame: though he stood taller against courtiers too loyal to draw themselves up to a full height that looked down upon a Highness.

"Fra," he said. "Oh, Fra..." And quickened by those cornflower eyes and those corn-blonde curls, he dropped to his knees to embrace her.

"My sweet Hally," she said, dabbing at his bare shoulders with billowy saffron skirts. "My sweet, sweet Hally..."

"I feared you might not come."

"I thought you feared nothing."

"I fear that."

"Ah..." She raised herself to meet him, her arms about his waist. "When I do not come, it is only because it would endanger us. I am so often watched." That was half the truth. The other half was that Mrs. Turner would stay her, declaring easy meat the enemy of appetite.

"*You* are watched!" He had five hundred who believed that by watching him they served him—though God alone knew how many watched to serve other masters. The King of Spain. The Bishop of Rome. Aye, and the King of England.

"Sometimes I ask myself... would you not be a happier man without this secret to hide?" Frances played her game.

"And what answer do you sometimes give yourself?" Henry played his game.

"The only answer I want, my love, is from you." Familiar fingers teased for it. "Mmm?"

"Mmm..."

Their laughing lips touched. Across Frances's mind danced a picture of that firelit bedchamber in Mrs. Turner's house in Paternoster Row where, as though to celebrate his majority, they had progressed from such glee into a horizontal galliard that had enslaved their bodies, bewitched their hearts and mortgaged their souls. Henry had been surprised, even alarmed, to discover her a virgin. He had never believed the court whispers of Essex's inability, and now he found himself beholden to Frances in a way he had not anticipated. She had been surprised, even alarmed, to discover him not a virgin. She wanted him to love her first and last: she had no wish to be the middle feather in the Prince of Wales's cap. All she could get out of him these five months was that he had dallied only with married women, as though that amounted to absolution rather than sin. The first was at fifteen, and there had been "one or two" more. Henry would not tell her who, which could mean only that she must know them. He would give her no clue, even when she pouted and said she didn't believe he had ever lain with anyone else. He would laugh and say perhaps he hadn't after all. And she would laugh and say she didn't believe that either.

Judged by her maidenhead, her own innocence was self-evident, and there were no old lovers for him to wonder about in return. But though her hymen had been virgin, her eyes had not, her lips had not, her limbs had not, her mind had not. Did he but know it, her confession would take till Latter Lammas Day. Most of it would be occupied by Robert Carr, Viscount Rochester, the King's favourite and the rich prize at whom so many noble mothers had set their daughters' caps. This despite the certainty of some that his rise from obscurity was for services rendered between his Majesty's sheets: services which obliged him to remain a bachelor even at twenty-five. It clearly delighted the King to bestow upon his favourite the affection for which his son had no appetite, but Frances had good reason to doubt the gossip. While her boy bridegroom was away across the Channel for three years, hopefully broadening his education to fit himself for service at Henry's court, she and Rochester had often found themselves together; and one sultry afternoon in his chambers by the Cockpit at Whitehall they found themselves alone. That had been the beginning of a voyage of discovery for them both. He had charted the twin brown stars on her belly, and circumnavigated her globes. She had explored horizons unknown to many good wives who had brought forth a dozen children and buried three husbands. Yet in all those wanton months, Frances had never let Rochester have her virginity, though she was sure she would have had he even once said he loved her. She was intact still for Essex to claim on his return. He did say he loved her, time and again, like a desperate litany as she shrank from his grasp into her own hollow in the mattress. Now that she knew what could be, she knew she could never live as wife to this stranger with a goat in his armpit and a mouse in his breeches. The frolics with Rochester went on until Frances caught the eye and the heart of a Prince who had hitherto seemed more interested in push of pike than of pizzle. And at that turn, Rochester had tiptoed away, for he wanted neither as an enemy in the path of his climb. The secret would be as safe with him for his sake as with Frances for hers.

Now they came out of a long kiss. Frances put her fingertips to Henry's face and looked into his hazel eyes. "Am I the first you have really loved?"

"The first this afternoon."

"Oh, you always say that." She dropped her hands and sat back on her heels.

"Oh, you always ask it."

"Should I not be forewarned which jealous women to be wary of?"

"You might forewarn your dear mother, too."

"I would *not*..."

"...and telling my Lady of Suffolk would be like a proclamation at every street corner." Henry smiled at the idea.

Frances, petulantly, did not. "Do you think I would want my own mother to know I am just another of your...your..."

"My?"

"Ladybirds? Wenches? Shuttlecocks? *Whores?* Which would you have me answer to?" She lowered her eyes and squeezed at a tear that would not oblige.

"Frances." He lifted her chin. "I would not have you answer to any. I would not hazard myself for any. I am here because I love you. I am here because I would sooner hold hands with you than have any woman on earth."

She drew him close and rested her head on his shoulder so that she would not have to lie with her eyes. "Believe me, I have told only my dear Anne Turner about us. I would trust her with my life."

"I hope so. You are trusting her with mine."

As Frances stroked the hair curling at his neck, Henry found himself accepting that he could forgive her lying more readily than he could forgive himself forgiving. Their love was born in deceit: perhaps made even more exciting by the secret meetings, the cryptic messages, the lies upon lies to family, to servants, to friends. Pray God it would not be murdered by deceit. No doubt she had confided in her mother, though she had probably spoken falsely about that only because she would not expect him to share her lifetime of trust in her clan. His assurance, however, rested on the fact that the Countess of Suffolk was desperate to bridge the widening gulf between the Howards and the heir to the throne. They could see their immense wealth and power at the mercy of a prince who had already contrived to have not a single Howard among the gentlemen of his court, unlike his father, who could hardly make a move without them. They did well to tremble. Their new ally, the glittering Viscount Rochester, would do well to tremble with them. If they sought to wax as fat upon a foolish son as they were doing upon a foolish father, not one of them would be left to piss against a wall. After three hundred years of grace and disgrace, fame and misfortune, the fourth century of the Howard dynasty depended on this girl upon whose face the Prince of Wales now gazed, wondering if those eyes that had no right to such innocence had long been the windows of a soul with no better right. Were they no more than reflecting back to him his own image of the woman he wanted her to be? And the woman he more and more wanted her to be was his queen, though that dream had never been spoken.

Sometimes Henry attributed this to a mutual fear that breaking the silence would break the spell. At other times, when he was alone and his blood could run cool, he knew it was because he was then made unsure by what had first made him sure: this tide of passion that drowned all doubts, only for its ebb to expose them as no more drowned than seaweed. But he told himself that it would not be thus once their love was no longer unlawful and could emerge from the shadow that would already have withered a lesser love. It had to last only until next spring to declare itself forever. Then damnation to his father's scheme to auction him off to the Catholic princesses of Europe: blinded by debt to the certainty that two religions could never lie happily in one bed. The destiny of the first-ever Prince of Great Britain was to make war on these devils, not make love to them.

His thoughts ploughed a furrow across his brow, and Frances moved to jolly it away with thirsty lips and hungry hands. Soon she edged back, one playful pace with each knee, the better to appraise her handiwork and the excitement in his eyes as, relinquishing him for a moment, she opened the lacing at her throat and freed her pale breasts to the sun. He saw them as though for the first time, and marvelled that this should still be so.

"Oh, Fra." He shaped his hands to her like a sculptor to clay. "You are the most delicious creature. Would that my tongue could serve you better."

"It serves me well." She opened her mouth to him again.

Henry reached for the hem of her gown, gathering with it a froth of saffron petticoats and drawing them over rose garters and ice-white thighs to the jet body hair whose secret wildness mocked the elegance of her public tresses. Now she lay unveiled to the navel, and he traced a finger between those twin birthmarks, like tiny stars pointing the mariner's way to the Pole. He bent to kiss them, and it. Frances melted, and the sun glistened on her as she spread herself for him. Henry missed a breath and moved above her, then luxuriously into her.

"I please your Highness?"

"Oh, you please me. By sweet Jesus, you please me."

They watched each other in thrall. Frances pressed her lips as her head moved in a shivering arc of ecstasy. Henry's eyes filled with tears, not for sadness but because it was so good.

THE SWEAT ran into the beard of the long man on the big bay. He could hear himself breathing as he sat uncomfortably in the saddle, tugging to ease his breeches as he moved off. His eyes were full of the snakepit of white limbs he had watched until the writhing ceased and his mouth dried. Soon he had Anne Turner in sight, and at the sound of his trot she turned her golden head in its lace collar. Once alongside, he reined to match the walk of her mare and that of the palfrey with the empty sidesaddle trailing behind.

"Your servant, mistress."

She stretched out a gloved hand. He took it and put it on his thigh, where she let it rest. It had lain there before.

"Peeping Tom."

"Peeping *Arthur.*" He corrected her. "And I do not peep for myself, sweet Anne."

"What will you report to him this time? One notch on a tally stick is much the same as another."

"Only to the tally stick, I am sure." Sir Arthur Mainwaring, of Ightfield in the county of Shropshire, doffed his steepled hat and addressed her with mock gravity. "I will say, 'Sire, you command me to speak what no torture could compel my lips to tell another.' I will say, 'Sire, his Highness and the Lady Frances met again today by the river.' And I will say no more."

Mrs. Turner raised an eyebrow. "He thinks that all they do is *meet?*"

"Well, my love, who knows what a king thinks? But I judge that he would not thank me for painting him a picture of our St. George piling his clothes under a bush and swimming the Thames to tilt at another man's target." He put finger to lip. "By my discretion, I serve the King, I serve the Prince, I serve your Lady Frances—and I serve myself."

"Spoken like a Jesuit." Mrs. Turner smiled.

"Perhaps, my dear. But you would know that better than I."

Indeed she would. Her husband, the learned Dr. George Turner, had lived and died a Catholic, though Queen Elizabeth herself had trusted him enough to waive that disability and allow him to become an Elect of the College of Physicians and thus sit in council among the eight greatest doctors in the land; while coreligionists endured the physic of fine and forfeit, and their priests the surgery of rack and block. Late in life, he had married the vivacious Anne Norton as his second wife. She had brightened his days and nights as she had brightened those of Sir Arthur Mainwaring since she was widowed two years ago (and for two years before that). She had been left at thirty-three with a modest estate, though hardly one to interest the already wealthy Mainwaring, who had managed not to take the hint when the old doctor bequeathed him ten shillings to buy her a ring. His aim was somewhat higher. An earl's daughter, perhaps. Or, richer and therefore better, an earl's widow.

Anne Turner accepted this, as she accepted so many of the cards life dealt her and life withheld: so many, but not all, for she was ever bitter at the fate that robbed her of her true inheritance. Her mother had been a St. Loe, sole surviving daughter of the rich Sir William, who held much fine manor land in the West Country. Though he was Captain of the Guard to Queen Elizabeth, his prowess at arms was no defence against a cunning woman. Such a one was Bess of Hardwick, the widow who snared him into his second marriage and put his aging hand to a will leaving the St. Loe fortune to her brood and not his. Those riches had been destined to descend to young Anne, who could have won with them not an old doctor but a young lord, as that Bess who robbed her went on to win an earl for herself and earls for two of her daughters. Indeed, the product of one of these marriages was Lady Arabella Stuart, the King's only cousin and, after his children, first in line to the throne—which was why he had locked her away in the Tower these two years since discovering she had secretly married. His fear of a rival line was such that Lady Arabella would doubtless remain his prisoner until death. The wicked old Bess was gone now, but Anne Turner cursed her and the host of step-cousins who wore coronets today with the help of the bounty that was rightly hers. Some day, somehow, she would get even with them all.

The single asset she possessed to bring such consummation nearer was the eager West Country smile that was her only St. Loe legacy. Before it, all obstacles melted as her generous lips opened on even, white teeth and her head inclined beguilingly. So, she smiled her way into the hearts of Frances and the noble Howards. Into the hearts of Mainwaring and his friends at court and the Inns of Court. Into the hearts of the fine ladies who patronised her talent for costume and her supply of the new saffron starch from France; and her key to the underworld of fortune-tellers who could see a baby coming or a lover going, and of quacks whose pestles could grind mixtures to lose the one and keep the other. And into the hearts of their fine gentlemen, especially when Mainwaring was God knows where, doing God knows what with God knows whom. But he had paid her so much closer court since she told him of these clandestine meetings between Henry and Frances, and as he was able therefore to place the King himself in his debt, she would surely reap Mainwaring's gratitude in turn. The young lovers probably enjoyed the secret as much as the romance, but the King would have come to know sooner or later—and if he really disapproved would he not have put a stop to it in the month since he found out? So no harm was done. No harm at all. The game might even end in weddings all round. Oh, just imagine it! Queen Frances... Lady Mainwaring... *Lady*... *Lady*...

Sir Arthur's prospects were good, perhaps not yet up to his dreams of nobility although he was already Clerk of the Pipe to the Exchequer, the valuable tax-collecting appointment that had descended through his mother's family, the Mores of Loseley. One maternal uncle was Lord Chancellor of England and another, through whom the King had placed Mainwaring as Gentleman Carver to the Prince, was Receiver-General of Henry's revenues and Chancellor of the Order of the Garter. True, on the opposite side of the scale, one brother was a pirate captain risking Execution Dock as he grew fat on Spanish treasure eight years after the war was supposed to be over, but the family didn't talk about him.

"Anne, my sweet. How long before Frances looks to your return?"

"How long would you keep such a girl when you were Henry's age?"

"Oh, the best part of an hour." He caught her eye. "Quite the best part."

"Do you think, then, you might put it to such excellent use as his Highness?"

"Aye. If you think you might put it to such excellent use as her Ladyship."

He took her ready hand and gently, finger by finger, eased off her glove.

HENRY and Frances lay still now, catching the sun as it found a way through the willow ceiling. He was thinking of the year that history would remember for the execution of the Gunpowder Plotters, literature for the first night of Macbeth, the New World for the grant of a Royal Charter to the Virginia Company—and he himself for the day he danced with Frances at her wedding. He could still picture that pretty little bride of thirteen, hair loose to her waist, and the kiss her lips formed for him as he returned her to that lanky bridegroom. Who could have known she was merely on loan to Essex until she grew old enough to fall in love? Today more than ever, Henry hated his father for what his folly had done to those children.

"Grumbling Essex," they called the fellow. It was the only soldierly attribute he had inherited from his legendary father, unlike whom he had little ambition but to be kindly looked upon and kindly spoken to. This one would never be sung of as Sweet England's Pride, the dashing blade who could out-swish any don and out-swive any dildo. In the end, it had taken three strokes of the headsman's's ax to cut him down to size. He had become Earl Marshal of England and the Queen's other self in Ireland, but had fallen out with her and decided that promoting the claim of James of Scotland was a better bet. In fear that the old woman would not die soon enough, he had risen against her with what he deluded himself would grow to a triumphant army but, in the event, shrank to a forlorn hope. At thirty-four, he left a widow who had already been the widow of another dazzling Elizabethan, the soldier-poet Sir Philip Sidney, and he left a son of ten. Within a year of coming to the English throne, James paid his debt by restoring that son in blood and honour to the earldom his father had forfeited, and declaring that young Robert Devereux's destiny was to be "the eternal companion of Prince Henry." It proved to be like so many of the King's vain speeches: the Prince had little of Essex's company, and the bride hardly more. The Masque of Hymen, staged by Ben Jonson and Inigo Jones, was the wedding night climax. Following it, Frances went home with her mother and Essex was soon shipped abroad to put the flesh of Europe on the bare, beaten bones of his Eton schooling. In his travels, he wrote to vow "faithful service to my most Princely master to the last breath of my life," and treasured the warm reply from "your very good friend, Henry." However, when Essex returned three years ago there was no more a place for him at St. James's Palace than on his wife's pillow. Henry wished Essex freedom as much for the poor devil's own sake as for that of the wife who now lay purring by another man's side.

"Hally." She opened bright eyes, and he propped his head to look into them. "What will you dream this night?"

"What would you have me dream?"

"Since a Friday night dream is sure to come true... your heart's desire."

"In that case," Henry humored her milkmaid superstition, "I shall dream of waking to another such day as this."

"My poor darling." Frances sighed.

"Your poor darling?"

"Tomorrow it cannot be. I have to journey to Chartley. I have to."

"The Devil you do!" He sat up, enraged by the thought of her playing the wife at the Essex ancestral seat a hundred miles away. "How long have you known this?"

"Three days... four days." In fact, a month or more.

"It is cruel that you leave it until the last to tell me."

"No, it is kind. I would not have you suffer in vain four days when you need suffer in vain but one. And all along, my hope was that I might get him to go alone."

"Fra." Henry kissed her forehead. "You *must* get him to go alone. Else God knows when we shall next be together."

"My mother says I must heed the lawyers." She laid a calming hand on his. "They warn that withdrawing myself from my husband's house now could lose me the nullity. He must be unable, not me unwilling."

"But you and he..."

"You need not worry. Mistress Turner will share my bed if he seems ardent."

"Ardent!" Henry picked up the word like a flung gauntlet. "You mean he *tries?* You have kept that from me."

"No, no, my love." She smiled desperately and fought to stop her speech from racing in alarm. "It is only that he will sometimes make bold when his men are about. They must not know he cannot do a husband's duty."

Frances thought Henry might hate her if she told him all they had done to keep Essex from claiming her the once that would bind her for all time. Even before he first took her to Chartley, she and Mrs. Turner had crossed the river to Lambeth where, safe from the jurisdiction of the College of Physicians, the notorious Simon Forman dispensed medicines as magical as his horoscopes. Mrs. Turner had every faith in him. Who else could have supplied a philtre so efficacious that it brought Sir Arthur Mainwaring riding helter-skelter fifteen miles through a thunderstorm one moonless night, scarce knowing what he was at until he was in her bed? The women had taken away with them powders and potions guaranteed to render any man impotent. They had left behind a miniature wax figure girdled with a black hair from the Earl's comb and pierced between the legs with a thorn. Mrs. Turner had inquired if so small a thorn would do, and Forman had replied that in this case a little prick seemed quite appropriate. No, Mrs. Turner had said to the anxious girl, this was truly not witchcraft, since witches worked only for evil. But once at Chartley, Frances had shut herself in her chamber, blocking out the light and stirring only at dead of night when the household slept. She recalled it now with a shudder. How she hated the gaunt manor that had been the prison from which Henry's grandmother, Mary Queen of Scots, had made her final journey to Fotheringhay and the scaffold.

"Hally." Frances was strangely pleased to see his face a mask of misery. She had never been so sure of his love as now, when he revealed how much he feared to lose her. "Hally, if you so command me, I shall not go to Chartley. I shall think of some excuse."

"I so command you. Make any excuse—or none. Just be here with me tomorrow."

"My love, I long for the day I can be with you every tomorrow."

They kissed and then fell silent. Frances soon had her excuse. She would send a messenger to Essex at their lodgings in the Tiltyard, telling him to go on alone: her mother was taken ill and had sent word for her to come to Audley End.

"It is as well you will not be away," said Henry, lying back content, hands behind his head. "I should have had to turn my thoughts to the beautiful princesses my father keeps urging upon me."

Now Frances was relieved by the mischief in his voice. "They can't all be beautiful."

"Oh, I have it on the best authority. The ambassadors say so."

"Their ambassadors, of course."

"Ours, too, if they have been paid enough... attention. Savoy is certainly paying enough to Sir Henry Wotton. He is falling over himself to send word that their Princess Maria is the most beautiful of all. And she has quite the biggest"—he watched Frances's eyes widen—"dowry so far offered. Seven hundred thousand crowns. Now *that* would pay a few of my father's bills. And he reckons they could be persuaded to put up more, and Spain more yet. Though, damn him, today he wrote to me that in the end Christina of France might be the most desirable match."

"Desirable! She cannot be much above six years old."

Henry reached out a finger to tease first one nipple then the other. "Perhaps you could help me wait for her to ripen."

"I could *not*." She put out her tongue. "So there."

"Ah, well. I suppose I shall just have to wait without you." He returned the gesture. "So there."

"Shall you?" She dipped to ply from mouth to south. "Shall you?" She rested a cheek on his belly and watched him rise again. "Shall you?" She turned her head and lifted liquid lips. "Shall you?" She moved astride him and drew crumpled skirts clear to her hips. For some moments she stayed like that, matching his gaze, then matching his gasp as she slowly impaled herself upon him. *"Shall you...?"*

MAINWARING surrendered rapier and cloak before he was ushered into the King's Privy Chamber at Whitehall. God's lieutenant on earth could not abide the sight of steel, and his oversize doublet and breeches were quilted like armour against the daggers he saw in all men's eyes.

Perhaps James was like this because he had dwelled in the valley of the shadow before even his first breath, when a pistol was pressed to the pregnant belly of Mary Queen of Scots on the night her husband and his men burst into her chamber and with fifty-three thrusts slew David Rizzio, her too-private secretary. At James's birth three months on, there were those who said behind their hands that he should have been named Solomon, for was he not the son of David? Mary swore to her husband, *My Lord Darnley, as I shall answer to God on the great day of judgment, this is your son and no other man's.* But Darnley stayed away from the baptism, and seven weeks later he was dead: strangled and blown up by the Earl of Bothwell, her new lover, though there were those who said behind their hands that he was in truth her old lover and that the baby was rightly named neither Solomon for Rizzio, nor Henry for Darnley, but James for Bothwell. Mary was dethroned after hastily marrying the Earl and, at thirteen months, the boy was taken from his Catholic mother to be crowned the first Protestant King of Scots. He was never to see her again (nor would he seek to lest it prejudice his claim to be the next Protestant King of England) in those twenty imprisoned years to her execution. Four young ladies were appointed to take turns rocking his cradle of black damask, with headpiece and pillows, too, fringed with the colour of death.

Such was the man Mainwaring now approached, slowly because sudden movement alarmed this survivor of attempt after attempt by sword, powder and kidnap. With each escape, James grew yet more unsure of yet more men: to which number had been added, since the tide of acclaim that began with his investiture as Prince of Wales two years ago, the name of his son and heir. The King of Great Britain, France (upon the coins of this realm if not that) and Ireland stood like the hind legs of a carthorse that had drunk a drop too much, as indeed he had from the flagon of sweet white Canary on the sideboard. His sparse beard and thin hair framed the baby skin of his forty-six-year-old face as he looked hard into eyes that had spied upon royal fornication.

"Again? He has been to the girl again?" His mouth seemed too full of tongue, and his brogue tumbled over it like a Highland waterfall.

"Again, your Majesty."

"Across the river?"

"Across the river."

"You were not seen?"

"No."

"As perilous as being seen would be to tell one single soul."

"I tell no soul but you, Sire."

"Which tells me you know the way to prosper."

"I seek only to serve…"

"Take a drink afore you go. Aye, and mark well that if any other body does come to learn of this, it will not be me who told them. Therefore I shall know whom to hang, shall I not?"

That was all. James turned his back and looked out on the fountain playing to empty galleries around the darkening Privy Garden that stretched south to the orchard wall.

Mainwaring was unabashed. Those to whom the King was civil had more to fear than those of whom he was certain enough to abuse to their face. Bolting his drink, he bowed unnecessarily low to a sovereign who was looking elsewhere, and accomplished with self-satisfaction the courtesy of withdrawing backward from the royal presence. In his time of spying upon the Prince, it was the King he had learned most about. Here was a monarch to exemplify Sir Francis Bacon's remark that it is a miserable state of mind to have few things to desire and many things to fear, and yet that commonly is the fate of kings. Here was an Argus-eyed father whose every word and deed must be measured against his suspicions of a son who had been most secret even as a child. Here was the highest and mightiest coward in the land, itching for confrontation yet afraid that it might provoke Henry to bury him alive. Perhaps that was not unwise: for though there were peacocks a-plenty to fawn upon the settling sun, there were men of adventure who had more to hope from the rising sun. For them, no expectation of a hand in the royal till or a kingly gift of forfeited Catholic estates could match the promise of steel and shot, of gold and glory, that the Prince embodied today. Unlike his father,

Henry would sooner harry Spaniards in the Indies than roebuck in Enfield Chase. He would sooner drive Hapsburgs out of Flanders than partridge out of Norfolk. He would sooner open up the hinterland of Virginia than the crust of a marrowbone pie. But the son's time was not until the father's was done. And it would never be done while the puppet-master could yet perform. Mainwaring looked at his own finger ends, and knew that the strings were there though he saw them not.

[2]

Saturday the Fourth of July

THE PEREGRINE'S SILVER BELLS trilled sweetly, a semitone apart, as she stirred on the King's fist. He stroked the back of her head through the plumed hood.

"We know a hawk from a heron, do we not, young Essex? Aye, that we do. But human birds of prey, now, they look no different from their quarry. They ought to have bells on, too, that's what I say. Give the rest of us fair warning... eh?"

The Earl supplied the requisite nod as he rode alongside his sovereign, who had sent a message commanding that he break his journey to Chartley and come hawking at Theobalds, a dozen miles north of London. The King had now drawn him away from the others, so he was about to find out why.

"How's your sweet wife, young man?"

"She has not been able to come with me to Chartley, Sire." Essex shifted his narrow shoulders. "She had word that her mother is sick."

"The Countess of Suffolk has a dutiful daughter, then."

"It would seem so."

"But why, tell me, does the Countess of Essex seem not to have a dutiful husband?"

"Sire?" Essex had feared that this would be the agenda. Had the Howards not tormented him enough? Did even the King have to turn the screw?

"Laddie, let me talk to you like the dad you were robbed of. I know what it's like to have need of a father."

James snuffled and spat. Essex would have liked to have snuffled and spat, too, at the idea of this man who was in nobody's eyes much of a father to his own sons, offering as wealth the poverty of his expertise.

"Majesty," said Essex as the King's watery eyes looked to him for response. "I... I do not deserve yet more kindnesses at your hands."

"You must tell me true. Is she yet a wife to you?"

"No." Essex gazed to the woods beyond the King's shoulder.

"You have never once had her?"

"No. At first, we were just children. Then, when I came home from Europe after three years, we were strangers. Then I was ill. Smallpox. I couldn't... I couldn't do... anything. It is as though a spell is on me when I lie with her."

"You feel no want for her?"

"Nor she for me."

"Have you never had a woman, then? I mean, do you not know what's what, laddie?" James giggled.

"I was in France. I had women enough there." Women enough. Was once with that Picardy whore woman enough? Stained body and stinking bed. Breasts like bruised lard, and greasy thighs he would sooner have paid to get beyond than between. Yet should he not be grateful to that ready creature who meant that he could today assure his King and, more important, himself that he was indeed a man—if only for half a minute five May Days ago?

James grunted. His own need for women had rarely surpassed the kingdom's need for heirs. With the virgin Elizabeth, the barren Mary Tudor and the boy Edward the Sixth, the people of England had been three reigns and half a century without a child in the royal nursery. If not for him, there would be a legion of lesser claimants, from Lady Arabella Stuart to Philip of Spain, at their throats. Only now, with Henry, Baby Charles and sweet Bessy, did the people have an assured future. They should be on their knees daily to give thanks to God and James of Scotland for the blessed peace of a secure succession. Yet more and more did he doubt that they would thank either to be ruled by the willful Henry, especially with the willful Frances at his side. When the Howards first sought the royal ear for an annulment, would he have heard them so readily had he known that their secret treason was to free the girl for his son? Indeed not. And James had not kept his head and his crown nigh on fifty years by being outwitted by the likes of the Howards. Much could happen between now and the summoning of a divorce commission. For a start, if Essex did his duty to Frances, then nullity there would be none.

"I have it, friend Essex!"

"You have it?"

"Listen. May you not be forgetting that in truth she's a shy new bride still? Waiting for you to show her a thing or two."

"Sire, it is not that." Essex felt like striking the fool. "When I came back from France, I wanted to love her. But she did not want to love me. Nor ever will she."

"Ah, but love follows when you do a husband's business, laddie.

I had never even set eyes upon my own wee bride before I went to Denmark to claim her. I had no Danish, she no English. All we had was Cupid's dart...eh? And Cupid's quiver...eh? And love came for us, as it will come for you—even this night—if you heed what an old married man tells you. Chartley will wait. Go to your sweet wife now. And send me word in the morning that, because of your King's wisdom of the ways of women, all is now as it should be for his dear young friends."

He beckoned Essex closer and whispered, though there was not a soul within thirty yards.

"Sire?" Essex reddened and cleared his throat.

"Oh, they like that." James nodded busily. "They like it well." He halted, waving to the others to catch up. "Master Falconer!" he called without turning his head, and Sir Thomas Monson trotted forward, a peregrine at his gauntlet.

The party scanned the sky. Monson was first to spot the heron, black against a lonely scud of cirrus clouds; though before calling out he gave it further scrutiny, mindful of the disgraced predecessor who once cried *à la volée* for a dragonfly.

"There! A heavy one!" Monson judged that the big bird was on passage home, weighted with his catch of fish and frogs. Good. Just let him get a little past so he would not see the hawks too soon. Then...

"À la volée!" The King whipped off his bird's hood, raised his fist and cast her off. Monson followed suit.

Dark eyes, unblinking at the sudden sunlight, marked the quarry in a moment. Two hundred and fifty yards high. A quarter-mile wide. Up and away the pair spiraled in the classic pattern of the high mountee, their wings like full-drawn bows as they gathered speed and elevation.

"He sees them!" The heron, head normally drawn back in flight, had signaled alarm by stretching his long neck to empty his larder, lightening himself to soar for his life with wings the span of both pursuers together. Their practised response was to divide, the King's falcon circling wider yet faster to cut off the straining heron from any hope of escape.

"She's above him!" Monson clapped his hands.

"Whoo-whoo-whoop!" The King led the chorus as, poising herself, his bird tucked back her wings to drop like a lead plummet. Her talons raked a great scream from the heron, vainly stabbing his beak as she swung up for another stoop. But her partner had reached a pitch above them both, and down she came; missing, towering up again and striking in a single flowing movement.

"Whoo-whoo-whoop!" Now came the leader's second stoop, this time binding hard and tight to pull the stunned heron down. Her partner joined in the savage embrace, and the three sank together until, at treetop height, the falcons let go. Their victim crashed to destruction, surviving only long enough to hear their bells as they fell upon him again while the falconers made in to lure them off before they gorged themselves useless.

"Well then, Essex?" The King nudged him. "Who'd be a heron if he could be a hawk, eh?"

ESSEX took his leave, reining toward the London road, where he must sooner or later encounter his wife's party on its way to Audley End. Later, if Frances had the sense to wait for the midday sun to pass. His eyes caught those of Rochester. Essex had been warned that the favourite was one of many who paid much court to Frances while he was away, and since his return. But then, Essex had heard that said even about Henry: as if that noble Prince who never let an oath pass his lips would be the thief of another man's wife. And, anyway, was it not alleged that Rochester had won his way into the King's favour not by the front door but by the back passage? Huh! A wife would be safer with such a fellow than would her husband.

How else could this glittering Ganymede have won such preferment? His forebears, the Kers of Ferniehirst, in the grim forest of Jedburgh, may have been lairds by the standards of Scotland but by those of England they were no better than murderous, sheep-shagging reivers. No wonder he had abandoned his born name for Carr, though cur would have better matched the stink of it on the Border marches. To look at him now, riding so huffingly in plumed hat, boots of white leather and jeweled rapier, who would think that he had left lousy Scotland in blue bonnet, old cowhide and with a basket-hilted black blade at his arse? Young Master Robbie had never known his father, and Essex would not have been surprised if his mother hadn't, either. Before the laddie was born, old Sir Tam, who had spent half his years making enemies and the other half running from them, died a prisoner in the castle at Aberdeen. He was there under charge of shooting dead the Earl of Bedford's heir, who had come with a flag of truce to settle a Border dispute. True to their nature, the in-laws had tried to drive the young widow Ker off her land, and it seemed that when she died some kind soul had found her orphan son a page's place, first with the Earl of Dunbar and then at the Scottish court. The lad did not continue with the royal household when it came to London, but was dispatched to France to learn better manners than were taught in Scotland; returning at much the same time that Essex was dispatched there to learn better manners than were taught in England. He came back to catch the King's eye by the stratagem of getting his horse to throw him in front of the royal dais at a pageant in the Tiltyard. His leg apparently broken, he was carried off. James rushed to fuss over the pretty lad and was at his sickbed each day. Very soon the leg was better, with no trace of a limp, and Master Robert was dubbed Sir Robert and appointed a Gentleman of his Majesty's Bedchamber. And for the Devil knows what in the five years since, the King had raised him to a viscountcy, to the most noble Order of the Garter, and now to the Privy Council. He had augmented his coat of arms with the royal lion *passant gardant or*. He had bestowed upon him the castle at Rochester to go with his title, and the castle at Sherborne forfeited by the imprisoned Sir Walter Ralegh. He had made him Keeper of the Palace of Westminster. He had given him thousands upon thousands of pounds. He had loaded him with plate. He had festooned him with jewelry.

The King would pinch Rochester's rosy cheek, stroke his trim *pic devant* beard, smooth an invisible ruffle at his shoulder, and look into his merry brown eyes; all the while addressing remarks to those who stood by, concealing their thoughts with the skill that was a prerequisite of service at the court of a king who delighted more in the company of his favourite than in that of his own son. Indeed, James called Rochester simply "the friend I love above all men." Essex thought it would not be hard to hate above all men this upstart, this pirate, this tartan catamite. God! When Henry came to the throne, Goldylocks would be stripped of his loot and bundled back to the borders with only the threadbare breeks in which he had set forth.

Rochester raised his jeweled cap and bowed his head to Essex: the almost-mocking obeisance of a man who does not expect to remain inferior for long. To be a third earl, Essex had needed only to be born in his mother's bed. To be first viscount, and the first Scot ever to sit in the House of Lords, required rather more. Even in this age of youth, no man had risen so high so fast.

"My lord." Essex acknowledged the salute.

"My lord." Another bow, completed with a flourish of frizzled flaxen hair that a princess might envy.

"I hear that you have not been too well, Essex. I trust you fare better now."

"A morning such as this is the only physic I need."

"We have missed your wit, my lord."

"You jest." Essex weighed the laughter against him.

"It could only be jest if you had no wit for us to miss. But what we miss more is the Lady Frances. The court is a duller place while you keep her away. That is no jest."

"If you are ever minded to take a wife yourself, my lord"—Essex turned to ride off—"you will discover that her place is where her husband pleases."

Watching him spur into a gallop, Rochester shook his head. "I suppose I should have asked if Frances is yet with child. Though, in truth, she can hardly be with child before she is with husband."

The dark, sardonic Sir Thomas Overbury joined in the applause no less for the fact that the wit was really his. But then, so much about Rochester was. The more the King turned to the favourite to ease himself of the burdens that had doubled the hump on the back of Secretary Salisbury (until that worn-out "little beagle" had rolled over and died six weeks ago), the more the favourite turned to Overbury. For precious Rochester knew precious little of politics, of Parliament, of the Privy Council, of the Church, or of the duties of the Secretary of State. His English was still too Scotch, and he had barely enough Latin for a motto.

Whose words were they that the favourite conveyed to the King as his own succinct appraisal when he found his table piled high with parchments he could never hope to digest? And cipher dispatches he had not the brain to master? Whose words but those of Sir Thomas Overbury, scholar of philosophy and logic at Queen's College, Oxford, barrister of the Middle Temple, confidential courier to Secretary Salisbury, and diplomatic observer in France and the Low Countries? For that matter, whose witty letters and pretty speeches were they that opened for Rochester hard hearts and easy thighs? Whose but those of Sir Thomas Overbury, poet, essayist—and his tutor these five years in the art of the courtier? Would the raw Scot have survived had he not learned from the suave Englishman to honour nothing but fortune, admit nothing but beauty, and love nothing at all? So what was one jest more or less on the long account of what Rochester owed him? And now the favourite had grown greater than any subject in the kingdom: great enough to repay by proposing soon to the King that he need look no farther than Overbury for his next Secretary of State.

The country judge's son would have come a long way in the thirty-one years since his childhood in the Gloucestershire village of Bourton-on-the-Hill. Long enough to become a fit husband for a daughter of Sir Philip Sidney. Overbury had loved the good and gentle Elizabeth without hope until suddenly, ten days ago, she became a widow: free of the sacrament of misery that was her thirteen years of marriage to the profligate Earl of Rutland. Now at last, Overbury could come nearer to her than the verse with which he had set the boundary of his love: *He comes too near who comes to be denied.*

But Rochester's new display of interest in Frances Howard worried him greatly. The last time he lost himself under her skirts was bad enough; this time could be the ruin of everything. The nullity was no secret at court, and if the cunning Countess of Suffolk now used her daughter as a lure to bring Rochester into the Howard camp, there would be no future for Overbury. They would soon have him off the stage and into exile as commissioner to Virginia or ambassador to Muscovy. Unless they could find him a more distant post on earth. Or under it.

He rode alongside Rochester and put a gauntleted hand on his forearm. "Was that wise, my friend? Half this company will sup free tonight on their tale of your entry into the lists for Frances..."

"I was merely toying."

"...and the other half tomorrow."

"I could do worse than a Howard heiress. She is perfect."

"Aye, perfect in lying down."

"Which nobler lady have you in mind for me?"

"Anyone but that whore."

"The Howards would have you in the Tower for that."

"She would still be a whore when I came out."

"You might not come out."

"ROBBIE!"

Rochester wheeled at the King's shout, and saw him with one hand clasped to his eye and the other swinging at anyone who tried to come to the rescue.

"Robbie! Help me, for Christ's sake!" As Rochester rode up, the King took hand from head and blinked painfully. "Oh, man, is there not room enough in my three kingdoms but this treasonable fly has to land in *my* eye?"

* * *

ALL WRISTS and ankles, like a wretch on the rack, the Earl of Essex had been cooling an hour in the corner of the bay-strewn hall at Cranford le Mote when Frances and Mrs. Turner came in, hand in hand and bubbling merrily.

"Oh!" The high colour left the girl's cheeks and she clutched at a throat gone dumb. She felt the evidence of her afternoon with Henry issuing like a fanfare from every pore. Her thighs were still sticky with him.

"Oh!" Mrs. Turner broke the guilty silence. "Fancy finding you sitting here like a ghost. We thought you must be well on your way to Chartley by now."

"And I thought"—Essex looked at his muted wife—"you must be well on yours to your mother's sickbed."

Frances's mind raced with a dozen lies, each one collapsing under interrogation on the way to her tongue. Again, Mrs. Turner came to the rescue.

"Frances felt too faint to ride. It's *sweltering,* isn't it? We went down to the river for some air." Her voice gathered speed as though it were conviction. "The horses can't bear it, either. There's not a breath of wind on the open road. Not a breath. The sun beats down and the dust rises in clouds. Perhaps..."

"Frances." Essex began to rise, but Mrs. Turner cut him off and gave the girl her cue.

"*Now,* my dear. Won't you feel better if you go and lie down?"

"I...I think so."

"So do I. We don't want your mother to have to be your nurse instead of you hers."

Mrs. Turner took Frances's elbow as far as the foot of the wide stairs, then excused herself from Essex's presence and found a maid to go up with basin and ewer.

Essex was on his feet when Mrs. Turner came back, his palms together as in effigy.

"Well, my lord?"

"Well, madam?"

"What business brings you here?"

"No business of yours."

"That I do not doubt, since my business is Frances's happiness."

Upstairs, Frances was waving the maid away, preferring to be alone as she shed her crumpled clothes, leaving them where they fell. She sat on the floor, drawing up her knees and completing a cocoon with head and arms. Eyes closed, she savoured the musky scents of love that still clung to her, and breathed them deep again and again before she moved reluctantly to the basin and soaped away that hour in the meadow. Then she took a pale green nightgown from the wardrobe and slipped an arm into each sleeve as she crossed to the long gilt-framed mirror on the wall. She watched her reflection as she drew the gown open to perfume herself with sandalwood. She wished Henry were with her.

"Frances."

She saw her husband's gray face in the mirror, secured the gown about her and whirled round as he shut the door behind him and stood there, hands raised in peace, judging that any advance might alarm her.

"Frances—we could still be happy."

"We could not." She turned her back.

"We could try."

"We have tried."

"We were happy on our wedding day."

"We were children."

"Why do you always speak as though nothing has been good?"

"Your absences have been good."

"I wish to God you would not seek this divorce."

"Would you rather I sought death? We are both young enough to begin life again. Divorce must be better."

"For you, yes." He sighed. "Many men would rush to marry you. Rochester..."

"He loves only himself."

"The Prince..."

"He can take his pick of princesses."

"But Frances"—Essex walked round to face her—"who would marry *me* once I am proclaimed to the world as impotent? You have told enough already. How else does the King know? *Impotent...*" He spat the word in despair, and sat on the bed, head in hands.

"Robert, listen." She would try to soothe him. "It is not like that. Our depositions have gone to the bishops. It will be they who have told the King. But they all say it is *my* fault. I am the one who will be branded."

"You?"

"Because it is clear that some misfortune has made you impotent only with me."

"Who could believe that? You are the most desirable woman on earth. I see the way all men look at you. I..." He turned his glance away. He could not look at her himself.

"Please! Not that again, my brave lord. You had all those women in France. You made me listen to the lewd tricks they performed. And when I would not do them, you taunted me that I was an icicle. But if you wanted a whore you should have married one."

"Some say I did."

"Some? Some? Who are these some?"

"If I fetch a Bible, will you swear you are virgin still?"

"You ask me that?" She slapped his cheek. "I shall never be anything else, shall I, until I am free of you?"

Essex put a hand to his stinging face. "The King thinks otherwise."

"The King indeed!" Frances snorted. It had to be a lie.

"The King indeed, madam. He sent for me this morning. He commanded me to return to you—and to try again."

"Did his gracious Majesty advise you what to try with?" She should have known better. However many lances a man might observe, only a woman could compare them in tournament array. And, maid or mistress, wife or widow, at her peril would she cause any man to think that nature had endowed him with fewer or feebler inches to the yard than some foregoer—and that lechery had endowed her with more than enough opportunities for appraisal.

"Dirty bitch!"

"Dirty dog!"

She drew back her hand again. He caught it as it came up. She moved the other to follow. He caught that, too. Her gown fell open from neck to ankle, and her body rippled with rage. He tried to kiss her. She jerked her head away. As she struggled, Essex felt a stirring in his loins that had never begun in all the nights she had lain dead-legged beside him. He tightened his hold, locking her hips into his.

Listen, the King had said. *They like a bit of rape, laddie. They like it well.* For once, the old fool was right. This is what the bridegroom should have done when he came back to claim his bride a thousand nights ago. Frances twisted round to get free, and Essex used his weight to force her forward over the bed, crushing the breath from her as he dropped heavily astride her back. She moved to spit out a mouthful of pillow and gasp in some air.

"Ugh..." He stank like a stable lad.

"I want to love you, Frances." He planted a wet mouth on her shoulder. "Frances, please. *Please.*"

She pressed down into the quilt, pulling elbows close, legs tight.

As soon as she had breath enough, she screamed. Surely Mrs. Turner would hear. The tangled gown tore, and tore again, as Essex dragged it up to her hips.

"Beast!" She screeched over her shoulder. "Beast! Beast!" God, *what* was he doing now? His hands were at her buttocks. Could this be why he was the way he was: his need not for a woman but for a boy, or a woman who would be a boy for him? She screamed again when his fingers wedged between her thighs to pry them apart. Now it was he who cried out as she abruptly turned under him, trapping his wrist until he could pull free. "Beast! Get *off* me."

"But, Frances, I love you."

"Christ, do you think this is love?"

"This is." Essex unbuttoned.

"*That* is?" The three-inch fool.

"Let me—damn you." His hands were at her throat. "Damn you." He pressed harder. "Damn you." She saw the wildness in his eyes, and was afraid. In despair, she encircled him with cunning fingers. Each stroke lessened his grip until he let go altogether, pressing his lips to her neck in atonement. "Oh, wait..." Already too late, he shifted to open her. "Oh...*oh*...I love...you."

"I *hate* you. *Hate* you. *Hate* you." Clenching her teeth, she slid her hand down to grasp at him: converting her agony into his, his ecstasy into hers. He cried out and struck at her. Her ear took the blow, which she repaid with another wrench before he hauled free, clutching himself as he fell heavily to the floor. She pulled the ruined nightgown around her and ran out, leaving him writhing.

Essex was unable to comprehend why nature should be so hypocritical as to harbour under so sweet a countenance so wicked a heart. Heaven help the man who got her next. He rather hoped it would be Rochester.

Mrs. Turner looked down at him from the open door. "You filthy bugger," she said.

[3]

Tuesday the Seventh of July

AT THE WICKET DOOR in the Great Gate of St. James's Palace, a yeoman of his Highness's guard yawned as he leaned on his halberd. His partner gave it a kick to rouse him.

"Up all night again, Taff?" No answer. "I said, *Up all night,* you bloody Welsh dormouse."

"Aaah!" Taff shook the sleep out of his eyes. "You're just jealous, boyo. You've got no bride to be up."

"Jealous. I can get a wench without having to marry her."

"There's no wench like my Gwenny. She's like butter."

"Wouldn't know, Taff. Never tried butter."

The sound of horsemen caught their ears. They looked across the park toward the Palace of Whitehall to make out some fifty of his Majesty's guard escorting the King and twoscore courtiers on their unheralded way to St. James's.

"Nobody tells nobody nothing," said Taff.

"They'll bloody tell you something if you don't get on and call out the guard!"

The Welshman lowered his halberd and ducked through the wicket to shout a warning. "The King is coming! The King is coming!"

And from across the courtyard yeomen of the guard flowed like a scarlet stream in spangled coats, badged front and back with the rose and crown imperial.

"Open the Great Gate!"

"Go tell the Chamberlain! Quick!"

Ambling between Viscount Rochester and the Scottish Duke of Lennox, the King saw the oak gates begin their long swing back. "Was I supposed to wait like a humble petitioner for an invitation to my son's table? Christ's wounds, I would be tarrying till doomsday—eh, Robbie?"

Rochester laughed. "I trust they'll find a crust of bread for the Prodigal Father."

"Oh, they sup well enough at St. James's, I hear. My son has a rich dad." His son had also a cunning dad. Poor Essex having sent no word, it was clear that he had been unable to rise to the occasion, even by royal command. Frances would soon be free, so other ways must be found to keep her secure from Henry. Today, a cunning dad would try one or two.

By the time the royal party reached the open gateway, a tall avenue of the Prince's guard was at attention, and at the other end of it Henry was waiting with twoscore of his own gentlemen as though there had been months, rather than minutes, to prepare a welcome. As he bowed to his father and advanced bareheaded, his household was swinging into action. From pastry to poultry, from saucery to spicery, cooks were raiding casks and larders for delicacies in stock for other than an ordinary day's dinner—and putting away the pork because the King could not abide it. Gold plate was getting an extra polish and, if the sergeant wasn't looking, a spit also to bring up the shine. Lesser gentlemen of the Prince's staff were being told that today they must fend for themselves to make room in the Presence Chamber for the King's party.

"I bid you welcome, your Majesty." Henry's worn gray Welsh frieze contrasted with the rainbow splendour of his visitors' clothes. For him, magnificence was for state occasions. He had led his court to abandon the French dress because he could no longer endure the changes of fashion that seemed to come every day from Paris.

"That's too mean for a king's son. You should not keep even a rich suit so long."

"Indeed, father."

The King sniffed and moved to dismount. Henry held out a hand, for his father was steadier on a horse's legs than on his own spindle-shanks.

"You've got good spies, son." The King nodded at the successful turnout. "I made up my mind to dine with you but an hour ago."

"What need would I have of spies in Whitehall?"

"Oh, no more than I in St. James's."

As the courtiers followed their masters into the Palace, a squad of grooms led the horses through the archway to the stables.

"See that, Taff?"

"See what?"

"Them gold stirrups on the King's horse."

"Look there—Rochester's got some with diamonds."

"He'd bloody better watch it, hadn't he, Taff?"

"And you'd bloody better watch it, boyo. If you don't give over calling me Taff, I'll have the other end of my halberd up your English arse."

THE KING assumed Henry's monogrammed chair at the head of the high table. On the wall behind hung the great embroidered crest of the Princes of Wales since the fourteenth century: three upright ostrich feathers that the Black Prince took from the slain King of Bohemia at the Battle of Crécy. With it came the German motto, *Ich Dien,* which was never rendered into the English, *I Serve.* And encircling the crest was the emblem of the supreme order of chivalry, the Garter, instituted by the Black Prince's father and carrying the motto *Honi soit qui mal y pense,* also never converted into the English, *Shame be to him who thinks evil.* No one but heirs apparent—and only ten of them—had ever been invested Princes of Wales. But such were their fortunes that no more than five had lived to inherit the crown and, of those, three had been murdered in prison: Edward the Second, with a red-hot needle up his guts; Richard the Second, by starvation; and Edward the Fifth, who was one of the Princes in the Tower. The survivors were the only two Henrys in the line, the fifth and the eighth kings of that name, and each went on to win fame that today's Henry was determined to excel.

James took little notice as gentlemen waiters paraded a score of delicacies. Pheasant with ginger. Goose with garlic. Mallard with black sauce. Hen with white. Lark with cinnamon...on and on they came, each dish so heaped that man might eat for a week to discover the plate it rested upon. A narrower choice would have dishonoured the host, though the chief guest would settle today for roast meats, with a morsel of bread, and then pick a path through offerings of fresh fruit. Knowing this, he studied not the procession from the groaning sideboards, but the men Henry had about him. They matched the accompaniment provided by the dozen trumpeters and the pair of kettledrums. It was the son's favourite music, after the sound of gunfire, although hardly to the father's taste. The Prince's household were men apart from the lute and viol courtiers of Whitehall. These were mostly sons of the old Tudor nobility. Young gallants born to great fortune. Fit, noisy and bursting with strength.

"You'll taste our new Spanish wine, father?"

"Aye, if it's sweet enough."

"I've sons enough here of fathers who'd tell them it was never sweeter than bought with steel."

"Fools. Better the lesson of those fathers run through before they could infect their sons with such bombast."

"Better yet the lesson that peace was ever the harbinger of war."

In Elizabeth's day there had been the *tercios* and *flotas* of Spain for a young Englishman to sharpen his teeth on. James's years of peace had deprived the nation of any enemy its men of adventure had come to need. For honour and glory. For trial of arms. For treasure. And for refuge from the enfeebling chains of domestic ease. With this Prince, chivalry would flower anew. He was Alexander. He was Ajax. He was Hannibal. He was Hercules. The Protestant crusader prefigured in the Apocalypse to trample underfoot the triple diadem of Rome: to which end, when his moment came, he would rake the old world and the new.

His armies would cross the Narrow Seas to the side of Maurice of Nassau, and clear the Hapsburg Archdukes from the Netherlands. On they would march to rally Henry's future brother-in-law, Frederick of the Rhine, leader of the princes of the Protestant Union beset within Holy Roman Germany. Spain would be prised out of Naples and Lombardy, and its threat lifted from Venice and Savoy. Then on and on to wherever dragons be. Henry would launch a procession of fleets across the Atlantic to build up England's new Jerusalem. It was five slow years since the Virginia Company made landfall on the white sandhills that reminded them of the Downs, and named Cape Henry for "the great Captain of our Israel." He could hardly wait to drive south to Spain's Florida outpost of San Agustín, and strike at Havana and the fat *flotas* ferrying treasure to replenish Madrid's war chest. Then north to Maine and Newfoundland, beyond where the Prince—now named Supreme Protector of the Company of Discoverers of the Northwest Passage—had this spring dispatched three ships to confirm the short route to the Orient that Henry Hudson had died without finding, though not before naming Prince Henry's Foreland. Conquest of the oceans would be assured by the Prince's will to advance the affairs of the neglected Navy royal, ever the brazen wall of this island. Already, he had begun to campaign for a universal pardon to allow some three thousand pirates to augment the mariners of England. Meanwhile, like those buccaneers for whom such course would have no appeal so long as James reigned, because peace never filled a belly like plunder, the young courtiers waited.

Waited... and studied deeds of arms, and the arts and sciences of war: siegecraft, discipline, alarms, watches, encamping, entrenching, fortifying, undermining. *Waited*... and planned stratagems, ambuscades, scalings and approaches by land and by sea. *Waited*... and built up intelligence of strongholds such as French Calais, and Spanish Milan and Venetian Palma. *Waited*... and marched and drilled, and leveled cannon to the white. *Waited*... and charged on horseback with pistols, each man's knee locked with the next in line, and practised breaking such attacks with squared ranks of pike and musket. *Waited*... and played the war game at a long table set with regiments of cavalry and infantry, placing to advantage Light Horse, Vanward, Main Battle, Wings, Sleeves and Rearward. *Waited*... and drank in the experience of veteran officers their Prince honoured at St. James's: dragoon colonels from Holland, fortress engineers from Germany, fencing masters from Huguenot France, artillery captains from Poland...

The King was noting these alien faces when Sir Arthur Mainwaring dropped to one knee and presented a plate of roast beef, cut daintily so that his Majesty hardly need stop talking to chew.

"My thanks to you, Sir John."

Henry leaned across and whispered the correction. His father had dubbed nine hundred and six new knights in his first four months alone—more than Elizabeth in her entire reign—but he must be getting old if he could not remember even the Carver to the Prince.

"Of course! I mean Sir *Arthur*. I'll be forgetting my own name next." He laughed and, because a king's jokes are always funny, those about him joined in and those about them followed suit. The King's eyes surveyed the long tables as he nudged his son. "No candy soldiers here. Your men are lean. Mine are fat."

"Tilting must make better men than tippling."

"Aye, son, but will they be content to tilt at the quintain forever?"

"We would all sooner level the lance at your enemies, father, than at men made of wood."

"But I have no enemies." James stuck a piece of beef into his mouth and mumbled. "Have I to make some?"

TWO HOURS LATER, the King waved away more grapes, washed his throat down with thick, sweet Frontignac and banged his empty goblet on the table for the hovering cupbearer to refill.

"I will speak a few words to your household."

Henry signaled to the Chamberlain, who rapped his tall staff three times on the floor to halt the hubbub. "Pray silence for his Majesty!"

James hauled himself to his uncertain feet, propping his thin thighs against the table edge. "My good lords and gentlemen—I would thank my son for his great hospitality but, since he learned that art from me, I shall thank myself."

Loud laughter, not least because the King clearly meant every word.

"... you may wonder how you can best thank him for his goodness to you, for a place here in his family that many a young Englishman might covet. Aye, and some young Scotsmen—though we are not brought up to sup as rich, nor dress as fine, nor sleep as soft. Are we, young Rochester?"

All eyes swung to the favourite, whose handsome face gleamed like a rapier hilt. "Indeed not, your Majesty. But we are striving night and day to reform."

At the foot of the table, one of Henry's Gentlemen Ushers whispered to another. "Well said for a laddie who left Scotland with fourpence."

"As much as that?" said the other.

"... what you all can do to repay my son's favour is help his old dad teach him patience. For no prince can be king until his father is laid to rest, and no good son would wish to bury his father ahead of his time, would he now? But before my old bones lie under Westminster Abbey I want to see Henry happily settled with a wife—the right wife—so that we may know our posterity is assured and the nation may sleep o' nights and not fear the future."

James stretched to award his son a pat on the shoulder but avoided his eye. Henry's mind churned. Was that his twisted way of saying, *I know about Frances?* But, no, if he did, could his blabbering mouth have kept silent? The remark was more likely meant to find its certain way to all those ambassadors whose masters were concerned that the Prince of Wales displayed yet more indifference to yet more negotiations for yet more princesses.

"... Henry's royal mother was my fortunate choice—a princess through and through. I pray her son may choose as well. He needs a woman of such virtue. Such breeding. Such beauty. Such *suitability.*" He played the jester with a mock-furtive glance over each shoulder. "A princess to make him eager to toil through the night to get a flock of bonny wee princes, eh?"

The King pumped an arm obscenely and got his laughs, though entirely from his own party. Henry's men took their cue from their Prince, struck silent by his father's vulgarity.

"... eh?" The arm went up and down again.

Another loyal round from the Whitehall courtiers, which served only to make the silence from the rest of the chamber seem hostile. The King sensed the atmosphere and did not like it.

"...I pray, gentlemen, that you will encourage him to choose well. For if he chooses ill, he may pay a high price."

The warm glow of feasting was altogether doused. Spread among the Prince's household, the King's men sat like enemies in a foreign camp. Albeit this was July, their backs chilled as though it were January.

"...you young gentlemen of St. James's may have learned much about the dreams of princes, but you have forgotten more about the reality of kings. Hear me well, now. Hear me well. I remind you that kings are God's regents on earth. Like gods, they possess the power of life and death. The power of raising up and casting down. The power to exalt and to abase. The power to make their subjects like men at chess: a pawn to take a bishop or a knight."

James lifted his goblet and thrust it violently against his son's, knocking it on its side. The red wine spilled across the table.

"So! A king is still like any other father in that he may dispose of his inheritance at his pleasure." James looked round the chamber, at every face but Henry's. "Aye, like any other father, a king may choose to disinherit the eldest—and prefer the youngest. He may make one a beggar—and the other rich."

There was not a sound now: the room might have been empty. James began to feel that he had perhaps been unwise to open his mind so freely in this company of men sworn to serve his son. He held up his hands, palms soothingly outward.

"Mind you, a king may restore his own children to favour as he would any penitent sinner. And it would indeed be a foolish father who would disinherit or destroy his children without trying first to educate them in wiser ways."

Only now did James catch his son's eye. Henry folded his arms and looked back evenly until his father turned his gaze to Chaplain Hall, at the end of the high table.

"Enough! Chaplain, pray for the Almighty to guide us all. If it is not too late."

Joseph Hall did as well as he could: reserving his doubts about this King who styled himself God's regent, this Prince who yearned for the helmet of Mars—and, indeed, this Chaplain who prayed for their great and manifold imperfections to be rewarded by great and manifold blessings.

* * *

THE KING beckoned Rochester to ride ahead with him as the party made its way back to Whitehall. "A little bird tells me," he confided, "that the Prince is casting glances in the direction of the Lady Frances."

"Few men do not." Rochester concealed what he had known these six months. The King, who smelled plots everywhere, would smell one more in Rochester's failure to pass on such knowledge without prompting.

"A word is enough to the wise. Half a word is enough for me. Enough to divine the *true* reason the Howards are all of a sudden so beseeching of their nullity. If you are fool enough to believe it is for the sake of the lassie, you are as great a fool as they take me for. The rascals! I'd like nothing better than to disappoint them. But—you know me—I have not the heart to disappoint that sweet girl. So she shall have her nullity. Is that not bountiful of me?"

"Truly so."

"Truly so, indeed. But she shall not have it to wed the Prince. Oh, no!"

"Does your little bird tell you"—Rochester's heart thumped—"that things have reached that pass?"

"No, no, laddie." The King detected his concern and doubted that it was for the stability of the nation. "No, no. Just glances and such. But I know these Howards."

"To forbid would not suffice?"

"With the Howards, perhaps—as long as they think I have my eye on them. But with Henry I need to have a care what I forbid, lest he fight me over it for that reason alone. Therefore we must ensure there is nothing to fight over. We must marry Frances to someone else."

"Sire?"

"To you, laddie." The King belched. "Don't try to look abashed. I've a good idea of what the two of you were up to while Essex was away. You will make a pretty pair. I'll be giving you an earldom for a wedding present. You can go to bed an earl—and get up a countess. Eh? Eh? Eh?"

"As your Majesty pleases."

"Don't give a thought to the Howards. They will love you as long as you are my favourite. Which shall be as long as it pleases you...to please me."

"Then as your Majesty pleases." The prospect grew rosier by the moment. Neither he nor Frances could make a richer alliance, in bed or out. Already, he was embellishing his silver-pearled viscount's coronet with the gold strawberry leaves of earldom. How soon before a marquisate? And then a dukedom?

"Mind you, Robbie, not a word to a soul till I say. Not a word."

The King congratulated himself. By God, you had to be sharp to outfox not only the Prince of Wales but the Howard clan, too, in half the distance between St. James's and Whitehall. He belched again. The favourite gulped and forced up a loyal belch to keep his master's company.

"It's that damned Spanish wine of his," said the King, and farted. The favourite stood in his stirrups and did his theatrical best to follow suit.

"Forgive me, Sire. I fear that one puts me yet further in your debt."

"Saucy devil," said the King.

[4]
Wednesday the Eighth of July

THE LOYAL PORTRAITS in the long galleries of the land captured a golden-haired beauty whom the Queen's own looking glass no longer managed to reflect. It saw neck more goose than swan. It saw hair so sparse now that it took on the pink of scalp. It saw a nose too long to be classical, with a bridge too low to be imperial. That reckless wit, Overbury, had remarked that it looked down to see how many of her teeth were amiss, and never could get up again—and favoured painters needed no telling to avoid the profile and favor the full face. It saw a lonely wife who, more and more these days, could hardly hold steady for the drink that blunted the hurt of her husband's indifference.

Anne's bride-bright eyes had dulled over the last dozen years of the old century and the first dozen years of the new, since James had sailed to Denmark to marry her. Four anniversaries had passed, with much murmuring about whether the King had the will to do with her what rumour had him do with his favourites (and Elizabeth's spies had him do with Lady Glamis) before the purpose of the marriage was achieved. The heir was named Henry for the King's father, and Frederick for hers. Two years later, Anne gave the nation a daughter, Bessy, and four years on a second son, still Baby Charles after eleven birthdays. There would have been a prince and three princesses more, but Robert, Margaret, Mary and Sophia all died in infancy; the last, five years ago, since when the King and Queen were rarely together but for state occasions, and kept mostly to their separate households.

Today she was at Hampton Court, her favourite palace because it was the other side of London from her husband's favourite palace. Perhaps too late, mother and son had tried to grow closer as the King widened the gap between himself and each of them. Now they sat on either side of a plate of bonbons in a window seat above the knot garden; the son renewing his hatred of his father for his mother's wretchedness, and the mother uncomfortable, in spite of everything, at any criticism of her husband other than her own.

"You should not be so hasty to judge your father. He looks at you and sees all he was denied." Anne spoke one alien language with the accent of another, for her English had long been overlaid more by the tongue of Scotland than of her native land. The flagon of Alsatian wine, half empty even at ten in the morning, slowed her speech to make it more distinct, rather than less.

"Mother, there is much that he denies me."

"He would love you—I am sure—but he does not know what a father's love is."

"Neither do I." Henry dashed his hands together like cymbals. "Yet Rochester's father was dead before he was born, and he knows a father's love. My father's."

The Queen chose not to hear. She could abide neither sight nor sound of Rochester, or that Overbury who whispered poison about her into his ear for him to whisper into the King's. She had hoped to have seen the last of Master Robbie Ker when she had him sent packing as too graceless a page for the English court. The King was his own Fool to have him back.

"You must not forget that your poor father had no love for half his life. He had neither father, mother, sister, brother—nor wife till he was twenty-three. Already you have all these but a wife. And I pray every day that gap shall soon be filled."

"My father"—Henry snorted—"would fill it not with love but with the princess whose dowry weighs most."

"Try to understand these matters." The Queen—daughter of a king, sister of a king, wife of a king—patted her son's hand. "The dowry is more a recognition of your value than your bride's. What would Spain think if we said the dowry was of no importance? They would be sure there was something wrong with you."

"Yes, mother." Henry let it pass. There was no more point in distressing her over a Catholic Infanta he did not want in his bed than a married countess he did. He watched as his mother took yet another drink, and let that pass, too.

"You know, your father was so much thinner than in the portrait they had sent us." Anne was looking through the open window at the simmering Thames of this summer but seeing the frozen fjord of that winter James came to marry her a month short of her fifteenth birthday. "His clothes were so gay, yet his eyes so sad. I told him that—and he said I would make them happy." She sighed. "He wanted a million pounds as my dowry. Did you know that?"

"I know you are worth it—and more."

"He did not get it..."

"Oh."

"But he said he would love me better than he could love a dowry. He said, 'Silver is a cold bedfellow.'" She laughed. "And he said there was enough of me here"—playfully she cupped her bosom, which sat low in her green gown—"to make up the difference. He loved me well then, my dear. He loved me well then." She held up her glass without noticing that Henry had already filled it, then withdrew it with a nod of thanks as though he had. "But it has never been right between us since the day you were born."

"It's *my* fault?"

"No, his." She sipped her wine. "It was a Tuesday. He hates Tuesdays. He came to my chamber, but it was not to see me. He stood over your cradle and looked down at you for an age. He pushed back the clothes to examine the colour of your hair. He pulled back your eyelid to see the colour of your eyes. He opened your little fist to study your fingernails. And, as you began to cry, he turned to me for the first time. And"—she made an effort to moderate the rising scream in her voice—"and he said to me, *'Is he mine, Annie?'* Jesus Christ help me, that is what he said. The people were daft for mirth because at last an heir was born—and, Jesus Christ help me, that is what he said."

"Mother..."

She waved him down. "Not for years did I find out that his own father had asked his mother the same question about him. He thinks all women must be like her."

"Then, for once, I pity him." Every single thing Henry had gathered about Mary Queen of Scots made him abhor her. Not a man loved her but was destroyed by her. Had James loved her, he would surely have gone the same way. But he had lifted not a finger to save her from Elizabeth's executioner: thus at one blow freeing himself from her threat, and from the Catholic umbilical cord that could deny him the English succession.

"I really believe your father hoped my answer would be no. I really believe he hoped the answer of your hair, your eyes, your fingernails wold be no. But you *are* his, my dear. No other man has ever known me." She sighed. "More's the pity."

"He is cruel, so cruel. Yet he is a coward. More ready to break a heart than a bone."

"He must never break yours." The Queen put her hands on his shoulders and looked into the face of the one man who could stand against the King. The man they had both made. She prayed she would live to see him rule. She prayed this not so much for her son's sake as for the fact that it could come about only with the death or deposition of his father.

"He will not break me." Henry covered her trembling hands, lifting them down to rest in her green lap.

"He would never let me be a mother to you." A tear spilled down each cheek. "He was afraid I would bring you up to hate him. Why else would he take you from my arms almost as you were born?"

Henry listened, feeling pain to match that in his mother's voice. This tale he knew well, for she had told it to him time and again. However much she established her innocence in his mind, she had yet to convince herself. It went back to soon after his baptism, when the King had him removed to Stirling Castle in the care of the Earl of Mar, hereditary custodian of the heir to the throne of Scotland. James's old oak cradle was brought out, and James's old nurse put in charge, under James's old governess, the Dowager Countess Annabella. What was bad enough for the father was to be good enough for the son.

"I had left my country, my family and my dear friends for your father, and all I wanted was my baby in my arms. If he would not grant me that, he would not grant me anything. I was so crazed, I devised a plan to take you back. What was so wicked about that? But his spies got wind of it, and he wrote out in his own hand the warrant that robbed me of so much of you all these years..."

Henry would never forget it either, for it had robbed him, too.

"...My Lord of Mar." She recited the words forever imprinted in her mind. *"Because in the safety of my son lies my own safety, this I command you: except for any order from me, you shall not deliver up the Prince. And if God call me at any time, see that neither for the Queen, nor the Lords nor the Church, do you deliver him up till he be eighteen years of age, and he command you so himself..."*

"Mother." Henry put an arm around her.

"...I was so ill. I miscarried. But your father was long in coming. He said he was afraid of me. *Afraid!* That if I would plot with his enemies to seize you, then I might plot with them to seize him. I said that if he wanted you to be a motherless babe then I would put an end to myself. I took a dagger from under my pillow..."

"Poor mother."

"Do you know what he did? He just fell to his knees and spread his arms wide. 'Strike me down first, Annie,' he said. 'I could not live without you.' I wish I had struck him down. But he swore things would be different. And I believed him. Like a fool, I believed him."

In fact, the Prince had remained at Stirling Castle until Elizabeth's death presented his father with the crown of England, and with that the might to cast out his fear of rebellion in Scotland.

"He can always make people believe him," said Henry. "Especially you."

"Not anymore, my dear. But, yes, he could be very loving when I fought him. Sometimes I wonder whether that was why I did it." The Queen shook her head, and smiled for no reason other than that the wine had found its mark. Henry was sad at the ease with which he had come to accept that it was too late to wish her different. "He says I'm silly if I say anything," she said. "*Any*thing at all." She shook her empty glass, listening as though it might rattle. Henry went over to the sideboard for a fresh flagon. He took the glass from her to replenish, then fitted it carefully back into her still outstretched hand. "*Any*thing at all," she said as he set the flagon on the small table beside her and walked quietly out. His mother could not help him. She could hardly help herself. "*Any*thing at all," said the Queen of England to the empty room.

[5]

Thursday the Ninth of July

"ALMIGHTY GOD," prayed the Archbishop of Canterbury, kneeling alone in the chapel of his palace at Lambeth. "I beseech thee, save our faithful land from Satan's messenger."

George Abbot lowered his chin to his clasped hands. Philip of Spain had sent Don Pedro de Zuñiga back to London. What treacheries, what horrors would follow his mission this time? It was seven years ago that Zuñiga had arrived to establish the first Spanish embassy to follow the peace treaty. The ink was hardly dry when merciful Providence had uncovered the Gunpowder Plot, with Guy Fawkes and his band of renegade English Catholics only hours from blowing up Parliament, and the King and Prince Henry with it. The Fifth of November would live forever as a day of infamy. Only God and the Devil knew what share Zuñiga had had in that business. Though from where else but a Spanish arsenal could the plotters have shipped in thirty-six barrels of gunpowder? From where else but the Spanish Netherlands would their armed legion of exiled recusants have swarmed across the Channel to put the throne in the hands of a Catholic puppet and tear down the Church of England? Aye, and put its bishops to the flame the way they did the last time they had the chance. Thus had Mary Tudor avenged her father's divorcement of her Spanish mother, Catherine of Aragón, and thus had she sought to please her Spanish husband, Philip the Second. Bloody Mary had given way to Protestant Elizabeth only four years before the Archbishop was born, so the Church of England had now been restored for barely half a century. It was still but a babe at the mercy of the old dragon of Rome, with his Jesuit teeth and his Spanish jaws, and no Pope would rest until England was back again in the fold to which it had belonged for almost a thousand years.

Spain had tried war. Spain had tried assassination. And Spain had tried marriage. What sort of people were these who could let it be known when the Queen was ailing that an Infanta might be reserved for James? The noble Prince Henry knew the answer better than his craven father, and had stood implacably against every attempt to plant such a princess in his bed. Had the father the son's courage, he would have sent the Spaniards away with fleas in their ears, and not permitted them to believe to this day that a marriage was yet possible if the price was right. And he would never have allowed again into the kingdom this ambassador Zuñiga, who was rumoured to come now with a new trump in his pack—namely, the monstrous suggestion that Philip the Third himself, newly widowed at thirty-four, should take to wife Henry's sister, sweet Bessy, not quite half that age and promised anyway to the young Protestant Frederick of the Rhine. Who could doubt that a marriage to Philip would soon be consummated by the murder of both Henry and Baby Charles to clear the way for the King of Spain to become King of England? This Philip would not let slip this throne the way his father had done, by believing it enough to marry Mary Tudor without destroying her heir presumptive, Elizabeth Tudor.

It was no wonder that Spain persevered. They knew, as the Archbishop knew, that so many of the nobility and gentry of England paid but lip service to the Protestant church. Even in the King's Privy Council were ministers betraying secrets to wives who knelt at forbidden masses, conducted by fugitives treasonably committed to Rome's decree that it was no sin for an heretical monarch to be murdered by his subjects. Elizabeth had dealt with such in the only way they understood—three hundred priests had dangled in her forest of gallows trees. But her successor had neither her blood nor her steel. While his reluctance to send more than a token few to the block reinforced the traitors' spirits, Spanish gold reinforced their pockets. James played a strange and dangerous game, certain even now that he could fill his bare coffers with a million dowry crowns—enough to halve his debts at a stroke—and sacrifice nothing in return. He seemed determined to blind himself to the reality that not one of the Pope's princesses would be permitted to change her religion, even to become the bride of the next King of England. Nor would he see that the Church of England, the Lords and Commons of England, and the people of England would brook no successor with a wife whose first allegiance was to the Vatican. With any such princess, the bride-price must be at least toleration of her Romish practices in private. Which inevitably must lead to easing, then repeal, of the penal laws against Catholics. Which inevitably must lead to their being able to hold office again. And, if there were Catholic Justices of the Peace, Catholic Members of Parliament and Catholic Privy Councillors, then how long before a Catholic heir and a Catholic king? Aye, and the Catholic Inquisition, and the smoke of the *auto-da-fé* darkening the English skies?

This morning, Zuñiga was to come before the Privy Council with his master's message and his master's mischief. It was noted that he showed no hurry to return to Madrid, and the Archbishop's spies had reported that, in the fortnight since his landing, Zuñiga had secretly disbursed some fifty thousand crowns. But to whom? And for what? When a poor Guildford cloth-worker like the Archbishop's own father had laboured from sunrise to sunset to earn a single crown (and sung hymns at his bench in thanksgiving), Zuñiga's thousands were neither for small fry nor small favours.

"I pray thee, make his bribes turn to hot ashes in the traitors' hands. And their powders and their poisons, their muskets and their daggers, turn inward upon themselves. May it please thee to guide our anointed King, and to grant to our Prince of Promise, our Palladium, a bride of the true faith."

"Amen," said Nightingale, the Archbishop's old servant, from the door. "Amen, amen, amen." Tears ran down his cheeks.

The Archbishop braced the fellow's trembling shoulders. "Fear not, good man. The Lord will look after his own."

OVER IN THE CITY, on the site of the old Barbican tower, there now stood the house of Philip the Third's resident ambassador, Don Alonso de Velasco, formerly Inspector-General of the Galleys and Fleets of Spain. Where, in centuries gone by, watch had been kept for the enemy, today the enemy kept watch on England—from behind high walls that scowled back at Cockneys less eager than their king to be at peace with these dark-eyed devils.

In the wide courtyard, Don Pedro de Zuñiga—Marqués del Floresdavila these three months, but ever Zuñiga to the English—put a polished toe into a groom's linked hands and swung into his saddle. He surveyed with the eye of an ex-general the turnout of his retinue of half a hundred black-liveried horsemen as they stood ready to escort him to Whitehall for his special audience with King and Council.

"Wish me well, Don Alonso. Were I on such an errand to our own sovereign, I would expect to leave the presence on a skewer."

"Ah, but you are the master of our trade, Don Pedro. You will find words to place their king in your debt for doing your duty to ours."

"Pray God you are right." Zuñiga spruced up his moustache with both thumbs. "But is it not fortunate that we have a friend or two at the Council table?"

"If our *confidentes* prove insufficient, we shall close our purse. That would teach them a lesson."

"They would learn a better one if the purse remained open—but with it their master's eyes. If they choose to be of no further use to us, let their king see to their downfall. Why soil our own hands?" Zuñiga brushed his gloved palms one against the other.

THESE TWENTY LORDS and others of his Majesty's most honourable Privy Council, waiting to take their places on the long benches on either side of their table at Whitehall, were the governors of England: the more so since an exasperated James had dismissed his first Parliament eighteen months ago. He found he could happily do without the babbling of the Commons about the rights and the privileges, the grievances and the petitions, of every Tom and Tib but James. He was surprised that the great Elizabeth and her mighty father before her had ever permitted such an institution—five hundred bodies without a head—but there it was when he arrived from Scotland, and he confessed himself obliged to endure what he could not abolish. Unfortunately, his predecessors had encouraged the Commons to believe they were an indispensable estate of the realm. Members were rash, suspicious and over-busy, whining unceasingly for things he was certain to deny. There came the time when, once and for all, he had had to show these harebrained squires and double-tongued lawyers who was master. So away he had sent them—and if he never again had to summon them from city, borough and shire, that would be soon enough for him. He would manage perfectly well without that factious crew, unless he needed to call upon more funds than the Privy Council could harvest without them. He did not need the Commons to force up the revenues from crown lands, nor to come down harder on recusant fines and forfeitures, nor to create two hundred baronetcies at a thousand pounds a time for the hereditary privilege of ranking above all knights but those of the Garter. The prospect of recall would recede still further once the dowry for Henry was obtained. And by the time that was spent, Baby Charles would be old enough for one.

Unlike the Commons, the Privy Council gave the King no trouble because only he elected its members. Each one confirmed the criticism that he preferred mean men for great place, so that when he chose to turn them out they should have no legion of friends to fight their cause, but rather a legion of enemies to rejoice. As long as they suited him, he would reward them well. The fatter they grew on monopolies, licenses, grants and charters, the more they would be bound to him for the wherewithal to sustain their great houses and their high lives, their ambitious families and their greedy wives.

The single embossed chair at the head of the table sat empty today, awaiting one of the King's rare visits for business he considered more important than hunting and hawking. The Archbishop, who usually presided, placed himself at the chair's right arm. From Henry's investiture as Prince of Wales, it should have fallen to him to be president in his father's absence. But James, faced with the choice of reducing deer herds less or enlarging Henry more, had the Archbishop take the chair, having already kept his heir waiting nigh on a year and a half even to be sworn a Council member. When the Archbishop had suggested that the Prince should assume his rightful place at the head of the table, the King had refused, looking at the man as though each word he uttered was to be a faggot at his stake. The King had compounded the insult by naming Baby Charles next in line for the other vital office to which the heir publicly aspired: Lord High Admiral. And when Henry made clear his displeasure, his father had responded by adding to the Council roll the name of Viscount Rochester. From that day, Henry had chosen not to attend rather than acknowledge his father's minion as a fellow councillor. He would take his seat only when expressly commanded.

The Archbishop watched to see where the Howards would sit today: they always managed to separate themselves at Council, as though even an accidental grouping might proclaim too provocatively the existence of this formidable alliance of blood and avarice. At the far end of the table, behind a long white beard, perched the Howard Earl of Nottingham, still Lord High Admiral on the strength of the Armada victory a quarter-century ago when he was a stripling of fifty. Another survivor of five reigns and seven decades, the cat-faced Howard Earl of Northampton, now Lord Privy Seal, sat a distance from his beefy nephew, the Howard Earl of Suffolk, Lord Chamberlain and father of Lady Frances—and, too, of Lady Elizabeth, who was cuckolding old Baron Knollys here with lovers nearer her five-and-twenty. The four others whom marriage had placed, or would soon place, in the Howard family tree were the last at the table. The Earl of Shrewsbury, whose son-in-law was the Howard Earl of Arundel. The Earl of Pembroke, richest of all the peers, who was Arundel's brother-in-law. The old Earl of Exeter, whose grand-daughter was courting one of the Earl of Suffolk's vast brood. And Viscount Rochester, whom the King had yesterday confided to the Archbishop would be Lady Frances's new bridegroom when the Essex knot was untied. As though to confirm the secret, Rochester made sure today that he sat next to anyone but his future in-laws—a task of some difficulty, even with the Scottish councillors absent, as usual, on the King's business in Edinburgh.

As Don Pedro de Zuñiga and his escort trotted up Fleet Street on their way to Whitehall, a shabby horseman edged out of an alleyway and doffed his cap in deep salute. The ambassador warmed to this rare gesture of welcome from a common citizen of London. In return, he ceremoniously took off his own hat, richly plumed and with a splendid diamond gleaming in a band of black velvet. In a single movement, the ruffian let his wool cap fall to the cobbles, grabbed the ambassador's and, sticking it on his unkempt head, spurred his nag away up Chancery Lane at the gallop. Tipplers under the triple-feather sign of The Prince's Arms shook with laughter and, pots in hand, moved to block the way of the escort as it waited for the command to give chase.

"Stay!" Zuñiga raised a hand. "I would not lower myself to keep even a thief's king waiting."

THE THIEF'S KING had toothache. He held a fist to his inflamed jaw as he tramped testily through the lesser chambers of Whitehall to join his waiting councillors. He wondered who was the bigger fool—himself, or the physician who had led him to suppose that stuffing the cavity with a bitter paste of fenugreek seeds held in place with wax would cure the King as it cured the King's horses. Clearly, these barmy quacks judged the remedy's efficacy by the fact that the horses never complained.

"Cornwallis! Have you any message from my dutiful son and heir?"

"His message to *me,* Sire"—Sir Charles, ever the diplomat, accentuated the word to reduce the chance of offence—"was that were I to favour a match with any princess unless and until she had consented to renounce Rome, he would regard me as a traitor."

"And were *I* to favour it, what then? I, being wiser in the ways of women, and knowing therefore that once in a Protestant land, once in the bosom of a Protestant family and once in the bed of a Protestant prince, she will convert her religion as eagerly as she converts her virginity—what then, eh? What then?"

"Were I to presume to put such a question to his Highness, I would surely merit a greater rebuke from your Majesty than for failing to do so."

Cornwallis had advanced his career at court by avoiding every opportunity to tell the powerful what the powerful might not wish to hear. Though now Treasurer to the Prince, he had served as an intermittent envoy for the King, journeying to Madrid to conduct marriage negotiations which expired and revived as the high winds of high politics blew cold and hot across Europe. And over all these tense years since the peace (God, how much simpler was war!) poor ambassadors were set to work spinning webs that were meant to entrap sovereigns, but which threatened mostly to entrap themselves. It made plain dealing a game for gulls. It made honesty the path to ruin. It robbed words of their meaning. It perfumed the lie and made the truth stink. And yet, the peace of nations depended upon the craft of ambassadors. War was the consequence of their failure to prevent the conceits of kings from becoming the criteria of conflict. To this end, their duty was ever to take on their shoulders the blows meant for their employers. And, with James adding the pain of his rotten tooth to the pain of his defiant son, Spain's decade of deceit in the marriage negotiations would mean blows a-plenty today for Don Pedro de Zuñiga. Especially since England's brave King would sooner thrash a don than his master.

This month, Spanish double-dealing had produced a spectacular double deal that could rob Henry of the two ripest and richest princesses in the world. For it promised to engage the elder Infanta to the boy king of France, and his eldest sister to the boy heir of Spain. Yet, with the contract due to be signed in Paris in the middle of next month on King St. Louis's day, Madrid was still striving for one English marriage or another. Cornwallis dared not breathe to James the report that they had been further encouraged in this by a secret message from his own Queen that sweet Bessy was ready to turn Catholic for the widower Philip. This could well be a dirty Spanish lie, or even a clean English lie. Either would be better than the story proving true, which would prove also that Anne's papist proclivities had not ended with the nine secret communions she was rumoured to have taken before she left Scotland for England. It was no secret, though, that she avoided the Protestant ritual at her Coronation, and no clergyman of the Church of England could be found to state that she had even once since received his sacrament. Some in her household said the Queen's Catholic sympathies were the real reason James had removed the baby Henry from her care. Others said she had turned to the Jesuits, for her comfort and to her husband's discomfort, only after her son had been taken away. There was, however, little doubt that Zuñiga was today empowered to try to match the younger Infanta with Henry to keep him from the next princess of France, lest that alliance diminish for Spain the strength of the new double-knot she was tying with England's other historic enemy. But, since both girls were but six years old, it would be a decade before either's dowry could relieve the wants of England's monarchy and either's womb could carry the next of England's line. Thus were the Machiavellis of Madrid winning even the hands they seemed to have lost.

"Cheer up, Cornwallis! It will gladden Zuñiga's black heart to see you wearing your worries on your brow."

"As your Majesty pleases." Loyally, he locked his face in the beginning of a smile.

"Anyway, man, I'm the one who should look down in the dumps. I'm the one with toothache."

FIFTEEN PAIRS of cold eyes followed Zuñiga as he bowed between the double doors, made his dignified way up the middle of the chamber to the foot of the council table and there bowed again. The sixteenth pair, less cold, did not move to him until the last of his footsteps had echoed from the wooden floor. Cornwallis had no wish to contribute to the ordeal of a diplomat whose impossible task was neither to win this encounter and insult King James, nor to lose and inflame King Philip.

His face like an El Greco mourner, Zuñiga waited for the usual permission to be seated. The King did not give it. His greeting was to pound the table so that the quill leaped out of the Archbishop's inkstand.

"Has the ordinary ambassador not told me enough ordinary lies? Has there to be a special ambassador to tell me special lies?"

"My royal master intends nothing in my instructions to cause your Majesty displeasure." Zuñiga's tones were level, but so low that the ancient Earls of Nottingham and Northampton each cupped hand to ear.

"You must give me leave to be the best judge of that. What *are* you here for, anyway? To bribe my people? To win me for the Pope? To poison my wine?"

The first was true. The second was devoutly to be wished. The third would, however, lance the boil of James only to raise the boil of Henry, by far the greater threat to Hapsburg Spain, to say nothing of the Hapsburg Holy Roman Empire. But Zuñiga brought to bear the deaf ear that traveled in every ambassador's baggage. "I am directed simply to give your Majesty satisfaction over the matter of the marriage negotiations."

"Negotiations! Hark at him! Negotiations!" The King threw up his hands. "They were not negotiations, Master Zuñiga. They were a trick to keep me talking long enough for you to arrange to deprive my son of the two most suitable princesses in the world."

The Archbishop caught Cornwallis's eye. They both knew the King's deepest anger arose from the fact that when negotiations opened, Henry was still boy enough to do as his father ordered. Those days would never come again.

"But your Majesty! It is my happy duty to state that our contract with France is not yet signed. Were it your Majesty's wish, the Infanta Ana could yet become engaged to the Prince of Wales."

A good stroke, thought Cornwallis. Nevertheless, he made a mental note to ensure it became known to the French ambassador that Spain was ready to dishonour its bargain. No doubt it was ready to substitute for Ana the Infanta María, whose mere six years would be no bar to King Louis since it would be September before he was nine.

"Zuñiga, you box of tricks!" James laughed in exasperation, and his councillors at last let their long faces shorten. "But you have led us up this blind alley before. We respond to your beckoning finger, then you say, '*Ah,* but we must accommodate the small matter of religion.' And we go so far as to agree that perhaps we may provide for your Infanta to practise her rituals privately. Then you say, '*Ah,* but she must have her own chapel.' And we go so far as to agree that perhaps even this may be arranged. Then you say, '*Ah,* but her children must choose their own religion.' Then '*Ah,* but this," and '*Ah,* but that.' And when every possible compromise has been achieved, what then? You say, '*Ah,* but your Prince must become a Roman.' Is that not true?"

"True," nodded the Archbishop. "True, true, true,"

"Were you Spaniards honest men, you would have raised at the beginning the impossible barrier you raise at the end. But you do not choose to do so—because the truth was, is and ever will be that you want the negotiations, but you do not want the marriage."

"True." The Archbishop was still nodding. "True, true, true."

"And now you pretend again to offer a marriage! But you do not tell me, Zuñiga, whether your demands are still those that insult me as supreme head of the Church of England. My son would not turn Catholic even if your Infanta were sole heir of the monarchy of the whole world."

"My master, Sire, would not wish your Majesty to hear from him any demand he would not judge fitting to be propounded to himself."

"Man, are you telling me your king is more certain of the truth of his religion than I am of mine?"

"My master would take it as a compliment were you to see him as no less certain than yourself."

And were Zuñiga a fencer, thought Cornwallis, he would be the finest of all. The ambassador, however, was not yet ready to applaud himself. The great test was still to come. For he had designed, with Madrid's approval, a gambit to save the English king's face before the English king's Council.

"Your Majesty, I am further directed to state that my master's regrets would be even greater had the proposal originated from him."

"But, God's wounds, it *did* originate from him!"

"To serve my master's recollection, Sire, might Sir Charles Cornwallis confirm that it was he himself who came to Spain a year ago to present your Majesty's kind and affectionate salutations, and to inform my master that your Majesty's instructions were to propound a marriage for Prince Henry with the Infanta Ana?"

"It's a wise man that knows himself, Don Pedro." James was scornful. "When it comes to the truth, you do well to seek it of another."

"If your Majesty pleases." Cornwallis rose. "Following your instructions, I gave particular notice to the King of Spain that the overture to this whole business was doubtless by his resident ambassador in London, Don Alonso de Velasco. By him was your Majesty advised that should you be pleased, according to the custom by which the intended bridegroom is to speak first, to begin a motion for marriage with the Infanta, then it should have all kind acceptance by Spain. That was the motive that caused your Majesty to propound the match. That, and that alone."

"Velasco tricked me!" Again, the King thumped the table, and again the Archbishop's quill went flying. "I was ever telling him that the peace treaty was strangely followed by the willingness of you people to harbour Englishmen ill-affected to England. God! Let us not mince words! There were fugitives from the plot to blow me to kingdom come sheltering in the Spanish Netherlands, and you wouldn't deliver even those monsters up to me. I began to wonder whether the peace was not a device to cause us to lower our guard while you built up an armada for another war. And—your damned man Velasco threw it back at me!" James put his fingertips together and lowered his head, but not his eyes, to mock Velasco's words: *"Oh, Sire, how it grieves me that you can think so coldly of my king. But will he not think as coldly of your Majesty if you continue to turn aside the opportunity to unite our great nations with a great marriage?"*

Rochester led the dutiful laughter that the King's performance demanded. In Council, the favourite would laugh when the King required laughter. The favourite would nod when the King required assent. The favourite would shake his head when the King required dissent. But he would say nothing. Whatever he had to say—about the stubbornness of Abbot, the cunning of Northampton, the stupidity of Suffolk—he would say when there could be no argument from them. He would save it for the quiet of the King's privy chamber, and the dark of the King's bedchamber.

"Velasco accompanied his challenge of coldness on my part with an assurance of warmth on your king's part if I would request the Infanta for my son. But it was a trick to cozen me—a Spanish trick!"

"A trick," muttered the Archbishop. "A Spanish trick!"

"Your nation, Master Zuñiga, showed no disposition to hasten in the matter. That should have served to warn me. Your ministers protested how much they desired amity between the crowns of England and Spain. Yet then, after an age, they informed us that only the Pope could rule on the final difficulty of religion."

The Pope! England's Archbishop shuddered at the name and rubbed goose-pimpled forearms through white lawn sleeves.

"Zuñiga," said James savagely, "you cannot look me in the eye and say that your Velasco could have given me such encouragement to proceed—*had not your king already tried the Pope's inclination!* I know the ways of kings. Especially Pope's kings."

"My king, Sire, would no more practise such deceit than would your Majesty."

"I have you, then! Either Velasco took it upon himself to speak his own wishes in his master's name—or he spoke the truth but you have now disavowed him. So either he is unworthy of his place by his own knavery, or he is made unworthy by his master."

James nodded triumphantly. Zuñiga let him have his moment, and then played Spain's gambit.

"Since it pleases your Majesty to take that view"—the ambassador sighed as as though accepting a burden—"it must be my duty to withdraw Don Alonso de Velasco forthwith from employment in this country."

Cornwallis joined in the chorus of satisfaction though he knew well that the temporary discomfiture of Velasco in exchange for the frustration of Spain's greatest enemy was no defeat for Madrid. The Archbishop lifted his eyes to the moulded ceiling between him and heaven. What humiliation for the ambassador! James sat back, folded his arms and noticed that victory had extinguished his toothache. Never mind the ambassador. What humiliation for Philip of Spain! To have a daughter whose sex gave her the privilege of being sought, and to lower himself to offer her only to have her rejected. James felt he had demonstrated to his Privy Council that with the passing of Queen Elizabeth they had not seen the last English sovereign to put Spain in its place.

"Master Zuñiga, have you no further instructions?"

"None, your Majesty."

"Well, get out, man. Get out—or I'll have your guts for garters!"

OUTSIDE, Cornwallis found Zuñiga waiting for his escort to assemble. "You did well in there."

"I would have liked to have done better. To have come away with an offer for the second Infanta."

"Henry needs a woman to love. What would he want with a bride aged six?"

"My King esteems her as much as the other. He would give her as big a dowry."

"A million would not make her riper."

"But, Sir Charles, we both know that in the matches of great princes there are commonly greater inconveniences than the disproportion of some few years." Zuñiga spread his hands. "And there are very few kings' daughters left in Christendom."

"Perhaps so. But instead of your Spanish olive, I would rather Henry found an English rose." Cornwallis smiled. "They have longer stems."

"I will take your word for it, Sir Charles. I have never got beyond the thorns."

[6]

Wednesday the Fifteenth of July

WHEN an assignation needed to be arranged, Henry would send a message through Sir David Murray, the man he most trusted, to Anne Turner, the woman Frances most trusted. Murray, first of the Prince's Gentlemen and now Groom of the Stole and Keeper of the Privy Purse, was more like a wordly-wise uncle to Henry than a high officer of his household. He had been at Henry's side since he was the six-year-old Prince of Scotland, and one of his prime concerns had been that Henry should learn to take his pleasure, slake his lust and make his love with women rather than men. In this, he would be better served than was his father, whose initiation had been at the cousinly hands of the Duc d'Aubigny. James's boyish devotion was the beginning of the reputation that his ever-after fondness for handsome favourites did nothing to diminish. Nor even premarital mistresses such as Murray's own kinswoman, Lady Glamis. Nor even the begetting of six lawful bairns.

Yet it would not do for the Prince to resort to the poxy doxies whose half-crown haunches rotted too many noble marrows. Nor would it be politic for him to play havoc among the maiden daughters of the great families whose loyalty he would need to buttress a reign that was not going to be easy after the jellyfish years of James. So it was Henry's good fortune that, after four neglected court wives, whose discretion equaled their allure, a beauty such as Lady Frances was eager to serve him. Since she had a husband, whatever the tales of his ability, her hopes of the Prince could not include marriage. There needed to be no such opportunity—just in case Henry should be foolish enough to fall in love and decide that he was not content to pluck the fruit, but must pluck the entire tree.

Murray's letter arrived as Frances was in the middle of a merry debate about whether the pearl earring she lost in the meadow yesterday might turn up today. Mrs. Turner glanced at the seal of the Murrays of Abercairny, and teasingly let the message lie on the side table.

"You were saying, Frances?" She would be amused to see how long the girl could keep curiosity at bay.

"My father says that when you lose an arrow, the best thing is to let fly another the same way to find it for you. I wonder if that's the way to discover my pearl?"

"You mean wear another just as yesterday, find the same spot in the meadow and go about the same exercise?"

"Yes! And if it doesn't succeed, I shall just have to try it again the next day. And the next day, and the next!"

"You might forget what it was you were looking for."

"Oh Anne"—she moved to hug her—"I think I've forgotten already."

They both looked at the letter and laughed. They both stretched to pick it up. Mrs. Turner reached it first, broke the seal, took a deep breath and began to read:

Good Mistress Turner:

My duty calls me to accompany his Highness upon a private visit to his Majesty's ships at Chatham. Therefore, I pray you will find the kindness to accept the postponement of our special business until I may wait upon you at Paternoster Row this Saturday afternoon.

Your most devoted servant,
David Murray

"Oh, three more days to wait..." Frances's eyes brimmed, and Mrs. Turner put an arm about her shoulder.

"Be patient, my dear. You will be free in the spring."

Frances went to the window to let her tears overflow. She looked across the shorn green and tried to imagine its spring carpet of crocuses, but the picture declined to form.

"If the King finds out...he will see to it there is no spring for us."

"If I were the King"—Mrs. Turner spoke to the girl's back—"I would make sure I did *not* find out. I would not care to be the father who looked into the eyes of this Prince and forbade him to marry the one he loves."

"But this father has the cunning of the Devil."

"And when it is for your sake, my dear, so do I. You know that."

"I do. I *do*. But my nightmare is that Henry will not be strong enough. The King may make him believe he can fulfill both his duty with a royal bride and his pleasure with a noble... *whore*." She squeezed the word out, and shut her eyes at the sound of it.

"Then, girl, you ought to leave him in no doubt that unless his heart is set upon marriage he will never again lay so much as a finger upon you. Never so much as a finger."

Mrs. Turner thought, but did not add, *like Anne Boleyn,* for that Howard girl had not this widow to save her head. To chart the course by which she might keep such as Essex at bay, such as Rochester bridled, and such as Henry besotted. To whisper to her those bawdy secrets that would leave a lover gasping yet leave a belly flat. To engorge her imagination on those painted Japanese scrolls Mainwaring had got from his pirate brother, with bedscapes of tangled limbs, insinuating hands, eager orifices, glinting pubes, wanton tongues and tumid flesh in many conjunctions more than that designed to perpetuate mankind. And, not least, to safeguard her womb with barriers of oil and wool; with concoctions of honey, vinegar, onion and peppermint; with infusions of willow, saffron and walnut; with pills of olive and quicksilver. Each and all more likely than the tales old wives were brought up on: of jumping and sneezing to expel semen; of holding the breath to the point of collapse; or of doing it standing up. Each and all less forbidding than the travellers' tales carried home with such grotesque souvenirs as sheaths of goldbeater's skin from France and of hemmed fish membrane from Greece: none a safe armour against impregnation, all a safe armour against love.

Frances thought, but did not add, *like Anne Boleyn,* for the very name was enough to shrink her neck into her shoulders. Nevertheless, it was true enough that Boleyn's gift of herself did get her royal lover to the altar, trampling a Catholic millennium into the dust to have and to hold the girl whose terms were marriage or never again so much as a finger.

"But, my dear"—Frances turned anxiously from the casement—"I do not know that I can take back what I have given. When I am with Henry, I am lost."

"You managed not to be lost with Rochester."

"This one *loves* me."

"Love you, love you not... he will hardly need to marry you, will he, if you are always as ready as the village shortheels? Grow up, girl. It is not the bait that catches the fish. It is the hook."

"He may turn to hate me."

"Mark my words, he will love you all the more."

"I don't know..."

"I *do* know, Frances. He's a man, isn't he? Men have to be shamed—tell him you fear to be with child. Men have to be made jealous—tell him Rochester has sent you that new necklace. Men want what they cannot have—tell him he cannot have you."

"But..."

"But nothing, my dear. Your fate is to win him. Simon Forman cast that the stars would free you of Essex and bring you your heart's desire. And Simon was never wrong. Ask your own mother."

"My mother?"

"Yes, but when your father's out of earshot, mind—he wasn't the one Simon was right about!"

It crossed Frances's mind to wonder whether Mrs. Turner had tried hook as well as bait with her own tardy lover, but a new concern was furrowing her brow. "Anne, I must ask, have you confided in Mainwaring about the Prince and me?"

"Rest assured, my dear. Would I do anything to harm my chances of being First Lady of the Bedchamber to the next Queen?" Mrs. Turner curtsied deep into a sea of the saffron she loved. "And Mainwaring will be quick enough with a ring then, I'll be bound."

Frances took a hand to lift her. "Then arise, my Lady-to-be...I shall bless you all my life."

Mrs. Turner folded Murray's letter and held on to it. She must try her own advice. Mainwaring took her too much for granted between and beyond the sheets, and it would do him good to discover—accidentally, of course—such a harmless message and conclude that perhaps he was not the only ram with a horn.

"HIGHNESS."

Henry turned to Murray from his contemplation of the cobalt sky through the windows of St. James's, glad that in the heat of this endless sun they would be spending tomorrow on the water.

"Highness, would you spare a few moments for Master Drayton? He awaits permission to dedicate to you his new book of verses. Ten thousand lines! Must have taken him years."

"Better fetch him in before he writes any more, though if they're half as good as his Agincourt I won't mind." *Fair stood the wind for France*...now there had been a prospect more heroic than wondering whether fair stood the wind for Chatham.

Murray signaled to a page, and the short and swarthy Michael Drayton was ushered into the Presence Chamber. He saw reborn in this Prince his hero of Agincourt, the young Henry the Fifth upon St. Crispin's Day, and his throat filled with awareness of it. He bent his head low.

"No—it is I who bow to you, Master Drayton. You are prince of a world in which I am but a serving man. My poetry is poorer even than Sir David's."

"In truth," said Murray, "I fear that to be a poorer poet than me is one of the few achievements beyond the reach of your Highness."

"Master Drayton." Henry smiled and motioned him to proceed.

"Highness, I humbly offer you my *Poly-Olbion,* a discovery in couplets of the glories of the kingdom to which you are heir." He came to a halt, dabbing at his eyes.

Murray tried to help. "Shall I read out your dedication?"

"Oh, no, Sir David. That must be my privilege." He held at arms's length his bundle of the first pages to come from the printer, and declaimed in hard Midland tones:

> Britain, behold here portrayed to thy sight,
> Henry, thy best hope and the world's delight;
> Ordained to make the eight great Henrys nine,
> Who, by that virtue in the treble trine,
> To his own goodness in his being brings,
> These eight glories of those eight English kings:
> Deep knowledge, greatness, long life, policy,
> Courage, zeal, fortune, awful majesty.
> He, like great Neptune, on three seas shall rove,
> And rule three realms with triple power, like Jove;
> Thus in soft peace, thus in tempestuous wars,
> Till from his foot, his fame shall strike the stars.

Drayton lowered the pages, and his eyes streamed again. Awkwardly, he fell to his knees, took the Prince's hand and kissed it. Henry raised him and put an arm round his shoulders. Today, he would reward Drayton with an annuity of ten pounds; tomorrow, he would reward him with another Agincourt. Murray looked on wryly, accepting that it would be too much to expect a court poet to acknowledge the less Jove-like, though no less worthy, qualities of this loving, affable, tender-hearted, slow-to-anger Prince. Neither Drayton nor any other was ever going to scan him truly without seeing, too, the flaws that made him a man as other men. Yet how was any outsider to see when those inside ensured, like Shem and Japhet, that their master's naked self was forever concealed?

Mrs. Turner carefully placed Murray's letter under a single scarlet carnation on her dressing table, where it would be certain to catch Mainwaring's eye while she was out of the room. The moment she returned, he bore her to the couch like a privateer renewing claim to a threatened prize, hauled up her gown and spread her from behind to take her with a vengeance that made her earrings jump. She had time only to lift her mischievous eyes to note that the carnation had been moved aside.

The contrived formality of the letter had made Mainwaring more jealous than a courtier's normal gushing flattery would have done. He had never got on with Murray, his superior in the Prince's household, who too often seemed to peer at him as though he wished he could peer inside him for proof of the suspicions he clearly nourished. And now, what devious game was Murray playing with Anne? Or she with him? Mainwaring laid a parting slap on her moist rump and slid from her to fetch some wine.

"Ow! What's that supposed to be for?"

"To make your cheeks blush for whatever *special business* it is that you do with David Murray this Saturday afternoon."

"You shouldn't read other people's letters."

"Not even from my rivals?"

"You see rivals everywhere. When Murray writes to me it is never more than Henry's device to send a private message to Frances." She poked out her tongue. "Disappointed?"

"No." He handed her a glass of sweet wine and sat alongside her. As she sipped, he bent to kiss the pink rose he had raised on her fair skin. "Not disappointed at all."

She drained her glass, wriggled playfully under his beard and turned onto her back.

[7]

Thursday the Sixteenth of July

IT WAS five in the morning and the sun glared low in an empty sky. St. George jiggled on the blue Garter ribbon at the Prince's breast as he led his company down the Privy Stairs to his gilded barge. The dozen oars of the scarlet-coated watermen remained upraised in salute until Henry gave the signal to cast off. He ignored the cushioned benches in the windowed cabin, preferring to stand at the prow like a live figurehead at least until they had shot the arches of London Bridge. The Thames was coming awake now with craft intent on passing through before the ebbing tide lowered the river to expose the starlings: those menacingly broad foundations that squatted on the riverbed like twenty-one sunken boats between which the current boiled as it forced its way. It was well said that the Bridge was for wise men to go over and fools to go under.

On Henry's larboard, as he made for the crown of the river, the north bank was a parade of noble homes, each set in orchard gardens and stretching back from porticoed stair on London's great wet highway to gatehouse in the cobbled Strand. Most stood as monuments to ambition overreached and monarchs undervalued. Essex House, once the home of the present Earl's executed father. Arundel House, once the home of the executed Lord Admiral Seymour. Somerset House, once the home of the executed Protector Somerset—and today Denmark House to harbour the Queen and honour her fatherland. Durham House, once the home of Sir Walter Ralegh, who had now wasted nine years in the Tower on trumped-up charges of encouraging a plot with Spain.

The men at the oars shed no tears for the ghosts of the north bank. When one vain lord lost his head or his fortune, another took his place: what difference did it make which supplied a humble boatman with cakes and ale to fill out his livery? And with a few coins to save up for the pleasures of the sinful south bank? There, between Lambeth Marsh and the Bridge, in the divers streets and winding lanes of the Bishop of Winchester's freehold, the flock of whores known as the Winchester Geese went about their business. Many a shilling was handed over for the privilege of stuffing many a goose, and as many more to stuff the pockets of quacks when passion paid its dividend in pox. Bankside offered bears and bulls fighting mastiffs for their lives in the arenas of the Paris Garden and the Bear House; and players fighting hecklers for their lines on the boards of the Globe, the Rose and the Swan. There was drink at the signs of the Tabard, the King's Head, the Flower de Luces and a mine host of others. And there was prison at the signs of the Clink and the Compter.

Now Henry's barge came to the Bridge—a street on stilts of stone, as crowded as any on land with houses and shops lining either side of a press of carts, coaches, cattle, horsemen and folk on foot. At gaps between the buildings people leaned over the parapet to watch the river traffic. Thirty more heads, long pecked clean of flesh, looked down from high above the Southwark gate where they had been impaled as a perpetual warning to enemies of the Crown.

"God save the Prince of Wales!" The triple-feather ensign was spotted, and the cry went up. Windows were thrown open wide as families craned out to watch the barge steadied and aimed at the central arch.

"Ship oars!" Henry commanded, and the dozen long blades lifted clear in line with his upstretched arms. The cheering crowd raised their arms to match and, merrily holding them high, bounced across the carriageway to cheer again from the other side when the oars touched down as one and pulled east into the rising sun.

"MAINWARING! You look like the cat that stole the cream." James himself, still nightgowned and as yet neither combed nor costumed, scented nor shod, did not look much the king that a cat might look upon. But he had told the fellow never to delay intelligence, so he made no complaint about the hour.

"Your Majesty, I have managed to secure this copy of a letter from Sir David Murray arranging a special meeting between his Highness and..."

"Give it here, man. Do you not think I can read? Mmm...*Paternoster Row*. Mmm...*Saturday afternoon*. Good work, my friend. You'll do well."

"I am happy to serve your Maj..."

"I don't suppose you had time for breakfast."

Mainwaring's heart raced. An invitation to eat alone with the King! His imagination sired a dynasty on the strength of it. "No, Majesty. I hastened to Whitehall at first light."

"Well, on your way out be sure to send to the kitchen."

"Oh..."

"And one thing more."

"Majesty?"

"Pray tell my wee page to present the King's compliments to my lord of Rochester, and request him to share a lonely old man's porridge."

Four more porridges, and the lonely old man would be starting his annual summer Progress, removing his court to lodge with a succession of noble hosts in the counties. Between now and then there was business to be done that could not wait the seven weeks until the court returned to town. The King slumped in his chair and closed his eyes, the better to calculate step by step how he might move the actors in this drama.

One: Frances was cast as the damsel in distress, Essex as the dragon. *Two:* Henry presumed he would play St. George, but this was in the gift of the author, and the part would fall to Rochester. *Three:* As long as Henry remained in ignorance of that, he would make no sudden move because, like all concerned, he took it that the damsel could not be freed before next spring. *Therefore four:* Rochester must bear the damsel away while Henry was still awaiting his cue. *Therefore five:* The divorce must secretly and speedily be brought forward. There could be decree and betrothal while Henry was still nodding offstage. *Therefore six:* The author must now write an earlier scene for the bishops.

The King padded to the window table, and drew pen and paper to him as he sat down. He tried the quill point between finger and thumb, and found it too stiff. Anointing it with spittle, he rubbed it back and forth on his sleeve until it was biddable.

Good Archbishop,

I pray you prolong no further the torment your poor King has borne these six long years since he allowed himself to be persuaded to match the misfortunate Earl of Essex and the Lady Frances. Justice and mercy dictate that the matter of the divorce shall be resolved forthwith.

Accordingly, you shall wait upon me at Theobalds this Saturday with the good Bishop of London. This matter is for the ears of none other. I repose myself upon your faithful and secret handling of the business.

James R.

As always when the Prince was aboard, the bargemaster now eased the helm to bring his course within three oarslengths of the Tower wharf. As always, Henry scanned the ramparts for the tall, still-soldierly prisoner who took his exercise on the walkway between his quarters in the Bloody Tower and the Lieutenant's lodgings. There he was! Striding with a zest that belied his sixty years. Catching sight of the royal barge as he turned. And raising his velvet cap high to circle it in the air, the sun glinting from his bejeweled fingers and the gold and diamond buttons of his black doublet.

The Prince cupped hands to mouth. "God love you, Ralegh! God love you!"

The last of the magnificent Elizabethans heard, and was strengthened for another day, another month, another year... however long it would be before this Prince could bring him liberty. Then Ralegh would repay. He would lead a fleet to Guiana and up the Orinoco to the legendary land of El Dorado, where gold and precious stones could be plucked off the mountainside like grass. He would bring home wealth enough to build Henry the greatest navy the world had ever seen. It would carry four thousand Englishmen to drive Spain out of the Americas, where they were hated more by the sons of the conquered than even the English by the Irish. With no more New World gold, bankruptcy would harry its troops from the Netherlands, too, and back behind the Pyrenees where the King of Spain would be reduced, as of old, to a king of figs and oranges. Then would Ireland be subdued and France humbled. Then would the Holy Roman Empire quake and the Pope quaver. Then would Henry become mightier than Alexander and, in the making of such an emperor, would Sir Walter Ralegh finally fulfill his own destiny.

Henry turned and made his way between the oarsmen, clinging to his sight of Ralegh like a lad to his receding kite. He took his seat by Murray and gave a heavy sigh.

"David, I swear that man will be out of that place within one hour of my accession."

"Amen to that! And yet, when we came down from Scotland, I shared your father's fears of Ralegh. I would have ridden a hundred miles to see him hanged. Now his enemies have proved to be your enemies, and I would ride a thousand miles to save his life."

"Only my father could keep such a bird in a cage."

"It's that bastard Rochester who should be in one."

"That bastard..." The hour that would see Ralegh freed would see Rochester in Ralegh's prison, and there let him take what rest his conscience would allow before he put his head on its last pillow and the executioner saw to it that such a soft, warm neck lay not too long on such a cold, hard block. Through Ralegh, Rochester knew well

what fate Henry would deal him. For the Prince had not long since fought and won the disarmed old soldier's battle to save his estate at Sherborne, all he had left to show for a quarter-century of valiant service. While Ralegh languished in the Tower, the King had seized his beautiful new manor house, with its young Virginia cedars and tropical shrubs now taking confident root in his green Dorset acres, and proposed to present it to his landless favourite. The high-born Lady Ralegh had gone on her knees to the King. He had averted his head and muttered, "I must have it for Robbie, woman. You would not expect your king to break a promise, would you?"

Ralegh had written to the favourite from the Tower:

> It has come to my knowledge that you have been persuaded to give me and mine our last fatal blow by obtaining from his Majesty the inheritance of my children. Seeing that your day is but now in the dawn and mine coming to the evening, I beseech you not to begin your first building upon the ruins of the innocent. I therefore trust, sir, that you will not undergo the curse of them that enter the fields of the fatherless.

To this, Rochester had made no reply, thereby acknowledging that there was none that would do. Henry had intervened, protesting until his father accepted that the King's son must for once have precedence over the King's favourite. James then agreed to let Henry buy Sherborne for twenty thousand pounds, which went straight into Rochester's eager pocket. Now the Prince held Sherborne in his own name for the day he would present it to a liberated Ralegh.

Meanwhile, he had been going regularly and publicly to visit his father's prisoner in his father's prison. No man could tell him more about wars and the winning of them. No man either, he found, could tell him more about women and the winning of them, or that victory in love could cost more dearly than defeat. The Prince had come to admire Ralegh more than any man living. There was no secret he would not confide in him. Until Frances. Henry did not wonder why. He knew why. Though he forgot it in the sight of her, the sound of her, the smell of her, the touch of her, the taste of her, the juice of her, perhaps Frances was not the good and gentle bride the common folk of England would cherish. They would see her as a Howard adventuress with one husband too many, and would think the less of Henry for following Essex into her bed. These were doubts that, in duty, a prince should test. But he could not. Uncomfortable with this awareness, and knowing well that Murray would never have been an accomplice to his liaison had he seen it as anything more than a better way than some for a lusty young Prince to purge his passions, Henry sought once again to press it out of mind.

"We should make Tilbury by nine, David."

"Aye, Highness. The tide is running for you."

FROM his wardrobe of threescore doublets and ten, Viscount Rochester eventually approved a combination of ash and pink, and wrinkled his nose at having to settle for an imperceptibly less than perfect match of ribbon roses on his satin shoes. He arrived to find the King had finished breakfast and lay sprawled across his high-backed chair as though content to spend the day in his nightgown.

"I beg your Majesty's pardon."

"Granted, granted." James shrugged. "I might as well start getting used to you keeping your old King waiting. Soon you'll have that young Frances in your bed, and what new husband can deny the dawn call of the stiff catzo? *Ah,* when I was your age..."

James, forty-six a month back, sighed for those gone-forever days. Once the mere thought of a couple throbbing under hump-backed sheets would have distended his codpiece, and out of habit he moved a hand to ease a discomfort that now existed only in the memory. As his desire had diminished, so had his need to bestow affection grown: though he could never see (and no one dared tell him) that every touch, every embrace, every kiss he lavished upon his favourites redoubled the whispers about his true nature. If he behaves thus in public, said rumour, how must he behave in private? And there was a ready parry to the counter that, in his classic textbook on kingcraft, *Basilikon Doron,* James had published his condemnation of sodomy as "a horrible crime that we are bound in conscience never to forgive." That, insisted rumour, was not disproof of his propensity, but proof of his hypocrisy. Rochester had long been aware of the gossip, but did not much care. He welcomed the King's attentions. Who wouldn't, accompanied as they were these five years by favour such as no man had received? And, anyway, from his boyhood in the wild Border country to his manhood in the wilder bedchambers of Whitehall, there was a growing multitude of witnesses who could swear that the only mark at which he had ever aimed was the one the Almighty intended.

The King stretched one leg over a stool, displaying a deathly white calf, and motioned to Rochester to help himself from the table. The favourite uncovered a now-lukewarm dish of porridge, made a face at the sight and smell of it, and chose instead to carve for himself a hunk of coarse bread and a wedge of Cheshire cheese. The King held out his cup and Rochester filled it, and then his own, from the pitcher of Scotch ale.

"Bless you, laddie. It always tastes sweeter when you pour it." He drained the cup noisily and held it out for more. "So I had better make the most of your company while I yet have it."

"Sire"—Rochester poured again—"you know I shall make no move to take a wife until it please you." As he said it, he became aware of a surge of anxiety lest the royal whim change. For, Rochester's calculating head having accepted that he must do the King's bidding, his accommodating heart was by now convincing him that no bidding was needed.

"Oh, it *will* please me, Robbie. You will be allied to a great family and breed a yet greater line. And my perverse son and heir will need to look for a bride where I wish him to look."

"But it would not serve your Majesty for me to earn the Prince's enmity. I beg you to make known to him that this match is to be *your* pleasure."

"No-no-no." James flapped both hands to dismiss the thought. "We all know the laddie's been making eyes at Frances, but that's as far as it's gone, take it from me. He'll wish her well—and he'll dance at her wedding."

"He usually does."

"Ha!" The King let out a horselaugh and wagged a finger. "Henry'd have your head for that."

"Then he would have the wrong head. If the quip is to merit such reward, honour requires that it go to the author."

"Your witty friend, Overbury?" The King's eyes narrowed.

"My witty friend, Overbury." Rochester would have given a thousand pounds to call back the last ten seconds. His bitterness at Overbury's attack on Frances had been seething since that day of the hawking at Theobalds, but oh, what folly to damn his man before his monarch.

"Your witty friend is a whit *too* witty." A snarl edged into the King's tones. "I have never cared overmuch for Overbury. I wonder that you still keep him."

"He is a most excellent secretary..."

"So? There are other most excellent secretaries."

"He knows my ways..."

"Others can learn your ways."

"He has served me well..."

"Clearly not well enough to profit by the lesson of last time. Fourteen months has not been long enough for me to forget. Or for the Queen. What makes Overbury think *he* can afford to?"

With so little in her slow life to remember, the Queen would indeed find it hard to forget that May Monday afternoon in her garden at Greenwich Palace. Rochester had been walking with Overbury, telling him of the King's anxiety about keeping his secrets safe from the Spanish ambassador's spies. Overbury had suggested there was no better hiding place than between the Queen's legs, for not even the King himself would hunt there, and we all knew, didn't we, that there was no braver man than he. They were laughing themselves as helpless as schoolboys when, unseen by either, the Queen had appeared at her open window and taken it that their guffaws were at her expense. The fact that they were did not help. Neither did the fact that the pair were too confused to offer the same answer to her demand to know just what was so funny. And the fact that Overbury, laughing still, presumed to leave his hat on in her presence confirmed her belief. She began by trying to laugh back at them but immediately turned to tears and ran to the King, screaming for him to commit them to the Tower for contempt.

He avoided the challenge by setting his Privy Council to hear the complaint. At Overbury's cunning dictation, Rochester confessed to the lords that he could not, for chivalry, have repeated to her Majesty the jest that had convulsed them, though in truth it was a crumb fallen from his Majesty's own table just the other day. Having endured the labyrinthine sermon of the old Bishop of Winchester for an hour, the King had informed the man that his contribution was like farting a hornpipe through a keyhole: prodigious in itself, but unlikely to bring mankind a step nearer salvation. The lords of the Council collapsed with mirth, and went to beg the King to bear himself the burden of explaining the indelicate misunderstanding to the Queen. Realising that her will was not going to prevail against Rochester, she had turned all her spite on Overbury, whom she knew the King would be less concerned to protect. Especially when she screamed: "You may think you rule Britain, Jamie, but Rochester rules you—*and Overbury rules Rochester.*"

James decreed that Overbury would be banished from the court. It was five months before much labouring by Rochester persuaded the King to admit him again, and even then he was advised to disappear from the Queen's sight whenever she was about. That privilege, said Overbury with an untamed grin, made the whole exercise worthwhile.

To the King it was now apparent that the man had not been dealt with effectively enough. "I have made up my mind, Robbie. Overbury shall go as ambassador to Brussels."

"But, Sire..."

"Not far enough for you?" James lifted his bare foot from the stool and stamped it temperamentally on the floor. "Damn it, then. *To Turin.*"

"But..."

"Not far enough?" The foot went down again. "Damn it, then. *To Muscovy.*"

"Your Majesty." Rochester dropped to his knees and clasped the King's hands to beg for the crutch he was not yet ready to dispense with. Now that he was acting as Secretary of State, how could he manage without the man? The thought of those cipher despatches alone was enough to make him fight for Overbury's career as though he were fighting for his own. As indeed he was. "His tongue, Sire, is impetuous in the company of those he trusts. His only fault has been to believe he could trust me. If your Majesty, in his wisdom, is minded to punish him for that error, then so be it. But he has ever been a faithful and discreet friend to me. And therefore"—Rochester looked soulfully into the King's troubled eyes—"I am resolved to share with him his fortune, good or ill, as he has willingly shared in mine."

"Laddie, laddie, there's no need to grieve," said the King, though it was his own eyes that filled. Rochester said nothing, knowing he had said sufficient. Now the old fool lay clammy hands on his shoulders. "He is fortunate to have such a brave, such a true friend. And as you are to yours, I shall be to mine."

Rochester squeezed his eyes tight, as though to stem his tears. "I thank you."

"You can best thank me by putting a bridle on your insolent friend. He laughs too much. One day he will laugh his head off."

"I will make it my mission to help him laugh less."

"Off your knees then, sweet boy." The King waved him up. "For it's high time you make it your mission to win that sweet girl. And the sooner you begin, the sooner I shall make you Earl of Somerset."

"Somerset..." That title would do him great honour. It had been borne by a son of Henry the Seventh, by a son (albeit a bastard) of Henry the Eighth, and lastly by the Protector of the boy King Edward the Sixth. James waited with amusement as Rochester savoured again the exquisite bait of an earl's coronet, surmounting it first upon the unremarkable Ker shield of three red mullets on a silver chevron, and

then impaling that upon the rich Howard coat of arms of three silver cross crosslets either side of a bend of gold.

"Now then, Robbie—I trust you have no commitments for the morrow?"

"I had looked forward to hunting with your Majesty at Theobalds."

"I would rather you hunt without me in Paternoster Row." He tapped the side of his nose confidentially. "I have reason to believe you will find your lonely Frances waiting for you at the house of the widow Turner." Aye, and let the girl explain Rochester's visit away to Henry when he knocked at the same door the next day. Better, let her conceal the fact, so that the lie would seem all the more monstrous when Henry found it out... which he well might.

"Your Majesty knows much, then." Much, but not all. Not how simple this errand was bound to be because Frances had always been wax in his hands.

"True—and I know much about the female race that you don't." James poked in the chest the lucky fellow about to get the benefit of his advice. "You've only ever ploughed a ploughed field. So you may well mistake a virgin's coyness for... coyness. But a lassie of quality is not like your tavern punks. She must be wooed. The sweet word. The chaste kiss. The deep sigh. The whisper in the ear." He wet his lips. "Only then, the hand at the dumplings. The finger in the pie." He waggled one to illustrate the suggestion. "So off you go—and on Saturday you will join me at Theobalds and tell me all about it. *All* about it, mind."

"I shall do my best."

"Do your worst, if needs be. Just so long as you make your mark with the lady before we set off on the Progress. What you do not lay claim to tomorrow, you will not secure in the seven weeks the court is away. And if I know you, laddie—and God knows I *do*—you'll be so busy swiving milkmaids from St. Albans to Nottingham that you'll have worn it out by the time we ride back in September."

"You flatter me. Sire."

"I'll flatter you with the back of my hand in a minute! Go on with you!"

By nine that morning, Henry's barge was at Tilbury Hope, twenty-five miles downriver, under a sun already high enough to dry the sweat on the aching backs of the royal oarsmen as they eased up to deliver their Prince to the waiting pinnace. Pennants flying, she sailed out from the estuary, sniffing salt long enough to turn twelve starboard points and bear the leeward tide in with her to the mouth of the Medway, home of the Fleet, by five that night.

Soon it would be ebb tide, leaving most of the ships of King James's Navy marooned in the stinking ditch between the mud flats; just as the tide of war had gone out with Queen Elizabeth, leaving most of her seamen disarmed, abandoned and prey to the elements until England might again require their lives at the going rate of ten shillings per lunar month (less twopence for the surgeon, fourpence for the chaplain and sixpence for the Chatham Chest to relieve comrades broken by sickness and wounds). Elizabeth had built up the harbourage at Chatham, safer from wind and weather than the exposed Channel stations; though such as Ralegh held that, for setting forth against Spain, Chatham was a rusty scabbard and Plymouth a drawn sword. Sir Francis Drake, greatest of the great Queen's great admirals, had been raised on a hulk here, amid the tang of tar and salted oak, and the music of bilges slopping and ropes slapping. Then, much as now, with the last war over and the next not yet in sight but as certain as every next war since the Creation, two dozen decaying but salvable battleships and one dozen too far gone were moored athwart the stream between the castles of Rochester and of Upnor.

James had been bequeathed by far the finest fighting fleet in the seven seas. But the blessings he had his sights on were those held out to the meek and the peacemaker, though critics no less mindful of the fifth chapter of St. Matthew judged him already qualified for the kingdom of heaven by poverty of spirit. Even before his coronation, he had recalled all Elizabeth's licensed privateers, lest they scuttle the treaty he was offering the enemy who had gone to war for her crown and his inheritance of it. He determined that the coasts of his new Great Britain needed no heavier guard than four vessels in the Narrow Seas. And his reign had so far added but a single new-built warship to the Navy Royal.

For fighting men, the peace of James passed all understanding. There was nothing for them here. Such as Captain John Smith went off to found Jamestown, observing that those who had plundered well in the Queen's name might rest upon their treasure, but poor men left with nothing between hand and mouth had little choice but to abase themselves to penury or to "turn Turk." This latter did so many with such success that pirate admirals Peter Easton and John Ferne alone were now mustering forty sail and two thousand men. From Cork's Roaringwater Bay the breadth of the Atlantic to Virginia's Chesapeake Bay, and from the Barbary Coast the length of the Mediterranean to the Levant, it had to be acknowledged that none made finer pirates than the English. Nor finer schoolmasters of pirates, as so many merchants had cause to moan when pillaged by corsairs trained at the hands of masters, boatswains and gunners unwanted by a Navy that now required but two hundred and eighty men for sea service—and no longer ventured abroad unless for such giddy adventures as a voyage to Calais to fetch Don Pedro de Zuñiga and his ambassadorial retinue.

For ten now too frail even for that, there was the relief of Sir John Hawkins's almshouse at Chatham. And those who could still get about went down to join the crowd at the dockyard pale for a glimpse of Prince Henry as he came ashore to take supper in the parlour of the Clerk of the Cheque. The front rank opened to let through one who perched on a square board with a rough wooden wheel at each corner, and bent forward to claw himself along with calloused hands.

"God save you, Captain."

"And God save you." Henry thanked him silently for the title as he looked down, smiling to mask the pity that welled up for this jetsam of war.

"There's not much left for God to save, Captain."

"Where did you lose your legs, my brave friend?"

"On the *Warspite* at Cádiz, Captain."

"With Ralegh?"

"Aye."

As the royal party moved on, Murray caught the Prince's eye and reached inside his doublet for a gold angel. He dropped it into the old sailor's hands, but it bounced to the ground and a ragged companion lifted a bare foot to capture it.

"Get off—it's mine!"

"Not if I tell him the truth, it won't be. *Warspite,* my arse! Whore's spite, more like. Garn! You'd have them legs still if you hadn't been sneaking out the top window with Black Lucy's wages when her fancy man caught up with you."

[8]

Friday the Seventeenth of July

ROCHESTER pulled the sheet over his head to shut out the morning sun streaming into his chambers at Whitehall. He wished he could as easily shut out the pictures streaming into his mind. In a few hours, he would be calling at that house in Paternoster Row for the first time in half a year. Had Frances by now tripped up that staircase with the Prince, too, her back closing the bedchamber door behind him as she turned the key that freed them and made the rest of the world a prison? Watching the Prince, too, as he watched her ease every stitch from her body and sink her sleek haunches impishly into the warm puddle of her clothes? Extending an arm for the Prince, too, to raise her from her wanton curtsy, her breasts bobbing thanks as she tiptoed across the cool floor to that bed?

Rochester lifted the sheet and snorted at his perfidious self for responding to his hot imaginings, despite the cold jealousies that begat them. But why mock the one part that never dissembled? It was no respecter of conscience, logic or edict. It was the one true signpost, and inclined where honesty bid. Perhaps it was all that remained of the real Robert Ker of Ferniehirst. The rest was vainglory. The rest was scarlet and ermine, crest and mantling, coronet and Garter. The rest was royal warrant and letters patent, gold and diamonds, and castles and forests. The rest it was that, when the Prince came on the scene, had bowed farewell to Frances lest it all become forfeit as the price of his Highness's displeasure. What would return to her today, by the King's command, was the real man. The one who could now see that, in his heart, he had never been away. The one who had surely always loved her, but was only now willing to admit the pain that told him so.

The real man flung back the covers and yelled for his breakfast.

THE DAWN TIDE swirled into the Medway, and the bare-rigged warships groaned like old men getting up as the flood raised them from their muddy beds. Once they were riding high, the Prince was rowed into midstream to begin his private survey with the ships rated Royal,

Great, Middling and Small in the lower reach. The Clerk of the Cheque had followed as far as the longboat, at which point Murray had advised him that the presence of the Navy Board would already have been requested had it been required.

Now Henry came to his own four-master, *Prince Royal,* the figurehead of a mounted St. George gracing her beak, and his Highness's three gilded plumes, each the height of a man, blazing at her tall stern and echoing in an upper canton of the ensign on the quarterdeck. She was two years old and the mightiest in the Fleet—her twelve hundred tons half as much again as *Ark Royal,* England's flagship against the Armada. Though she stretched little further than a tennis court, she could serve death point-blank at four hundred yards from the fifty-five cannon on her three decks. The plan had been to give her eighty guns, but the Prince had heeded Ralegh's plea to lighten her lest she go the way of Henry the Eighth's *Mary Rose.*

Even then, *Prince Royal* had stuck too low in the Woolwich dock gate at the appointed hour of her launching. The King wanted to return the next day, and went sourly to bed when his son would not leave with him. And at two o'clock in the morning she had come clear, in thunder, lightning and a gusting sou'wester. As the black skies trembled, Henry had stood on the galleried poop with his trumpeters to christen the ship: cheering as he emptied the gilt standing-cup across her half-deck, heaved it overboard according to custom, and threw his hat to the full moon while the rain ran down his face and lanterns flickered the way for the first new warship to sail under the united crosses of St. George and St. Andrew.

When the hour came for *Prince Royal* to fulfill her birthright, she would carry a company of half a thousand. Here, her crew needed to be no more than a score. The boatswain was hustling them below as Henry came aboard to be greeted by the shipwright who built her, Phineas Pett, and her master, John King.

"Mercy!" The Prince drew a breath through his teeth. "Did you ever see such pitiful rascals?"

"Mercy indeed," said Pett, rugged of beard and tongue. "For in truth your Highness's ship has the pick of the Navy. These others in harbour count themselves blessed to have one per watch who can tell futtocks from puttocks."

"Aye," said Master King, "but who can blame any able seaman able enough to pay the pressmaster rather than serve with our ragged regiment of tinkers, tailors, robbers and rogues?"

Pett growled. "Those the clerks foist upon us would not have the stomach to fight their meat in an easy gale. Highness, they are even less use than their invisible shipmates."

"As bad as ever, is it?" Henry watched Pett and Master King nod in unison. "Tell me, how many such are put down to *Prince Royal?*"

"Well, sir," said Master King, "if you lift the hatches and shout below for John Panson, Tom Windsor, Simon Hodge, Dick Tonge, John Warner and Hugh Morton, I promise you'll get no answer. They serve in the ship's book, sir, but they serve not in the ship."

Round the fleet-in-waiting were nigh on a hundred like fellows, with names answered but once a month at the Chatham pay board. Add to that twice as many in the accounts of the four King's ships at sea, and you had some five thousand pounds a year going into the pockets of the parties to the deception.

"Highness." Pett sighed. "Nothing is going to change unless we first press a new Lord High Admiral. Nottingham's an old hulk now. How much shot has he got in his locker at three score year and fifteen?"

"Wrong tack as usual, Phineas!" Murray ribbed him. "He's put enough shot in his new wife's locker to father two bairns in a twelvemonth."

"Would that warships were as easily got," said Henry.

"Would that you were Lord High Admiral," said Pett.

"Be sure I shall not long be kept from it."

Murray read Henry's glance: as clear a signal of battle forthcoming as striking the main topsail. Yet only a few months ago he had won his father's word on this. Nottingham was to be pensioned off. Baby Charles was to be titular Lord High Admiral, and Henry was to be commissioned to execute the office with full powers during the six further years of his brother's minority. But suddenly the King changed his mind: Nottingham would continue for life. The turnabout was effected at the very time that Henry began openly to dig in his heels against all pressure to take a foreign princess. Could it be mere coincidence that this was, too, the very time that Henry began to pay court to Frances? Could it be that the King had searched out that secret?

"Have no fear, my hearties!" Henry was bracing his men as though they were the only ones here who might need it. "In peace, for sure the meanest ketch in the Thames is better manned than the Navy Royal. But when the press is for war and not for playing at sailors in the Medway mud, then we shall have the seafaring men we want."

"And the ships, Highness?" Pett's hands prayed. "Shall we have the ships?"

"Aye, Phineas. All the ships we want."

"Meantime"—Master King was not entirely convinced—"we have few that could safely go as far as Plymouth."

"Something *must* be done." Henry thumped fist into palm. "Something *will* be done." In went the fist again. "David, make a note..."

Murray readied his writing board and aimed quill at inkhorn. The Prince had adopted as his own the Northwest Passage Company motto, *Juvat Ire per Altum*—He Delights to Go upon the Deep. But it was nowhere more obvious than at Chatham that there would never be waters deeper than these, and never delight upon them, unless and until he could seize the helm for himself.

"Here, David." Pett led the party to the bow. "Look. Our anchor cabling is thirty-five fathoms too long. And nineteen-inch where eighteen would suffice. So not only are we burdened with two surplus tons but, at thirty shillings the hundredweight, that's sixty golden pounds down the drain. And the same goes, more or less, for every ship in the Fleet. The waste on cabling and rigging alone would pay for two new ships a year."

"Aye," said Master King, "but you'll be lucky to get one by the time our Comptroller has had his share. And our Treasurer his. And our Surveyor his. And our Keeper of the Stores his. And our Clerk of the Cheque his..."

"...and our Royal Shipwright his!" Henry laughed, though not as loudly as Master King, and his pointing finger challenged Pett.

"True, Highness." He lay hand upon heart. "But them as has to buy dear must find it from the next man."

"Phineas, I'll not weep for your poverty so long as that belly"—Henry gave it a prod—"threatens every button of that doublet!"

Master King's guffaw took into account that much the same could be said of Pett's *Prince Royal*. No ship loomed more fair, but she had too much belly, drew two foot beyond a sensible sixteen, was too lofty by far and sailed like a gilded slug.

Murray's notes grew with Pett's enthusiasm, with Master King's pessimism and with the Prince's impatience as they moved from ship to ship. Few had been caulked in a year, or graved and ransacked in five. Not that anything could now halt the decay of *Elizabeth Jonas, Garland, Mary Rose, Quittance, Charles, Tremontane* and *Advantage*.

All were quite beyond repair, and destined to join *Triumph* and *Bonaventure* at the breakers.

The Prince waited for Murray's pen to stop scratching for a moment. "Phineas, tell us how many ships are serviceable—or can be with no more than six months' work."

"Up to a score, I'd say, Highness. Plus the four already at sea—*Rainbow, Crane, Adventure* and *Lion's Whelp.*"

"I see very little activity to give me much confidence of that."

"Well, *Assurance, Antelope* and *Speedwell* are being readied for the next half-year's sea service."

"So I saw." Henry snorted. "I'll lay you five pounds to one they won't be fitted out in time."

"Twenty to one and you might tempt me," said Pett.

"Done!"

"Ah..." Pett was alarmed by the Prince's alacrity. "Well, I'll take you in shillings."

"The great gamester!" Henry rolled his eyes.

He did not offer odds on when the rest of the Fleet might get the attention it needed already, or the further attention it would need by the time the shipwrights got round to the task. *Dreadnaught, Defiance, Due Repulse* and *Merhonour*—the fastest sailer in the Navy—were still suffering from the last bout of repairing. *Vanguard* and *Antelope* were spewing so much oakum that they were hardly more watertight than a pauper's shoe. *White Bear* and *Nonsuch* were iron sick, their bolts so eaten by rust that they stood hollow in the timbers. *Warspite* and *Red Lion* were camber-keeled with long lying at anchor. *Anne Royal's* foremast and mizzen were cracked.

Murray completed his note of cabling overtarred, boltsprits sprung, main knees broken, keelsons insufficient, beams asunder, girdling required, pumps defective, cockboats missing, anchors oversized...

"It would be a day of rejoicing in Madrid if they could look over my shoulder," he said glumly.

"Not if they look over their own shoulders first," scoffed Pett.

It was not until they were ashore, walking through an avenue of gleaming trumpets and beaming officials, that Henry found his smile again. He had caught sight of Pett's chubby little wife.

"How's my noisy young namesake, Mistress Pett?"

"Noisy, sir." She curtsied and kissed his hand as he raised her up.

"What's the boy going to do with those nine sovereigns I sent him for his ninth birthday?"

"He's that proud of them, Highness. He swears he'll never, never spend them."

"Never spend them, madam? If I'd known that, I'd only have sent him nine half-sovereigns!"

THE COMPANY were washing down grapes with Rhenish white when Sir William Monson, Admiral of the Narrow Seas, presented himself at the Prince's table, hard-ridden and sweating like a turnspit.

"Pray forgive me, Highness. Through some oversight, I was not informed of your visit until this morning."

"No oversight, Sir William. I wished to see through my eyes and not yours."

"Your Highness will no doubt shield me from his Majesty's anger at my failure to be here to present the Navy's respects." Monson inclined his head.

"Well, we must see that your journey is not wasted, mustn't we?" Henry looked from Monson to Murray, who hoped without hope that mischievous gleam was not the precursor of a tasty tidbit for this Howard dependent to set before the King. "So sit yourself down, Sir William, and let us suppose—just suppose—that I wanted ten of the raggle-taggle ships I have seen out there made ready for war. How much would the Navy Board require to accomplish that?"

"Highness?" Monson's high colour drained away. "How long would this war be lasting?"

"Come, man! How can anyone know that? Just give me your estimate for a year at sea, and I'll be in a position to advise the enemy how long we can afford."

"As your Highness pleases. Well, it's men that cost most, and you'd reckon on one King's seaman for every two ton of King's ship. Say three-fifty men for *Due Repulse* down to one-twenty for *Adventure*. All in, that's near on two and a half thousand for your ten men-of-war. Plus four hundred more, of course, for your ten transporters of victuals and munition. Mmm?"

"Mmm," nodded an impish Henry, and Pett lifted a hand to mask a black-toothed grin.

Monson, went on, "You'd need to press a couple of thousand from the shires, and half a thousand from about London. The rest would be made up by men already in service."

"Not the men I've seen today, it wouldn't!" Henry's fist made the point.

"As your Highness pleases. It doesn't affect my arithmetic—what we are talking about already in wages, victuals and the rest is, mmm, sixty thousand pounds." He looked to see if the Prince wanted him to stop. The Prince did not. "Well, there's grounding and graving, and putting into serviceable order. There's suits of sail, flags, ensigns. There's all manner of sea stores. There's anchors, masts, yards. There's pinnaces and longboats. There's shot and powder and, aye, matches—mustn't forget the matches! And there's two shilling per ton per month for the hire of your ten transporters. And at the end, there's the five shilling to see your pressed men discharged and home—as many as may be left, that is."

"And what does it all add up to, Sir William?"

"Mmm, I fear you'd have precious little change from seventy thousand pounds."

"Make a note of that, David." Henry clapped his hands. "We'll keep him to it."

Good God, thought Murray, this young-blood talk will give the King something to think about.

Monson's feet scraped like impatient hooves, though he knew no one was going to race him to the royal ear. Nor to the ear of Don Pedro de Zuñiga who, three weeks before, when Monson brought him to Dover, had grumbled that Spain got little in return for the annual one-and-a-half thousand crowns it had paid England's Admiral of the Narrow Seas since the peace.

THE TERRACE of shops and houses in the long north shadow of St. Paul's Cathedral was still called Paternoster Row, though rosary beads were no longer sold here, any more than Psalters of the Blessed Virgin were to be had in neighbouring Ave Mary Lane. For the King's Justices of the Peace were empowered to search out such Popish toys for burning, and to exact for each a fine of forty shillings, of which the informer would reap thirteen shillings and fourpence.

The law of Protestant England was such that a crucifix seized from a recusant's home would be taken to Quarter Sessions to be ceremoniously defaced, and restored in that state to the owner as though the original had been insufficient a symbol of sacrifice.

Garbed this afternoon in an outfit indicative more of a city grocer than a peer of the realm, Rochester ambled his least splendid horse along the busy row. He went by Mrs. Turner's handsome double-fronted house without halting, and kept on well beyond the sign of the Golden Lion before reining about and passing Mrs. Turner's again. He had seen nothing and nobody suspicious, but he could take no chances. A dozen yards behind him, therefore, rode two of his men, alert for eyes as watchful as their own. Their task was to be ready to follow whoever might be spying on this private visitor to Lady Frances, and to discover for whom he spied. They were to silence any in the employ of Essex, who must have no evidence to prove his wife false; of the Archbishop, who would head the divorce commission; or of the Prince, who must not be made yet more jealous of his father's favourite. Any who turned out to be on the King's business was to be left to deliver the intelligence that his Majesty's darling had, as always, dutifully carried out his Majesty's instructions.

Rochester dismounted by the churchyard gate and gave his reins to the first of the eager lads who, scaring the fat pigeons into flight, thrust forward for the lure of a silver groat. Still cautious, he swept the row with a glance as he moved not yet to Mrs. Turner's but to the stalls of the stationers who had made St. Paul's their quarter. Rather than go empty-handed, perhaps he would find a present here for Frances. She had no more appetite for literature than most of the lightsome ladies of the court, and no less appetite for flattery; so she would be more delighted by a compliment to virtue pretended than to virtue possessed.

Here was Ben Jonson's new comedy, *The Alchemist*. Here, John Webster's new tragedy, *The White Devil*. He flipped through its pages:

> To sow kisses is to reap lechery;
> I am sure a woman that will endure kissing is half won.

Here, under his hand as though eager to be sworn upon, a stack of the new Bibles, translated by King James's command into the English of the day. Rochester lifted one up, and it fell open at Proverbs:

> There be things which are too wonderful for me, yea, which I know not: The way of an eagle in the air; the way of a serpent upon a rock; the way of a ship in the midst of the sea; and the way of a man with a maid.

Here—ah, yes, this would serve for Frances—Will Shakespeare's *Troilus and Cressida:*

> Women are angels, wooing;
> Things won are done;
> Joy's soul lies in the doing.

He thought sixpence enough to be asked for a mere forty-eight quarto pages, but he paid up, tucked the volume under his right arm to leave his natural left free to go for his sword and walked quickly up the row to Mrs. Turner's.

* * *

IN THE BUSTLING GARDENS of Chatham Hill House, the Prince's master gunner, John Reynolds, stood ready to touch off the powder charging a final salute to match Phineas Pett's final toast.

"I must confess I do not know to which sweet and noble lady I raise my glass, though it's high time his Highness did." Pett looked at the Prince, who shook his smiling head in acknowledgement that impudence was to be expected of rascals. "But let us drink to the health of whoever fortune shall one day—soon, we pray—favour as his bride."

Fifty elbows aligned with Pett's. Fifty voices called, "His Highness's bride!" Fifteen chambers fired. Henry looked into the gunsmoke, seeing Frances's face as, about this hour tomorrow, it would shine up at him from that bed in that room in that house in Paternoster Row.

"His Highness's bride!" piped up little namesake Pett. Henry lifted the lad in his arms and kissed his forehead. Mrs. Pett wiped her eye.

NOW Rochester and Frances faced each other across the chequered marble floor of Mrs. Turner's hall like pieces set for chess, sharing the delusion that they were not pieces at all but players, and that the King was not a player at all, but a piece. After these five months apart, the gap that seemed to have grown as wide as eternity was suddenly no more than two squares of black and white. Frances, her pale breasts quickening in her vivid orange gown, knew she must do nothing, say nothing, to acknowledge that in some bygone enchantment she and this stranger had lain navel to navel. One glad glance, one touch, one halfway step toward Rochester would take up the game where it had been adjourned before they both lost. Tensing herself to send no such signals, she was resentfully aware that she would be welcoming him back with all of them, were it not for the precarious love of a prince who, God help her, might be forced to put his destiny before his mistress if it came to the push too soon. As ready as a greyhound and—how it all flooded back—as fierce and as gentle, Rochester still disturbed her. Mrs. Turner was right: new love did not really bury old, though it might take its place, or even take a place alongside it. Only hate could bury love, and Rochester she would surely never hate. But she had learned to read him, and today she could read a difference. Today she could read fear. And, reading it, she found herself for the first time a little afraid of him.

Rochester's anxiety was that he might not find this to be still that girl of February—the girl he had loved selflessly enough to back away from when she took the Prince's fancy. The girl he had loved selflessly enough to leave *virgo intacta* for the divorce commission that would free her from bondage. His heart therefore disbelieved his eyes when they observed a new leanness about her cheekbones, a new assurance about the set of her shoulders. And disbelieved his head when it told him: Ah, yes, this was that girl, but is not now.

"Your hair"—of course, *that* was the change, it was like a bride's—"you never used to wear it down."

"It has been down and up and down again a hundred times since you last cared to see it." *Damn him.* "I dare say it will be down and up and down again a hundred times more before I care you to see it next."

"I pray not." Rochester moved forward a square.

Frances moved back to maintain the distance between them. "Why are you here?"

"For your sake."

"For *your* sake, if ever I knew you."

"Frances..." He said her name caressingly, alert for even a scintilla of the old warmth in return. "If ever you knew me, for your sake *is* for my sake. I am here because you are in need of my protection."

"As I recall, my brave knight, your notion of protection was not to put on your sword but to put off your breeches." She tossed her bright mane.

"Frances..."

"I beg you, let me be. Go find a girl as silly as you found me. Go find someone else to...to *protect.*" Her skirts hissed dismissively as she swirled into a bishop's diagonal move across the gleaming white squares to the stairs at the far corner of the hall.

"Frances, you are in danger. Great danger." Her echoing footsteps halted. She put a hand to the ruff at her throat. She did not turn round. "The King fears that his son is plotting with you."

"Plotting?" Now she swung to meet his eyes.

"He has learned that Henry foolishly believes himself in love with you—that he is resolved to go against him and make you his bride once you are free."

Foolishly believes...the words were like cymbals clashing through her heart. "How could the King learn any such nonsense? Henry has shown me no more courtesies than any lady of the court."

"The King comes to know every such nonsense. His is a kingdom of eyes and ears."

"But they cannot see what is not there. Nor hear what is not said."

"Did they hear wrong when they heard that I would find you here today?"

"You have found me here before. It is no secret." Oh, but it was. Except to Henry, Murray and Anne Turner. Essex, like the servants they had left at Cranford le Mote, believed she had gone to her mother at Audley End. Her mother believed her still at Cranford le Mote. So, she must have been followed. But by whom? And for whom? She crossed to the sunlit window and looked out—straight into the eyes of a young fellow with a lopsided beard, who thereupon bent to fiddle briefly with his shoestrings and moved off.

"A friend of yours, Robbie?"

"No."

"Then perhaps it is you the King has sent him to spy upon. What could he discover of me but my innocence?"

Rochester moved to take her hands as they hung uncertainly at her side. She left them limp in his, not wanting to discourage any answer that could reveal where else she had been followed—how deep was the abyss, and how near.

"My dear Frances, I told his Majesty I would stake my life that, whatever flimflam he had heard, you could never have been a party to the Prince's folly."

"But..." Frustrated that she must not fall into the trap of denying what she purported not to know, she squeezed his hands without having meant to, and froze when he squeezed back.

"The King asked for what reason the young and callow Rochester presumed to know better than his old and wise master. And I said, 'Because, Sire, it is Rochester with whom the Lady Frances has long been in love...'"

"No!" She pulled her hands free and clenched them into trembling fists.

"'...and Rochester who has long been in love with her.'"

If only she dared scream *I love Henry,* it would put an end to this. But it would light too soon the fuse that must not burn until Henry was ready. He was entitled to expect for his queen a woman who would not betray him whatever the plight, whatever the provocation, whatever the pain. She made herself calm.

"You spoke false for me, Robbie. Should I be surprised that you speak false for yourself? I do not believe you have ever loved anything but your own ambition."

"Nor did I, until I loved you." He bit his lip and lowered his gossamer lashes, finally lifting them as though to allow a tear to descend each soft cheek. No tear came.

"Did you think to tell the King you had never once bothered to inform me of this so-called love?"

"I had feared you might spurn it as long as you remained married in the eyes of God."

"Huh!" Could any man fear that of a girl who had let him under her skirts like some moonstruck milkmaid behind a haystack with the farmer's son? She knew the turn she had served then. What turn was she to serve now? What else but Rochester's urgent need for an alliance with the Howards as Henry grew more and more a threat to his greatness? "Come, Robbie. You could not have stayed away from me five hours, let alone five months, had you been in love."

"Come, Frances. I did it, as ever, for you. I knew Essex's spies were everywhere. Your nullity would have been at risk each moment I was with you. My sacrifice was the measure of my love. To speak it would have lessened it."

"You would charm the very Devil." She shook her head and could not help but smile at the hurt on an open and honest face such as no open and honest man could ever aspire to own.

"But not you?"

"Not me."

"Though I swear I love you?"

"I do not believe it. I do not believe it."

"Then you will be less surprised than I that... *neither did the King.*"

"Oh!" Sweet Jesus, which was worse: the King disbelieving it and dooming Henry, or believing it and dooming her?

"It is given to few courtiers to tell the truth"—Rochester spread his palms apologetically—"as well as they tell a lie."

"You seem set upon ruining me with either."

"But, sweetheart, I have not ruined you. I have saved you. I *made* the King believe." Spurred by desperation, the new lie galloped away with him. He could not allow her willfulness to cause him to fail the King now. "I dropped to my knees—and begged his leave to marry you when the divorce is through."

"Marry me?"

"Marry you. Only then did the doubt vanish from his eyes. And do you know what he said?"

"No..." She hardly knew what Rochester was saying now, let alone what the King might have said yesterday.

"He said"—Rochester thickened his voice to ape the royal brogue, and leaned his head to one side the way the King would do—"'Laddie, that's good to hear... you shall both have my blessing... aye, and I'll give the bonny bride away myself...'"

"You had no right!" Her fists beat a tattoo on his shoulders. "No right! No right! No right!"

"But Frances, I saved you. Can't you see?"

"Saved me! I need to be saved from you, not by you. Do you think I seek to be free of one ass only to be chained to another?"

"God! I would need to be an ass to go back to James with that message. It would convince him his misgivings are true. And worse..."

"Worse?"

"...and worse, that I had been conspiring with you to hoodwink him. Our feet would not touch the ground. He would have us both in the Tower before dusk."

"Robbie"—Rochester had overplayed his hand; she could be bold now—"it is only you who are in peril."

"Me!"

"I shall go to the Prince and tell him you are spreading lies about him plotting against his father. And we shall see what the King thinks of that. My God, I would not care to be in your shoes."

"What makes you think the King will take your word before mine?"

"He will not take your word before that of the Prince of Wales."

"Do not rest assured of it, madam. Much more defiance from that impatient young man, and the King will likely disinherit him with one snap of his fingers." He matched the words with the gesture. "Then you, and you alone, will have undone Henry the Ninth. And who will you, and you alone, have set in his place as the next King of England? B-b-baby Ch-ch-charles, that's who. B-b-baby Ch-ch-charles."

A picture of that porcelain Prince, barely the height of boys half his eleven years, flashed before her. Charles take Henry's place? Never. He could count himself fortunate if he lived to see his big brother crowned.

"Robbie, why, *why* will you not see? If you are too stubborn to undo your mischief, what choice am I left but to undo it myself?"

"Before you consider any such madness, I make you a solemn promise." He paused ominously. "Place me in jeopardy, and I shall draw the bishops a map of your belly."

"You bastard! Oh, you bastard!" Instinctively, she masked with closed fingers the site of those twin stars at the beginning of her secret hair. Say Rochester carried out his threat? She would lose the divorce. Henry. Everything. Helpless and humiliated, she burst into tears. She knew it had been a blunder to threaten this man. She had made him more dangerous with every no. That was never the Howard way to deal with enemies. The Howard way was first to make them think they were not enemies. She lowered her head in submission, then faced him with damp eyes and troubled lips.

"Forgive me. You know I could never do you harm."

"Nor I you, Frances. But why do you make me cruel?"

"I learn from you."

"I would rather you learn love from me. *Remember?*"

She did not resist as he drew her to him. *Remember?* Her pulses throbbed with the danger as she put her arms round his neck. *Remember?*

"Will you"—she spoke over his shoulder—"will you then tell the King that his young and callow Robbie presumed too much too soon? That you found me not of a mind for husbands old or new—whether earls, princes or viscounts?"

"If that is your wish."

"It would please me." She brought her head back to face him.

"It will not please the King. He will be angry at first—I know him. But not for long. Then he will mock me that I let infatuation carry me away. He will say I know nothing of the ways of women. He will say I should have made sure of you before I made sure of him."

"And you will say?"

"I will say I have every confidence that, in time and with patience and love, I shall make sure of you. And I will give thanks to the father of the nation for finding time to be a father to me, too. There!"

"A brave speech, my dear. No father could but forgive."

He hugged her close. She found herself moving her hips against him, asking the oldest question. She felt the oldest answer. And, with it, both triumph and despair. For in accepting that the gossip about Henry was mere gossip, Rochester would accept accordingly that the way was still open for him after all. Now, in his ardent embrace, dare she go on to deny him when every hesitation must revive suspicion that she was indeed in love with the Prince? Dare she withhold even the favours she had once allowed? Or should she win the time that was needed with favours no greater? Favours that would mean nothing. Henry would remain the only man who ever truly possessed her. For Henry, she would lift the shadow that could make Rochester destroy them. For Henry, she would render the few empty caresses, the few meaningless moments, that would send Rochester away with a smile on his face for the seven-week respite of the Progress.

He slipped his hands below her waist to clasp her yet closer. She looked past him to the door. Anne Turner would not be back for at least an hour.

"Mistress Turner will be back any minute."

"Then Mistress Turner will just have to wait her turn, won't she?"

He laughed. Frances gave him the mock-shock face required by the role in which she had cast herself. He kissed her hot eyes, took her by the hot hand and led her to the stairs. They did not speak. There was nothing more to say. Inside the bedchamber, he turned the key and took her in his arms again. When she let him open her lips, he knew his punishment for ever leaving her was over. Their tongues fenced. His fingers reached into her bodice, and she swayed back to let them delve. He gasped with delight as her nipples betrayed her. Soon he took both hands to bunch her gown, drawing it clear with her petticoats and looking over her shoulder to observe in the mirror set in the wainscot as he turned her other cheeks again and again and again.

THE PRINCE rode between Pett and Murray as far as Gravesend, where the royal barge awaited.

"Phineas, you have my solemn word that I shall not rest until a dozen new keels are laid. There has been neglect enough to satisfy the Councillors of Spain, never mind the Councillors of England."

"May God put a hook into their nostrils!" Pett shook a fist. "May God haul them into the pit they dig for us!"

"Chatham must have a dry dock. Two dry docks. And new wharves. And more storehouses. And an extra mast pound."

"But first, Highness, a brick enclosure wall"—Pett pulled his wild beard into a reluctant point and let it spring gratefully back into shape—"or every accursed splinter will vanish overnight."

"Huh! If I know my father's Council, they'll tell him there's perhaps money enough for a dock, or perhaps money enough for a wall, but not money enough for both."

"So which shall it be?" asked Murray.

"Both," said Pett.

"That's the spirit!" Henry applauded. "After all, we're the ones who'll do the fighting—not that scum."

"Aye!" roared Pett, and spat into the ditch.

"No." Frances put her hand in his way.

"Still my virgin wanton?" Rochester smiled down at her, so white against the crimson spread. "But, my darling, I have been patient this long—I can be patient longer." He kissed her sweetly on each eye, each cheek, each lip. He let his head dwell on her shoulder, and she softened with his gentleness. Her arms went gratefully round his neck, and suddenly he was inside her.

"Oh, no, no, *no*..."

She let out a great groan. He took it to be at the hurt of her breached hymen. She threw her head from side to side, keening tearfully at her folly. He took it for passion, and playfully pinned her wrists at full stretch so that she lay crucified beneath him. She thrashed in despair; he thrust in delight, ceasing only to let her bucking hips take him to the paradise they fought to deny him.

Happy enough to believe himself her first and last lover, Rochester lifted away to look at her stained face. It moved him like a rose after rain. "My beauty," he whispered, soothing her hair back from her damp forehead.

Frances stared unseeingly at the damask canopy. She realised that she was caressing his neck, but did not stop because she did not know what else to do.

THE YOUNG FELLOW with the lopsided beard had been aware he was being followed almost the moment he walked briskly from Mrs. Turner's window. Out of Paternoster Row he had led the pair down Carter Lane, hoping to lose them by flattening himself against an entry wall in the day-long darkness of Do Little Lane, but turning over his shoulder as he emerged after an eternity to find them waiting across the street. Now he began to run, and in doing so endorsed his own death warrant. For, at this, his pursuers were certain he was not on his Majesty's business. Any King's man would know he had no more need to flee from Rochester's men than the King himself had to flee from Rochester.

Into Knightrider Street. Past the Boar's Head tavern. Would he be safe there in the crowd, behind a pot of ale? *No*—he must keep on. Away between the wetfish stalls, over cobbles slippery enough to proclaim that this was Friday. Still they had him in sight. He doubled back, and back again, in a desperate dance through thronged streets until at last he came panting to the Thames at Puddle Wharf. No sign of them now. God be thanked. He was alone at the quay but for a single wherry plying for hire. Slumping heavily onto the cushioned stern bench, he gasped the cloying river air into his lungs.

"Lambeth Stairs, man—and move yourself for mercy's sake!"

The ancient waterman leaned on his oars and yawned. This young customer looked as though he might be persuaded to pay a little extra for his hurry.

"I don't know, sir. I'll be done for the bloody day pulling you that far against this tide."

"Would five shillings give power to your elbow?"

"One elbow."

"Ten it is, then, and the Devil take you for a rogue." He saw his pursuers round a corner and run on to the quay. "Pull, man! Pull! *Pull!*"

The flung dagger caught him in the back of the neck, severing the spinal cord. He was dead before it completed its travel, and he toppled forward into the waterman's lap. Desperately, the old man pulled away, until the second dagger went straight into his heart. He fell across his passenger, and the tide swept the loose oars flush to the wherry's side and sucked it into midstream. In a few minutes, the little boat would be dashed to driftwood against the Bridge. The bodies would be lost in the swirling undercurrents until they rose again down river for the kites to pick clean.

STILL WARM with the glow of the newly pleasured, Mrs. Turner made her way home along Paternoster Row. She went on many a Friday to the public lecture at the College of Physicians, to keep in touch not with the still-modern disciplines of Galen and Hippocrates, but rather with the fashionable medical men who had been colleagues of her late husband. Today she had ridden away in the new coach of the dapper young Huguenot Paul de Lobel, apothecary to their Majesties' First Physician and brother-in-law not only to him, but to each of their Majesties' apothecaries. As always, Mrs. Turner had inquired after the well-being of the lumpish Madame de Lobel, whose husband, by way of reply, had mischievously arched his single eyebrow as he reached forward a familiar hand to each of her familiar knees and gently eased them an inch apart. Madame, he had said, liked not the summer heat of the city and was again away at her sister's in the country. Perhaps Mrs. Turner would care to take some refreshment at his fair house in Lime Street. By way of reply, she had moved her knees a matching inch under his hands. Now, having been twice refreshed, she tripped gaily across her chequered floor to find Frances sitting, head in hands, halfway up the stairs.

"Frances! *Frances!*" Mrs. Turner moved beside her and put an arm round trembling shoulders.

It took half an hour of sobbing and coaxing, of raging and comforting, to get it all out of her. Mrs. Turner permitted herself an inward sigh. The poor girl could not know that she had yielded to secure a secret the King already knew.

"Oh, Anne, what can I *do?* Rochester has me like a hooked fish."

"Nonsense, my dear. *You* have him."

"But..."

"But nothing. So long as he thinks you may be his bride, Rochester will shame you to neither the King nor the Prince, nor Essex nor the bishops, nor any man on earth. So who is the hooked one—you or he?"

"I never thought..."

"It is as well. The thinking is best left to me. I have seen you thus far; I will see you all the way."

"I am so fearful of tomorrow. What *can* I tell my Hally?"

"The truth."

"The *truth?*"

"Well, so much of the truth as he may hear from other lips. Tell him Rochester called out of the blue—which he did. Tell him he said he had asked the King's blessing to marry you—which he did. Tell him you answered that you will permit yourself no thought of marriage until the bishops have set you free—which you did."

"Henry will not be pleased."

"Not be pleased! I hope for your sake that he is white with anger. If he is not, then he does not love you enough." Mrs. Turner stood and looked down at her. "Is that why you are afraid of tomorrow?"

"I don't know." Frances turned her face to the wall. "I don't know..."

"You will know tomorrow. If he is not going to fight for you the moment the first trumpet sounds, then better you know it before the last. Anyway, if the King's son is not ready to marry you, then the King's favourite is. Would to God my chances were one half as bright!"

"It's no good." Frances got up and shook her head frantically. "I *cannot* see Henry so soon. He will read the truth on my face."

"Sweet Jesus!" Seizing her by the shoulders, Mrs. Turner forced Frances to look at her. "Does your father read it on your mother's face? No. Does old Lord Knollys read it on your sister's face? No. If Mainwaring comes to me tonight, will he read it on my face? Of course he won't. Yet it is hardly an hour since I left the bed of Monsieur de Lobel. If I avoid Mainwaring, only then will he read it."

"Anne, I do not have your strength."

"Indeed you do, as well as your own." Mrs. Turner held Frances's arms, then slipped down to take her hands and fortify her more. "You have the steel to be Queen of England. Settle for less, and you know you will regret it every time you curtsy to some chinny Spanish bitch or some French dwarfess. Every time a Hapsburg or a Bourbon spawns an English prince that a Howard should have bred. Every degree your family slips from the favour you could have advanced. God! What is today's mad moment set against your whole future?"

"Please..." Frances led her to the stairhead and threw open the bedchamber door. "I tell you, Anne, I tell you there are two things I do not have the steel for. One is to lie there tomorrow with Hally; the other is to refuse to. I beg you, find another way." She pulled the door shut, and silently they went down to the hall.

"I have it." Mrs. Turner clapped her hands. "I will send word to await Murray the moment they are back from Chatham. I will say we must forgo tomorrow's arrangements because... yes... because I fear the house is watched. Mark my words, Frances, your eager Prince will soon see to it that Murray sets a new meeting. Oh, how much easier it will be once the Progress begins on Monday! No King and no Rochester to bother the pair of you for three whole weeks."

"*Dear* Anne, I would be lost without you." Frances thought to mention the young fellow with the lopsided beard but, weary of conflict, kept quiet rather than be chided for not telling of it sooner. How odd that with men she was a woman, yet with women just a girl.

[9]

Saturday the Eighteenth of July

JUST AFTER MIDNIGHT, the second candle flickered and went out. Still no word from the young fellow with the lopsided beard. A much troubled Sir Thomas Overbury sat on in the hot dark. To confirm where Rochester had been going in such secrecy should have been a simple enough task. Almost as simple as the one that waited on the information—the delivery of an anonymous letter to Lambeth to advise the Archbishop at which address his proctors could find evidence that the forthcoming petition of the Lady Frances was not that of a virgin wife but of a rank adulteress. Had the noble Viscount concealed his ignoble tryst to the point of murder? Or was Overbury's spy a captive, at this very moment under torture to reveal the name of his employer? Had he by now gasped it out, and would Rochester's hell-hounds be baying at this door before the night was through?

Yea or nay, ruin was still the prospect for Overbury, He could not sleep for the knowledge that freedom for Frances would soon banish him from Rochester's side, and lose him not only the post of Secretary of State but also the hand of the widow Countess of Rutland. How could he hope for that if Rochester married Frances? The good and gentle Elizabeth would never ally herself with the confederate of the man who had stolen Essex's wife, for the simple reason that she and Essex had come, though by different fathers, from the same mother's womb. In the forest of family trees, a slender branch was easily obscured. So many thought of Elizabeth of Rutland only as daughter of the wondrous Sir Philip Sidney, cut down in his prime on the field of Zutphen, and offering his water bottle to a wounded soldier with the immortal "Thy need is greater than mine." But she had then become step-daughter of the unfortunate second Earl of Essex and was tied by blood to the unfortunate third. Elizabeth's distress at her half-brother's hurt magnified Overbury's hatred of the slut who was its cause. This Frances was a poison that could finish them all. The only antidote was that, somehow, the world should see her for what she was.

Overbury went to his bed. He was still awake when the new moon rose at ten minutes to four.

WITH London and daybreak an hour behind them, the Archbishop of Canterbury motioned to the Bishop of London to trot ahead of their retinue so they could talk privately. A half dozen more dusty miles north along the Newmarket road and they would sight the golden weather vanes and the golden lions that sprouted them, glinting in the sun above the eight turrets of Theobalds. A half dozen more dusty miles and they would kneel to face his Majesty's wrath unless, after a life of serving their own consciences, they could find it in themselves to serve his instead in this matter of the nullity. The greatest churchman in the land, and the greatest in the capital, knew each other well enough not to feign optimism today. They had been friends since Oxford thirty years back. Each had gone on to become Vice Chancellor of the University, and at George Abbot's elevation to Canterbury last year, John King had succeeded him as Bishop of London. The bachelor Archbishop had long been a welcome guest at the Bishop's family fireside. He had taken boat to stay with them at Fulham last night, grateful more for the opportunity to talk lightly with Joan King than weightily with her husband...

About the wedding prospects for Princess Bessy and young Frederick of the Rhine: only three months now and he would be here to claim her. About the worrisome lack of prospects for Prince Henry: with Baby Charles at the mercy of every puff of wind, Frederick would be a mere accident from finding himself King of England. About the galloping licentiousness of the playhouse: after complaints about lewd jigs at the Fortune, the justices were to ban them throughout Westminster. About that notorious baggage, Moll Cutpurse, who tippled three quarts of sack on her way to do penance at St. Paul's Cross for going about in men's apparel and drawing a sword and a pipe with the best and worst of 'em. About anything but the subject that had busied these two lords of England's spiritual estate so many hours in their libraries at Lambeth and Fulham, as they tumbled books and flagged pages in search of defences to the King's demand for their presence today to speed the divorce.

The Archbishop turned to satisfy himself that they were out of earshot. "Heaven help us, we have a foul and strange business in hand."

"Heaven will help us."

"And heaven will need to help me, Bishop, for I have not kept faith with you."

"Your Grace?"

"If the King tells me a secret that you should know if you are to be a judge in this matter, am I to betray his trust in me? Or yours?"

"If a man suppress the truth, it be as great a lie as denying the truth."

"Then even greater for an archbishop."

"Then even greater for a king."

"Then—will you permit me to share this burdensome secret with you, my friend?"

"Do so at peace, your Grace. It is already no secret from the King of Kings."

"What I had from his Majesty's own lips"—the Archbishop sighed heavily—"is that a new husband is already provided for the Lady Frances."

The Bishop was first to break the lingering silence. "And for what man's desire does the King make himself party to a wife's treason?" The thought struck him. "Pray God, not the Prince!"

"No, never the good Prince. The new husband is to be my lord of Rochester."

"Thus the stink is complete. I shall never give my vote for the nullity. *Never.*"

"Nor I, Bishop, as well you know. The Devil would fetch away my soul."

"Your Grace, I fear that as long as there are creatures like our brother of Lichfield—and as long as there is fear and favour—the King will find ways to drum up a majority."

"I fight on!" The Archbishop thrust a fist into the air. "Even one on God's side is a majority."

"Then the longer the King believes he can leave such as Lichfield out of it, the better. If his Majesty but lets us, we would be wise today to fight only for time."

"Aye, Bishop, time. Time for God to open the King's heart. Time for truth to open his eyes. Time for us to open his ears."

"Time for Rochester to fall."

"Or Essex to rise?" The celibate Archbishop mocked himself with a disapproving frown as they reined to let the company catch them up.

MRS. TURNER'S heavily sealed letter was waiting for Murray when he arrived back at St. James's. Having read it to himself, he took the Prince aside and read it to him. Henry put one hand to his rapier, the other to his dagger, and gripped their hilts until his knuckles showed white.

"I don't care *how*. I don't care *where*. I don't care *when*. Just do me this service, David—get her to me before this day is out."

"Highness..."

"Highness be damned! If you fail me, I shall ignore Mistress Turners' fears and I shall ignore yours. Whether Essex's men are on watch, or the King's men, or everybody's damned men, I shall go to Paternoster Row myself."

"I..."

"Take her this." Henry pulled from his finger a ring of nine diamonds.

"I beg..."

"Just do as I command, sir!" Henry pushed the ring at him and turned on his spurred heel.

Murray's chest felt hollow. He had never thought it would come to this.

THE ARCHBISHOP led his flock through the gates and up the furlong avenue of elm and ash, at the end of which the three-storied turrets of the King's favourite palace usurped the horizon. More glass than wall, with magnificent stretches of mullioned window set in rose brick, Theobalds had belonged to the late Earl of Salisbury until James besought it from him in exchange for Hatfield House—with the encouraging jest that Theobalds was too rich for a king, let alone an honest Lord Treasurer. Too rich indeed: the Archbishop had journeyed from London in the two hours it would take to encompass this vast high-walled estate of deer park, forest and garden. All was now at its fairest, with the white musk roses of July trailing their rich scent after the earlier reds that kept their fragrance to themselves, knowing their beauty sufficient to fill any man's senses.

The troop trotting away from the palace came to within fifty feet of the Archbishop before he recognised the flaxen hair of the favourite and the unworried bulk of Lord Chamberlain Suffolk. Archbishop and Bishop exchanged glances. In truth was a new husband provided for Frances! What business could this pair have just left but the business that was intended to allow Rochester to replace Essex as the Lord Chamberlain's son-in-law?

"Good morning, Archbishop."

"And to you, my lords."

Hats were doffed and tapped back into place with neither party pausing on its way, though when Rochester looked over his shoulder he met two holy pairs of eyes doing the same.

"His Grace looks surprised, my Lord Chamberlain."

"Bishops, Robbie, are born to be surprised. They are great for but one generation. Not bred to the ways of kings."

Unlike the Lord Chamberlain. Not surprised, though summoned at dawn to be instructed whom his daughter shall next marry. Not surprised, though commanded to keep it close the while, lest the divorce commission be distracted from its business. He wished he felt surer that his wife would welcome the news, and abandon her dangerous fancy that the Prince himself would declare for Frances the moment she was freed by divorce, or Henry by his father's death. Whoever had put that into her head? It could well be a legacy of Simon Forman, by whose horoscopes the Howard women swore; as indeed did sea captains of the Lord Chamberlain's acquaintance who ought to know better, having more honest dealings with the stars than did the entire galaxy of astrologers. But it needed no magic to prove his Majesty right: Rochester was indeed the fellow to tame Frances. To plant a son in her belly on their wedding night, and once a year thereafter.

"You are certain of her willingness?" The Lord Chamberlain looked hard at the man.

"Doubly certain, my lord. As much as a maiden can, she has given me to understand so."

Her father pictured his dear daughter allowing Rochester a chaste kiss and modestly restraining his impatient embrace. Rochester pictured her startled eyes as he invaded her yesterday, and he eased himself in the saddle as his body signaled renewed doubt that it could wait seven minutes for her, let alone the seven weeks till the Progress ended. To the King he had reported that the afternoon at Paternoster Row had gone according to his Majesty's instructions. The Lady Frances was assuredly won. His Majesty had squeezed him for proof, and would not be satisfied until he had the secret of the twin stars on her Ladyship's belly. Rochester's reluctance had confirmed the King's belief that this was indeed a love match, and he had rubbed his damp hands as his plot moved on. The next scene, in which the divorce was made ready, would be rehearsed this day.

"Your Grace." The Bishop of London stayed the Primate as they reached the archway to the first of the five courtyards that formed the palace. "The eyes of our whole Church are upon you—and expect you will show yourself a worthy man."

"With God's help, that I shall."

"Then do me the honour of expecting as much from your humble servant."

Halberds at the shoulder, two liveried yeomen stepped forward to greet them, sweat shining their faces between black Tudor bonnet and white ruff. His Majesty awaited their Lordships in the summerhouse.

From the terrace the length of the south facade, flights of steps led down to broad pathways weaving for two miles through a garden paradise bounded by a shrub-lined moat. Some walks lay between tall hedges, recessed here and there to provide an arbour where politics or passion might thrive. Some trailed through tunnels of trellised clematis. Others were sun-dappled alleys pleached with willow and whitethorn, honeysuckle and rosemary. The yeomen conducted the visitors past a maze commanded by an assembly of fantastic sculptures in privet and yew. There were centaurs, sirens and serving maids with baskets of real flowers. Dragons, leopards and bulls with gilded horns. Pyramids, obelisks and poles topped with perfect spheres like heads on pikes. Looking down upon it all, and crowning a man-made hill, was the spectacular summerhouse. Inside, the Twelve Caesars in white marble formed an arc about a massive table of black touchstone. And waiting between Claudius and Nero, with one leg cast over the side of his chair, as always when he was pleased with himself, sat the man who succeeded where Rome had failed: Jacobus Rex, first ruler of all Britain.

"Aha! The Abbot who isn't an abbot—and the King who isn't a king!"

Archbishop Abbot and Bishop King returned a faint reflection of his smile to the Defender of the Faith who, in this dark matter, bid rather to be defender of the faithless.

"Your Majesty is well prepared." The Archbishop indicated the tome-laden table as he knelt to kiss hands.

"Indeed I am, your Grace... the books are for *your* benefit."

"We come, Sire, to yield frankly to such truth as they shall show us."

"Good." The King swung his leg down and walked over to a side door. "Good." He drew it open, looking not at the pair revealed but at the response on the Archbishop's face. "You will be glad, then, that I have brought in two of like frankness."

So... after Frances's father and intended husband, now two conspirators more. The Archbishop wondered, God, how far has this business gone?

"You are a long way from Lichfield, my lord."

"His Majesty does me the honour of believing I might be of service."

"Indeed." The Archbishop's eyes were cold. This Richard Neile was the last bishop one would wish to weigh in the balance on a matter involving Frances Howard: his wife was cousin-german to the girl's mother.

"Well, your Grace"—Lichfield condescended—"Chartley *does* lie in my diocese, and the Earl of Essex and his lady *are* two of my flock."

"And you, Sir Daniel Dunn, are a long way from your Court of Arches."

This bowed old man, forty years in the law, had been Dean of England's chief ecclesiastical court and principal civilian to a succession of three archbishops, each of whom had sought to dislodge him as corrupt. But neither Whitgift nor Bancroft then, nor Abbot now, could be rid of this royal appointee any more than he himself could be rid of his limp and his Welsh accent.

"When our sovereign requires, my lord Archbishop, this Daniel will always come to judgment." His lips curled over black and broken teeth.

The King resumed his seat to end the preamble, and flapped both hands to beckon them all to the table. The Archbishop and the Bishop of London having, as seniors, taken stools on his right hand, the Bishop of Lichfield and Sir Daniel Dunn placed themselves on his left.

"I have gathered us today, having talked privately with my lord of Canterbury these many months." The King did not notice the Archbishop's sniff at the deceitful implication that he was thus a party to what might come. "We were of a mind that a divorce commission would sit in the spring, but I am troubled that this poor girl has been on the rack long enough. It would not be Christian to stretch her more when the law allows otherwise—would it, Sir Daniel?" The author motioned for the principal actor in this piece to speak his lines.

"The fact is, my lords, I have advised his Majesty that precedent permits such matters to be considered once the parties have been together for three years after reaching the full adult age of eighteen. Now, since poor Essex was twenty-one last January"—he waved a baptismal certificate—"there is no good reason why the matter should wait."

"Save *one,* Sir Daniel." The Archbishop drew at the lawyer the bow he dared not bend at the monarch.

"Save *none,* your Grace—in your single year at Canterbury or in the thousand years of your predecessors."

"Save *one*"—the Archbishop would not be deflected—"for is it not law that the requirement is to share the same bed for three adult years, not merely to share the same universe? And is it not the fact that the Earl did not return from France to claim his bride until the January of 1610? And is it not, therefore, the reality that it cannot be until *next* January that there will have been opportunity for carnal copulation for three adult years?"

Eyes lowered, Dunn shuffled his papers as his mind strove for an answer. The Archbishop turned to Lichfield.

"Is that not so, my lord, and within your knowledge as their bishop?"

Lichfield, too, said nothing. The Archbishop pressed neither, content to let their silence do his work.

"Archbishop, I ask you"—the King sighed like a weary tutor—"within his knowledge or without his knowledge, does it matter?"

"My only concern is that Sir Daniel shall not abuse your Majesty's ears with false advice. For, as I see it, if it is to be not three years for an earl but two and a half, then next it will be but two for a marquis, and then but one and a half for a duke."

The King recognised that the Archbishop was on sure ground, and that Dunn had been pitched into the mire. Let him get himself out of it.

"Well?"

"Lawyers, Sire, have the sense to learn from kings to be of the world we live in. Archbishops grow too great for any world but their own. If his Grace will not take it from me, I trust he will take it from you: that if nothing were done unless it had been done before, then nothing would ever be done at all."

"But, Sir Daniel, before you bring his Majesty into your argument, will you not see that if this is done in haste, others will expect equal haste? Will you tell them that it was fit for my lord and lady of Essex but is not so for them? The law knows no persons. The law must be indifferent to all."

"There is conscience as well as law." Dunn looked for support to the King. "What a disgrace it will be to my Lord Chamberlain and his daughter if this should not now go forward."

"Aye, what a disgrace." Lichfield shook his head sorrowfully.

"Do you, Sir Daniel, tell your Archbishop that to save any man from disgrace he must send his soul into hell?" The Primate's voice rose, and Dunn masked his satisfaction. At last he had provoked the choler that bubbled never far beneath the man's skin. "Heaven knows, if it be a disgrace they put it upon themselves! They should have looked to that before they began. *We* were not the ones that set the matter afoot."

"No." The King drew the word like a sword from the scabbard. "*I* was the one that set it afoot."

"Indeed you were, Sire." Dunn wrinkled his nose at the Archbishop as the King went on.

"And why? Because I was distressed at the torment of my poor Lord Chamberlain. What it is to see a great man reduced so! This was the brave captain of the *Golden Lion,* who faced the Armada without flinching and saved our island for the likes of you and me. Yet, in this matter of his daughter, he wept—aye, wept—when he left me not an hour ago. He lies on a gridiron, broiling till the matter be accomplished. And, I tell you all, I lie there with him. For I, more than any man, bear the guilt of his daughter's supposed marriage these six long years. How may I ease that heavy load? How else but by myself launching this process of nullity? It is to you that I look for *my* salvation as much as theirs. I pray that I do not look in vain."

The King sought each pair of eyes in turn. Strange, thought the Archbishop, that Lichfield and Dunn, who would do the King's bidding without question, looked down, while London and himself, with much to fear, held their gaze. The righteous knew that God was on their side.

"Your Majesty"—now Dunn rose—"I trust that no *reasonable* man would set any impediment in the path of your wishes. We are but four troubled souls seeking a lawful and expeditious way for you to free two young folk from their chains." He swayed, thumbs in armpits, addressing the troubled souls not as though he were one himself but rather an advocate going through the motions in a cut-and-dried case. "May it please your Majesty, for the convenience of all, I have thought it helpful to have at hand the draft of the petition to be submitted to you."

Canterbury and London were heavy of heart as Dunn searched out the document. The meat had been carved before the diners were summoned to the table.

"Since the pretended marriage, as time and place did serve, during the space of three whole years after the said Earl had attained the full age of eighteen"—Dunn raised his eyebrows triumphantly at the Archbishop—"the said Frances Howard lived together with the said Earl at bed and board, and lay naked in the marriage bed. Desirous to be made a mother, she again and again yielded herself to his power, and as much as lay in her, offered herself and her body to be known, and earnestly desired conjunction and copulation."

Committed as he was, the Bishop of Lichfield could afford to admit only to himself how false a picture those words painted of imploring eyes, beseeching lips and entreating limbs. He had seen the couple together at Chartley, with those eyes scorning, those lips belittling and those limbs eager only to transport her from the side of her husband to that of any man who signaled encouragement, of whom there were many. Was it any wonder that when such a wife lay with such a husband, Master Mouse would not come out to play?

"And also the said Earl again and again did try to have copulation, which she refused not, but used the best means she could. Notwithstanding all this, the said Earl could never carnally know her, nor have that copulation which the marriage bed allows. No, not once."

Strange, thought the Bishop of London, that the son should be thus when the father's appetite was a legend still. Stranger that a nobleman of such blood had been persuaded to allow his insufficiency to be declared to the whole world.

"Yet, before the pretended marriage, and since, the said Earl has had, and has, power and ability to deal with other women and to know them carnally. He has felt the motions and pricks of the flesh but, peradventure by a perpetual and natural impediment, he has been so hindered that he can have no copulation with the said Lady Frances."

"Do I hear aright?" The Archbishop pulled himself to his feet to face Dunn. So this was the trick they had used to cozen Essex.

"I trust you do, your Grace. My Welsh tongue is sometimes challenged, but never misheard."

"Then I hear a novelty unheard of in our Church, unknown in our kingdom. We have registers in every diocese. We have acts and records of the days of our forefathers. But—I tell you—no memory of man can express unto me the name of one husband whose marriage was annulled for impotency towards his wife *when he was able to copulate with any other woman*. It is today's imagining, Sir Daniel, for all our yesterdays knew it not."

"If you sit down, your Grace, I will continue." Dunn spoke as though to a man in second childhood.

"If you name me that one husband, then will I sit down."

"Oh, sit *down,* man!" The King waved his command, and it was obeyed. "Ignorance of the married state may stop up your heart, but it is too early in the day for you to permit it to stop up your ears. Sir Daniel, pray continue."

"And furthermore, the said Lady Frances has been, and is, fit and able to have copulation with such a man as may carnally know her, though she remain at present *virgo intacta."*

The Archbishop doubted it, and noted that Dunn had significantly not offered to satisfy the commission as to that virginity by the inspection of a jury of seven midwives and matrons. The King was thankful that his Grace was not armed with Rochester's intelligence of the twin stars on her belly, or Mainwaring's of her secret trysts with Henry.

"And therefore she petitions that this pretended matrimony may be adjudged and declared of no effect, and she may be quit and free from all knots and bonds of it, by your sentence and authority."

"Before you sit"—at the King's words, Dunn, who had in fact resumed his seat, rose again—"is it not possible that since we are all gathered here, we may pronounce upon this matter without further delay?"

Dunn reached awkwardly across the table for a book that rested at the elbow of the Bishop of London, who made no move to help him. How would the rogue know where a particular volume lay unless it remained where he had left it at rehearsal?

"Your Majesty is learned in the law," said Dunn. "By your commission, we may indeed hear this case summarily." He found the bookmark he was seeking, and opened the pages to read. "Here we are. It says that he who has power to hear a matter summarily is in the nature of an arbiter chosen by both parties, and therefore may judge in discretion as he shall think fit... and so on, and so forth."

"Before you put your book away, Sir Daniel..."

"Your Grace?" Dunn answered the Archbishop, but looked at the King.

"Does it say, lawyer, that discretion may dispose of a matter without evidence? Without examination? Without search for precedent? Without reference to scriptural authority? Without doubts being resolved? Without even the husband's answer to each and every article of the wife's petition?"

Dunn waited, book in hand, until the chill of the stone table struck through his silk breeches to his thin thighs. But the King was not going to rescue his instrument.

"I never said it did, your Grace."

"Then my mind is set at ease..."

"I am sure I should not want it otherwise, your Grace."

"...for any commission upon which I sit shall want proof of the lady's virginity."

"Do you suggest such a noble lady would perjure herself, your Grace?"

"No more than you would, Sir Daniel. But we must protect her noble name against any who might so allege, must we not?"

"May we take it for granted that Sir Daniel will also arrange for the Earl's name to be similarly protected?" The Bishop of London moved in support, and the King shifted restlessly as the formidable alliance asserted itself. There would be no divorce today unless these two could be budged, which task was clearly beyond Dunn alone.

"Be warned, Bishop." The King wagged a finger. "When you mock poor Essex, you mock his King's pity for him."

"Your Majesty, I beg you to accept that no such offence was ever in my heart."

"Huh! I beg you—and you take no notice. You beg me—and I am supposed to forgive any insult. Do you wonder that I grow angry? You have spoken with the Earl but once or twice in your life. What do you know of him? Has he told you, as he told those close to him, that he even intended to go to Poland to see whether some wise woman there could unwitch him?"

"Sire!" Dunn leaped in triumphantly. "If he sought to be unwitched, it follows as day follows night that he must have been witched. That is the *proof* of this impediment!"

"But surely, lawyer"—the Archbishop's tone was scathing—"we shall require better evidence than that."

"Your Grace," said Dunn, "I can see that we shall require no better evidence that you are prejudiced in this case beyond hope of redemption."

"I challenge you to support that *wicked* allegation."

"Why challenge me when you can so readily support it yourself? Does not every sound you have uttered this morning declare that there are *no* circumstances in which you will set your hand to a divorce for this unfortunate lady?"

"If that be so"—the King saw a way out—"then it would be no more than mercy to rid his Grace of this troublesome business."

"Or this business of his troublesome Grace." Dunn sat and rubbed his cold thighs. The Archbishop was a fool if he did not take the King's hint.

"Archbishop?" The King was encouraging. If he would volunteer to withdraw, the Bishop of London would surely go with him. There could be a new beginning with a new commission—and without scandal. But the Archbishop chose diplomatically to deliver his answer to Dunn.

"Since I am an archbishop of his Majesty's making, I should be the last to quarrel with his Majesty's choice of archbishops. It ill behooves you to be the first. Kings less tolerant of your long years and your short temper would award you a month in the Tower for such contempt. For my part, I am determined that, in me, our sovereign shall have chosen a dutiful servant as Jehoshaphat, King of Judah, chose his, minding them thus: *Take heed what ye do, for ye judge not for man but for the Lord. Let there be no iniquity*"—he looked unflinchingly at the King—*"nor respect of persons"*—pityingly at Lichfield—*"nor taking of gifts"*—contemptuously at Dunn. *"But deal courageously, and the Lord shall be with the good."*

"Amen," said London, and Lichfield joined in before he could help himself.

"So, your Majesty, I shall never abuse the trust you have committed to me. For if I vary from justice, I leave God and show myself worthy to lie in the flames of hell. And *cui bono?*" The Archbishop held out his palms in supplication: but Dean, Bishops and King offered no more answer than the jury of twelve marble Caesars. "To what end should I transgress in judgment for either side, when I have no reason to be partial for either? The Lady Frances may remain wife to Essex: it is nothing to me. She may marry another: it is nothing to me."

"By your leave." Dunn was back in the fray. "Is it also nothing to you that, without this nullity, the noble Essex line will die out? Is it also nothing to you that, without this nullity, poor Lady Frances will be forever denied the satisfactions that are the right of the humblest wife in the land?"

"Answer!" demanded Lichfield.

Dunn flashed him a look for interrupting. "Is it also nothing to you, my lord Archbishop, that declaring yourself against the divorce lays a grave imputation upon the conscience of those who declare themselves for it? *Not least*"—he swept his arm theatrically—*"the King himself."*

At last I have him, thought Dunn. Lichfield mentally tried Canterbury's mitre for size. London offered up a silent prayer. The King folded his arms. The Archbishop breathed heavily as he considered his words.

"Sir Daniel, I know not whether you be the most vain of men or the most foolish. But I do know that only one or the other would presume to put such ill words into the mouth of a king. For majesty is well aware, if you are not, that no man who is false unto God can be true to his monarch. Were any Primate of All England to go against himself, could any king ever after expect true service of him? Furthermore, you are perverse in insisting that I am unwilling to give judgment for this nullity. God knows, I *am* willing..."

"Ah!"

"...when, Sir Daniel, there has been opportunity for consummation for the required three full years."

"Oh!"

"And when, Sir Daniel, I see with my own eyes and hear with my own ears the witnesses and the proofs that must precede such judgment."

"And so say I." London cast its die.

"Meantime, my prayer is that a reconciliation might be laboured between these young people. Surely no achievement would become us more in God's eyes?"

Lichfield intervened. "They are better known to me than any here, save his Majesty. I implore you to accept that such a proposal comes too late. If we force them together, we may be the cause of their destruction as surely as if we put poison in their hands."

The King nodded. "Such good sense is the stuff of which archbishops are made. Eh, Archbishop?"

The Primate let it pass. "Your Majesty is witness that the most bitter of breaches can be healed. Your own intercession did give an end to that between England and Spain. What could it not achieve between this husband and wife?"

"I fear that I, as their Bishop, can hold out no hope that reconciliation is within the capacity even of our blessed peacemaker." Lichfield inclined his head like a good dog, but no pat was forthcoming.

Dunn sensed the King's impatience. "Now that prospect has been disposed of, your Majesty, it surely remains only for his Grace to resolve his conscience on some points of divinity and give his consent. Then we lawyers will bear the burden of making the nullity firm."

"Lawyers!" The Archbishop was contemptuous. "How ready they are to counsel divorce with all that passing of money into their capacious pockets! Whereas those of us who practise divinity are as ready to give counsel for reconciliation at no expense."

"I pick no quarrel with his Grace over the value he puts upon his advice."

"Enough, Sir Daniel. Enough, all of you." The King pushed back his chair, and they stood with him as eleven chimes began to ring out from the clock tower. "You will complete your task with more dispatch if you do not need to mince words for my digestion. I hope you will reach agreement within the hour so that you may dine at my table." He turned, halfway to the door. "If not, I shall take it that you do not wish your debate to be interrupted by such trivia as food and drink." He turned again in the doorway. "But rest assured that later, if needs be, I shall send you candles."

WHEN SHE RAN to answer the bell, Mrs. Turner's guess was that it would be Paul de Lobel, eager to repeat yesterday's prescription. But, at the door, to be delighted by her glad greeting, stood Sir David Murray. The warmth rose in him as her loose-tied bodice billowed its own salutation. He savoured the nectar of her, and she drew him into the hall, nullifying his intention to insist that he was in haste.

"For people who correspond much, we meet little." Her smile lingered between rebuke and regret.

"I serve a royal master. You serve a noble mistress. There is little time for such as us to serve ourselves."

"Then such as us must serve each other." Her eyes were frank. "Perhaps I may begin by serving you... a glass of Muscatel?"

"I treasure the invitation, but for another day. You must not make me forget why I am here."

"Oh, it is not to see me?" She laughed.

"It *was* not." He spread his hands in surrender. "But I confess I am suddenly become my own ambassador as much as my master's. For him I command, for myself I can but beg, that you attend at St. James's this very afternoon to see The Prince's Servants perform a play for his Highness's pleasure. You—and your nephew."

"Nephew?" she teased, realising full well what he meant.

"Aye. Frances needs to be Francis to serve this turn. All else is arranged. A coach will be at your door at two o'clock. I myself shall accompany it to see you both safely to St. James's. There will be young pages and boy actors a-plenty about today. One smooth cheek more will not be noticed."

"I had best hurry then, since you allow me but three hours to become an aunt."

"I shall ever be in your debt, madam. As much as shall the one who sends this ring for Lady Frances."

He passed her the circle of nine diamonds. Then, lifting her hand to his lips, he held it there long enough to abandon the punctilio that had always distanced them until now. Their eyes mingled. He kissed her mouth, which she opened to him like a scented promise.

"Sir David..."

"*David,* please."

"Do you know you have not yet managed to tell me the play we are to see?"

"Forgive me. I had hoped it would be of no matter."

"Indeed it would not—if you have other plans to occupy me." She put a hand on his arm. He covered it, and she covered his.

"Sweet Anne. I can think of no delight but how I might occupy you better than Will Shakespeare." Now his hand went to form a half collar about her fine neck, and she locked it in for a moment with her cheek.

"What could excel *As You Like It?*" She widened her eyes.

"Only *Measure for Measure.*" The hand slipped gently into her bodice, and she let the thumb stir her nipple before she eased him away in a gesture slow enough to indicate not rejection, but postponement.

"I shall be as happily occupied with either." She moved into his arms, neatly tailoring her hips to his. "Or both."

By God, he thought as they kissed again, if Frances was this heady creature's pupil in the ways of love, no wonder Henry was bewitched.

Mrs. Turner picked the moment to tear herself away and up the stairs without a backward glance at her new conquest. She burst in upon Frances, who sat burnishing her already gleaming hair in front of the mirror. "Stir yourself, nephew. You have a busy afternoon ahead."

WITH THE KING went the last restraint upon the four commissioners. The summerhouse was now a bear pit, with the keeper gone three hours and the animals rumbling with hunger. Dunn cleared his throat as the clock chimed two.

"Had the King but listened to me, your Grace, he would have dismissed you from the commission. And your pet bishop also. Then we would be spared this comedy."

"Had the King but listened to you, Sir Daniel, he would be a bigger fool than you. A scandal is the last thing he wants."

"George"—the familiarity put the Archbishop on guard—"we shall be here forever unless we are reasonable. Look, I'll give you your damned inspection of the girl's virginity—though I tremble to think

what her noble father will make of that insult—and in return you give me the three years' cohabitation. What say you to that?"

"I say thank you, *Daniel.* I accept your offer. But canon law does not permit me to give what you ask in return. You know that."

"I know that there are no words in English or Latin to convince the King that he must wait six months."

"Why not tell him—in English or Latin—that the Church is used to such haste only from pregnant brides?"

AS THE COACH came through the park to the gatehouse of St. James's, Anne Turner reached into the pocket within her bodice and fished out the ring of nine diamonds.

"He sent you this."

"Oooh!" A trill of delight sprang oddly from the gallant in the bottle-green doublet. "I'll wear it for*ever!*"

"Forever, Frances. But not today, I think."

"He will take it amiss."

"Good. Then put it in your pocket so you can wave it in front of his nose and tell him you will most gladly wear it—if he will himself put it on your wedding finger."

"Do you think he might?"

"If your news of Rochester's proposal does not make up his mind, nothing ever will."

"But say I lose him?"

"You won't. He is wild for you."

"But say I do?"

"Then better you lose him now than when Rochester has found a wife elsewhere."

Murray rode ahead of the coach through the archway whose spandrels bore a double cypher: H for the Henry who built this palace, and A for its first mistress, Anne Boleyn, grand-daughter of the second Duke of Norfolk. From a window looking down on the throng in the inner courtyard, today's Henry watched the arrival of Frances, grand-daughter of the fourth. He was reassured at her disguise. Minus paint, and with hair safely swept up from her standing collar into a roomy cap, she made a convincing page once she had got down rather too carefully, as though still in a skirt. No one arriving for the play paid special attention as Murray escorted his guests to a side door, but Henry knew he had been impetuous to override the man's caution. He would need to choose the field of battle with more cunning than he chose the field of love.

Getting out his keys as he led them up the cased stairs, Murray unlocked the dim gallery looking down on the Great Hall, made a little game of dusting the bench and secured the door behind them. The audience had been growing in number and noise for an hour, and the lutes and viols, flutes and drums were losing their fight. The Prince controlled his household like a fine regiment of soldiers who would accept the strictest discipline knowing they could unbutton at such entertainments as this, from which he would tactfully absent himself. Listening to the hubbub from their tiring room, the players lifted their pots for a last pint of courage to go forth and face the foe. Mrs. Turner looked over the rail to see if brother Eustace might be in the throng. But no, the Prince's Falconer would have little time to spare in mid-July. As she sat back, the clock struck three and trumpets blasted a fanfare. Bowing low, an actor advanced to the front of the stage amid cheers, boos and catcalls.

"By his Highness's favour... The Prince's Servants, come over by command from the Fortune playhouse, will this day perform for you *The Two Gentlemen of Verona,* by Master William..."

A chorus of groans drowned the author's name, but the actor turned them to laughter with a mock retreat to the rear stage.

"I don't think they care for it," said Murray.

"I don't blame them," said Mrs. Turner.

He put his lips to her ear and explained the exits and entrances of the other drama that had brought them here. Now that the bulk of the household had come to the play and the palace was almost empty but for the guard, he would convey Frances to the Prince's chambers. He would return for the girl at the beginning of Act Five, which would be signaled by the third musical interlude of the afternoon, the King of Denmark's Galliard. With all windows thrown wide on this sweltering day, it would be easily heard. In the meantime, Murray was happy to place his own chamber at Mrs. Turner's disposal, should she herself prefer a galliard, or perhaps a coranto, to this poor advertisement for the genius of Will Shakespeare. Mrs. Turner thought she well might. The first of the Gentlemen of Verona was putting it aptly even now:

> Indeed, a sheep doth very often stray
> If the shepherd be a while away.

"Baa," went a sheep in the front row, and the flock took it up from all over the hall.

Murray tapped Frances on the elbow. It was the moment to go.

* * *

DUNN sighed heavily. At this pace, they would still be at it on Judgment Day. "Archbishop, do you or do you not accept that marriage is for carnal copulation and procreation?"

"I grant you that, Sir Daniel."

"And that it is the intention of those who contract matrimony to receive such satisfaction?"

"Agreed."

"And that, if the Earl of Essex be unable to perform those marital rites unto the Lady Frances, then he does her a grave injustice to retain her as his wife?"

"Agreed."

"And that, if we do not free her from this yoke, we shall perform as great a cruelty toward her?"

"Agreed."

"And that we are bound in conscience to do this, since without consummation it is no more than a pretended marriage?"

"Agreed."

"Then, in heaven's name, what more do you require before we starve to death?"

"Proof," said the Archbishop. "Proof, proof, proof, proof, proof."

FRANCES lengthened her stride to Murray's as he acknowledged a halberd salute at the Guard Chamber. Their footsteps echoed on up the wide stairs to the Presence Chamber, deserted now but for the minimum two Pages of the Presence on call, day and night. They moved to rise from their bench as they recognised the Groom of the Stole, but he waved them down before they had straightened their backs, and ferried Frances through to the lobby and across to the no-woman's-land of his Highness's private wing. Only the elite of the Prince's household were permitted here. Lesser ranks had to leave even coals and laundry at the door for the Grooms of the Privy Chamber to handle. Commanded by Gentlemen Ushers, these trusted young esquires, exalted enough to rate servants of their own, saw to every humble duty: making the bed, warming the Prince's apparel, looking to the fires, airing the rooms, removing the close stool and keeping all sweet and clean. Last thing each night, they would set four pallets for Gentlemen of the Chamber to lie at the Prince's door, rapier and dagger to hand lest any foolish intruder find a way past the guard to try his luck against a Prince whose skill at arms was the talk of the town. Even at sixteen, he had dazzled all beholders at his Investiture display of chivalry, with three hundred and sixty consecutive sword strokes to defeat eight consecutive challengers. Murray glanced each way to make sure the lobby was still clear. Then, unlocking one of the wide double doors, he pushed it inward to let Frances through without a word, pulled it to and locked it behind her.

He sighed as he slowly paced his way back, hands clasping and unclasping behind him. He had been Henry's sworn servant longer than any at court: how well was he serving him now? It would have been greater loyalty by far to decline to pander thus to the vassalage of Prince Henry at the court of King Cock. A good servant would do duty to those weaknesses that distinguish princes from ordinary men: lust for war, hunger for empire, thirst for glory. But never to those that pull down into the gutter noble with nobody, master with man, judge with judged—and, aye (thinking wryly of the delicious widow Turner awaiting him), knight with knave. In the blood that descended collaterally with the founder of this Palace, this Henry had clearly inherited a like appetite for Howard mutton. Pray God, this throne, this land, this people would not face a like outcome as the result of Murray's blind obedience today.

IN THE GREAT HALL the audience was won over from cracking nuts and peeling oranges by the welcome entry of Speed, half the pair of clownish servants who redeemed the unreality of the play's precious heroes. He held the stage with a droll mockery of his lovesick master:

> How know I that you are in love, sir? Well, you sigh like a schoolboy that has lost his ABC. You weep like a wench that has buried her grandam. You watch like one that fears robbing. You walk alone like one that has the pestilence. You whine like a beggar at Hallowmas. Now you are metamorphosed with a mistress, I hardly know you as my master...

Mrs. Turner felt a tap on her shoulder. She inclined towards it, found nobody there and swivelled the other way to meet the grin of Sir Arthur Mainwaring.

"Well, well, madam. Twenty to one I surprise you."

"Twenty to one you surprise yourself. You said you would be out of town today."

"I am on my way now. You won't catch me sitting through *The Two Gentlemen* again—it's too far-fetched. Would you believe it, the heroine disguises herself as a page to meet her lover!"

"I believe everything you ever tell me."

"Then you will believe that I have just observed your friend Murray sneaking through the Guard Chamber with as pretty a page as St. James's has seen for many a day."

"My dear, be *careful*—he will be back here any minute. He came to my house this morning to *plead* with me to bring her. Poor Hally cannot do without her—isn't that *wonderful?*" She laid a hand on his arm. "I am more sure now than ever that he will find a way to marry her as soon as she is free. It will be the *making* of us."

"Or the breaking of him—if he is mad enough to challenge his father."

"You will not tell the King too much? Please. *Please.*" She stroked the hairs on the back of his hand. "I will be so nice to you."

"Anne, trust me. As I trust you." He patted her shoulder in a brief farewell. If he galloped hard, he could be at Theobalds by five o'clock.

HENRY and Frances simply looked at each other. Then they simply held each other, until the ache of their parting eased from the eternity it had seemed to the four days it had been, and then to no ache at all.

"Hally... oh, my darling Hally." Frances tightened her arms round his neck as they stood in the centre of the richly hung Privy Chamber.

"Afraid?" He spoke over his shoulder.

"Only for you."

"No need, Fra. I am as brave as you."

He spanned her waist as she leaned away to loose her cap and the combs that imprisoned her long hair. Two shakes of her head tossed it free. Henry smoothed it to frame her face, and she covered his hands as they came to rest on her cheeks.

"Bringing me here—that is more madness than bravery."

"It is more love than either."

"Sometimes... I think it is just a game to you."

"No, Fra." He was grave. "If it were a game, I could bear to lose—which I cannot. If it were a game, I could as well play it with another—which I will not."

"Then tell me this: how many *pages* have been brought to you this way?"

"You are the first this afternoon."

"Oh, you *always* say that." She snorted.

"Oh, you always ask it."

"I must know."

"Then you must know you are the first ever."

"Hally, I want more to be the last."

"That you are already."

Through the open windows floated the music that marked the end of the play's first act. Henry began to whistle the tune, Master Griffith's Galliard, and offered an arm to Frances. She stood her ground. She should be telling him of Rochester's call.

"Sweetheart, I want you to listen..."

"Sweetheart, I want you to dance..."

"But there is much danger..."

"*Not* if you watch where you place your toes."

He lifted her hand to his wrist, patted it into place and danced round her with springing steps, making her squeal with mirth as he added a series of goat-leaps and clapped his heels in the air. One-two-three-*four*-pause-pause, they progressed clockwise round the big room. Then one-two-three-*four*-pause-pause through to another, and once round that. Then one-two-three-*four*-pause-pause through to his inner chamber, where he lifted her in his arms, flipped the doors shut with a nimble foot and fell laughing with her between the open curtains onto the huge bed. He was still whistling the galliard as his fingers took it over, unbuttoning her tight doublet with a one-two-three-*four*-pause-pause down its twenty buttons, and another when, having tugged her shirt out from her breeches, he playfully went to unbutton her navel. She giggled, and stretched so that he could get the doublet over her arms, then brought them back round his neck for the last of the tender kisses and the first of the wild. Six more beats for six more buttons, and her breeches were undone. She arched so he could push them to her knees, then lifted her legs in the air for him to tug off breeches, hose and shoes in what was meant to be one sweep but grew merrily to three. The music stopped as she lay there hot and heaving with laughter, naked now but for the loose shirt rucked up about her ribs.

"Ah, Master Griffith's Galliard is done," said Henry.

"And Master Hally's is beginning," said Frances. She did her dry best to whistle the tune again as her fingers went to his waist to trip their own measure.

ON STAGE, Speed and his comic partner, Launce, were reviewing the courtship of one Gentleman of Verona and his sweetheart:

SPEED: Why, then, how stands the matter with them?
LAUNCE: To be sure, when it stands well with him, it stands well with her.

There were roars of approval as he tottered back, feet well astride, and mimed his meaning. Mrs. Turner rested her hand above Murray's knee.

SPEED: But tell me true, will it be a marriage?
LAUNCE: Ask my dog. If he says aye, then it will. If he says no, then it will. If he shakes his tail and says nothing, then it will.
SPEED: The conclusion is, then, that it will.
LAUNCE: Oh, no! You shall never get such a secret from me...

The audience, so many of them lesser servants, guffawed at the blockheadedness of lesser servants. Mrs. Turner put her lips to Murray's ear.

"And you shall never get such a secret from me."

"My dear Anne, there is no such secret to be got. He cannot marry her."

"Cannot?"

"Cannot."

"Is that what he told you?"

"He does not need to tell me. We both know his father."

"But Henry is strong."

"Aye, madam, strong enough to say no to his father's choice—but not to his father's veto."

"We shall see." She patted his thigh confidently, then moved her hand higher and leaned warmly against him. "David, does the play not weary you?"

He covered her hand. His mind was too full of anxiety to revive his earlier offer. To whom else might Anne Turner declare this perilous business?

"Better another day, Anne."

"Oh."

"There are too many eyes here. I swear I saw Mainwaring snooping by the back stairs. Wouldn't trust that man an inch. He's too often waiting when you come round a corner."

"Mainwaring?"

"Yes, the Prince's Carver. Surely you know him?"

"Not really. He was a patient of my late husband."

"Hmmm...I can guess what for."

She giggled, and moved her hand. "The matter stands well with you," she said quite soon.

* * *

Sir Daniel Dunn limped round the summerhouse to place the big Bible in front of the Archbishop. "Go on, your Grace! Turn up the page where it says there must be three years' probation. Go on!"

"It is nowhere in the holy scripture."

"Ah!"

"It is also nowhere in the holy scripture, Sir Daniel, that a man is forbidden to marry his sister's daughter. So do you also propose to allow every uncle in the land to wed his niece?"

Henry felt no paradise could surpass this basking in the afterglow of love, well knowing that before the world went on its way there would be love again.

"Fra... open those sweet eyes for me."

"For you..." The cornflower irises turned to him. Full of the moment, she parted her lips and sighed with happiness.

"I could look into them forever."

"I could want nothing more than that you do."

Those eyes. Maybe one day he would find the way beyond them. Then would he truly fathom her, though in the process he got too deep ever to return. And though any fool mariner knew himself better employed sounding not the depths but the shallows: for that was where grief chose to wait. Now she shut those eyes to lock in the rapture as his hand began a circuit of her body. From cheek to collar to nipple to navel. From hip to wrist to shoulder. From upper brow to lower, where his fingers spread to tease the damp, dark curls.

"Oh, *forgive* me"—Henry had found a bruise on her thigh—"I would not mark you for the world."

Frances leaned up to look, only slowly attributing it to yesterday's episode with Rochester, so well had today's with Henry canceled it out, as though it had been some other girl there in Paternoster Row and that a thousand years ago.

"My darling, there's nothing to forgive. It's a medal for me to treasure." She took his hand and rubbed the bruise hard with it. "See—it does not hurt."

"It hurts me."

She knew she must soon begin to tell him about Rochester's visit. As much of the truth as he may hear from other lips, Mrs. Turner had said.

"What do you think?" She stroked his arm, soothing him before the blow. "Rochester waited upon me yesterday."

"The Devil he did!" Henry tensed.

"He turned up at Paternoster Row without so much as a by-your-leave. And do you know what he came to say?"

"Not a word you can trust. That is sure."

"He came to say"—she watched him anxiously—"that he had asked the King's blessing to sue for my hand when I am free."

"The damned jackanapes! I'd like to have seen his face when you told him to go to hell."

"I would be unworthy of you if I were such a fool. Nobody—least of all the King's favourite—must suspect that my heart is already spoken for."

"You think it better for him to suspect you are his for the asking?"

"Oh, no! I made him understand that I would permit myself no thought of marriage until the bishops have delivered their judgment."

"I'd have delivered a boot to his bum."

"What for? He knows I can soon be a bride. Why should it surprise you that he might aspire to marry me? Am I such a dragon?"

"Not enough to deserve Robert Carr." Henry teased her frown into a smile, and bent to kiss her. Impatiently, she pushed him off.

"But say you tire of me?"

"Never."

"But say you settle with your father for some foreign princess?"

"Never."

"Huh! It's easy enough to say *never,* but should the day come I shall be glad of such an offer as Rochester's—if he is still waiting. There will not be many rich and handsome noblemen clamouring to wed the Prince's cast-off punk."

"Fra, you know how it saddens me to hear you talk thus."

"It saddens *you!* What do you think it does to me, contemplating sharing my sister's fate, warming the cold bones of some ancient widower. The only thing old Lord Knollys can give her is forty years. I would rather be buried than be such a wife." She shuddered. It's like milking a dead cow, Elizabeth had said.

"Frances, you would never be here unless I loved you."

"You send for me the way you send for your barber."

"You *must* believe me. I love you more than anything."

"But not as much as you fear the King." She patted his hand. "Oh, my dear, I should not reproach you for that. It is right for a man who will be king to know that kings must be obeyed. But I have a life to live—so if you love me, then love me enough to let me go to a man who wants me as a wife."

"I..."

"Do not be sad. I will always come to you when you need me. You know that."

"Fra, I know only that I shall marry whom I please as Prince—or I shall not marry till I may please myself as King. But you must see that I cannot declare myself for you until you are free. If I show my hand too soon, my father is cunning enough to blackmail the bishops into denying your nullity forever. We must lie low until that wickedness is beyond him."

"And then?"

"I dare not speak it. And neither dare you." He lifted her hand to his lips. "Where is the ring I sent you?"

"In my pocket."

"It was meant for a finger."

"I wanted you to put it on."

"Then give it to me."

She stretched across him to fish among her discarded clothes on the floor. He smoothed her long hair down her back.

"I have it." She wriggled round and held up the ring, its nine diamonds a-glitter. He took it from her, and placed it on the finger that Essex's ring had occupied until the nullity was mooted.

"Now you are pledged to me, Fra. And I to you. But, for both our sakes, I beg you never to wear it on that finger unless we are alone."

She fluttered her hand in the air to let the diamonds catch the sunlight. Without taking her eyes from it, she sank onto her back. Her heart throbbed with the impulses of romance, and her head with its notions, though her words never managed to match. Her limbs spoke best for her: she spread them eloquently, opened them sublimely. He eased slowly into her, then back as slowly; fascinated by the gleaming span lengthening, shortening, lengthening between them. She drew back her knees to her shoulders, the better to watch him watching their conjoined flesh with eyes half closed and lips half open.

"Fra, you are heaven for me."

"And you for me."

"I will love you always."

"Then truly, sweet Highness, you do love me as I love you."

"Then truly, sweet Fra, you could not love me more."

Now she surrounded him with arms and legs, and held him deep in her as the spasm overcame him and his head sank to rest on her shoulder. There came the stately strains of the second interval pavane.

But Frances heard only the music of Henry's breathing. She stretched her hand high once more, and waved the ring to make it sparkle again and again. She had never been so happy.

ACT FOUR, Scene Four. The heroine declaimed her dilemma. Numbly, Sir David Murray recognised it as his:

> I cannot be true servant to my master
> Unless I prove false traitor to myself;
> Carrying the message I would fain refuse,
> Praising the love I would fain dispraise;
> When Heaven knows I would not have him win her.

It was time to fetch Frances. He lifted Mrs. Turner's hand from his lap, and rose to slip away.

"DEAR ME . . . *dear* me . . ." The King, his voice full of dinner, stood in the doorway and surveyed the summerhouse scene. "Are you not yet agreed?"

"His Grace is deaf to all reason." Dunn threw wide his hands.

"Then his Grace has need of fresh air to unblock his ears." The King beckoned. "Come, Archbishop, walk with me." He took his arm to lead him down the spiral path to the maze. "I lean upon you, confident you will not let a poor Christian stumble."

James knew every turn of this labyrinth of seven-foot hedges, and the pair reached the bench at its centre without being balked by even one of its twenty stops.

"Sit yourself down, man." The Archbishop sat. "Eat, man." From inside his doublet, the King produced a napkin which he unwrapped like a present to reveal bread and cheese. He waited only until the Archbishop was chewing his second mouthful. "I have been thinking . . . is it not high time we put forward your brother for a bishop's mitre?"

"It is within your gift, Sire."

"Then it is as good as done, eh? It is not impossible that he could succeed to York itself when the time comes. Imagine . . . two archbishop brothers. Imagine."

"You are too kind to me, Sire."

"I to you as you to me." He clasped the Archbishop's elbow. "You have fought a brave fight today. You have won my admiration, my respect. You can now give way to your King with honour."

"Majesty, that cannot be."

"Cannot?"

"My conscience is more to me than all the gold in India."

"Your damned conscience is less to me than a turd!" He looked at the Archbishop's half-eaten bread and cheese as though he would snatch them back, and the man so far forgot himself as to remain seated when his sovereign sprang up and stormed away. The King was soon out of sight among the evergreen walls but he could be heard cursing from one direction, then another and another, all the way out of the maze.

Abbot's heart thundered as he hauled himself from the bench. What now? The guard dispatched to consign him to the Tower for treason he had not committed? Or a messenger bearing a letter accepting the resignation he had not offered? Whatever, he would not await his fate. He would go forth to meet it. But he stumbled into blind alley after blind alley, craning at hedge-tops to get a bearing on the elusive pavilion. After an age, he found himself back where he began. Hot with effort, cold with apprehension, faint with thirst, trembling with exhaustion, the Primate of All England fell to his knees. He closed hands and eyes to the world, and opened heart and mind to heaven: *Oh, God, I know not how soon I am to be called before you, and I am loath against that time to give a wound to my soul. Poverty, imprisonment, death itself, are things contemptible to a resolved mind—and my mind is resolved. I choose to die an honest man rather than a clever one. If we have no further proof, I shall never, never give sentence for the nullity. I shall strive to batter it to dust. I shall not be tongue-tied. I shall not yield before ten thousand. I am in no way afraid, because you will never forsake me if I turn not from you . . .*

LEANING BACK on his elbows, and with one leg crossed untidily over the other, James was at ease on the terrace steps as a dust-stained Mainwaring finished reporting upon the disguised visitor to the Prince's chamber.

"It is said, Sire, that his Highness now has a mind to marry her the instant she is free."

"By whom is it said?"

"I . . ." Mainwaring mopped his sweating face again.

"By *whom,* man? Have you secrets from your King?"

"I . . ." He could have kicked himself. The news of the girl's visit would alone have been enough to fill the King's ear. But now, if he pleaded honour, the King would set another to find out and Mainwaring would have lost his every advantage for nothing. Anyway, surely better for Anne that the King did not wonder why her name needed to be concealed. "By Mistress Turner, Sire. No one is closer to the Lady Frances."

"Ah, yes. The pretty widow." The King read in Mainwaring's hesitation that no one was closer to Mrs. Turner. Fair enough. False friends such as she deserved false friends such as he.

"Is it said that I might permit such a match?"

"It is not, Sire."

"Is it said, then, how the Prince might achieve it?"

"It is not, Sire."

How, how, *how*? The King paraded the possibilities. No member of the royal family could lawfully marry without his permission, but Henry might seek out a treasonous chaplain for a de facto wedding that would be kept secret until the right moment. Or he might fly the country with the girl. To Denmark, his uncle's kingdom. Or Brunswick, his cousin's duchy. He could marry her abroad and busy himself breeding heirs while he waited for his father's death—his new Howard bride and his old Stuart impatience doubtless combining to compass how it might be hurried. True, Baby Charles could be substituted as Prince of Wales, but Henry would with ease raise an army to deny him the throne when the time came—though with that frightened wee bairn, raising a voice would be enough. *And yet*... Henry could not marry Frances, unless and until she was quit of Essex. And here was this ass of a king hammering his ass of an archbishop into an early grave to secure her freedom this very day!

"Quick, man. Help me up." He stretched out to be hauled to his feet, nodded thanks and shambled away to the summerhouse at something approaching a trot as Mainwaring unconsciously wiped his fingers on his sleeve.

The Archbishop was not there. Jesus, was he still in the maze? Unerringly, the King threaded his way to him like a hound picking up an old scent.

"Off your knees, good Archbishop."

"Sire?" Abbot's damp eyes looked beyond the King, expecting to see the scarlet of the guard. Stiffly, he made to rise. The King bent to aid him.

"Your prayers are not in vain. Nor your wise words, however much I might have seemed to scorn them. I have given them much thought, and I conclude that you are right. Your conscience shall be mine. There can indeed be no consideration of this nullity before January. And, indeed, none then if there be no proof."

"Hallelujah! Oh, hallelujah!"

"Amen to that." It would do for a start. Frances would never now be free until Henry was securely married and she could not abort his destiny.

"The young folk will have time to try again to make a success of their marriage, Sire. A period of prayer and fasting will surely stop them making fools of themselves."

"Aye, and fools of others."

The King put an arm round the Archbishop's bowed shoulders. "Now let us acquaint our friends with your victory—and then you shall all have meat and drink."

"The sight of Sir Daniel Dunn's face will be meat and drink enough."

As the King's feet led him gawkily out of one maze, his mind led him nimbly out of another. Rochester and Frances's father would be back here tomorrow, ready to join him for the start of the Progress on Monday. Time enough then to bid them be patient until January when, if needs be, there would be time enough to bid them be patient again. After all, it was not as though Rochester were in love with the girl. If his King commanded, he would give her up more readily than he would give up his damned Overbury. Even if it took a whisper of what Mainwaring had observed in the meadow. But—*God!*—there was going to be too much opportunity for such trysts with Henry not due to join the Progress until it was almost halfway through its course. And if he now dared smuggle Frances into St. James's, though the King's court was on his doorstep, what mischief had he in store for when it roamed the shires?

Since the Spanish match began to totter, England's ambassadors had been carrying out their brief to revive negotiations for a princess of France, of Savoy or of Tuscany. How would they fare if Europe's ambassadors sped home the news that the intended bridegroom was of so foul a nature as to keep a mistress in the very palace, even the very bed, he sought a royal bride to share? By heaven, a stop must be put to this forthwith.

THE KING'S MESSENGER cursed as he wound through the endless wagon train trundling the royal household baggage towards St. Albans for the start of the Progress. God help travelers for the rest of the summer as the court went on its circuit of the stately homes of eight counties. The traffic was heavy enough now, but it would grow worse after twenty days when the Prince's retinue joined the Progress at Belvoir, and worse still after a further twenty when the Queen's joined at Woodstock. By then, the highways would be clogged with nigh on a thousand carts.

He was still bemoaning his lot when, having delivered the dispatch to the Captain of the Prince's guard, swilled a tankard of the Prince's ale as his horse was changed and grabbed a roast chicken from the Prince's kitchens to eat in the saddle, he was back on the road before nightfall. It was one thing dallying in London town when you were getting paid for it, but since the Privy Purse had run dry again before the poor posts got their overdue pay, a man with empty pockets might as well be home with the wife.

Alone with the Prince, Murray watched his frown deepen with each sentence of the King's letter, until he finally tore it in two, letting the halves float to the floor as he crossed to stare into the empty fireplace. Murray picked up the pieces and held them together:

My Son,

I must needs speak with you of matters that will not wait until you were to join me. You shall therefore set forth to Theobalds at first light to take your place at my side from the start of this Progress. Thus shall you be reminded where your place lies. Thus shall all be reminded. And thus shall be dismayed those who engineer mischievous hopes that the Kingdom is weakened by some falling out between its now and future Kings.

Your loving father,
James R.

"Highness, I had best give orders for the morning." Murray made to go.

"No, David."

"But, sir, you are commanded."

"No, David. He cannot expect my entire household to be set on the march with one snap of my fingers."

"Come, sir! You do not so undervalue us as to believe we should ever need two snaps."

"Anyway, there is too much business to complete for me to go yet." The Prince's shoulders heaved uncomfortably as he began to dissemble. "It would be grave enough for me to disappoint so many in my own name. The King would surely not forgive me for doing so in his. I shall reply accordingly."

"The courier was instructed there would be no reply." Just as well, if this was the best the Prince could manage.

"Then no reply shall there be." Henry took the torn letter from Murray's hand and ripped it yet again. "Two can play at that game."

"No, Highness." Murray shook his head. "At the game of kings, only one can safely play." History was spattered with princes who had convinced themselves otherwise. This one would be no different if he tested fate before fate was ready. Which would not be until his head knew better than his heart. And his heart better than his loins, still too hot to be cooled by any counsel that would distance them from those of Lady Frances.

"But, but, *but!*"—Henry quickened like a drowning man sighting a raft—"did not the King charge me to ensure that all is properly arranged to receive Frederick when he arrives to marry my sister? Now if I go on Progress tomorrow, I shall have no time to fulfill that duty because he lands only forty days after we are back in London. What an insult to Frederick that would be!"

"Indeed." Murray nodded tactfully. "Such an argument must surely win the King. But since he bids you ride to him tomorrow, then ride you must. I'll lay odds that he'll more likely release you if you persuade him than if you defy him. In truth, Highness, he requires no more of his son than you will of yours."

"I shall not require my son to be bought and sold."

"Sir, no wise general fights another day's battle."

"It cannot be another day's forever." Henry clenched his fists. "You know it is Frances I want. Must I wait till he is in the grave?"

Murray bowed to dismiss himself. "Then I shall order horses saddled for daybreak?"

"All right, David, but for no more than an escort. Give no orders to advance my plans to join the Progress, because I am not going to advance those plans. Come what may."

[10]

Sunday the Nineteenth of July

JANE DRUMMOND, First Lady of the Bedchamber, stood sentinel within Denmark House in the Strand as, for the first time since Holy Thursday, father Agustín Pérez was able to hear the Queen of England confess her sins: the gravest of which was, again, that she prayed for the destruction of her husband. Today, Pérez did not counsel her to pray rather that James should live to lead his people back to the Church into which his mother baptised him. For, in those few weeks since Easter, this pusillanimous King had been persuaded to allow the martyring of priests after eighteen months' respite.

The Archbishop and his like had grown worried by the burgeoning confidence of the Catholic community since the death in May of their great persecutor, the Earl of Salisbury, and since the renewed talk of a Spanish marriage for the Prince. With the Commons in abeyance, the laws governing Popish recusants were more than ever honoured in the breach than the observance. The number of secret priests in the kingdom was rising to the eight hundred mark. The ambassadors of Spain, France, Flanders and Venice were defying all warnings forbidding their private embassy chapels to subjects of King James. On feast days, brave English communicants swelled the congregation in the Spanish Embassy alone to half a thousand: so great was the crush that not a soul could move between sacristy and altar. Perhaps James had thought the Archbishop was asking no more than a cautionary turn of the screw—perhaps the cunning Archbishop *had* asked no more—but, in the event, a Benedictine and a secular had been plucked from among the twenty-eight priests rotting in the gaols of London and delivered up to the Pentecost assizes. In vain had the Spanish ambassador sought an audience with the King, pleading to be allowed to take the priests abroad, never to return. The next day, a royal secretary had been sent to tell him that, to avoid a feared breach of the peace, an officer had thought fit to bring forward to five that morning the executions that would customarily have taken place at eight. The ambassador would appreciate that, even with the best will in the world, there was no way of commuting a penalty already carried out. Those who, like Pérez, had been on hand to ride behind the sledges dragging the condemned pair to Tyburn, would recall that royal reply every time they recalled the last prayers from the scaffold, beseeching God to destroy all who stood in the way of this nation's return to the Catholic faith.

Today, therefore, Pérez told the Queen it was no sin to pray likewise. How else would come the blessed day when her confessor would no longer need to confer the Holy Sacrament in layman's garb while her lady-in-waiting kept watch at the doors?

The Queen dabbed at an eye with her scarf as she let it fall about her shoulders. Much moved himself, Pérez helped her from her knees and sank to kiss her hand.

Jane Drummond answered his treble-knock with another to signal that all was clear, and Father Pérez edged swiftly past her to go down by the back stairs to the busy Presence Chamber—there to resume his public role as *Señor* Pérez, secretary to the Spanish embassy, calling this day with the special ambassador for an appointed audience with her Majesty. When Zuñiga came to present Pérez, the Queen contrived not to catch his name for the music of the viols. Zuñiga suppressed a swell of admiration, for fear it confuse his loyalties.

"You look sad, Don Pedro." She ferried him to an alcove where they might talk beyond earshot of the courtiers, and she might still hold the arm of a friend much missed in his two years away.

"How else but sad could a Spaniard look in England?"

Jane Drummond arrived with sweet muscatel. Zuñiga noticed how readily the Queen drained her goblet, and how well Mistress Jane knew to wait on and fill it again before setting down the flagon and curtsying away. The Queen caught Zuñiga's glance and shrugged.

"I know... I drink too much for my own good."

"I drink... I know too much for my own good." He emptied his cup in sympathy.

"But you are good for me." She squeezed his arm.

"I only wish I were good for myself." He sighed. "You know, when my King was looking for his first ambassador to London after the peace, he was determined to have someone *esparcido*"—he snapped his fingers for the English word—"sparkling. So whom did the cap fit? Who else but the bold Don Pedro? Alas, there was not much sparkle left by the time I was called home. The cork had been out of the bottle five years. My health was not so good with your English winters. My estates had gone to ruin with our Spanish summers. And my poor wife had died waiting for me to return. Then my King comes again to look for a new ambassador—and decides that this time there might be more success with someone *no esparcido*. So whom does the cap fit? Who else but the dull Don Pedro?"

"Dear rascal!" The Queen clapped the air. "You deceived your King to come back to me."

"Dear Majesty." He lifted her hand to his lips. It trembled in his palm like the leaf of the aspen—as renowned for its thirst as this Queen had become. A glass or two more into a communion-empty stomach, and that aspen tongue might flutter such secrets as all Madrid's spies could not learn. And Spain needed to know beyond all doubts what lay deep in the minds of King James and the Prince but a heartbeat from his throne. "I fear I may not remain longer than there is hope for my mission, and there seems little when his Majesty sends me away with a flea in my ear."

"His speech is harshest when he is afraid."

"Can a poor ambassador make a great king afraid?"

"This great king was born afraid. He rails at me that were there not so much rumour that the Queen is a Papist, then the King need not strive to demonstrate to Parliament that he is not one. He even blamed *me* for those poor priests..." The tragedy of it touched her heart as the muscatel began to touch her head. "Oh..."

"May they rest in peace." In a continuous movement, Zuñiga crossed himself and renewed her drink.

"Amen." As she reached for it, the Queen stared through the windows to the waterside beyond the rosemary hedges, no more needing to survey her hand's journey to her goblet than her goblet's journey to her lips.

"May I ask, dear Majesty"—Zuñiga waited patiently for her attention to return—"may I ask, were it your misfortune and not mine to be Spain's ambassador, how would you conduct this business?"

"It is a wooing, yes?"

"Yes."

"Then I would hardly conduct it as if it were anything but a wooing."

"In all these years, though, Spain has yet to discover how this king might be wooed."

"Like a woman, Don Pedro." She smiled at some private recollection. "Would you begin your courtship by demanding all? Then demand it not of him. Ask not for Henry's conversion. Ask no more than that the Infanta be permitted to practise her religion in private."

"I fear it is too small a beginning."

"Is any beginning too small if it be enough to bring an end to the persecution of our flock? If it be enough to obtain a marriage from which will flow all I pray for each day?"

THE QUEEN talked on—and drank on—until an hour had passed. The viols also continued to converse as older members of her court, weary of standing, moved from the centre of the chamber to rest against the walls.

The Countess of Suffolk, not long come from Paternoster Row where, upon crossing her heart, she had been vouchsafed a glimpse of the ring of nine diamonds, whispered into the ear of Agustín Pérez. "Father, I know why Don Pedro is here—to try to match our princess with your king."

"That arrow is flighted too late, my lady. Spain will not rob your little Bessy of her little count from Heidelberg."

"But why else would the ambassador linger on when the match for Henry is lost and gone forever?"

"Oh, I would not call it lost while her Majesty has a tongue and his Excellency an ear."

"You would not think that if you knew the secret I know." The Countess smiled a little-girl smile.

"The Prince is already sold to France?"

"No."

"To Savoy? Tuscany?"

"No—nor Germany, nor any of them."

"My lady?"

"Oh, no, Father! I cannot confess it even to you. *That's* how great a secret it is..."

NOW Zuñiga half-rose, judging that the Queen would bid him stay.

"Please." She clung to his arm.

"Dear Majesty, in such times I may serve you best by not dwelling overlong at your door."

"Please."

"Your Majesty is most gracious." And quite soon her Majesty would be most drunk. In the maudlin meantime, her Majesty would be most indiscreet.

"Stay awhile. What can the King do about it? Make me unhappy? He makes me unhappy now. Make me wish I was dead? No—not while I can wish him dead first and my bonny lad on the throne. My bonny lad..."

"Majesty, your bonny lad earns our greatest respect, but he is very much a stranger. Perhaps that is why my King inquires of me whether Henry was ever as willing as represented to take a Spanish bride. We say, *Es muy bien que el galán busque a la dama*—It is far better that the lad shall seek the lass. Yet we cannot but observe that Henry makes no such motion."

"Why should he—when the lass's father is so stiff-necked?"

"Why shouldn't he be—when the lad's father has set the example?"

"Then, Don Pedro, you and I must bend them both. Before it is too late..."

"Too late?"

"Listen." She swallowed still more muscatel, and he had first to listen to that. "Listen, dear friend. You must first end your King's doubts that England wants a Spanish match. So tell him this privately from me: Were it Baby Charles we were dealing with, everything would have been signed and sealed by now. There! Will that not impress him?"

"Indeed, Majesty. And I trust my answer will be as impressive when he asks why what can be achieved with the one cannot be achieved with the other."

"Tell him that in the years you have been away Henry has grown too strong to be commanded. Puh! You ambassadors think you see everything. You see the King's struggle with the Puritans and with Parliament, but you fail to see that it is not they who have him loose with fear. It is Henry."

"Majesty?" Zuñiga spun her on like a whirling top.

"I know my own husband, I know my own son. And I tell you Spain will rue it forever if she does not make this marriage while there is yet time. I doubt that even the terms you scorn will be available once Henry has the keys of the kingdom. And"—she swayed—"soon he will have them, or soon he will take them."

"Take them?" Zuñiga breathed the words from a mouth gone dry.

"Oh, I suspect they will need little enough taking. My husband knows well the fate of Stuarts who do not bow to the inevitable. When Henry's challenge comes, Jamie will see the wisdom of making him Regent and retiring to the pleasures of the chase. Deer wear no sword..."

"Unlike your son..."

"Unlike my son. Remember that. He will be far from well inclined toward your nation if you deny him the highest princess in Christendom. What fools you are to require that he humble himelf before his people to qualify for a Spanish bride. *Fools!* You must tell your King that if he does not make Henry a friend he will make him an enemy. And such an enemy..."

"Majesty, Spain has cause to be grateful to you. England, too. I shall send a dispatch to my King this very day."

"Ask him this: If Spain does not think it worth an Infanta to save us, is it not worth an Infanta *to save Spain?*"

"Majesty..." Zuñiga rose to take his leave.

"Don't go yet." The Queen rolled in her chair. Jane Drummond sighed, and rustled to the rescue.

"Majesty, I must."

Zuñiga lifted her hand to his lips. This time, the fingers that trembled were his.

As Henry and his escort trotted through the gates of Theobalds, Zuñiga was coding the final sentence of his dispatch and adding, *Vuestra Majestad mandará en esto:* May your Majesty command in this matter. Soon, an express courier would be sweating down the Dover road on the first stage of his eleven-day race to the Palace of El Escorial with information too vital to take three weeks or more with the ordinary post.

He would not be the only horseman riding this day on the business of a bride for the Prince. He would be passed between Canterbury and Sittingbourne by a French messenger already cursing those small English saddles designed for a tribe with as little between their legs as between their ears. In his pouch was a letter of instruction from the Queen Regent for her ambassador, the Seigneur des Bisseaux. Since Spain was dishonestly dangling the bait of its first princess to encourage negotiations, then France would play the same trick. A second courier from the Queen Regent was on his way from Paris to her nephew, the Grand Duke Cosimo de' Medici, counseling him to cool his efforts to match his sister Caterina. Was Tuscany's intelligence so weak that he was the only ruler in Europe unaware that England had no intention of any such marriage, and was encouraging his bid only to force up the auction? Nevertheless, the Grand Duke's own courier was carrying orders to secretary Andrea Cioli in London to press the offer, requiring merely the Pope's implacable condition that Henry be converted. For Tuscany was now playing either for a match or to obtain a general caveat from the Vatican that would put rival Savoy out of the reckoning.

Ambassador Sir Henry Wotton, however, was in no great hurry

as he crossed the Splügen pass on his way home from Savoy with the sure offer by Duke Charles Emmanuel of his daughter Maria. Once over the Alps, Wotton thought, he might well break his journey at Basel, at Frankfurt and perhaps at Cologne. After all, Savoy's dowry of seven hundred thousand crowns was not likely to be equaled by Spain or France—and Maria asked no more than to hear mass *privatamente*. The Pope would not be pleased, but he had less need of a powerful ally than had Duke Charles Emmanuel, with Spanish troops on one border and French on another. Wotton rode with a smile on his face. The Duke had whispered that Savoy's gratitude to him for a successful conclusion would be all of twenty-five thousand crowns.

HENRY advanced down an indoor avenue toward the dais upon which his father was seated beneath a golden canopy. The sixty-foot Great Hall at Theobalds was lined with a dozen columns so skillfully endowed with the bark and greenery of oak and pine that birds fluttered to them through windows opening on the gardens. The lofty ceiling was an imitation sky, contrived so that by night the stars of the twelve signs of the zodiac were illuminated, and by day a gilded sun was propelled through its course by a mechanism which, today, had stuck shortly after dawn.

"Ambuscado!" the King yelled—and in response a figure sprang with a matching yell from behind each of the last pair of trees. Henry, rapier half-drawn, gave a cry nearer relief than delight as he swung round to see his brother and sister running open-armed to embrace him. He held Elizabeth warmly; he had always felt of one blood with her. Unlike Charles.

"H-h-hally."

"What is it, Baby?"

"I h-h-have a new silver p-p-pistol."

"Well, mind you don't stand at the wrong end."

"I will g-g-give it you... if you l-l-like." Charles tugged at his big brother's sleeve and looked up with adoring eyes. But Henry had turned to Elizabeth and was admiring her newly swept-up amber tresses, adorned with eglantine roses and a cascade of jewels.

"Bessy, you should *always* wear your hair like that."

"You don't think it too old-fashioned for me?"

"Only if it is old-fashioned for a princess to look like a princess."

"It was mother's notion."

"Pity she had no notion to be here to see it, then." The King shifted in his chair. "Still, she is not qualified to attend meetings of the Nineteenth Legion, eh?"

James chuckled alone. The children had long ceased to be amused at the ways in which he managed to exclude their mother, even for her failure to be born on the nineteenth of a month, as were James and all three of them. On the next nineteenth, thought Henry, his sister would be sixteen. It might be the last birthday he would ever see her: the coming marriage could well remove her to Germany forever, as their mother's had taken her at much the same age from Denmark. Three nineteenths later, and Charles would be twelve. How strange of fate to decree that, unless and until there was a beginning to the business of breeding, this miserable little fellow should be his heir presumptive. Reading Henry's face, Charles blushed and went to seek the comfort of his father's arm about his skinny shoulders.

"And what are you laughing at, sirrah?" the King asked of Charles who, as usual, was not laughing at all.

"N-n-nothing."

"Then your sister shall supply you with something." Elizabeth held out her arms, but he lowered his gaze and stayed where he was. She smiled encouragingly, nonetheless, and carried on. "Well, dear Frederick's steward arrived the other day with letters from Heidelberg, and presented Henry with the one"—her face creased with glee—"saying his heart would melt clean away if his eyes could not soon behold me. And me with the one hailing a new brother-in-arms!"

"Laugh, Baby Charles!" The King chucked him under his eggshell chin.

"W-w-why did he not write to *m-m-me?*"

As their laughter enveloped him, Charles hid his face in the crook of the King's elbow.

"Father." Henry seized the moment. "I must advise you that I have many arrangements still to complete for Frederick's arrival."

"And therefore, I suppose, you will be compelled to deny yourself the opportunity of spending a little more time at your father's side? Are you afraid you may learn something?" He stroked the hair of his younger son, whose eyes now emerged to study the proceedings. "Or are you afraid I may?"

"I am afraid only that if I am called to the Progress three weeks sooner than expected, Frederick's first impression of his new family may be less than we would wish. I require—as I know you do, father—

that he shall encounter nothing but excellence in our land. What better way to ensure that such shall continue to be our Bessy's due when she goes into his?"

They remained eye to eye until James looked away to his daughter and knew he could not prevail, though victory need not be entirely Henry's.

"Well, Bessy?"

"Oh, father, please...*please*..."

"Then—for you, sweetheart—so be it. There is nothing I would not do for my little Bessy, even if it puts her brother's education yet further in arrear. But we must look on the bright side! If the good Lord continues my kingship until the Prince of Wales has learned all that his dad can teach him, then I am fated to live as long as Methuselah."

Henry snapped at the bait. "Is it necessary for a Prince of Wales to be a professor? Better, surely, to be a soldier—a man of the world."

"But, son, soldiers in peacetime are like chimneys in summer. And what use is it to be a man of the world of the untutored? Your little brother is already farther advanced in his studies than you were at his age. Perhaps I should leave him the crown."

"Father, your letter said you would speak with me of matters that will not wait." Henry did not have the patience for his father's games. He could see Frances: breasts swelling as she sat up on crumpled sheets to bid farewell with lips and limbs that would draw him down again to bliss the moment he returned.

"All in good time, sir! Next you will be departing before you arrive." Charles laughed at last. The King patted his head and pulled him awkwardly onto his knee. "Ah, Baby, would that I had known a father's knee to sit upon, a father's footsteps to follow in. I was left to discover my own enemies. Fall into my own pits. Bind my own wounds. You would think, would you not, that your brother might thank God every waking hour for sparing me to light his way. But he reckons he can find it without me. True, he can play war games on his table—but the art of kingcraft he can acquire only at my table. What is it your father says, Baby, of princes who prefer to learn from themselves?"

"They have a f-f-f-"

"Fool."

"For a t-t-t-"

"Teacher."

"Father!" Elizabeth stamped her foot. "Charles will never get anything right if you say it for him."

"Forgive me, Bessy. My sons do not care for their father to keep them waiting."

Henry tried again, warily. "Father, I meant no discourtesy, but it was at your urgent command that I rode here at dawn."

"Oh!"—the King had still not looked up from the boy on his knee—"I thought he'd gone, Charles."

Elizabeth moved in to help. "Let me take him into the garden. We'll find a nice little pebble to pop into his sweet little mouth so that he can exercise his poor little tongue. Come on, Baby!"

"Off he goes, then." The King launched him ungently, shaking his head at the boy's rickety gait as he went down the garden steps hand in hand with his sister. "What *shall* we make of him?"

"If he is as learned as you say, then Archbishop of Canterbury."

"You have begun to make your dispositions, then?"

"Those legs need the mercy of a cassock."

"You are a hard man. Better move my old bones lest your mercy finds a premature sepulchre for them." James pulled himself up and massaged his thighs. "Here." He motioned to the vacant chair.

Henry, who wanted to sit nowhere but in a saddle on the London road, made a business of settling as if for the day. He could not, however, resist the imp that urged him to throw a leg over the chair arm, the way his father did.

"I am sure Frederick will make your sister happy."

"I shall run him through if he does otherwise."

"Rather should you run me through, for it has been my responsibility to rank him suitable. Such is a father's duty, and kings are fathers, too. Marriage is enough a lottery without adding to the odds. So I took much care to discover the nature of Frederick before I would consent to give him my little girl. Was that not wise?"

"Wise indeed."

"And would it not be wise indeed of any sovereign to take as much care to discover the nature of the Prince of Wales before consenting to give him his little girl?"

"I presume so."

"And do you presume that you will stand the test?"

"No Prince of Britain could ever fail the test of lesser reigns"—Henry swung his leg down—"and all other reigns are lesser, are they not?"

* * *

"BESSY."

"Yes, Baby?" She smiled encouragement, though Charles's speech always came easier when his brother was absent.

"He did not say whether he would like my silver p-p-pistol."

"Oh, I am sure he would love it."

"I would give him anything if he would l-l-love me."

JAMES breathed deep. Great was the temptation to challenge Henry outright with the secret that was corrupting him into a creature whom Heaven could surely never regard as fit to rule. Alas, so damnably proud was he, that even in an evil cause he would know but one response to a flung gauntlet. *And, Lord have mercy, what then?* So let the weapons remain those at which the lad was still prentice and the dad still master.

"I meant no harm, son." James spread his palms. "You know my silly comedies are only to tease."

"I would as soon they were beyond earshot of those who might not know."

"I can but beg your understanding. Children put away childish things when they become men. It is not as easy for their fathers."

"Then let it pass." Aye, let it. What words were there to make such a father see that private apology rather doubled than canceled the wound of public insult?

"I am in your debt. Perhaps I can repay with the reason I have summoned you. It is to acquaint you with my decision"—James milked the moment—"that you shall be Lord High Admiral. What say you to that, eh?"

"I thank you." Henry knew there would be more to it.

"You thought I might deny you? Dear, dear, I wish I knew who pours such poison into your ear. This shall show our mutual enemies—and mutual they most assuredly are—how foolish they are to hope for any jarring between us. They spread the calumny that I am jealous of your popularity! Even that I do not regard you as fit, else I would have promoted you as soon as you were of age. But they shall be silenced. For it shall be done before the year is out."

"Before the year is out?"

"I never intended to wait beyond the day we settle you down with a fitting princess. And now, at last, I have reason to believe you shall soon be betrothed. Then—that instant, you have my word—you shall become Lord High Admiral. There!"

"But father..." Henry gripped the arms of his chair.

"But?"

"I cannot see the difficulties over religion being resolved. Do you say that my Admiralty shall therefore be forfeit? That would go hard with me."

"Then all the more reason to see that they *are* resolved."

"Parliament would accept no promise made by Spain."

"Nor I, laddie. You should have been there when I put the fear of God into Zuñiga. Conversion! I told him I'd see you in hell first."

"I would see *them* in hell first."

"Of course you would. But our firmness will cause them to relent—or it will bring us a bride elsewhere. Do not be surprised if we are informed any day now that France is eager to bend to us. Savoy and Tuscany will not be far behind."

"And how far behind will be our people in wondering why their King is so set upon a Catholic Princess of Wales?"

"Ah, your dad is no fool." James tapped his nose. "Why do you think he deliberately chose the chief Protestant prince of Germany for a son-in-law? So that he can safely steal a Catholic princess for a daughter-in-law, that's why."

"Two religions can never lie happily in one bed, I always say."

"Yes, son, you always do—and how many times must I tell you there is nowhere better for them to lie? You will convert your princess twice a night. Thrice on Sundays." James widened his eyes.

Henry smiled to mask his contempt and, as though it had just occurred to him, began to set up his real question. "Father, the two most powerful nations in the world are both paying us court. Now if you favour the one, you anger the other. And if you prefer a lesser, then you make an enemy of both. So I cannot but think... would not the good folk of Britain be best served, and indeed be happiest, if their Prince were to find a bride from among the noblest of them—rather than any of the Pope's princesses?"

"You have someone in mind?"

"We are not short of great families."

"Son"—James shook his head patiently—"I would wish a thousand pounds for every noble daughter who wishes you her maidenhead. Aye, and a thousand more for every one who wishes she still had a maidenhead to give. But he who marries beneath his rank will ever be the less accounted of thereafter. I mean, when we take so much care to breed only horses and dogs of good pedigree, how much more careful should we be for the breed of royal loins?" He paced up and down, stopping only to wag a finger for emphasis. "I have never been privy to your innermost thoughts. But if you mark not my words, son, then mark well Christ's: *There is nothing so hid that it shall not be known. Whatsoever is spoken in darkness shall be heard in light.* I ask you, do you have reason to fear the light?"

"No more than any man."

"Ah, but you are not any man. You are a prince. And princes are, like it or not, set upon a public stage in the sight of all the people. Every eye is attentively bent to pry into their most secret recesses. Which should make princes the more careful not to harbour such thoughts as they shall be ashamed openly to avow. Me, I embark upon no action without examining how it might someday bide the touchstone of a public trial. I counsel you, the first fruits of God's blessing to me, to do likewise." He came to a halt in front of Henry. "Do you think I was never your age?"

"There are times..."

"But how else would I know what drives you to spit in the face of destiny with thoughts of marriage to blood that would thin our line? Son, I well mind my own fears of a match with a foreign princess I had never set eyes upon. I, too, was tempted to stand firm and find a noble lassie to marry for love. But God set me on the strait path, and I knew I should be cursed forever if I went the Devil's way. And so shall I give a curse unto you if you defy me. Rather you be *dead* than I the father of a wicked son. And—there's no call to look at me like that."

"Like what?"

"Like a son who deceives himself that if he cares not for his father's curse, then he deserves it not. I tell you, the curse, as indeed the blessing, of a father has almost ever a prophetic power. Do right by me in this, and I shall bless you. Do wrong, and I shall curse you."

A sudden whirring overhead adjourned the debate as the artificial sun began moving again across its heaven. Henry wondered how much his father did know. How could you tell, when his speeches were ever designed to alarm you that he knew more than you thought, or lull you that he knew less? But much the same lecture had been delivered to every royal generation in every kingdom, as though princes were doomed to perpetuate the misery of the loveless unions that begat them. He would be different. He would insist that his heart must be allowed to rule him so that it might better rule his people.

"I see you itch to be on your way."

"No-no."

"Then you'll stay for chapel?"

"Of course." Well, it would soothe the old man.

"And dine with me."

"Gladly." Well, he was not expected at Paternoster Row before evening.

"Good." And after that, my son, you will please your old dad by staying for supper. And then, my son, you will find it so late that you will need to stay the night. And in the morning, my son, you may resume your pursuit of perdition—but do not be surprised if it has moved on from Paternoster Row.

BEFORE going into chapel, the King drew his Lord Chamberlain aside. "Good Tom."

"Aye, Majesty?"

"I dare say you found our young Robbie sad at having to part from Frances all these weeks."

"He'll survive."

"I trust you do not think I would object if you wished to fetch her on the Progress with you."

"I hadn't thought..."

"Can't you just imagine the laddie's face when he comes in to dine at St. Albans tomorrow and finds his sweet nymph there!"

"Tomorrow?"

"Aye, tomorrow."

"Then I had best send word of your command posthaste."

"Indeed, Tom. But send word of *your* command. After all, it's *your* idea."

[II]

Monday the Twentieth of July

WHILE the Prince took his barge to Richmond, where he would hold court until he joined the Progress, Murray rode first to Paternoster Row. He was to arrange that Frances would, for the next three weeks, find herself conveniently at Cranford le Mote, where Henry would, as conveniently, find her (and, for that matter, Murray would as conveniently find the widow whose look alone could set cocks-a-crow at dusk).

He had to fight his way through the crowd overflowing the west yard of St. Paul's. It was the day of drawing the Virginia Company's lottery to raise funds for the First Colony. A roar went up as the winner of the chief prize of four thousand crowns was declared: one Thomas Sharpliffe, tailor. But there were groans, also, for threescore thousand hopefuls had drawn blanks—as was to be the fate of the Prince's man when he reached Mrs. Turner's door. After Murray had rung in vain a fourth time, a bystander came up, touching his cap.

"Begging pardon, your worship, but if you own the right name I might have a letter for you."

"Murray—give it here, man!"

"Begging pardon, but the good lady said your worship would surely find me a sixpence"—he sized him up—"or two."

Murray made the exchange, ripped open the row of Mrs. Turner's greyhound-head seals to get at the message and sucked in a breath through clenched teeth.

The bystander stood by for another expected caller from whom he might expect another sixpence—or two—for this other letter nestling inside his jerkin. Name of Monsieur de Lobel. God knows what London was coming to. Full of bloody foreigners.

THE BELL-RINGERS of St. Albans pulled six shillings' worth of chimes as the royal party wound through the cheering crowd.

"Which one's the King, then?"

"The one scratching his codpiece."

"Well, he ain't much like the head on my silver."

"I never get to look. The wife has mine off me afore I'm through the door."

"Your silver? Or your codpiece?"

Waving languidly to one side, the King turned to his Lord Chamberlain on the other. "How I *hate* the damned Progress. All these gawking people..."

"They have come miles to see your face, Sire."

"God's wounds, Tom! I shall pull down my breeches, and they shall see my arse!"

THIS OUT-OF-THE-WAY CHAMBER in Richmond Palace was dominated by a round mirror in which, legend had it, Henry the Seventh saw what was passing anywhere he wished, on land or sea. At his death, the glass was found cracked from side to side, and to this day it had been left just so, the shards enshrined in their crumbling frame. But Henry Tudor's true magic had been the intelligence conveyed to him in corners as private as this: much as Henry Stuart now looking into that mirror needed no better clairvoyance than Murray's report.

"Highness, forgive me. My disobedience would have served you better. Frances was most likely seen at the play. If only I had failed to bring her, the King would have been denied two and two with which to make four."

"I suspect he already had one and one with which to make two. Why else had he become so frantic to marry me off? And then yesterday—I confess—I as good as confirmed his arithmetic." Henry turned to meet Murray's eyes. "I told him it would be better that the people have an English bride to love than a foreign bride to hate."

"You wanted him to know! Sir, you *wanted* him to know!" Murray went cold.

"Be glad." The Prince clapped Murray's arm, unaware that he shrank at the touch. "Be glad it is a secret no longer. Because *knowing* the King knows is like having my chains struck off. *Knowing* the King knows is knowing that he dare do nothing except play these games."

"And knowing that princes may not marry whomsoever they please?"

"Is knowing that kings may"

So: a heartbeat from the throne was no longer near enough. From now on, it was going to be a drumbeat. And all for Frances, though if the Prince could forget that giddy creature's gender he would scarce bother to pass the time of day with her.

"David."

"Highness?"

"We are nearing the crossroads. Which way will you go?"

"Your way." God help us, what other after all these years?

The Prince turned to his splintered reflection in the mirror, and straightened his shoulders. Murray looked away, filled with foreboding.

BY CANDLELIGHT, the colours that show best are white, carnation and a kind of seawater green. By candlelight, the glitter of oes and spangs belies their little worth. Thus had written Sir Francis Bacon, the King's Solicitor-General and his host at Gorhambury Park this first halt of the Progress. And thus the Countess of Essex had chosen: aquamarine for her gown, and sparkle from piled hair to peeping toe. Also this night she wore, with a defiance that had Mrs. Turner in despair, the ring of nine diamonds that Henry had placed on her wedding finger. In the minstrels' gallery, the consort leader flicked his bow at a lutenist so dazzled by the girl that he was strumming his coranto in pavane time. Frances bloomed in the hot focus of every man's gaze and kindled the eye of every woman, not caring what might be whispered each time a fan went up to mask a jealous mouth.

"If that's the case, my dear, then I've been a virgin three times since Wednesday..."

"...and her mother said, which sex is he supposed to be earl of? Essex? It should have been Middlesex..."

Across the bustling hall, Rochester folded his arms, proud as a proprietor. Oh, how he loved her. What a couple they would make. But where Rochester saw a gulf of beauty he could hardly wait to drown in, the troubled man at his side saw a swamp of corruption that would suck them all down. Where Rochester saw an angel's face framed by rich gems, the troubled man at his side saw a devil's, hanged about with cheap beckonings like a tavern sign.

"Careful..." Overbury sought to hold him back by the elbow.

"Tom—I know what I'm doing."

Overbury doubted that. Rochester's passion was grounded in envy of the man rather than love of the woman. He was deaf to caution. Deaf to reason. Deaf to reminders that this catopard he now wanted as a wife was the same whose bawdy tricks he had once so gleefully inventoried. The lascivious whispers...the harlot postures...the spurring cries...and that thing she would do in the dark...

"Sweet lady." Rochester made his bow.

"My lord." Frances made her curtsy.

"You are so beautiful."

"Not so beautiful as you, my lord." Please, God, guard his daft tongue, Frances prayed. Everyone is listening.

He opened a hand for her to take as they joined the dance. Her mother had warned her that she must never be alone with him now—lest it further the King's fancy to match them, lest it hazard the divorce and lest mischief be made of it to the Prince. But a coranto was not alone.

"I want you."

"No." Her smile widened for the lookers-on.

"Now."

"No." Wider.

"Then later."

"No." Wider still.

The gay toss of her head made it seem to him like yes.

THE KNOCKING grew less discreet the longer it remained unanswered. Mrs. Turner left the side of the soft-breathing Frances and, drawing on a nightgown, went to get rid of the fool before he woke the whole of Hertfordshire. She opened the door of the outer chamber only a few inches, but Rochester leaned on it and lurched in, maudlin-high with wine. His bow almost knocked the candle from her hand.

"My sweet, sweet, *sweet* Mistress T."

"Come now, my bonnie laddie." She put a humouring arm round his waist. "It's long past your bedtime."

"Please, I must see her."

"She's fast asleep."

"Oh..."

"So come on, there's a good boy." She tried to steer him about, but he stood firm.

"I wouldn't harm her for the world."

"Of course you wouldn't."

"I'd kill anyone..."

"So would I, my dear."

"I love her." Tears began to trickle into his beard.

"Hush!"

"I only want to see her."

"And she only wants to sleep."

"Just one look at her sweet face, then. Just one."

"Promise?"

"Promise."

He crossed his heart, and Mrs. Turner bade him wait while she drew open the inner door and held the candle on high so that he could glimpse the still Frances, her hair fanning over the pillow. More tears followed. Mrs. Turner put her finger to her lips, and soon he let her tiptoe him away, though not turning his head from the girl until he was outside.

"What a clown." Mrs. Turner climbed back into bed.

"They're all clowns." Frances leaned up and blew out the candle. "All of them."

[12]

Friday the Thirty-first of July

THE LEVELLED HALBERDS of a dozen guards in the imperial red and yellow ploughed a furrow through the Madrid crowd for Juan de Ciriza, newly appointed secretary to the *Junta de Inglaterra.* Inside his doublet, Ambassador Zuñiga's dispatch simmered like these thousands lining the plaza for the festival of the bulls. The exhausted courier had proclaimed to Ciriza that this was a message of the highest importance, to be deciphered forthwith and borne to him of the highest importance: Don Francisco Gómez de Sandoval y Rojas, Duque de Lerma.

James had his Rochester, but Lerma had his Philip. And for the fourteen years this Hapsburg husk had been reigning, it was Lerma who had been ruling. "Alas," the old Philip had lamented of his heir, "I fear they will govern him." And Lerma, more than twice the new Philip's twenty, had fulfilled the prophecy by taking the hands that took the reins of the widest empire the world had known as it ambled down the hill from glory to decline. Philip the Good, they would call this one, as they did all kings for whom history had no bolder niche. And good he had certainly been to his *privado,* who came to office the poorest marqués of the forty-two and was now the richest duque of the twenty-four. Today, as most days, Lerma had left Philip stroking his pink chin at one of the two-and-a-half thousand windows of the palace of El Escorial in the cool Guadarramas, well away from the clamorous capital in which the plaza crowd, which had been piling in since dawn, were now counting the minutes to four o'clock.

Glass in hand, the Duque leaned an august head out from his balcony. At one elbow, his lustrous lieutenant, Don Rodrigo Calderón. At the other, the older and wiser, if plainer, Don Antonio de Arosteguí, principal secretary to the Council of State. Their side of the square would soon be in merciful shadow, though the others would scorch for a couple of hours yet. Every window was packed jowl to jowl, every bench cheek to cheek. Behind one gate, foaming at the mouth, half-mad bulls pawed the ground. Behind another, dry at the mouth, half-mad bullfighters waited for the mounted constables to cudgel away the last of the rabble.

"May it please your Grace..." Sweat suffused Ciriza's face as he proffered the vital dispatch to Lerma's back.

The Duque turned, close-cropped scalp contrasting with handsome moustache and beard. He looked Ciriza up and down, and turned again to the plaza as the trumpet signaled the first bull. Ciriza was new enough to this post to clench a fist in frustration, but Arosteguí motioned him to bring up a chair, help himself to a glass and be patient with the great man.

The plaza was hushed now as twenty thousand eyes watched the young *torero* go down on one knee. He extended each hand to display a long dart trailing a red banderole and, yelling his invitation as the gate was thrown open, fluttered the ribbons to offer a target. The bull was almost upon him when he swayed back out of range. From the four sides of the square came a gasp like swirling wind. He took the next two charges on his feet, each time planting a dart in the great neck muscle and spinning clear with a grace that had the crowd cheering. At the following pass, he used the bull's horns to spring nimbly upon its back. But the roar of acclamation stifled itself as he lost his footing and crashed to the cobbles. An angry horn skewered his thigh, and the plaza was on its feet, groaning with excitement as the beast shook its tormentor free for another attack. But now three comrades with raised broadswords were there, screaming curses to draw attention from the stricken youth. The first smashed a two-handed blow across the bull's eyes as the second slashed between the hind legs and laid it low. The third took his time, making a ceremony of positioning his sword point above the bull's slumped shoulders, and plunging it deep into the aorta.

Six mules dragged the bull away as its victim was taken off on a litter—to much crossing, giving way to shrieks of delight as he waved a trailing hand to show he was not done for.

"Brave boy!" Lerma rose to lean over the balcony and throw a purse of *escudos* to a constable. "Hey! See he has this medicine!"

Only now did he attend to Ciriza, showing impatience when the dispatch was not instantly in his outstretched hand. After a few lines, he came to the details of Henry's survey of the Fleet at Chatham and his fire-breathing talk with Admiral Monson. He sat abruptly, the better to bear the burden which, page by page, he passed to the standing Calderón and Arosteguí. This time when the trumpet sounded, Lerma did not hear: he was in another arena.

"You must tell your King"—Arosteguí broke the silence, his voice rising as he quoted the Queen's warning to Zuñiga—*"that if he does*

not make Henry a friend he will make him an enemy. And such an enemy . . ."

"What fools you are"—Calderón picked it up—*"to require that he humble himself before the world to qualify for a Spanish bride. Ask your King this: If Spain does think it worth an Infanta to save England, is it not worth an Infanta to save Spain?"*

"Henry grows too strong to be commanded"—Arosteguí again—*"soon he will have the keys of the kingdom, or soon he will take them . . ."*

"And the first key he turns?" Lerma offered the cue to Calderón.

"Will free Sir Walter Ralegh."

"And Ralegh free means?"

"War," said Calderón.

"War," said Arosteguí.

"War," said Ciriza.

SIR WALTER RALEGH, the proudest of men (though some swore that Overbury ran him damnably close), sighed at the unreadiness of these rooms above the portcullis of the Bloody Tower, his prison since the fourth month of James's reign. Hitherto, Murray had always sent Ralegh notice enough to have his servant bring out the finest hangings and silver, and to have Bess Ralegh bring in the finest dishes. Notice enough to receive the Prince in clothes more splendid than these that did for the hours in the garden shed where he cured his tobacco, and cured also those who sent for his renowned pills and plaisters and balsams—in particular for that Great Cordial whose efficacy against all fevers the Queen herself promoted. Notice enough to clear the table and floor of work on his History of the World, cataloguing from the year dot the comeuppance of unjust Kings—with the beseeching exception of his "revengeless and liberal" gaoler, whose heir held the promise of freedom from this place and for whose service the masterpiece was undertaken.

Indeed, hope began to open Ralegh's cage as he looked into the Prince's glad face. Henry read the signals and could have scourged himself. He shook his head.

"I'm sorry."

"You should be." Ralph's still-broad Devonshire softened the reproach. "I was halfway to Havana."

"You haven't changed."

"Ah, but I have, sir. Had my fancy not been so long confined, I would have been halfway home again—with the Spanish silver fleet in tow."

"I fancy that your fancy shall not be confined much longer. Things are coming to a head. My father..."

"Come, Highness." Ralph halted him, finger on lip to warn that the Tower's dead walls came alive for indiscretion. "Let us take a breath of Thames air while my fellow makes ready."

Henry motioned his host to lead him and Murray to the river terrace atop the inner wall. But Ralegh deferred to him, happier for his Prince not to see him limp up the twenty winding stairs, even with the wound that was his souvenir of the sack of Cádiz. Murray smiled to himself as he followed. Though nigh on sixty now, Spain's greatest living enemy had heart enough yet to strike those dons anew. To found more Virginias. To transfer the Spanish empire to the British empire. He had scourged Philip the Second on both sides of the Atlantic, and in the middle. He would happily do as much for Philip the Third. How Spain had cheered when, even before James's coronation, Ralegh had been brought down by the whispers of courtiers jealous that he would win the new sovereign as he had won the old. Majesty, they had said, Sir Walter was loudest for putting your poor mother to death. Majesty, they had said, Sir Walter is plotting to set your poor cousin Arabella on the throne. Majesty, they had said, Spain will never believe James truly desires peace unless and until this sole survivor of Elizabeth's Council of War of '88 is off the stage.

Therefore was Ralegh stripped of the great offices Elizabeth had bestowed upon him: Captain of the Guard, Governor of Virginia, Vice-Admiral of the West, Lord Lieutenant of Cornwall, Lord Warden of the Stannaries, Governor of the Isle of Jersey. Therefore was Ralegh beggared of the great revenues with which Elizabeth had rewarded him: not least his licences worth thousands a year from wines, tin, broadcloth and playing cards. Therefore was Ralegh evicted from Durham House: and, after the twenty years it had been his London home, with but fourteen days' notice, when even the humblest artificer merited a quarter's grace from his landlord. No wonder Ralegh could write to Henry from prison: *There is no man so assured of his honour, of his riches, of his health, of his life... but that he may be deprived of any or all the very next hour to come.*

And in this very next hour to come he might be deprived of hope, too. For Murray had persuaded the Prince that he must let Ralegh into the secret that was now no secret from the King. Murray gambled that, heedless of consequence, Ralegh would oppose this ambition for marriage to Frances. Then, please God, Murray would find the strength to save his own conscience, and stand with Ralegh to save that of the Prince.

"Well, then, Sir Walter." Henry tried to compose himself to look his hero in the face and tell him straight. He could not. He would come to it once his insides ceased churning.

"Well then, Highness."

"Just look at this I had today." Henry produced a letter and unfolded it. "From your enemy and mine—the King's best friend. Now, to cap it all, when my father would address me it is Rochester's ear into which he speaks. Am I expected to reply through the other ear?"

Ralegh held the paper away for better focus as he read out loud. *"...his Majesty observes...his Majesty wills..."*

Henry wound himself up. "Can't you just see that smirk on Rochester's face as he writes to me?"

"...his Majesty commands that his Highness set out his considered opinion on the renewed proposition for a match with the Princes Christina of France..."

"Hang him!" Henry took back the letter and flung it aside. "It is none of Rochester's damned business. And the King well knows my considered opinion. The girl is Catholic. She is secretly on offer to Spain. Is the first son of England to contend with the second son of Spain for the second daughter of France? By the living God, he is not!"

"Highness, is it an old man's wisdom you require?" Ralegh folded his arms. "Or an old man's agreement?"

"But surely..."

"Surely, I agree that your father could have secured you the first princess had he not been so busy being twice as clever as Spain that he was only half as clever as France. And surely, I agree it is a disgrace that the letter should have come from the hand of Rochester. Nevertheless, it would be wise to ignore him as you would any great man's ape. You can make your point by replying directly to his Majesty. And, sir, would it not be polite to reply in terms that do not transform this from an argument about whom you shall marry into an argument about who is King of England?"

"Perhaps that is the argument."

"Then perhaps that is the best reason for not stating it before you are ready."

"I am an inch from ready."

Murray caught the Prince's eye and willed him to come to the matter that brought them here. Henry shifted away. Murray tried to help by tacking the conversation closer to the wind.

"The only regret about Bessy's match with Frederick is that it seems to rule out his Highness, too, finding a consort from Germany. But you will not be surprised, Sir Walter, to learn that the ambassador happened to bring portraits of Frederick's three sisters for our Prince to cast an eye upon."

"Neither," said Ralegh, "would I be surprised to learn that all are shown to be beauties of the greatest magnitude."

"And the princesses of Brandenburg and of Hesse-Cassel have also been put forward, though so far we have had to manage without their likenesses."

"Ah, David, how easy it would be for his Highness if a sweet face and a glad eye were the only criteria." Ralegh stroked his beard. "I like these Germans. I have found them just and free from treachery. But the merchant does not hazard all his estate in one vessel, and no more do well-advised kings lay all their hopes upon one nation. Nor upon the likes of Savoy that are beset by enemies: Is not Ireland enough a grave for our best captains? Nor upon such as Tuscany: What can they offer but Medici money, which will not come into your hands anyway, Highness, but will soon be scattered by the King? No, you would do well to acknowledge that in the long run it may indeed be France that provides the answer."

"But..."

"I know the buts, Highness. The fact remains, there is already much French stock in our royal line. They are not our natural enemies, nor slaves to the Pope, as are Spain and those others. By alliance with France, we would secure the Low Countries, which will make us invincible. And they do seek your hand, whereas Spain shuns it unless you first convert."

"Be that as it may, I will have no Catholic princess unless *she* first converts."

"Then you will have no Catholic princess."

"And even if France pretends that their Christina may convert once she is here"—Henry's voice betrayed how thrown he was by the thought—"it still begs the question of what I am supposed to do while she grows from six to sixteen."

"Highness, I have advised my own sons, better to tarry than marry till they are toward thirty. Shall I advise you different?"

"Sir Walter, there is something else." The Prince looked out across the battlements.

"Something else?"

"I beg you, forgive me for not confiding it sooner. I suppose I feared you might not understand. And now that you honour me by speaking to me as the son I wish I were, I..."

Henry's eyes filled as he turned back to the river. Ralegh looked to Murray, who put palms together in a silent plea.

"Something else?"

"Sir Walter." Now the Prince met his eye. "I have to tell you that when last with the King, I made it clear I would rather marry a daughter of the Church of England than any of the Pope's princesses."

"You made it clear, did you?"

"Yes, I made it clear."

"And did you, I wonder, make it clear that you have some particular daughter in view?"

"No."

"But you do have some particular daughter in view?"

"Yes."

"Namely?"

"Lady Frances Howard."

Ralegh felt his age as he paced to the far end of the terrace and came back to lean out on the crenellated stonework. He closed his eyes and remembered Frances, no more than twelve when he last saw her but already too much a beauty, already too much her mother's daughter. His Bess had been a Maid of Honour at the same time as the then Catherine Knyvet, and knew her for the witch she was: her kettle never off the boil, her glance never far from a codpiece. He opened his eyes and saw on Tower Green the scaffold site where the two Howard adulteresses who had bewitched England's last Henry had died.

"So the annulment is no idle rumour."

"She was never his wife."

"Why must she be yours?"

"I love her."

"You love her." Ralegh sighed. "And how long before the King discovers?"

"I think he must know—more or less."

"Is she already your mistress—more or less?" Ralegh accepted Henry's silence as his answer. "And how long has this continued—more or less?"

"Five months. Six months."

"Yet, Highness, you have not felt able to trust me with it until today. Why do you think that is?"

Henry struggled. He could stand fast against all his father's chicanery. But he was weak against the candour of this man who had so much to gain by chanting as-your-Highness-pleases to every whim, yet held him dear enough to hazard telling him the truth.

"Believe me, it is as I said. I did not think you would understand."

"Oh? Am I more likely to understand when, even today, you could not face me with it until now?" Ralegh's voice stayed small and slow. "Why did we first have to have this comedy over Rochester's letter? Had you straightaway told me what you had been up to, I would straightaway have told you to seek no further reason for your father's action. Did you hesitate in hope that I would rescue you from the truth? That I would say: I have it, Highness! Why do you not find a certain way to dismay the Church, to dishearten the people, to dumbfound Parliament? To make every court in Europe think you knave or fool? To hand the King the means to diminish you? To be the butt of every filthy jester? And to reduce to despair all of us who love you and know you to be the hope of England's greatness?"

Ralegh's eyes watered, but he did not bend his gaze to spare himself or Henry.

"May a prince not love?" Every other argument stuck in his throat.

"Sir, I rejoice that you are too much a man to forbear to love without heed. But, I pray you, be enough a prince to forbear to link without heed. Though I know she be very beautiful..."

"Oh, she is, she is."

"...and though I know it useless to seek to dissuade you, or any man, from being captivated by beauty. Listen: When I was first at court, I fell in love with one of the Maids of Honour...

> Violet breath and lips of jelly,
> And of the softest down her belly...

Oh, I knew I would die if I lost her. But I did not die. I fell in love with another Maid...

> Sweet embraces: such delights
> As will shorten tedious nights...

And, oh, I knew I would die if I lost her. But I did not die. I fell in love with the Maid I was meant for...

> True love is enduring fire
> In the mind ever burning:

Never sick, never old, never dead,
From itself never turning.

That one was my Bess. That one I married. And every day for twenty years I have known that Heaven has blessed me not with a woman I could die for, but a woman I could live for. Which is why I say to you—as to my own sons—remember that if you marry for beauty you bind yourself forever to that which will not last, perhaps not even please you a year hence. Better adore such magic in a mistress—and when your desire changes you are free to choose again. As, indeed, is she."

The pain on Henry's face at those last four words made Ralegh wish he could call them back. The girl, true to type, had doubtless made him frantic by playing that card already, and would doubtless play it again.

"Sir Walter, the more you say, the more I know how much I love her."

"More than your destiny?"

"Perhaps she is my destiny."

Ralegh took palm from brow to point toward an ill-laden merchantman listing in midstream. "And what is her destiny, Highness? What but to tip arsy-varsy if the wind gets up? So what service would I do her master, had he the good sense to ask an ancient mariner's opinion, were I to bite my tongue and tell him all stood fair?"

"Come, David." The Prince turned to go. "I was right to fear he would not understand. He has been shut away too long."

"Highness, would it have been too long were I telling you what you want to hear? You know the King will never give permission—and poor Lady Arabella in the Bell Tower behind us is warning enough as to what befalls those of the blood royal who think they may marry without it."

"Come, David."

"No, sir." Murray stood his ground. He felt himself trembling, too aware that fortune was at the divide. No Stuart prince for two centuries had known a father long enough to learn how to be a father to his own son. What Ralegh had done this day was a father's act of unselfish devotion such as had long ceased to fashion Henry's line. They both were entitled to more from Murray than this standing cravenly by.

"Highness, I have followed you since you were a child. I have kept your secrets, even from the King who placed me at your side in order that you should have none. I have served you in many ways I am proud of—and in some ways I am ashamed of. I have played pander for you. Lied for you. God knows, I would kill for you. But if the good Sir Walter has not diverted you from the path of folly, he has diverted me." He shook his head. "I will not cry havoc for this."

Henry looked from one to the other. He needed them. But he needed Frances, too. "My dear friends," he held out a hand to each, "I am some way on this course. Maybe you will persuade me to turn about. Maybe I will persuade myself. But now is too soon—David, you know that."

"Aye."

"You must give me time."

"Highness," said Ralegh, "you can give yourself time. You need only put aside the thought of marriage yet awhile."

"So be it." It was not much to promise. Frances would not be free yet awhile. Even as King, he could not marry her before then.

Now, with the last of the slain bulls dragged away, the plaza was empty save for a few ragamuffins with nothing better to do than watch the bloodied square flushed clean...and save for the four doleful countenances on the Duque de Lerma's balcony. Like poor Don Quixote (whose chronicles of misadventure were this year being introduced to England) the shambling empire of Philip the Third was in no condition to do battle. Not even against a windmill such as the Virginia Colony, which Zuñiga recommended Spain to tilt into the dust lest it be a giant after all. Let alone against a windmill such as King James, whose son and heir Zuñiga recommended Spain to tilt into the dust while they were still able.

"Puh!" Lerma threw up his hands. "The Queen of England asks Don Pedro if it is not worth an Infanta to save Spain. But England already has a Catholic Queen! And she dare not declare her faith to save her nation, never mind ours. God forgive us, the last Infanta we sent them died in misery. Would our María be less humiliated by this Henry than was our Catherine by that?"

"Better fate take her first," said Arosteguí.

"Better fate take *him* first," said Calderón.

"Fate," said Lerma, "is not unused to being Spain's ally in such matters." He did not need to list William of the Netherlands and France's last two Henrys, all cut down by assassins; nor other enemies of Spain whose sudden ends were less spectacular, but no less convenient. "These English like to mock that we are men of small dispatch.

They say, *Mi venga la muerte de España*—Let my death come from Spain—for then it will surely be long in coming. Therefore, let us pray that misfortune to this Prince comes not from Spain—for then it will surely be soon in coming."

"His Grace has a plan?" Ciriza prompted dutifully.

"Yes, gentlemen, his Grace has a plan." Lerma's palm commanded attention. "A wise plan. A plan to leave all to our man in the field. Don Pedro knows England as well as he knows my mind."

"Our Don Pedro is a powerful *caballero,*" said Arosteguí.

"So is our Don Dinero." Calderón fetched out a purse of gold and jiggled it by his ear.

"Nowhere more than in England," Lerma scoffed. "It is like a shop: nothing is to be had there without money. And—as you will discover, Ciriza, when you have been longer with the *Junta de Inglaterra*—no people there have been more eager to shake Don Dinero's hand than the noble pair you will find enciphered as Beltenbros and Roldán. This very spring they were telling our ambassador they had been offered one hundred thousand crowns by the Grand Duke of Tuscany to influence a match between his sister and the Prince of Wales. Beltenbros wrung his right honourable hands and said that, naturally, they did not wish such a marriage against the interests of Spain—but one hundred thousand was a lot of crowns. So we were forced to give that much to them *not* to work for Tuscany!"

"I call it blackmail," said Arosteguí.

"Well," said Lerma, "I suppose that if the Earl of Salisbury could be called Beltenbros to suit his purposes, then blackmail can be called compensation to suit ours. The King of England's first minister served us well enough for his pension; it is our loss that the Devil has now taken him."

"It is as well that Roldán remains to us, your Grace." Arosteguí had begrudged twice a year since the peace the pensions he had had to find for the other dozen on the London list. "The wages of a hundred servants are not too great a payment for one such *confidente* in high places."

"Not at all," said Calderón, "though what does grieve me is that in the two years Don Pedro was absent from England, poor old Velasco paid her as much for nothing."

Lerma smiled. "I doubt that it grieves Don Pedro. He insists that the sauce for Roldán is *dinero*. But, the way his face goes quite pink when I mention the lady, I guess that *dinero* may not have been the only sauce flowing between them."

Lerma began to pace. Ciriza knew by now to recognise the signal that the great man was about to compose a dispatch. His question as to the identity of this Roldán would have to wait. He produced his table book and had completed the salutation before Lerma started to dictate.

"Tell Don Pedro—from his Majesty, as usual, eh?—that we have noted his report on the matter of the Prince, and his opinion on each point. Tell Don Pedro that we consider this has been well thought through, as was to be expected of one with his discretion. Tell Don Pedro that, since Henry is so poorly disposed toward our religion and so impatient to wage war upon our whole empire, it would indeed be a mercy if the hand of fate—rather than the hand of Spain—were to deny him that opportunity. Tell Don Pedro that the rest is up to him."

Ciriza would have this into the new cipher and into the pouches of two couriers before the sun went down. One would take the direct route by way of San Sebastián, through Huguenot land to Paris and on to the Channel ports. The other would ride more slowly and more surely in Spanish company on the supply road through mainly Hapsburg lands from the Mediterranean to the Flanders coast. Ciriza said a silent prayer to St. Christopher for the pair of them.

"WELL, why not?" The Prince helped himself to one of the three clay pipes Ralegh's man had brought up to them on the Tower battlements. "I can hardly be more in the King's black book."

"Not for me," said Murray, moving to ensure he would be upwind once they were a-whiffing.

"Still *virginia intacta?*" Ralegh ribbed him.

"When it comes to tobacco, I am the King's man. It is nothing but an expensive stink."

"That may be." Ralegh lit up, unhurriedly. "All I know is that I took a pipe the morning the King had me sent to the scaffold. And I had no sooner finished it than I was reprieved. So you will understand"—puff—"why I have been sure"—puff—"not to miss a day since."

Murray studied the Prince and Ralegh as they leaned against the river wall and blew smoke rings at a cast of ravens. The birds flew off to join their kind about the several towers that housed state prisoners whom only the King's pleasure could free. Murray reflected that there had been no representative of the house of Howard here since the Stuarts came to reign, though the Tudors had put away not just Henry the Eighth's two Howard wives but two Howard dukes, two Howard earls and a Howard viscount. Still, if the Prince's servants had done their duty well enough today, the next batch of Howards might not be long in finding their way through Traitors' Gate. By heaven, the rage of the Countess of Suffolk, once Henry picked the moment to dash her daughter's dream of marriage and leave the family to his mercy, would outdo the Three Furies in one.

Henry discharged a puff into the still air like gunsmoke and mouthed a boom to accompany it. Ralegh's insides stirred with a fearful eagerness.

JUAN DE CIRIZA's curiosity boiled over as he left the plaza balcony with Arosteguí.

"Don Antonio, who is this Roldán?"

"La Condesa de Suffolk..."

[13]

Saturday the First of August

IN THE PRIVY CHAMBER at Richmond Palace, Henry applauded with delight as Isaac Oliver unveiled his new portrait miniature. For Oliver, Limner to the Prince, saw him as a Huguenot refugee might hope to see the hero of Protestant Europe: in gilded armour against a background of soldiers, tents and cannon. The face would have been at home at King Arthur's Table. It was the face of a victor to whom conquest never came so hard as to bereave it of generosity, and that of a lover to whom conquest never came so easy as to bereave it of rapture.

"Master Oliver, your genius takes my breath away." Henry double-patted his shoulder. "Though I am not at all certain it does as much for Sir David..."

"It's a very fine portrait, Highness, I'm sure." Murray had no wish to upset the painter.

"What he is too polite to say, Master Oliver, is that it captures the Prince he exalts, yet not the Prince he beholds."

"But not too polite, Highness, to pray that, though I love them both, the former continues to serve as model for the latter."

"Amen to that, David. But now we must find a worthy subject for our gifted friend next to ply his pencils."

"I shall like it well if your Highness commands me to make a portrait of the lady of his choice. If I may be bold..."

"Go on."

"...it is being said among our community that you may favour a daughter of France."

"Well, it is no secret that I admired your late King Henry. I could wish to have such an enemy of Spain as my father-in-law. But now he is gone, I doubt that his widow would meet my condition that their princess convert to the religion I follow—and indeed, Master Oliver, the religion your family left Rouen in order to follow."

"Then perhaps..."

"Highness"—Murray decided he must interrupt before, God help us, Henry was prompted to commission a portrait of Frances—"no doubt I can make your wishes known to Master Oliver in due course."

"Very well, then." Henry took the point.

"And, sir, we shall all too soon need to bid *au revoir* to our friend, and attend to that letter we must have on the road to his Majesty before the day is much older."

With Oliver gone, leaving behind his plea to keep the hinged glass closed on the portrait lest some fool's dandruff ruin the perfectly ground colours, the Prince and Murray were soon applying as much art to that letter.

THE KING'S PROGRESS had now reached Kirby, the Northamptonshire manor of Sir Christopher Hatton. Rochester hardly cared that they had left behind them the Earl of Kent's seat at Wrest, Lord St. John's at Bletsoe and Lord Compton's at Castle Ashby. For he had left his guts behind him at each stop on the way, and had barely the strength to ride from one to the other, never mind attend to his King and pay court to his secret bride-to-be. Yet Frances and Mrs. Turner—and that spitfire Countess of Suffolk, who had taken over the chaperonage of her daughter—seemed to find his plight amusing. Especially when he blamed them for sacrificing to him their mighty portions of strawberries and cream as they refreshed themselves on the road from Sir Francis Bacon's that first morning.

"ONCE MORE, David." The Prince sat back and closed his eyes to concentrate as Murray read out his draft of the letter to the King:

Your Majesty's pleasure, signified unto me by my Lord Rochester, is that I set down my opinion concerning the proposition for a match with the second daughter of France.

The cause which induced you to proceed was the hope, given you by the French, of obtaining their first daughter for me by breaking off her match with Spain. I hold that it stands more with your Majesty's honour to stay your ambassador from proceeding any further in this.

No great negotiation should be set upon ground so unsure, and be dependent upon the will of the other party to go back on their word elsewhere. And, in the end, it will not be honourable for your Majesty that the world should see you break off proceedings for the second daughter when it becomes apparent that you will not obtain the first.

Whether your Majesty will continue to negotiate for little Christina, I leave unto your better judgment. But if you be so resolved, I entreat you to be certain that France would send the child to us without delay.

"Good, David! That will hold the fort. France has gone too far to break the match with Spain, and there is no chance that they will send Christina here for us devils to convert. I hear the Papal Nuncio told the Queen Regent that she should as soon consign her daughter to hell."

"Perhaps your Highness might consider that, with the Pope himself on your side, you need not be quite so sarcastic to your father. A touch of respect here and there would not blow away your argument."

"Do give over! If my father wants respect from me, he should not ask Rochester to obtain it."

Murray saw little point in persevering. This was the Prince of the Isaac Oliver portrait. Ajax before Troy.

HENRY remained as much that Prince after dinner when he drew aside Phineas Pett to talk privately in the bay window of the Presence Chamber. The matter at hand was no more than how the Navy might best be used to create the right impression of Britain's power from the moment his sister's husband-to-be landed, in eleven weeks or so. Nevertheless, the Prince was sure Pett bore scars enough to know the need to keep anything and everything secret from those who lived only to spite and to spoil. The date for Bessy's wedding had yet to be fixed—it might be any time between Epiphany and May Day—but Henry was eager to make some beginning before he had to join the Progress.

Three times during the afternoon, Pett was summoned back to answer particular questions. Henry envisaged a wondrous river pageant befitting the marriage of Thames and Rhine. Could forty pinnaces and the like be brought above London Bridge to set up a mock sea fight before the assembled company at Whitehall? Then there must be the finest fleet the Navy could muster, jubiliant with ensigns and pennants, to escort the couple across to Holland to begin their journey to Heidelberg. Which ships could be made ready in time? And lastly—the Prince apologised for calling Pett yet again, but the thought had only just come to him—there surely could be no theatre for the sea fight more imposing than Tower Reach, where mightier men-of-war could play their part in the spectacle. Which of the escort squadron could get up that high with the tide and ride safely at low water in the Pool of London, between the Bridge and Limehouse Point? The Prince required Pett's advice speedily and, at this juncture, without reference to others. Not even the good comrades at his table, John King, master of the flagship, and John Reynolds, master of the cannon.

Pett went out onto the terrace to compose his answers and himself. The order was for a tattoo, but the specifications were for a battle. He could picture London on the wedding eve, with a hundred thousand souls lining the great river bend between Westminster Hall and the Bridge as ordnance thundered and fireworks split the sky. But he knew, as did the Prince, that the stage below the Bridge would be too small to provide much room for actors with the displacement of *Adventure, Rainbow, Antelope, Speedwell, Assurance, Crane* and the rest. There had to be a more portentous reason to have them bristling by the Tower; inside which lay not only the greatest soldier in the land, Sir Walter Ralegh, but the greatest armoury in Europe, stacked with munitions enough to hold the realm for the King. Or against him.

As he presented his detailed answers, Pett was anxious enough for there to be lines on his face for the Prince to read between.

"Good fellow, Phineas! I shall see that the Lord Admiral gives immediate orders to prepare for the escort and the mock sea fight."

"Above Bridge *and* below?"

"Just above, for the present."

Pett looked relieved. He had five young children, with a sixth due about the time Frederick would be landing. Henry took his arm to walk him to the doors.

"My good friend, by all means be gloomy at the thought that if things continue as they are, our nation will sink into nothingness. But cheer yourself with the certainty that, one way or another, one day or another, we are going to see a new dawn. Your children and mine will grow up as citizens of an unbounded empire, not a mere shrinking island off the shore of Europe."

"Highness, I pray God to look after you."

"He will, Phineas. So that I may look after you."

HENRY had slipped through a side gate after supper to walk the riverbank by the light of the moon. The trumpets had now ceased to echo after him across the still night, but his head was yet too busy for the pillow. He allowed himself a sigh as he came to a halt at the spot from where he had crossed to meet Frances in the meadow when she came down from Cranford le Mote.

Only six days more, and he would see her again when he joined the Progress at her uncle's Belvoir Castle. After this fortnight apart, he ached with love unmade. The last time, he had pledged himself with that ring of nine diamonds. What words were there that would hold her if he now sought to move it to a neutral finger? *Christ, say she goes to Rochester*... He had been honest enough in telling Ralegh that now was too soon; but they, like him, must live with the reality that it would remain too soon as long as the flame of Frances consumed all doubts the instant she hove in sight. His clouded eyes turned from the river as Murray approached.

All this for that damned girl, thought Murray as they walked in silence back to the Palace. Let the reckoning be soon: account each plaint, each tear, each groan; each grief concealed by day, each torment unconcealed by night; and sum them all in one to present the price of soon-forgotten pleasure in long-remembered pain.

[14]

Wednesday the Fifth of August

THIS was the day the King had set aside each year for all time so that his people might give thanks to God for preserving him from "the wicked designments of those bloodthirsty wretches," the Earl of Gowrie and the Master of Ruthven. His salvation, achieved by the butchery of both those brothers, aged twenty-two and nineteen, had taken place in dubious circumstances while he was yet ruler only of Scotland. And when he came into his new kingdom three years later, he could not wait to enter London before issuing a proclamation for the arrest of the third and fourth brothers, who were schoolboys when the slaughter took place and had been smuggled across the border to be safe from his vengeance. The younger, Patrick Ruthven, had now lain nine years in the Tower without trial. The elder, William, was hunted still.

The King's new subjects did not care overmuch how many Scotsmen slew each other for any reason or none. Nevertheless, at Sir Anthony Mildmay's manor of Apthorpe in Northamptonshire, where the Progress now rested, the Almighty was today entreated to smite James's current enemies. The prescribed collects were followed by endless feasting, endless boozing and endless arguing about what really happened inside Gowrie House that bloody afternoon of the first Fifth of August of the century. Some settled for the King James version that the Ruthven clan were out to assassinate him. Some favoured the story that, the Queen being six months gone with Baby Charles, the King discovered that the Master might be the father. Others preferred to believe that death was the price the brothers paid for scorning his advances and threatening to dash his hopes of the English succession by informing Elizabeth that Scotland had a bugger for a King. The Fifth of August—like the Fifth of November anniversary of the Gunpowder Treason—was never allowed to pass without its hero frothing himself into a ferment of suspicion, and this day the royal finger pointed at the special ambassador of Spain.

"What's this? What's this?" The King drummed the festive board as Rochester whispered into his ear the message Overbury had just whispered to him. He rose to address the company. "Day after day, my lords and gentlemen all, I ask why this man Zuñiga stays on in London when there is no more business for him. Day after day, I am fobbed off with trash as to what a slowback the Spaniard is. But I know better. I know he is never slow except it be for some purpose. Therefore, at my command, a watch has been kept on the Barbican every hour of the twenty-four. And now, whom do we discover leaving Zuñiga's house the other night? Who but that arch-Jesuit, Blackman!" The buzz acknowledged that this was a discovery indeed: the Confessor of the English Colleges of the Society of Jesus in Valladolid and Rome. "And, what is more, papers found upon him reveal that two Jesuit superiors have been summoned to London to engage in secret conference with him—Holtby from Northumberland and Jones from Monmouth. Need I ask why else that should be but for them to offer their cunning to Spain for some new attempt upon my person?"

The courtiers swelled their chorus of sympathetic indignation to fill the pause as the King reached for his goblet and poised it for yet another toast.

"Stand up, Haddington! Stand up, Fenton!" The pair, whose lordships and lands had rewarded the part their swords had played on Gowrie Day, and their silence since, pulled themselves heavily to their feet. "I drink to your health, bonny lads. You saved me then. I pray you be ever ready to do so again."

They resumed their seats, Haddington wishing that the boon he was permitted to crave each Fifth of August had this time been one soft cushion, rather than a royal command for the Exchequer to hurry up with the five hundred pounds it owed him. James in this mood would talk on till their bum-bones cried out for mercy. Fenton, who had taken Ralegh's place as Captain of the Guard, stifled a yawn and feared to fall asleep at his post long before the King was done.

"Every plot against me has its roots in Spain, though it is thanks to me that they enjoy peace! And now they publish this book of Father Juan de Mariana, in which he extols the killing of kings such as myself. Does the Pope censure him for it, when he has already called in books by him on lesser matters? No, my lords and gentlemen. The Pope does nothing. *Nothing!* This is again a time of great blindness in Popery. In days gone by, though a man found his wife abed in her friar's arms, it was unlawful to suspect that the errand was other than confession and instruction. And now in our day, though the treason of those Jesuits who plotted to blow up me and my son and my Parliament that Fifth of November is verified, and they are duly hanged for it, yet does the Pope suffer them to be enrolled in the canon of holy martyrs! I say with Isaiah, woe to them who speak good of evil..."

The King paused only to drink up wine, and drink in approbation. Two hours on, he had argued in English, French, Latin and Greek. Two hours on, he had cited Nero and Nebuchadnezzar, the Whore of Babylon and the Holy Maid of Kent, Cyrus and Cicero, Attila the Hun and John the Baptist, Ethelbert and Barbarossa, the Archbishop of Salzburg and the wife of Socrates, Knox and Xenophon, Innocent the Third and Henry the Second, Calvin and Caesar, the Druids and the French Ladies, Diogenes and du Bartas, Agnes of Moravia and Ingeborg of Denmark, the King of Macedonia and the Queen of Sheba. Two hours on, the weary courtiers were now becoming more sparing with applause and amens lest their fuel keep the fire going all night.

"Such is the religion of these reverend fathers, in comparison with whom all the impiety of the infidel and all the barbarity of the cannibal may pass for pure humanity. How long shall we suffer this viperous brood to spit in our faces? Still they predict that God will bless their enterprise against me at some future date. They shall not think they can frighten me! They shall taste agony first! For when that date is upon us—as it surely will be one dark day or one dark night—be certain the Almighty will again give me warning. Because these Jesuits are the agents of Antichrist. Only God may make a king. And only God may unmake him."

The cheers of the company when James finally made his exit were as much from the bladder as from the heart. Rochester in tow, he moved upstairs to the quiet of the long gallery where, glass in hand and doublet loosened, he could descend from his oratorical peak. The pair lounged on either side of the fireplace, whose overmantel was a carving of David at the harp, and upon which was inscribed:

Composing for the body, soul and ear
That which sadness and foul spirits fear.

James's body, soul and ear, however, were harping on a string that would not soothe. Henry's defiant note about the match with Christina had him on edge. Good God! Which of them was the father, which the son? Which the master, which the pupil? Which the King, which the Prince?

* * *

THREE DAYS to go. As the Prince's arrival neared, Rochester grew more uneasy. He had not managed to be alone with Frances thus far along the way. One guardian or another was ever at her elbow, and there had been little but good-morrows to sustain his love. With the sixteenth good-morrow, his frustration had burst. He had sent a couple of his men to her door laden with roses and, since all this shepherding of Frances could be because her mother still entertained hopes of Henry, he had enclosed a note implying that his Highness's latest answer to the French proposal amounted to consent. Rochester's post-script promised that her first, last and only lover would visit her this night.

"A word with you." The Countess of Suffolk took him by the elbow as the company drifted in and out of the ball.

"Madam, the King awaits me."

"So does the Devil." She drew him into an alcove, keeping her hold. Though half a head shorter than Frances, even on double soles, she was very much her daughter's mother, and still aflame at five and forty. "I would like to stuff your stupid roses down your stupid throat." She spoke through clenched teeth. "Do you not know that there are a hundred eyes at every corner, a dozen bishops at every halt? What do you seek—to pash the nullity in pieces?"

"I did not think a few roses..."

"I did not think a few roses..." she mocked. "Your brains must be in your breeches. Do you want to ruin Frances?"

"The King favours my suit."

"The King favours my suit—pish! The King once favoured Essex! Now tell me that my husband favours your suit—and I shall tell you that my husband, too, once favoured Essex. They are the pair who picked the wrong bridegroom for my poor little daughter last time. And I let them do it. So next time I shall ensure that she has the right bridegroom—if you are not fool enough to prevent there being a next time."

"I shall hardly do that, since I hope to be that man."

"If it turns out to be you, Robbie, I will be happy for you both." She stroked his arm where her grip had held him. "First, though, let us see if it turns out to be his Highness."

"But I love her. And I am certain she loves me." Her mother could not know what they had been to each other.

"She is *not* certain—accept that from me. And if you truly care for her, you will not think her good enough for your wife, yet not good enough for your Queen. Meanwhile, leave her be, there's a good lad." She wagged a finger. "Or else"—now she wagged a pair like scissors—"I'll cut off your tail."

Sir Thomas Overbury, observing the scene on his way over to speak to Rochester, decided not to bother. By the look on the poor man's face, mother bawd must be advising him that the mutton was indeed dressed fit to make the mouth water but, alas, it was another's turn at the trencher this night. Anyway, Overbury had more to be concerned about. His dear Elizabeth was taken ill; some quack had dosed her with dangerous potions, and her life was despaired of. He would leave a message apologising that he had to break away from the Progress and go to her. Pray God he reached London in time.

[15]

Saturday the Eighth of August

THE PRINCE was full of Frances as he set off on the remaining miles to Belvoir Castle where, come sunset, they might be together again. It troubled him that, this last of his three weeks bereft of her, the imprint that had obsessed him awake and asleep had begun to blur. His eyes could not clearly summon up the sight of her. Nor his ears the sound. Nor his fingers the feel. Nor his nose the scent. Nor his tongue the savour. Yet still the yearning gripped him like Greenwich armour.

He had left it until late to quit Richmond yesterday, and had needed to spur his party to Hinchingbrooke Priory in Huntingdonshire, where they had sampled overnight the renowned hospitality of Sir Oliver Cromwell, Master of the Prince's Game. They had marveled, too, at his legendary matchmaking ability. He had secured his family fortunes by marrying himself to the widow of the banker Palavicino, his two daughters to her sons and his son to her daughter. It had been quite a merry evening, with much talk of employing his talents in making a match for the Prince. Sir Oliver had wryly supposed that whichever of the royal families of Europe was fortunate enough to win his Highness would likely call upon the Palavicino coffers to help out with the dowry anyway. He felt bound to add that they might be unlucky, since the family were still whistling for thirty-three thousand pounds lent to the late Queen Elizabeth, of most happy memory except where creditors were concerned.

In jest, Henry had rounded on his host for not thinking to save at least one daughter for him. Lady Cromwell had agreed that Catherine, Jane and Baptina would each make a perfect princess. No doubt, said Jane, but could the Prince really marry a subject? Could and would, Henry had replied, if that was where his heart led him. The gentlemen had been amused to see their sweet ladies so taken by a mere show of gallantry. The ladies had wondered, silently then, though noisily once he had left, which subject the Prince must have in mind. When the name of Lady Frances Howard happened to come up, all four made a face.

* * *

THE NEW EARL OF RUTLAND'S SWANS looked on from the Trent as a royal coach carrying the ambassador of Venice came to lofty Belvoir. The match for Henry was the reason the King had summoned Antonio Foscarini to join him on the Progress. Although the Serene Republic had no daughters to offer, its ears were the busiest in Europe. And his Excellency of Venice, having pumped their Excellencies of France, Savoy, Spain and Tuscany, knew more of the game than the five million good people of Britain or, indeed, their dread sovereign. Little Foscarini's haste to respond to the royal command had cost the lives of three carriage horses yesterday, on his first frantic leg of the hundred miles from London. He could hardly wait to advise the Doge and Senate of the honour the King had done their inky-fingered servant by sending his own coach for the journey to be completed, and by detailing his own retainers to see that his Excellency wanted for nothing. James had not long since paid the compliment of granting him equal rank with the ambassadors of kings: never had an envoy obtained higher esteem for Venice. By the time he was bowed into the presence, Foscarini was glowing fit to melt.

Music of voice and viol from the gardens accompanied the opening civilities about the weather ("The drought is so bad in Scotland that mountaintops are afire," said James) and about who might succeed the late Doge Donato ("Whoever is elected will be a true friend to Britain," said Foscarini). Then the King announced his wish to have private discussions with his Excellency, tipping a wink to Rochester as the chamber was cleared. James's only regret was that there would be no gallery to admire the master of kingcraft at work: obtaining the intelligence of five ambassadors for the payment of attention to one.

"Excellency, it will please me if you will permit me to address you as Antonio when we are alone."

"Majesty, it is not usual..."

"Well, you are not usual. Else I should not judge that I can be utterly frank with you—and I am right in that, am I not?"

"Indeed. Indeed."

"The cross I have to bear—ah, me!—is that so few suitable gentlemen will give up the pleasures and profits of this island to venture abroad in my service. Therefore my ambassadors are not all of the quality with which you have made your fortunate masters familiar."

"I do my best for the Republic."

"And I am going to plead with you—Antonio—to do your best for me. I do sorely need your advice."

"Majesty?" Foscarini shifted, aware of the tariff for treason to Venice: strangulation in the night, the corpse to hang by one leg on the high gallows between the columns of the Piazza San Marco.

"I place myself confidently in your hands," said James, reading him, "and you may safely do the like with me. We both know there is not the slightest question of touching upon any matters secret to the Republic. In faith, did I but think you such a man as to betray your masters, then I should know you such a man as to betray me."

"Pray rest content, Majesty. I do not have it in me to speak aught my masters should not hear."

"And I do not have it in me to give them the chance to invite me to share the cost of your embassy!"

"Which is little enough, Majesty. Venice blesses me with no purse to bribe matchmakers."

"Then Venice is itself blessed—for those who do are cozened. The only matchmaker in this is me." James chuckled and put off his hat to mop his forehead. "And I ask you here this afternoon because not only am I Henry's king, I am his father. I cannot sleep these nights for fear that if I am misinformed—or if I misunderstand through ignorance—then will I do the succession much harm. I need to be advised what is genuine, what is counterfeit. It will be no secret from you how ill-counseled I was over the Spanish offer. I'll wager *you* could have told me the trick they were playing."

"Assuredly I could."

"I can but scourge myself that the favour I ask today I did not ask then. Though now you have shown me such regard, you make it easier for me to beseech the benefit of your experience. Oh, nothing on paper, of course... just a private word over a friendly glass."

He hauled himself to his feet, unsuccessfully waving Foscarini down in the process, and fetched jug and glasses. "If my mere muscatel is not to your taste, I shall call for whatever pleases you."

"No wine is mere in a Venetian glass."

"Spoken like a true ambassador! I drink your health."

"And I yours, Majesty. If my poor opinions are of any worth, you may surely have them."

Have them, James did. Poor, they were not. For as well as exchanges with his fellow ambassadors, Foscarini could draw upon the treasury of intelligence from Venetian agents at every court in Europe: not least Rome, from where England's information was never better than third rate. James let Foscarini flow. By way of encouragement, he would lift an eyebrow at a revelation of chicanery as though he had not good reason to know it loose conjecture. The King's brain winnowed the cards as Foscarini dealt, and when it was done his pulses were throbbing like those of a player favoured with a sight of his opponents' hands.

First Tuscany...where Grand Duke Cosimo de' Medici is playing as though his deuces and treys are court cards. He lets it be known that he has six million of gold—and to achieve the Prince of Wales for his sister would think half of it well employed. But he does not have half of it, maybe not even one-third of it. And his father left no more than three hundred thousand for Princess Caterina's dowry. Why, then, does Cosimo talk of raising it to a million? Because he knows he will never be called upon to pay it. The truth is that he is a captive of Spain, and his bid is nothing but a ruse on their behalf to upset the French proposal. Nevertheless, he has the impudence to plead with the Queen Regent of France, as his aunt, to support him at the Vatican "for the honour of the house of Medici." She scorns this, doubting that England would prefer a daughter of Tuscany when a daughter of France is available. Anyway, there is no chance of Pope Paul granting dispensation. He breaks into burning words whenever the question is raised, and declares that he will not even consider it until he has the King of England's oath to allow any offspring of the marriage to be brought up in the Catholic faith. And—oh, yes—it is not without interest that Caterina's brother expects soon to become a cardinal. A fine brother-in-law for the future head of the Church of England!

Then Savoy...where Duke Charles Emmanuel is hard-pressed to improve his dowry offer beyond five hundred thousand, though he is ready to have recourse to his jewels. He is already overstepping his means by spending a hundred thousand on presents around the English court, but he has a long way to go to match Tuscany's bribes. He will send Cavalier Battista Gabaleone to London to negotiate the match for Princess Maria—the Lion of England should be aware that Gabaleone can be translated as "trick the lion." Indeed, the Duke's secret plan, should he fail to win Henry for his daughter, is to steal Christina of France for his son. The Duke declares he is a sovereign prince and has no call to apply to Rome or Spain. In this, he deceives himself if nobody else. For Maria is, of course, the King of Spain's niece, and he has promised the Pope to see that the religious conditions are obeyed. So Savoy is most unlikely—though it may be some consolation that Maria is not as lovely as the portrait sent to London might suggest.

Which leaves France... where the Queen Regent is zealous for this match because she needs to balance the double-match with Spain that so alarms not only her Huguenot community but many Catholic nobles, too. She is now ready to pay a quarter million on the nail and as much again when Christina reaches ten, at which age she would come to England to be brought up. If necessary, France will raise the dowry, lower the age—and say not a single word about religion. They are no more in fear of the Pope than is Venice. What does worry them is the fact that Zuñiga lingers here, and that Spain's second daughter could yet be offered on better terms. France is also anxious to foil the Savoy match because it would establish an axis between the bold (Foscarini forbore to say warlike) ideas of the Prince of Wales and of Duke Charles Emmanuel.

"Dear friend Antonio! I am forever in your debt." James, mightily pleased, rose to embrace Foscarini. He felt like dancing the man round the sunlit chamber to the strains coming in from the consort in the gardens. Christina of France it would be. Henry had presumed that they would never send the child here to be converted. Now he was caught on his own hook.

"Majesty, I am honoured if I may have been of some small service." Foscarini began to bow himself toward the doors.

"Take this"—James plucked a monogrammed watch from his pocket—"as a remembrance of my gratitude."

"Majesty, I..."

"And should it please you to do some favour to your friend the French ambassador, you might ensure that he does not believe I have no choice but to suit France's pleasure. The Queen and myself both think it desirable that Henry be betrothed as soon as possible." The King beckoned Foscarini close and whispered as though they were not the only ones present. "There is no time for French games. If you hear that Henry has begun to favor a certain lady of this court, you will hear aright—but, for God's sake, be sure your friend never discovers that it was I who confirmed it for you."

With Foscarini gone, James whistled through his teeth Master Dowland's *Me, me, and none but me* as the consort played Master Byrd's *O Lord, how vain*.

FROM THE MINUTE he arrived to find an invitation from Frances awaiting him, the Prince had become as deaf as Priapus. He put in an appearance at the revels for little longer than to acknowledge his father, ignore Rochester, have a couple of words with Foscarini, take a drink with his host, flatter his hostess and plead fatigue after a hard day's ride. Then Murray was conveying him from one courtyard to another, one backstairs to another, one chamber to another. And now Henry looked through the dark at Frances as she posed all a-glitter in the oblong moonbeam filtering through the lead lights. He had imagined her greeting him in loose hair and nightgown, and indeed she would have been, had not Mrs. Turner insisted that she keep on her full finery. Did she want to play tonight's paramour or tomorrow's princess?

Henry enfolded her, eyes closing to lock in the moment, nostrils widening to take in the balmy warmth of her. This was perfect bliss: in need of neither word nor deed. He was content for it to continue evermore, but Frances soon drew away to face him, and then away again as he moved to kiss her.

"I do not know why your Highness bothers with me."

"Of course you do." The games women played...

"Rather should you save your wooing for the French princess."

"In truth, you know nothing will come of that."

"In truth, Hally?" She unwound his arms from her waist. "Then why have you just given it your consent?"

"Consent! Who feeds you such nonsense?"

"It is all over the court."

"Which alone should be enough to prove it a lie."

"So you wrote no such letter to the King?"

"Fra, listen..."

"...to more lies?" She pushed at his chest but he caught her hand between his and began to soothe it.

"Poor darling...you have had the chance to listen to little else." He did not sense her resentment that he thought she could be gentled like a child. "Yes, there is a letter. But it is consent to nothing. The King wished me to set down my opinion. And now he is seized of all my objections—save, of course, this one." He brought her fingers to his lips.

"That does not ease the pain I feel—the *shame* I feel—when I hear of you being married off." Her anger was mounting because he would not share it. All he had come to share was the four-poster behind them. Yet, as long as this was their fate, where else was there for them but the bedchamber? They could not trip abroad with a hey, and a ho, and a hey nonino, like the humblest lover and his lass. Only alone could they be together: though, when hope was low, not even then. She freed her hand. "Hally, *please*—give the nay to France and be done with it."

"Sweetheart, such is not the way of nations. If the Queen Regent offers a daughter, the King of England does not tell her to go hang herself. We do not need to agree to the match, but we do need to agree to negotations—and that is all we have done."

"So much for your consent to nothing."

"That *is* consent to nothing! Can you not see? We had to go through the same balderdash with Spain, though the match was no more likely in the beginning than it proved in the end."

"Is this also going to take ten years?"

"Of course not."

"And then ten for Savoy? And ten more for Tuscany? By the time you are done, I shall be too old and cold for your pleasure." She measured her words. "Or anyone else's."

"Fra, we can do nothing before you are free."

"Hally, my dear, I am not the only one waiting upon freedom. These weeks apart give me pause to see that you are farther from it than I am. And, unless something happens, your wait has no end in sight."

"Then we shall have to hope that something *does* happen."

"But if hope is not enough? Would it not be merciful to give me leave to . . . to do the best I can while I am still young enough?" Frances watched his face harden. Good, she thought. Why let him believe he could forever choose to love her for an hour or leave her for a month according to his convenience?

"For Heaven's sake! Do we sneak round corners and creep up backstairs only to rehearse this? Does my word not suffice?"

"The nine diamonds you put upon my finger suffice"—she moved the ring back and forth—"but they do not make you free."

"I shall be free soon enough."

"My sweet Prince, you can be free tomorrow! You are brave enough. Powerful enough. Rich enough. If you want me enough, then go to the King. *Inform* him you have chosen me. *Require* his blessing. *Demand* that he bring forward the nullity. He dare not make a fight of it because against your strength he has nothing but your fears."

"Believe me, this is not yet the moment."

"When is?"

"You must let me be the best judge of that."

"Here"—she lifted his hand and tucked the ring into it—"you will be a better judge if you are no longer pledged."

"Frances!"

"But come the day you prevail, and you still want me—if by then I am not yet spoken for—then you know I will say yes with all my heart." She took his face between her hands and kissed him softly.

The silence lengthened. Here was escape. He need only turn and go. A month, a year hence, he might pray for so ready an exit. Today, he could not relinquish even his gaze. Her eyes went to his fist as he opened it and picked out the ring. Taking for granted that he was about to restore it, she extended her hand and began to separate her third finger. This signal of her belief that she could bend him to her will infuriated him. He drew back and flung the ring into the darkness.

"Damn you, Frances! I will do this my way or not at all. And you *will* wait. And you *will not* be spoken for. And you *will* tell me who feeds this poison into your ear." He gripped her shoulder. "Your mother?"

"No. No." Please God, let him not hate us.

"Then Rochester?" Of course. "Rochester!" he bellowed.

"I have hardly seen him this Progress. Nor did I need to—I told you, the whole court knows of the letter."

"It *has* to be Rochester. All my business passes through the paws of the King's spaniel now. But... to break the Privy Councillor's oath of secrecy is high treason. He shall hang for it!"

"Oh, no!" Despair racked her. In a spasm of folly, she was losing them both.

"Why do you display such great concern for his neck?"

"Why do you display such little for mine? Rochester is nothing to me—you know that—but if you would hang him for telling me what he did not, you would as soon hang me for listening. Anyway"—she caught at the next straw—"if any spaniel is to blame, it is more likely Rochester's than the King's."

"Overbury, eh? Tell me the evidence and I shall gladly rid us of the pair of them."

"Evidence?" Deeper still, and deeper. "Oh, my darling Hally... you could not hang a *cat* on evidence from me... so confused am I... all these *weeks* without you... my first and last and only love..." She threw her arms round his neck, moulded herself to him and began to sob on his shoulder, shaking her head at his proffered handkerchief and gulping tearfully. "I am all at sixes and sevens... so *afraid* to let you down...so *afraid* to say the wrong thing...so *afraid* to look at anyone when you are mentioned lest I give myself away...I doubt I even heard aright when that tale about the French match was told...I hid in a corner and *cried* my eyes out...oh, I did not want it to be like this...I want only to love you as I have *dreamed* every moment we have been apart...all this waiting and waiting and waiting...and then I am so *cruel* to you..."

Now she was moving lips and hips against his, inducing the symptoms of that fever better stuffed than starved. Now she was backing along the moonbeam toward the four-poster until her thighs met it and she perched on the edge. Now she was slipping off a shoe and patting the place beside her. Now she was lying back, feet a-dangle, as he knelt by her on the covers and bent to renew their embrace. Now her hands were priming him, having undone his seven vital buttons while he was coaxing the first of the jeweled clasps down her front.

"Tear them," she prompted through closed teeth, and ripped open the top fastening by way of example before resuming her urging elsewhere. The combination stirred him scalp to sole. Presently, ravaged gown and petticoats fallen away, she arched and spread to conduct him into her, and clipped hot heels across his back.

"Oh, Fra..." He buried his gasping mouth in the moist hair at her neck.

CANDLES burned late in the chamber across the courtyard as Ambassador Foscarini worked on his dispatch to the Doge and Senate. His main concern was not the destiny of Europe, but his expenses in joining the Progress when his grant for all extras was a miserable forty crowns per month. Since it took a five-sixths majority in the Senate to get back a lira more, the tactics of reimbursement required that his masters were duly informed what honour was done their servant, and what obligations that placed upon him to maintain the dignity of Venice before a sovereign of such power, a court of such magnificence, and a nation *tutto richissimo*.

"I have not failed," wrote Foscarini in clerkly script, "to scatter largesse wherever I went, with a liberal hand as becomes a representative of your Excellencies; so this infinitely supersedes my ordinary allowance. As the nobility and gentry flock in from the neighbouring country, the court has been much fuller than in London, and the cost far in excess. The splendour surpasses all belief. The sumptuous food and the abundance of comfits which they consume is amazing. Nor could the greatest monarch in the world inside his own royal palace shine with greater pomp. This castle at Belvoir is capable of housing the more distinguished part of the courts of both King and Prince, now come together and numbering upwards of one thousand mouths. The dining tables for persons of quality hold about two hundred, before whom the King was pleased to drink, with hat in hand, to the health of him who serves your Excellencies..."

MURRAY clasped and unclasped his hands yet again in the acute silence of Mrs. Turner's chamber, guarding the doors beyond which the lovers lay. This night's tryst was the most reckless they had yet managed. How many more stratagems to be devised, routes to be scouted, ruses to be made, escapes to be secured in the twenty-one days to the end of the Progress? His only consolation was that, since nature was going to run its course with or without his assistance, he might at least speed it on its way. Given his due season of rutting, the Prince, like the lustful stag, would piss his tallow and be surfeit of hinds for the year.

Anne Turner came awake in her chair from a quite vivid dream—recapturing that last short, if sweet, passage with that sweet, if short, apothecary de Lobel—to find Murray again at the window, scanning the grounds. He had mind only for duty: a man to be admired. She found herself comparing him with Mainwaring. Perhaps she ought to be setting her cap at this one instead, as close to the next King as she to the next Queen, and surely bound for the peerage. Lady Mainwaring had a ring to it, but Viscountess Murray...now that was a peal of bells. Mainwaring, however, would never have been alone with her in a bedchamber for a minute, let alone an hour, without laying her on her back or, as likely, her front.

"David," she said hopefully, "I think our lovebirds will be some time yet."

"HALLY, ask me what I wish."

"You are about to tell me, anyway."

"I wish you would put that ring back on my finger."

"First we have to find it."

"I doubt you will find it *there.*"

[16]

Tuesday the Eleventh of August

ELIZABETH, *Elizabeth, Elizabeth*... whispering the beloved name, Overbury watched her coffin being lowered into her father's tomb in the Lady Chapel of St. Paul's. She was twenty-seven. She had been a widow one month. He folded a paper on which he had penned the only poem of his she had not read, and let it flutter after her:

Why do I weep and moan
For my departed dear?
I should own
My greatest grief
Is for mine own mortality.

The sad sweetness of the choir accompanied his thoughts as he looked across to the family... mainly Sidneys... uncle de Lisle... aunt Pembroke... their unseeing faces like that row of gargoyles on the wall of his boyhood church at Bourton-on-the-Hill. There was the Earl of Essex: how perverse of fate to take his virtuous half-sister yet leave his vicious half-wife. Overbury felt a bond with him since they must both be mourning Frances's life no less than Elizabeth's death. Overbury, because all that remained to him, now that he had lost the only woman he had ever truly loved, was threatened by the only woman he had ever truly hated. Essex, because all that remained to him was to be freed of this creature, at the price of being proclaimed less than a man.

"A sad morning, my lord." Overbury moved to his side as the mourners spread out from the west door into the blazing heat of this last of the Dog Days.

"I am sorry, Sir Thomas—for I know she loved you."

"I thank you—for I know you can never have thought me your friend."

"You are too close to Rochester for my good."

"Or, I begin to believe, for mine."

"Why does he hate me?"

"Because he loves her."

"And she him?"

"If you think she is capable of love."

"I think she is capable of anything."

"My lord"—he took Essex by the arm—"may I speak frankly to you?"

"If you speak not for Rochester."

"I speak against him. He wants Frances to secure her nullity however much it shames you."

"I will bear it to be rid of her."

"But you can be rid of her without shame—and without letting Rochester take her from you to be his bride."

"No, there is nothing I can do."

"Listen, my lord. You know well enough that the Church allows remarriage of a party to nullity. And you know that Canon law forbids it of a party to divorce on the grounds of infidelity. But what you do not know is that Frances and Rochester can provide you with such grounds."

"You mean..."

"I mean thus can you obtain your freedom on evidence that will advertise not your insufficiency but her adultery."

"Adultery...for how long has this gone on?"

"Four or five years."

"Four or five." Essex squeezed eyes and lips tight. The pair of them had planned this even before he came home to claim her. How they must have laughed. But now, in a second, past torment was explained, future torment cancelled. He would not wake tonight, fearful that the bishops might require him to be searched by a jury of seven women, according to precedent in the archives of Canterbury, Ely and York, from which last a kind friend had thought to supply an extract...*The witness exposed her naked breasts and, her hands warmed at the fire, held and rubbed the penis and testicles of the said John. She embraced and frequently kissed the said John, and stirred him up as she could to show his virility and potency, admonishing him that for shame he should then and there prove himself a man. The whole time, the said penis was scarce three inches long and remained without any increase. All done, the seven women cursed the said John and departed...*

"My lord, if you will take this course, then gladly shall I seek to send word where your witnesses may discover your wife and Rochester in flagrant delict."

"Then so be it. She has given me hell. She shall have hell." He looked hard at Overbury. "But—why will you do this to Rochester?"

"Not *to* Rochester, my lord. *For* Rochester."

THE YOUNG ENGLISHMAN waving farewell to Boulogne from the stern rail of the little merchantman was not pleased with a Channel smooth enough to row a skiff across. It needed a decent wind on their quarter to drive them home to Dover in five or six hours, by which time the innkeeper might still not have realised that the Spanish courier was not dead drunk, but dead.

He had not wanted to kill him, a gentleman much like himself, seeking to make his way up from the junior ranks of embassy service. It would have been unnecessary had not the fellow woken from apparently exhausted slumber and begun yelling "Thief!" in as many languages as appeared in his diplomatic passport, signed by none less than the Duque de Lerma himself. In fact, the young Englishman surprised at his pouch was not taking, but rather restoring, the cipher dispatch it contained—having merely borrowed, unsealed, copied and resealed it. At first light, he had settled his bill, not delaying to argue with the innkeeper's swindling wife, and taken passage on the earliest ship in harbour. He hoped Viscount Rochester would make allowance for his inexperience. He had been careful to leave the impression that the motive here was common robbery, stripping the poor courier of money, rings and boots, but leaving the pouch and its contents discarded as valueless. Was it worth a life? Sir Thomas Overbury would tell them soon enough. He would have these ciphers unraveled quicker than shoe-ties.

ESSEX had crossed the Bridge to the Boar's Head, more aptly known to customers for ale and tail as the Whore's Bed. He fortified himself with a drink, and when the dark girl inquired as to his pleasure, he indicated the fair one who had just come down the stairs. In the twinkling of a thigh, she was on the way up again. At the bedchamber door, Essex paid her two gold crowns, for which she bobbed thanks and gave him her accommodating hand on the bargain. Soon it had him free, and soon it had him proud. Her harlot patter was poetry... *Christ, you're a big lad... Ooh, aren't I a lucky little girl...?* His hand her rudder, he steered her to the bed. She sheathed him easily, still lubricated from her previous transaction. It struck Essex that the said John would have done himself more justice with a jury of this one woman than of those seven, and he was grinning at the thought as she jounced him to completion. He fell asleep on her bosom. She looked up at the familiar ceiling and wondered which fine lady he wished she were.

[17]

Sunday the Sixteenth of August

TWO CANDLES flickered on the table at which Overbury was completing his task, and the draught from the opened door wafted the fragrance of sandalwood that told him Rochester had come in. It had taken from dawn yesterday until sunset tonight to break Lerma's dispatch to Zuñiga. Its brevity made the task not easier but harder, because a new cipher was in use. Had it not been prepared by a secretary clearly in rather a hurry for a Spaniard, and therefore failing to use the available options, it might have proved impossible. But while the rest of the court busied itself with the stags of Sherwood Forest (and Rochester, he supposed, with his woman), Overbury had bent to his duty in the blessed quiet of Sir John Byron's Newstead Abbey. And now the decipherment was achieved. The King would have it before Zuñiga received the customery copy by way of Spanish Flanders.

"What does it add up to, Tom?" Rochester put an appreciative arm across his friend's shoulders and looked at his work.

"It is not addition, Robbie. It is subtraction."

"Subtraction?"

"Seventy-one is to be gotten rid of."

"And who is Seventy-one?"

"The Prince of Wales."

"My God…"

"I shall have a fair copy in half an hour. The King had better see it straightaway."

"No, Tom."

"Are you mad?" To Overbury, the workings of Rochester's mind were as obvious as an open clock. *If Henry ever becomes King, I am done for. So why hinder any who might remove him for me? In which case, I must find some way to stifle this warning.*

"It fell into our hands too easily, Tom. Likely it is a forgery."

"To what end, pray?"

"Well—if the King's response is to light the beacons, then how would it go with me if I had let him be taken in by a trick?"

"A trick by whom?"

"By any who envies me or fears me... the Archbishop... the Queen... the Prince himself..."

"Or Archy, the Court Fool?"

"Before you scoff, remember that you yourself admitted this was in none of the ciphers we know Spain to employ."

"My dear Robbie"—Overbury sighed—"if the Archbishop or the Queen or the Prince or the Fool wants you to be gulled by a false dispatch, why put it in a cipher you are unlikely to break?"

"Perhaps they know how *clever* you are." Rochester took up Overbury's decipher and held it over a candle until it caught. He let go only when the flame lapped at his fingers. "Never, never forget, Tom, that it is on my legs you stand or fall."

"You never let me forget, do you? Though it is no less true that, left to their own devices, they would walk you no further than the Tower."

"They might serve me all the better without your weight to carry."

"You think so? How would you manage without my brains to tell you that, rather than risk the block for treason, the wisdom of this wickedness is to take to the King our man's copy of the cipher, and tell him the truth?"

"The truth?"

"Aye, tell him how it came into your hands. And tell him, without a word of a lie, that it is a new cipher not even your mighty intellect can break. Here, take it. Thank God that you burned the wrong piece of paper. And thank God that I cannot afford for the years I have invested in you to go to naught."

"Good man, Tom!" Rochester clasped his friend's hands warmly, as though that gesture should suffice to cancel their high words, threw in a smile for good measure and bore the document away. "Do not fret"—he turned at the door—"I shall see you right."

Overbury returned the smile, knowing that he was already seeing Rochester right. Why else had he advised Essex to begin his watch on Frances this night?

COMING now to the house where Frances was lodged in the Abbey grounds, Essex was gleeful at the prospect of catching her. Better that his valet, waiting here behind the trees to become a witness, see him as a poor husband given two horns than an even poorer husband unable to offer one. A couple more couplings at the Boar's Head (where he had proved himself with the dark girl, too) had confirmed his resolve: for as long as Frances lived, she would pay for gelding him these three years while Rochester swived the arse off her. The Howards would pay, too, and in hard coin. For while a nullity would have required the return of Frances's dowry of six thousand pounds, a divorce for infidelity would not.

"My lord, the pair of them went in not a half-hour ago."

"Damnation! Did you see who they were?"

"Alas, not from here—there is hardly a light in the house—but one seemed very much the lord, my lord, know what I mean?"

"Rochester." Of course.

"And the other—well, he was a bit older and half a step behind, my lord, know what I mean?"

"Overbury." Of course. "Come on, then. You know what to do."

Pistol in hand, Essex flattened himself at the side of the door. His man pulled the bell and stepped back holding out a letter so that from the window he might be taken for a messenger. He began to whistle as he waited, keeping the tune going disarmingly when the door opened a crack and Mrs. Turner's face glowed in the lantern light. As she put out a hand for the letter, he threw his weight at the door, drawing his sword as his master charged past him into the hall.

"Hold, sir!" Essex leveled his pistol at the seated figure shadowed by the branched candles at his back. "Hold—and no blood need spill."

"Treason!" Murray roared to warn the Prince upstairs and in that instant was upon the intruders: dagger in left hand, rapier in right and putting the valet between himself and Essex. In one sweep, he hacked the sword from the valet's hand and followed through to strike Essex's fist. The pistol discharged into the valet's back. Mrs. Turner screamed from the doorway.

Crumpling more in anguish than in pain, Essex looked the length of the blade at his throat to see not Rochester's man, but Henry's. And at the foot of the stairs, Henry himself. The good Prince whose "eternal companion" it had been his once-proclaimed destiny to be. The good Prince for whom he had prayed daily on his knees. The good Prince whose hands he had sworn to kiss to the last breath of life. The good Prince to whom that life was now forfeit, for never imagining that the highest in the land would be the likeliest to seek out the loveliest.

"Christ Jesus receive my soul. Christ Jesus forgive me as I forgive..."

"Let him be, David."

"Highness?"

"Let him be. He is my friend."

Prepared to be overcome by death, Essex was overcome by life. He collapsed in a sobbing heap.

"Leave us, David." The Prince moved to help the pathetic Essex to his feet.

"I'll have his sword off him first, Highness."

"No-no. He would never do me harm."

"Never." The Earl raised a sleeve to mop his eyes.

Murray's instinct asserted that the last man Essex had expected to discover here was the Prince. So who was the first? He motioned Mrs. Turner to go up to Frances as he carried the stricken valet away, leaving Henry to play out his gamble that mercy could silence the scandal that slaughter of his mistress's husband could only blazon forth.

"Don't worry. David will attend to your man." The Prince put a brotherly arm about the craven Earl and walked him clear of the scene. "Robert, I must confess that had our circumstances been reversed I would surely have been here on much the same errand."

"You would, sir?"

"And I confess, too, that I would most likely have misled myself in much the same way as to what might be found. Look, my friend, I'm not going to insult your intelligence. Knowing that you and Frances had put in your depositions, I was impetuous enough to begin to pay court to her. But no more. We have never been alone. Her honour and yours—and, for God's sake, mine—are unsullied. Believe me."

"Oh, I do, sir. I do."

"And believe this, too, Robert: If your wish is to keep her, I shall bow out with no ill feelings at all. You and I shall still be friends."

"Your Highness is truly noble"—Essex swallowed more tears—"but she has never been mine and never will be."

"Fate has played us a cruel trick, my lord. Fate—and my father. He is hell's own matchmaker, yet he believes he is heaven's. You and I, we are his victims alike..."

"That we are."

"...which is why we understand alike. Forgive alike. And, soon I pray, forget alike. Once you are free of all this you will marry soon enough, I'll warrant."

"And you, sir? And she, sir? Will you...will you marry soon enough?"

"My lord"—the Prince placed hand upon heart—"You need neither bullet nor blade to finish me now. You share the closest secret of my life. Thank God I can trust you."

"Always, Highness. I want only to serve you."

"And so you shall. Here's my hand."

Henry was pleased with himself. Forgive the man the wrong you do him, and he kisses your fingers. Could even his father have turned it better?

Essex was in turmoil. With steel at his Adam's apple, he had needed to accept whatever story he was told or go the way of his executed father. The Prince had striven more eagerly than honesty required: proclaiming honour unsullied when he had just been upstairs with the wife of another, and clearly not for the first time, because he would have been glad to gloss his lie with that truth. Nevertheless, Essex was sure Overbury had not lied to bring him here. The man simply could not have known that the Prince was sharing Rochester's whore. And since—God help England—the Prince intended to marry her, it was clear that he could not know, either.

MRS. TURNER came down from Frances to find Essex's man laid on the kitchen table, unconscious of the comfort of Murray's cloak, his face a waxen mask.

"Will he live, David?"

"Perhaps. Perhaps not."

"But say he does?"

"Then he does."

"And say he speaks?"

"Of what? He saw only you and me."

"Which spells your prince and my lady."

Mrs. Turner took Murray's dagger from its sheath and offered the hilt to him. He left her holding it as he drew the cloak aside and bent an ear to the man's heart. Presently he stood up and, with finger and thumb, closed his victim's eyes, his mind already organising consignment of the body to the river. Now he accepted his dagger and replaced it.

"The poor man," said Mrs. Turner.

Murray looked at her and shook his head at the blackness of their souls.

[18]

Monday the Twenty-fourth of August

JOAN TRASH'S GINGERBREAD and Madam Ursula's roast pig made the final furlongs the most aromatic of the Spanish courier's ride to Ambassador Zuñiga; and the most hazardous, thanks to the press spilling over from Smithfield's Bartholomew Fair to hold him from the haven of the embassy in the Barbican. In the process, he had managed to lose his purse. It had been there when he lifted to scratch a sudden itch at his ear. By the time his hand came down, the money had gone, along with one cutpurse and one accomplice with a feather on a stick. He had, therefore, been unable to respond to the get-penny cries advertising such sights as the bull with two pizzles, the morris-dancing dogs, the tabor-thumping hare—and the monkey that would jump its chain when its keeper shouted for King James and leap back again for Prince Henry, but display its bum for Philip of Spain and the Pope.

All day, every day for three weeks, Zuñiga had been awaiting this dispatch, certain that the direct courier must have become yet another traveler fallen to marauders. One hour after its arrival, he had the dispatch in plain text. One minute after that, he had reduced it to ash. England was to be lightened of its warlike Prince. Fate was to be the cutpurse. Zuñiga the accomplice with a feather on a stick.

As Frances and her mother joined the Lord Chamberlain at Grafton Lodge, he had no doubt they were celebrating something other than his fifty-fifth birthday. He knew well enough to leave them their silly secrets, though few could merit such whispering and giggling with Mrs. Turner all week as the Progress ambled from Nottinghamshire to Northamptonshire.

The spark was not so much the drama of Essex (even less the tragedy of his poor valet) as the affirmation Frances had witnessed from the stairs that Henry was determined to marry her. Essex had taken the secret into retreat at Chartley, and Henry had thought it prudent to stay clear for a while. On the strength of the Prince's hand on heart, mother and daughter had decided that the wedding would be at St. Paul's, rather than the Chapel Royal, and that the first son would be named Thomas for her father, rather than James for his.

The Lord Chamberlain's head was occupied by thoughts of who might become the new Master of the Bears: he had better get in ere long with his recommendation for Tom Badger, the finest bulldog man in England. As he lumbered off, the three women waved in comic unison, and laughed at themselves for it. Better to leave him in blissful ignorance that it was the Prince who would be his son-in-law. Likewise, leave the King. Likewise, leave Rochester.

ZUÑIGA thought he might learn something to his advantage in a fortnight, once the Progress had run its course. The Prince would be back at Richmond, the King at Whitehall—and Roldán at liberty to meet her old Spanish friend. Not much passed without the Countess of Suffolk coming to know of it. Perhaps she could throw light on this mysterious information he had from Father Pérez, who had it from the Savoyard secretary, who had it from the Tuscan agent, who had it from the French ambassador, who had it from his Excellency of Venice. Foscarini would not say from whom he had gained his impression that the Prince "inclined towards a lady of the court," but it was clear he brought the tale back from his journey to Belvoir. Whoever she was, she might need to hurry if she were to be a bride in time to be a widow.

[19]

Saturday the Twenty-ninth of August

TO BE HUNTED by the King was to be dubbed Hart Royal, which fatal accolade had fallen today upon the monarch of the great herd of red deer above the Prince's palace at Woodstock. By sunlight in these forests and by moonlight in these pastures, he had ripened for this since the third year of James's reign. He had grown from spitter to knobber, from brocket to staggard, from stag to hart of sixteen antlers—and now he was done to death. From the trees came the huntsman's horn sounding the mort: one short note and one long, like a last sigh summoning the King to lead the gallop to the last gory rites.

The previous time the Prince had agreed to go hunting with his father had ended badly, and he doubted it would go any better today. The King had mocked his lack of enthusiasm for the chase. Henry, preferring the courage of the stag to the lust of the howling butchers who pursued it, had shown resentment at being reproved—particularly in front of Rochester, as though it were not enough to bear that the favourite was next day to be installed a Knight of the Garter, side by side with Prince Charles. When James lifted his whip in anger, Henry had spurred away from the hunt, followed by the larger part of the company. Tearfully, James had attributed it to his son being no sportsman. But Henry knew it was the carnage, rather than the chase, which thrilled the King, never mind those protestations that what ravished his senses was the music of horns blowing, huntsmen hallooing, hooves beating and hounds in full cry. When the appetite for blood consumed him, all cares were gone, all aches forgotten. Anyone brash enough to intrude business into the field was branded a pantaloon. Could he not see his King was hunting? And, when the poor fellow had waited until the end of the day, could he not see his King was weary after six hours in the saddle? No wonder petitioners would pray:

> Then let him hear, good God, the sounds
> And cries of men as well as hounds.

Today's Hart Royal had doubled and wheeled up wind and down river, across hedge and along ditch, through grove and into covert. He had come to a halt in a thicket when he could run no more; sides heaving, eyes bulging, tongue hanging dry as he turned to face the full pack of baying hounds. He had lowered his antlers in futile threat, then lifted them in final pride. Crying "Ware haunch!" the keepers had hauled back Beauty and Bouncer, Dido and Dancer, Truelove and Tickler, Jollyboy and Juno, and the dozen more couple straining to break in. And, creeping stealthily from behind a bush, the huntsman had slit the deer's throat.

Now, with the King hastening from the saddle, blue Garter of chivalry blazing above his left boot, his huntsman lay the animal upon its back. Another held clear its forelegs, and another the pizzle, as the King took the knife placed ready and drew it eagerly from the brisket down the midline. Rolling back green satin sleeves, he opened the belly and plunged in up to his elbows to wrench out rewards for the hounds, warm blood spattering as entrails flew: the Tyburn executioner did his duty with no greater glee. Eyes shining, the King circled to daub the proffered faces of first Rochester and then other of his courtiers. They would not wash off these stains, but wear them proudly at the masque tonight as marks of the royal esteem.

The sudden impulse to besmirch his son, too, was sped by the confidence that it would be unwelcome, and he reached out, cackling mischievously. Henry held him off, gripping the skinny wrists until the bloody fingers gave up their flailing. With a shrug, James turned to the following ceremony, lifting his sword to cut off the head, to the yelping of hounds eager for the next course. Henry flung down his fouled gloves and led his men off, without waiting for the huntsman to blow the treble mort, signaling every horn in the company to sound the recheat and go whoo-whooping home.

The King threw his hat the way of Henry's gloves, and clutched at his hair, too angry to speak as he set off with Rochester to lead the leisurely return through the valley to Woodstock.

"My God, Robbie!" he said eventually. "That impatient young man cannot forbear me half an hour—he would have me off the throne as soon as look at me. My God! What prince moved by any reverence towards his parents, or touched with any fear of the Almighty, would cast out of the kingdom the father by whose loins he is himself heir to that kingdom? And what fate has he in store for me, I wonder? I suppose he might allow me my life—but so far from retaining any dignity, I should fall into greater contempt and misery than had I been born a peasant. My God! What fowl is more beautiful than the peacock? Yet bereft of his plumes he is more ridiculous than a jackdaw. The rude artificer, the packhorse porter, the base tinker, the homely cobbler, the infamous tax gatherer—all are happier in their liberty than a king held captive. My God, Robbie!"

"Majesty." Rochester knew that he was not required to respond. He knew, too, what favour he had done his master by destroying the intercepted dispatch that would put Henry on his guard against Spain's vengeance.

"Time was," said the King, "when leaving the field like that would earn a man ten on the bum with a hound-leash. Ha! He will never be the sportsman you are, my laddie. You do not mind a little blood. Nor do you laugh when you lose at cards. Nor play tennis like an artisan. Nor"—the King began to see a weapon against Henry—"think the sport that has no lookers-on is only for begetting, eh?"

"Perish the thought."

"So." The King waited a moment or two. "How goes your wooing?"

"Wooing! I cannot get near her for Mother Suffolk and Mistress Turner. They are so fearful about the nullity. Well, I suppose it's understandable."

"Aye, and it's understandable that you itch to go stargazing again, eh?" He winked, nodded and nudged without success. "*Star*gazing—you know."

"Stargazing? Oh, *star*gazing!" Rochester began to wish he had never let himself be pressed to betray the secret of those twin birthmarks, however much the King had demanded proof that Frances was won.

Baby Charles had long since tottered off to bed. And now, at last, the Queen and Bessy were gone, too. The King sat alone with Henry, his mind honing the blade he had drawn from Rochester's sheath. The blade that had been waiting all these weeks while Henry grew so bold.

"Son, I must thank you for leaving our little differences in the field. Your poor mother is unhappy enough that this is the very last Progress we shall all be together. She will much miss our sweet Bessy."

"She thinks you could have done better than the match with Frederick."

"And I suppose you agree?"

"Then you suppose wrong. I believe it a wise match."

"Henry, the older you grow"—stiff from two hours in this chair, the King pulled himself up and began to pace the long, dimly lit chamber—"the wiser you will discover your old dad has become."

"The proof, father, will be in the match that is made for me." The Prince's eyes followed the King into the shadows, losing him altogether until he emerged unexpectedly at the point he had entered.

"I trust my efforts for Bessy will not be the only ones to meet with your approval."

"You are not unacquainted with my views."

"Neither am I unacquainted with my own." The King came to a halt behind his still-seated son and drummed fingers for a moment on the high back of his chair. "But for once I am not speaking of your marriage. I am speaking of Robbie Rochester's—for him I have made the perfect match."

"You have risen that man so high, I am surprised there is one woman on earth fit to kiss the hem of his garment."

"There is Frances..."

Her name hung in the air like the sound of the mort, one short note and one long. The huntsman, relishing the moment, came round to confront the dead-run quarry.

"No—not Frances." The Prince hardly heard himself. "She would not give him the time of day."

"I tell you otherwise. And if you do not wish to believe your father, then ask hers. And if you do not wish to believe him, then ask the lady herself."

Surely she could not have been deceiving him all along: he would have seen through it. Yet, as surely, she had been lying to everyone else all along: and they had not seen through it. "All this is... just Rochester talking."

"And Frances not talking? Of course, we all know she once caught your eye. Perhaps it was more than once. Perhaps it was more than your eye. She doubtless thinks you too smitten to be told such news. Sweet lass."

"She has told me everything there is to tell. He called upon her some weeks ago to offer his courtship, pretending he had your blessing."

"As indeed he had."

"No matter. She sent him off with his tail between his legs."

"Between hers, from what I hear."

"From what you hear?" Henry shot up. His father retreated a step. "Must you hear every filthy innuendo Rochester spews into your ear?"

"It is clear he does not hold the monopoly on jealousy."

"And he will never hold the monopoly on slander as long as you are ready to let his lies trip off your tongue."

"Oh, dear... oh, dear." The King sighed and shook his head. "It begins to dawn upon me that Frances must be the English bride you were hinting at that day at Theobalds. What a pity you chose to keep her name to yourself. Had you no secrets from me, it would have saved you so much anguish. I would gladly have told you that Rochester had got there before you. Oh, dear... there you were, poor lad, so busy rehearsing Henry the Fifth—crying *God for Harry, England and St. George!* And, all the while, Robbie was no less busy playing Romeo—crying *Two of the fairest stars in all the heaven!*" A pause to let the words sink deep. "Ah, I see you have no notion what he was raving about. Never mind—neither did I. When I would not believe that he had won her, he became very cross with me, and asked how else would he have discovered the twin stars on her belly. Naughty lad! Mind you, he was honest enough to confess he had already gazed upon them a time or two while poor Essex was away. Aye, and since he came back. Must I go on for you to know she is for him and not for you?"

The knife went in at the brisket. The hounds yelped. The horns sounded the recheat. The company whoo-whooped. Henry slumped into his chair, images bursting in his head. He brought himself down to earth to find his father standing over him, eyes shining as they had this afternoon when he wallowed in gore. God almighty, the blood was still under his fingernails.

[20]

Sunday the Thirtieth of August

MURRAY shushed Mrs. Turner as she intercepted him on his way to tell her what had to be told. He drew her into the cloisters, aware that raised voices in this open quadrangle would echo four or five times to reach every window of Woodstock Palace. She heard him with face and fists set for a scream, though what came from her was a hiss.

"Lies, lies, lies!"

"Madam, we are done with lies. It is all over."

"And is our Prince done with honour, that he does not seek the truth of her?"

"He might throttle her in the bargain."

"She might do as much to herself."

"I doubt that."

"And her mother might do as much to him—casting Frances aside like an old glove."

"Should the Prince want a glove stretched by another?"

"She will quash that slander the moment she is heard." Mrs. Turner threw in an emphatic nod.

"And when that forces the King to call Rochester to give her the lie, do you imagine he will fail his master?" Murray's nod cancelled Mrs. Turner's. "Can you not see, Anne? The King does not give a fig who has had Frances or who hasn't. All that concerns him is to break Henry from her, any way he can, and get him married off to a princess before he is much older. If Frances is defiant, she will lose everything. And so, my dear, will her family—and so, my dear, will you."

"Blast you, David Murray! You were never so officious with your buttons undone."

"Thank you, madam. All I have to add is that it will be as well if some indisposition or other keeps Frances from the festivities tonight."

And first thing tomorrow the Prince would be returning to Richmond. The King had now found it convenient to let him quit the Progress early to prepare for Frederick's reception. Murray bowed farewell to Mrs. Turner; seeing her face that night she would have had him finish off Essex's valet. He held up his head. He, too, was a free man again.

"PRAY SILENCE for his Highness!" Three raps of the Chamberlain's staff commanded attention as late sunshine dappled through rose-decked boughs of this great summerhouse Henry had built to regale the court at quite the most splendid feast of the Progress. Murray noticed with satisfaction the empty place at which Frances was to have sat.

"Your Majesties"—a bow to their table—"your Highnesses"—a bow to his brother and sister—"my good lords and ladies and gentlemen. Only if I were determined upon unfavourable comparison would I attempt a speech of weight on an occasion when the King might possibly have a word or two to say." Loud laughter. "Therefore shall I content myself with a simple welcome at this first opportunity to entertain you at Woodstock since it became mine."

Murray was proud of Henry. This was his stage, and this his role. He was every inch a Prince of Wales, aglow with assurance and vitality. Masked was that wretch of last night, aghast at finding himself played false by the love for which he was making ready to call down the lightning. Thank God he had not been undermined by those who had expected so much of him all these years that they had proffered a false mirror, showing him a face not his own: invulnerable, infallible, immortal. And, for once, thank God he had for a father the craftiest old fox ever to wear a crown.

To the Countess of Suffolk, that empty seat was signal enough of the way things would now go for the Howards. There would be no room for them at the court of Henry the Ninth. Curse him, smiling away there as though it were nothing that he had made Frances a prisoner in her chamber, reduced to a tear-drowned wreck who could not have shown such a face anyway. Mother Suffolk's anger, so hot this morning that she could have pistolled the tyrant, ran so cold tonight that she could begin to consider more subtle means of riddance.

"And if God's blessings upon my throne continue for but the few months to Bessy's wedding," the King was saying, "then shall I be the only monarch of my line in two whole centuries to live long enough to see any of his children married. Aye, and perhaps I shall be spared to see my sons wed also—if Henry does not take too much longer in making up his mind."

The Prince caught Murray's raised eyebrows, and joined in the laughter for his own good reason.

"But I must not be impatient with the lad. And he must not be impatient with me, though he is the first Stuart heir in seven reigns not to find himself on the throne by now. Against that, I am sure he will set the benefit of being the first not to be cast adrift into such seas of wickedness as threaten to engulf us still." The King stopped to drain his glass. "Oh, we all know that fornication is thought but a light and pardonable sin by the most part of the world..."

"B-b-bessy." Charles tugged her sleeve. "What's f-f-fornication?"

"Nothing. Shush!"

"...but if we measure one sin by the rule of lust and appetite, and not of conscience, the same shall apply to the next and then the next until we be wholly corrupted. By the mouths of Mark and John, the Almighty placed fornicators with dogs and sorcerers, whoremongers and murderers, idolators and lovers of lies—and warned that none shall enter the kingdom of heaven. Therefore must we all counsel our sons to abstain from haunting the idle company of dames who are nothing but *irritamenta libidinis...*"

"B-b-bessy?"

"Dirty women. Shush!"

"D-d-dirty?" Charles wrinkled his nose.

"...and therefore must we bid them not to wait overlong to marry, for it is ordained that they quench the lust of their youth. Yet must we ensure they choose wisely, knowing that behind fair masks may lie infinite miseries. And knowing that they will find themselves coupled with a devil if they choose beauty without bounty, wealth without wisdom, friendship without honesty. I was fortunate. I chose all with all." He bent to lift the Queen's hand to kiss, cuing murmurs of approval. "May God grant Henry as sweet a *tourterelle...*"

"B-b-bessy?"

"Turtledove. Shush!"

The King paused for his choice of French to sink in. It sunk nowhere deeper than into the heart of the Prince. That battle was still waiting round the next corner.

"Well, we shall see," said the King. "And when we do see, what better example will my son and his princess have than that of his loving parents?" He smiled down at the Queen, who responded with a brittle laugh. "Our recipe for a good marriage is simple enough. Eh, Annie? I treat her as my own flesh. I command her as her lord. I cherish her as my helper. I rule her as my pupil. I please her in all things reasonable—though I teach her not to be curious in things that belong to her not." The Queen made a comedy of pulling her hand away. "Ha! As you see, this is not always to my Annie's liking. Yet—thank heaven—there is nonetheless such sweet harmony between us that she is as willing to follow as I to go before."

"And," whispered one of the Queen's ladies behind her fan, "she is as willing to dwell at Greenwich as he at Theobalds."

"The rewards God has bestowed upon us speak for themselves," said the King. "I call our witnesses—Henry, Charles and Bessy." He waved them to their feet. "Stand up, sweet bairns!"

The three linked hands. The company cheered, and banged goblets on the tabletops. The King and Queen were already dabbing at their eyes. Others soon followed, moved as much by that as by this picture of the royal children at their last Progress together.

Rochester and Overbury looked only at the Prince, and saw sand running from the glass.

[21]

Tuesday the Fifteenth of September

As the Spanish ambassador's black coach drew out into the Barbican, the man in the Spanish ambassador's black suit glared from under the brim of his black hat at the watchmen waving him to a halt. One on each side opened doors and peered under seats in case there might be another Jesuit or two to bring before the Archbishop. They paid scant attention to the plumber trudging from the embassy gates.

The coach turned left to bear Zuñiga's secretary on an errand no more important than giving the horses a run. Zuñiga himself hunched a shoulder to secure his toolbag, and turned right for the quarter-mile walk through Aldersgate, down St. Martin-le-Grand and into Paternoster Row. There, waiting for him at Mrs. Turner's, he would find Roldán.

THE PRINCE released a sigh. Again, he squeezed eyes tight to shut in a vision or shut off a tear. Again, Murray judged it wiser not to notice: the man must vanquish his torment alone, or remain its vassal. But this fortnight at Richmond had seen Henry grow short on temper, as though he had left his mask behind at Woodstock to be cleared away with the other braveries of that feast. Now he was spending hours by himself, walking early in the fields, swimming late in the river, dining on a few grapes in his chamber. It must be the fever getting worse before it got better.

Murray was unaware that what had made it worse was the arrival a week ago of a letter from Frances, enclosing the ring of nine diamonds. The Prince had read it again and again before burning it, but the ring was still in his pocket and every stroke and loop of her childish hand was still imprinted on his mind:

Sweet Hally

I am bereft of all hope of any good in this world while my silence allows you to believe what you were told about me. If it were true, I would never desire to see your dear face again.

You gave me this ring in all love. I return it in all love, so you will know

I look to you for nothing that you may not give. I cannot go on with your hating me. I will be your servant, your friend, your mistress for as long as you wish. And when you bid me go from you, I will be happy to please you even in that.

When I have done writing this, I will go to the house at Cranford le Mote, there to wait knowing that if you do not come to me in a week you will come to me never. I beg you do, though it be but once again, and that to say farewell for always.

Yours, never so unhappy. Love me.
Fra

Another sigh. Again, Henry asked himself, did it not dishonour him to condemn her without a hearing, on the word of the greatest liar since Ananias? Again, Henry asked himself, should he not see her that once, just that once? Again, he answered himself that what really beckoned him was neither honour nor sentiment, but the will-o'-the-wisp between her hot thighs.

THE COUNTESS OF SUFFOLK purred as Zuñiga lifted her from her curtsy and kissed each ring-laden finger.

"You," she said, "are very gallant for a plumber."

"I," he said, "am very gallant for an ambassador."

"Dear Pedro! How I've missed you." She drew him clear of the window to sit beside her on the wainscot bench by the stairs. A silver flagon of his favourite *tinto* was already at his elbow on the chess table.

"We must not let your King take you away again. You do more good than such donkeys as Velasco. More good for Spain. More good for us. More good for me."

She linked an arm in his. They were two old comrades in this secret war that had brought them closer than lovers, which they might easily have been, and which awareness was the reason she did so much for Zuñiga's reputation with Madrid and so little for his successor's. Velasco had lacked the grace to succeed with Spain's most valuable *confidente*. Having gone through his wife's fortune to maintain himself in office, he resented the rewards flowing to Roldán, and behaved with her as he would not dare with a whore—wanting what she had to give before he would relinquish his master's gold. With Zuñiga, the ducats were always a present, never a payment. He could smile with her that better the treasure Spain gave him to disburse helped make Audley End the grandest private palace in the land, than be wasted on a host of rogues.

But it was because of this greed that he could never quite trust her. For all that she swore she would die a Catholic, even if she could not live as one without setting both wealth and influence at naught. For all that there was no doubt that this influence alone, particularly with the late Earl of Salisbury, was such that the laws against the Catholic laity had never been enforced as strictly as their enemies wished. And for all that today he must enlist her aid in the salvation of the faith from its paramount threat.

"Ah, my lady, my lady." Zuñiga patted her knee. "You know I would remain forever to please you—though I hold it even more troublesome for a Spaniard to die here than to live here. But it is out of my hands. Your King has declared that he wants me gone. No man of rank may visit me. Pursuivants watch my gate. Embassy business is at a standstill. I do not serve Spain by staying on to feed the spite of her greatest persecutor."

"The son will be greater, mark my words."

"I have already reported as much to my masters."

"And?"

"Nothing." His shoulders acknowledged impotence. His palms apologised. "Alas, my King has yet to cease believing that the Almighty will inspire some Catholic marriage or other as the medicine to cure this ulcer. He assures us that the good people of England will then be as obediently Catholic under the ninth Henry as they were Catholic under the seventh, heretic under the eighth, Catholic under Mary and heretic again under Elizabeth."

"Then he should know what the good people of England are saying now: *Henry the Eighth pulled down monks and their cells, Henry the Ninth will down bishops and bells.*"

"My lady, greater men than your servant have failed to move Philip from his knees in this matter." Zuñiga filled their glasses, but the Countess waved hers away. She did not drink when she was working.

"You will be fortunate if Henry leaves even Spain Catholic. Do not be surprised if he uses his sister's marriage as the pretext for journeying to plot with your greatest enemies in Holland and Germany. He will fill their heads with grander designs than they ever dreamed of."

"God help us all!" Zuñiga could see armies massing from the head to the heart of the Rhine.

"Pedro, why is God deaf to the prayers of his most pious king—unless it is because God has another fate in store for this Prince of Wales?" She rose to cross to the window, looking at it rather than out of it for a moment before returning to Zuñiga. "Everything tells me it is our duty to destroy him before he destroys us."

"My dear, I do not want to sound like an old ambassador"—he must procure Roldán for this task, not she him—"but my orders remain to warn the Catholics of England against any rash practices that could perchance bring their ruin. No more Fifths of November."

"Amen to that."

"The embassy is instructed to advise that by continuing to be quiet and loyal the community will place James in their debt, and will more quickly enable him to return the nation to the bosom of the Apostolic See."

"I would say amen to that, too, were Baby Charles his heir—but never with Henry. He would have his father off the throne at the merest hint."

"He is in a great hurry for a young man bound for hell."

"All the more reason for us to help him on his way." She sat beside Zuñiga again, clutching his arm.

"My King will not order the death of princes. That is the province of heaven."

"And if heaven chooses to employ an earthly hand?"

"Then so be it, my lady. It would not be the first time. Or the last."

"Everything tells me... that I am to be that instrument."

The Countess stood before him, madonna-eyed, and sank to her knees. She knew this was divine inspiration because the way had opened before her like the Red Sea before the children of Israel. Zuñiga knew it was divine inspiration because, for once, she had not mentioned money.

"I may not offer you Spain's help, but I offer you mine."

"Pedro, I need only the help of Providence."

"Swear to me there will be no violence." He cupped her thin cheeks.

"I swear it."

"If he could but know, the King of Spain would bless you."

"If he could but know, the King of England would bless me."

HENRY'S SIGH was more for himself than for Frances by the time he reined into the forecourt of her rose-brick manor at Cranford le Mote and left his mount in the shade. He had intended to come the short way until he caught sight of Sir Arthur Mainwaring at Ferry Hill, boarding the horse-boat ahead of him. So then, after taking cover like some truant schoolboy, he had gone round by way of Kingston Bridge, his mind too heavy-laden to wonder what his truant Gentleman Carver was up to at the very hour he was due in the Presence Chamber along with the Gentleman Cup-bearer and the Gentleman Server, to receive instructions from the Gentleman Usher of the Day.

As the Prince crossed the hall toward her, Mrs. Turner remained in shadow, not wishing to proclaim herself a sharer in the secret of the letter that had brought him. It was she who had given Mainwaring the task of getting it into the Prince's hands, knowing that it would therefore reach the King's first. It was she who had calculated that his Majesty would bid Mainwaring postpone delivery until the week Frances had said she would wait for Henry had passed, and the counterplot was accomplished. Thus the Prince, who deserved his fate for keeping Frances on tenterhooks even that one week, would seem to the girl to have cared so little as to let two go by. Mrs. Turner bobbed the barest of curtsies as he looked past her for Frances. When she did not appear, an inclination of his head put the question and a shake of Mrs. Turner's gave the answer. He did not accept it.

"Go on then, madam. Fetch her ladyship." His thin smile acknowledged her entitlement to repay him for his delay.

"Her ladyship is not here to fetch... sir."

"Oh. Did she leave word when she would be?" Henry heard himself with dismay, aware of what this woman must be thinking as she shook her head once more, and looked at him as if he were ugly. She saw no prince come to court his lady; she saw ram come to tup his ewe.

"How long has she been gone?" He tried again.

"An hour or more."

"Tell me which way she went—I will catch her up."

"Better not, sir."

"Better not, madam?" He began to understand. "You mean she is not alone?"

"It's not for me to say, sir."

"Rochester?"

"It's not for me to say, sir."

The Prince berated himself. What a fool he was. What a fool.

Mrs. Turner offered to the door the curtsy Henry did not stay for, and fell laughing in a heap. To think that she had striven to keep Frances from sending that letter! Yet not only had it served to show her once and for all that nothing would move sweet Hally, it had served to move the King to move sweet Robbie. By the time Rochester galloped in, Frances was ripe for redemption: she had fallen into his arms, blessing Heaven that her only true love had come to her when she needed him most. Oh, how she had wept. Ah, how he had wept. And, after their week of honey days and moony nights, it would have served the Prince right to have turned up in time to see those beaming faces as they came down after lying abed till noon again. Frances had been unwilling to let go her darling's hand even while she embraced Mrs. Turner, wanting happiness to rub off, bless her, on the friend to whom she owed more than she would ever know. Away across the park the lovers had ridden, two on one nag, like a lad and his lass. And tomorrow he would be escorting her to Audley End, secure in the King's promise to see them wed before Lent.

HUGGING HERSELF to his back, her cheek against his shoulder, Frances matched her breathing to Rochester's as the horse took them at its own pace along the riverbank. She tightened her hold, and he responded with a hand over hers.

This morning, he had woken first, enraptured to lie just looking at her. Then her eyes had opened, and then the rest of her, as a marigold to the sun. This was the greatest gift the King could ever bestow upon him, albeit the hurry was bound to be in response to some renewed sign of the Prince's interest. The Devil must be inside Henry to make him so perverse. But what matter? Spain was going to have him off the face of the earth any moment of any hour of any day now. The Archbishop's men were already examining one Jan de Horneck who, though declaring himself an innocent Hollander, was suspected of being the Jesuit Abraham Vlaming, warned against by the British agent in Brussels as the founder of some secret order of martyrdom. Rochester had sped to Overbury with the news, only to be sneezed at with the logic that, if Horneck proved to be Vlaming, that would make him less, not more, likely the intended assassin, since Spain would not want any Catholic imprimatur on this work.

Henry came upon the couple as he rode over the ridge atop the meadow. Their meadow. With their willow tree. It was a moment or so before he recognised the loose-haired girl in bodice and kirtle, and the bare-headed fellow in shirt and breeches. They looked well together, the Lord Chamberlain's beautiful daughter and the King's beautiful Secretary of State.

"A perfect day, Highness!" The exuberant Rochester swept off an imaginary hat, and bowed his head to touch the crest of his horse's neck in due deference.

"Perfect." Henry nodded. The man could have no inkling of all that had passed, and in this very meadow, between his rival and his light o' love.

As Frances looked over Rochester's shoulder, her eyes caught Henry's. Please, they said, *please*... Henry cleared his throat, clipped his heels to command a trot, and rode away. Presently, he took the ring of nine diamonds from his sleeve pocket. He held it up, ready to drop it underfoot, but could not bring himself to let go.

Frances looked back as Rochester's nag took them on again. Then she dropped her hands to his thighs, and changed the subject.

ONLY NOW did Zuñiga assemble himself to take leave of the Countess of Suffolk. Only now was he satisfied that the task could be left to her. For only now was he sure that he knew her true motive. There had been no glimmer of it until he had held out to her Foscarini's tidbit that the Prince was showing an inclination to a lady of the court. She had snapped at it. The lady was, of course, her daughter. Who but Frances would be great enough a prize for him? But Frances had, of course, instructed him to show his inclination elsewhere. She had given her promise to Rochester (though that secret was for Zuñiga's ears only). His Excellency's brain had not been overtaxed to deduce that, since Mother Suffolk could never have allowed her daughter to turn aside such an opportunity, something had gone badly amiss. Especially when he added into the equation that "great secret" Father Pérez had reported her hinting at with glee on the morning Zuñiga had his audience with the Queen. Thus far, their best guess had been that Lady Arabella Stuart must be the intended bride. They had failed to take into account the gossip about Frances's nullity. But today it had become plain to Zuñiga that the Prince had seduced her: the Howard escutcheon was besmirched. Now that was motive worthy of a Spaniard, and therefore rare in this land where they had no honour save to own and to eat. When *el honor* was at issue the Spaniard reached for his sword, the Englishman for his scales. He would weigh in the balance that if the law punished him for taking revenge, then his enemy would be up two to one; and that, anyway, blow for blow made him merely even, whereas passing over the offence left him superior.

It took one such as Roldán to know that honour was not governed by the arithmetic of the grocer's shop. And it took one such as Roldán to know that this revenge required not the knife that flashed before the multitude, but the arrow that flew in the dark.

"Go with God, dear man." She stood on her toes, but still had to pull his head down to kiss him.

"And you, dear lady."

"Wait." She held him back as he began to open the door. "Do you reckon you will more likely be taken for a plumber if you forget your tools?"

THE PRINCE stroked his brow with the back of his hand as he came into his chamber to find Murray waiting. The look on the man's face said it all.

"Poor David."

"Sir, I prayed it was finished."

"It is—now."

[22]

Friday the Second of October

PLANTING HIMSELF in a chair between the open doors of his hunting lodge at Royston, the King scowled at the rain pouring down, and wondered aloud if God were about to break his promise to Noah never to drown the world again. James was not the easiest of men to please. Since Michaelmas, his moan had been that the weather continued to be too droughty for the hounds to pick up a good scent. He loved this Cambridgeshire border country, the best in all England for hunting the hare, and was eager to begin the season. A legion of leverets awaited, as yet ignorant of the cunning that had kept their parents alive, especially the doe, whose shorter and more frequent doublings and crossings gave her a longer span than the less-crafty buck (though superstition used to have it that all hares were female, possibly because, sleeping or waking, their lips never ceased to move).

The King was also out of patience with his ambassador in Paris. Having finally broken Henry from Frances, he wanted to waste no time in binding him to Christina. But since Sir Thomas Edmondes had been instructed to spur proceedings, summer had moved into autumn with still no conclusion—except the King's that the little man required a large firecracker up his fundament. James had no wish to take into consideration the fact that Edmondes, who had been England's man at the French court on and off for twenty years, knew their ways so well that Paris feared he knew them too well. Nor that Edmondes knew the ways of his master so well that he was not fool enough to come to terms for the second daughter until directed to abandon any remaining hope of the first.

"Come cheer me up, laddie." Without turning from the rain, the King lifted an arm over his head to summon the favourite.

"Majesty, here's the news to do the deed!" Rochester, already on his way with Overbury's decipherment of the dispatch they had been waiting for, was happy to be able to place it in James's beckoning fingers.

"A clever fellow, that Edmondes," the King said presently. "He does what I tell him." He let the document fall to his lap, all gloom evaporated, and wrung his hands in anticipation of the pleasure his next move would give him. "Bring pen and ink, young man, and I shall dictate a letter for you to send to my son." What had surely done the trick with France was that hint of the Prince's inclination to take a bride from among the ladies of the court. Henry could wriggle all he might: he was on the spit, and he would roast.

"Away we go then, Robbie." The King swung a leg over the chair arm, and relished his words as he issued them at the speed of Rochester's quill. "Write that—may it please his Highness—you are commanded to send him the dispatch from Paris, upon which his Majesty desires his opinion, and observes two things. First, that the match with the eldest daughter is utterly despaired of. Next, that the proposition for Princess Christina is so strongly apprehended that France will refuse no condition that with reason may be demanded. They will accommodate all difficulties and hindrances that in any way might interrupt a work so acceptable to and so passionately taken hold of by them. As to the dowry which, according to the example of the elder sister, is but five hundred thousand crowns, his Majesty thinks France so earnest that there may be hope of increasing the sum. Further, his Majesty wills that his Highness consider that Princess Christina cannot be made riper nor fitter than her age permits, which is no more than nine years..."

"Six, Majesty. It is the eldest who is nine."

"Whose side are you on, laddie?" The King unsheathed a smile. "Be a good fellow, eh? Just write down what I say. After all, she will be going on nine by the time they send her over, will she not?" He cleared his throat of that dissimulation to make way for another. "And, in conclusion, his Majesty states that the incongruity of age is the only inconveniency, and neither side can help it." He motioned Rochester to add his own salutations. "Et cetera, et cetera..."

Bowing away, Rochester wondered why he had bothered to correct the King. Six years old, nine years old; first daughter, second daughter; half a million crowns, three quarters of a million—what did it matter now?

The King sighed again at the rain masking even the first of the two-score miles north to Peterborough where, at his secret order, the body of his mother was this night to be exhumed for reburial in Westminster Abbey. He complimented himself that his timing would much please Paris and help set the seal upon the match for Henry. The English could not be expected to applaud, but the French had never forgotten that this Queen of Scots was also their Queen Dowager, and was dishonoured so long as she was not entombed among her peers. Indeed, she had begged to be buried at Saint-Denis with her first husband, their Francis the Second, or at Rheims with her mother, their Mary of Guise. Elizabeth had refused (so much for her protestations that she never intended her rival's execution) and the Queen of Scots, her head sewn back on, had lain a quarter-century under Peterborough Cathedral.

Like her journey there from the scaffold at Fotheringhay, this also would be managed in the dark to avoid commotion. Three or four days from now, the chariot conveying her lead coffin would be passing this way. James pictured himself standing by the London road, bareheaded in the flickering torchlight, to pay his first and last respects to the remains of his mother. But he knew he would not be there; the only obsequies he would ever attend would be his own.

Though parted from her forever at ten months, he was aware each time he looked at her grandson what she must have been like, and why she lost to Elizabeth. More had descended to Henry than the broad brow, the piercing eye and the defiant jaw of her portrait. Henry, too, was cursed with the fatal certainty that pride was reason enough and courage armour enough.

SINCE that afternoon the Prince had gone to Frances like dog to whistle, only to find another at the bone, Murray had thought it as well not to be far from his shoulder. Sigh by sigh, Henry was emptying his heart of the girl, but it was not going to mend so long as he was riven with rage at his father for his undoubted hand in this, and at himself for his undoubted foot in it. He had made some attempt at exorcism with a frenzy of tilting as though the quintain were a live foe, and tennis as though it, too, were a martial art. But he could not long sustain those sports on a diet of little more than fruit, and had turned to less demanding primero and gleek, sitting till late at the card table and then lying abed till nine.

So another day was passing without his Highness caring to bend his head for long to the urgent business of Frederick's reception. Too often when details were paraded for his approval or amendment, he would turn them away with the back of his hand. The Prince's officers were competent enough to deal with this traffic through the Presence Chamber, but it was the Prince himself all were looking to please with their schemes for the ceremonies and revels to greet England's first royal bridegroom in sixty years. Frederick was by now halfway from

Heidelberg with his train of eight counts, seven privy councillors and a hundred and fifty followers, and would be landing them from The Hague about the middle of the month. Henry must pull himself together, lest these Germans and Dutchmen discover the prefigured conqueror of their Catholic enemies to be no more than an echo of that hope. Lest they find not an Emperor of Europe in waiting but a pale apology who sighed each day away, uttering sometimes that he knew not why, sometimes that he was unaware that he did it and sometimes that it was not without cause.

"David, why do you look at me like that?" The Prince picked at a cluster of grapes in his chamber.

"Sir, why does your mirror look at you like that? Because it never before saw death warmed up—and reckons it high time it saw the face it used to see."

"Or high time I called in the physician. You know, I would not be surprised if all this is just an autumn ague coming on."

"The only physicians you need, Highness, are Dr. Diet, Dr. Quiet and Dr. Merryman. And the only physic you need"—Murray sniffed at those grapes—"you will more likely get from the kitchen than the apothecary."

Nonetheless, Murray thought he would ask the Prince's doctor to purge him. Else the moment his father set eyes on that spiritless face he would send in his own man. And much as the King swore by Dr. Theodore Turquet de Mayerne in the year since summoning him from Paris to become First Physician to their Majesties, it could not be gainsaid that the fellow had achieved a reputation for being uncommonly unlucky.

WITH Frances away at Audley End, Mrs. Turner today resumed her visits to the Friday lecture at the College of Physicians, so conveniently housed at the Amen Corner end of Paternoster Row. The hallkeeper made as much of the winsome widow as when her husband was successively Fellow, Censor, Elect and Treasurer here, and insisted on conducting her to the seat she indicated—there to glow in the frank delight of Paul de Lobel at finding her next to him after all these weeks. Now that Frances was finished with the Prince, Murray was never again going to look at her like that, and Mainwaring could be expected to have less of an eye for what was no longer his main chance.

As always, her first inquiry was after the well-being of Madame de Lobel. Ah, said Monsieur (in tones ever more English than the English), one feared apoplexy at the very least if one's coach went to fetch one's own family, rather than Madame's, to the banquet she was giving her distinguished brother. One would have thought, wouldn't one, that the great Dr. Theodore Turquet de Mayerne would buy a coach of his own, sooner than leech upon his apothecary. However, one's real difficulty was that one could hardly tell Madame one's decision was based not upon sentiment but upon avoirdupois. Madame's fat brother plus fat wife, Madame's fat sister plus fat suitor, and Madame's fat old mother would put such a strain upon one's still-new coach. Far more than would the neat little de Lobel sisters plus their neat little royal apothecary husbands—even with neat little father de Lobel, Botanist to the King, thrown in for good measure. Ah, lamented Monsieur, if only one could afford to be a mere physician, one could arrange to be called away to some sickbed and leave them all to feed their fat faces in one's absence. One was certainly not hungry for more of the great man's jibes. Physician's cook, indeed! Quacksalver! Gallipot! Grocer! Monsieur doubted that one would put up with it were it not for the sake of Madame—and, maybe to some extent, for the sake of the stream of red-ink prescriptions one's incomparable brother-in-law was gracious enough to send one's way.

But—Monsieur took her hand—no more of one's domestic squalor. How *was* dear Anne? Oh, that her wish for his company might be even a grain, scruple or dram of his unending ache for hers. Dear Anne shushed Monsieur as the lecture began and, drawing off her glove, mixed her fingers with his to rehearse with them the parts soon to be played upon the bed that was her stage.

[23]

Monday the Fifth of October

A BONE to pick with you, David Murray!" Scrolling up his calendar of plays for the nuptial season, Sir George Buck retreated from the Presence Chamber, more a short-shriven schoolboy than a long-headed Master of the Revels.

"Pick away, my friend. But don't say I didn't warn you the Prince was not at his best."

"Not at his best, eh? Then as well he didn't catch me out when he was." Buck cupped his ears. "Whew!"

"You found him on his mettle?" Please God..., prayed Murray.

"Aye, that I did. Would that you had pointed out before I went in that only an idiot would put *The Dutch Courtesan* on the list. The Prince was on to it like a shot. Did I not realise his new brother-in-law is half Dutch?"

"Ha!" Murray was going to enjoy this.

"And did I not take the trouble to discover that he brings with him four counts of Nassau? And was it my judgment that they would find it amusing to hear some misbegotten actor declaiming that Englishmen love the Low Countries because we would rather wage our wars there than on our own doorstep?"

"Heaven forfend!"

"Mind you, David, he did grant me that it was marked to be played after the wedding and not before..."

"Ah, that must be what saved your head."

"...but find some other comedy, he said, there's a good fellow. And go through every single line of every single work in your calendar—*you*, sir, not your clerk, nor your comptroller, nor your yeoman—and then come back and assure me there will not be one word out of place to disturb my little sister's happiness. So there, David. What do you say to that?"

"Hallelujah! Your thick ear is a small price to pay for our old Prince back." Murray went inside the Presence doors and stood, arms folded, observing Henry in conversation with his Gentleman Ushers at the big bay window. Yet too pale. Yet too lean. But at least, and at last, eager once again.

"Sir..." There was a small cough at his elbow as a page offered a letter. Murray snapped the King's seals. Oh, no. The Prince had gambled that France would never send the child Christina here to be converted—and the Prince had lost. Whatever conditions he asked or refused, the Queen Regent would go along. And, as though the message were not enough, the subscript would whet the goad: *So, humbly taking my leave, I rest. At your Highness's command—Ro. Rochester.*

"Good news, David?" Mainwaring loomed up.

"Mind your own business, Carver." Murray folded the letter away.

"No need to bite my head off. I mean it's good news that his Highness is to take dinner with us. I require no licence from you to rejoice that he has found his appetite. We are all the Prince's men, you know."

Murray watched him slide away like a shoved ha'penny. He was now convinced this was the spy in the camp—the scab keeping the King ahead at every turn. For as soon as Henry had offered the thought that Mainwaring might have been in wait on his last visit to Cranford le Mote, three old suspicions had leaped into place. One, Mainwaring snooping as they smuggled Frances into St. James's. Two, the King who forgot nothing making such a point of forgetting the man's name at the Prince's table. Three, Mrs. Turner's insistence that she knew him only as a patient of her late husband. All in all, it was enough for Murray to set off inquiries about the pair of them—which was how he had learned that Dr. Turner's will contained a bequest of ten shillings for Mainwaring to buy a ring for Anne engraved with the old physician's last prescription, *Fata irriguntum amantes,* hinting that destiny had now cleared the way for them to marry. Since she most likely whispered into her lover's ear everything Frances whispered into hers, there was no secret about the affair that the King could not have come to know. And yet it was politic to let Mainwaring remain in the Prince's household, because the King would only replace him—and better the spy you know than the spy you don't. Meanwhile, this knave who selected the very meat for his Highness's mouth would stir neither hand nor foot nor carving knife unobserved.

TRUST the King to blow an ill wind just when Henry's topgallants were filling again. For his part, Murray had let the message wait until after a good dinner, and the Prince was at ease in his chamber. And now they sprawled, their silence amplifying the occasional rustle as

Henry swung the letter in a loose hand, his thoughts bounding beyond how he might reply. He accepted that he could no more hope to rally Church, Parliament and people against marriage with France on these terms than he could have for marriage with Frances on any. Therefore he was going to need as much cunning to thwart the one as his father had employed to thwart the other.

"David, I never bargained that the French would be so obliging."

"That will teach you to rely upon the Pope for salvation."

"But he had already saved me from a Spanish match."

"Ah, there are no Huguenots in Spain for Philip to appease..."

"...as there is a king in England for me to appease." Henry got up, motioning Murray not to. There was mischief on his face as he crossed to a cabinet displaying his father's works. From between *Demonology* and *A Counterblast to Tobacco,* he fished out the italic *Basilikon Doron,* dedicated to the infant "appointed by God (I hope) to sit on my throne after me," and charging him ever to follow its precepts or be cursed. "Here we are, David. His Majesty's instructions to his dearest son. Listen...*I would rather have you marry one fully of your own religion. For although the number of princes professing ours be but very small, yet have you deeply to consider how you can be of one flesh and keep unity betwixt you, being members of opposite churches...Neither pride yourself that you will be able to make your wife do as you please. That deceived Solomon, the wisest king that ever was—and perseverance is not a flower that grows in our garden...*" Henry shut the book with a flourish, and restored it to the shelf. "Now is that not most excellent advice?"

"Fit for a prince."

"And will I be damned if I ignore it?"

"Aye."

"Then damned if I will! Why pay attention only to the royal houses of the Romish religion when for all these years I have been commanded to do the opposite? Bessy's marriage to the Prince of the Rhine can no longer be allowed to mean that I may not look to Germany."

"France and Spain will mislike it."

"What better reason do we need? They shall have their double marriage—and we shall have ours." Henry applauded himself as the plan took him. Bessy would soon persuade their father to send him to escort her to Heidelberg so that her new people would see how great a princess was coming among them. And, once there, she would seek out a German lady for him to lose his heart to.

"Frederick has three sisters," said Murray, reading his mind. "George William of Brandenburg has two. Otto of Hesse-Cassel has one. I doubt we shall be home for some months."

"The more the merrier, David. There are things I will not be sorry to leave behind me. You know..."

"I know." By the time they returned, Frances would be married to Rochester.

"I can hardly wait to be on our way! Just imagine. Flushing to Arnhem. Cologne to Coblenz. Oppenheim to Heidelberg. It will be difficult not to observe what good soldiers ought to observe of Holy Roman Germany." He clapped Murray on the shoulder. "Eh?"

"Highness, I am loath to march you back to Richmond, but we do need to frame a reply about the French princess."

Henry was not his father's son for nothing. Far from being cast down by the ambassador's message that there would be no reasonable conditions Paris would not accommodate, the Prince now hailed it as his trump card. With Frances shuffled out of the pack, his hand was no longer being forced. He could play for time—and the exchanges as to how early would be "reasonable" for Christina to be sent to England would alone take longer than a journey to Heidelberg and back. Murray was soon ready with his draft—a masterpiece of denial by delay. The Prince nodded approval and begged his pen to add a final sentence, speaking the words as he set them down:

"And besides, your Majesty may think that my part to play, which is to be in love with any of them, is not yet at hand."

[24]

Sunday the Eighteenth of October

SOON, London would hear the eighty-gun salute from the Tower as the royal barge brought Frederick the Fifth, Count Palatine of the Rhine and Prince Elector of the Holy Roman Empire, into the last reach of his journey to claim his bride. Torches shivered in the east wind at the Whitehall stairs, along with halberdiers who lined the terrace to the Banqueting House on the coldest day of the season. Inside, the Queen noticed Henry shiver, too, though the throng was generating warmth enough to melt every brow, let alone hubbub enough to drown the consort in the gallery. The pillared hall was the more crowded because the Master of Ceremonies had failed to pass beyond a few the word that farthingales would not be welcome—and through a sea of silken tubs, each sprouting a gilded lily of the court, wallowed the purposeful bulk of Dr. Theodore Turquet de Mayerne. Henry tracked the great, balding head as it bobbed his way and, catching his mother's eye for a moment, guessed that she had dispatched the First Physician to him.

"Sir, the Queen is much concerned about you." Mayerne regarded the damp ivory face.

"I thank her, monsieur—and I thank you—but it is no more than a chill. It will pass soon enough if I stay clear of physicians."

"You should have kept to your warm bed. When did you last see your Dr. Hammond?"

"Only yesterday."

"And?"

"And I packed him off home, monsieur—he did not look at all well to me." Henry smiled as much for the humourless Huguenot as at him. "But I confess to you, I was a trifle aguish a few days since. And the good Dr. Hammond has thought fit to dose me with sufficient physic to empty a regiment."

"Sir, sir"—Mayerne wagged a fat finger—"he will not be pleased that you hazard your open body abroad so soon. It is as well I have to tell you that the King has sent your brother out to the river stairs in your place."

Now the Tower cannon began echoing, and the crush gravitated toward the entrance through which Baby Charles would be leading his new brother-in-law. Henry was glad to find himself left with breathing space by the far windows for the few minutes before he needed to take his seat on the canopied dais.

He felt a hand in his, and did not need to turn to know whose it was.

"Hally..."

"Are you stark mad?" His gaze stayed ahead. It was as much as he could bear to see her reflection sparkling in the glass.

"I still love you."

"That game is over and done." Was it? Then why, even now, could his mind calculate that all it would need to bring them together again was persuading Bessy to take Frances to Germany as a lady-in-waiting?

"I had to come. I heard the Queen sending Dr. Mayerne to you. I was so worried."

"Worry about your lover."

"You are my lover." She willed him to look at her, but he would not.

"I *saw* you. Remember?"

"Robbie was no more than a sweet brother—making me laugh when you made me weep."

"Laugh, aye!" Her hand was somehow still in his. He lifted it and let it fall away.

"I know you love me. I will wait for you as long as I live."

"Your wait is ended, Frances." Only now did he turn to face her, seeing the hope leave her eyes as they read his. "You are dead to me."

Trumpets and drums proclaimed that Frederick had arrived. The Prince of Wales went forward to do his duty. The Countess of Essex looked at herself in the window, watching the torchlit tears run down her cheeks.

ANTONIO FOSCARINI'S JAW hung open at the splendour of it all. From his favoured stool in the row of ambassadors, he duly noted for his dispatch the swarthily handsome bridegroom, who brought a blush to Bessy's fair skin with a kiss of unexpected boldness. He joined in the delighted applause, his mind more on arithmetic than romance. He was already composing a paragraph to help his Venetian masters appreciate how expensive it was for their servant to maintain the prestige of the Republic amid such pomp and majesty. To get a vote of ten thousand lire he would need to make a case for twenty, so even this magnificence would require to be magnified. The eighty-gun salute would be doubled, as would the half-million crowns set aside for the nuptial term. The rest of his report would be to scale.

"The arrival of the Prince Palatine has attracted an extraordinary number of people to London," Foscarini would write to the Doge and Senate. "This has caused a great rise in the price of everything—food, dress, upkeep of horses. For the sake of your Excellencies' dignity, I must put my household into new liveries, besides some clothes for myself. Also, I must get more horses, as I lost three when I was honoured by his Majesty's command to join him on the Progress. Moreover, there are expenses for banquets, masques, ballets, tourneys and other entertainments incidental to such rejoicings. All this is very troublesome and causes me anxiety on account of my private fortune diminishing by such expenses during the eight years I have been in your service. Nor can I—nor ought I to—speak of this to others, nor look for any help save from your Serenity and your Excellencies. The Dutch envoy has just received a large donation from his masters. The French, Spanish and Flemish ambassadors are also in receipt of assistance. I am constrained to lament that my private fortune is not such as to permit me to compete with them, as they have their masters' purses behind them. I will, however, do my best. My remarks are merely to express my duty, so that either a resolution may be passed to assist me—or I may be pardoned for the nature of the efforts I shall be forced to make..."

"Foscarini." Ambassador des Bisseaux of France leaned over. "You are impressed?"

"The English are good at this."

"They have to be good at something."

"What are the French good at, seigneur?"

"Finding better matches for our princesses than counts who count for nothing."

FREDERICK had not needed to count very far to work out that the man who came to marry the King of England's daughter was but two strokes of fate from the succession. He had halved that the moment he was greeted at the river stairs by Baby Charles, so fragile that shaking his hand enthusiastically might rank as an assassination attempt. And then he had come upon a Prince of Wales who looked to him more embalmed than alive, hardly stirring in his chair except to shiver. Too excited to sleep, though thankfully unbuttoned after a day of ceremony, Frederick now lifted a glass to Uncle Harry of Nassau, Count

Prefect von Solms and Colonel Count von Schomberg. The unspoken toast was this suddenly real prospect that the landlocked prince of a fragmented Protestant state beset by enemies might one day find himself sharing the throne of this mighty island, upon which no invader had set foot in six centuries.

Their eyes swung to Dr. Christian Rumpf, the Palatine's chief physician, who joined them after stopping for a word with a friend he had not seen since their years at Heidelberg university.

"So?" Uncle Nassau voiced the question in five minds. "What does the fat Dr. Mayerne have to tell you?"

"That our Frederick is a most fortunate prince."

"Amen to that," said Count von Solms.

"The Princess Elizabeth will give him many children."

"Amen to that," said Colonel Schomberg.

"The Prince Charles?" Answering his own question, Dr. Rumpf's hands went up and down like a pair of scales.

"And the Prince of Wales?" Uncle Nassau inclined his head.

"Mayerne says it will take a lot more than a touch of ague to keep him from his destiny."

Frederick said nothing.

FRANCES had crawled into Mrs. Turner's empty bed at Paternoster Row and cried herself to sleep, still in her Banqueting House finery.

"Poor baby," whispered the Countess of Suffolk, drawing the coverlet clear of her daughter's tearstained face. "Why are you such a fool?"

"She loves him." Mrs. Turner shrugged.

"Though he tells her she is dead to him?"

"She knows better."

"Anne, my dear..." The Countess linked an arm in hers to take them outside the chamber. She closed the door quietly behind her. "We are all dead to him. There is no hope until... he is dead to us."

IN THE HARBOUR at Calais, Ambassador Zuñiga was going ashore from his Majesty's ship *Rainbow,* the same in which Admiral Monson had carried him from here to Dover sixteen weeks before. The King had not neglected to send the customary present to a returning envoy. In Zuñiga's baggage was a parcel of silver-gilt. It was the King's final insult that the pieces numbered thirty.

The ambassador's departure had become urgent when he received a message from the Countess of Suffolk. It had occurred to her that the opportunity for which she prayed would present itself amid the hustle and bustle of the German prince's visit. With her cipher letter was her farewell gift of a jewelled dagger inscribed with a single word—*Durindana*. It was the name of the holy sword borne by the legendary paladin of Charlemagne, known to the poets of England and France as Roland, the poets of Italy as Orlando and the poets of Spain as Roldán.

[25]

Sunday the Twenty-fifth of October

GIVE NOT *thy strength unto women, nor thy ways to that which destroyeth kings...*"

From the pulpit of the Prince's chapel at St. James's, the aged Scottish tones of the Reverend Robert Wilkinson offered the last chapter of the Book of Proverbs. Murray returned the momentary lift of his master's eyebrows. Yes, someone or other must have scurried to the King with a tale of that overseen interlude with Frances at the Banqueting House. And the consequence was this arrival on the sabbath following of the dutiful Wilkinson, one of his Majesty's chaplains since his Highness was an infant in Scotland. Thus the parishioners of St. Olave's at Southwark were doing without their rector this morning so that he could deliver King James's message in King Lemuel's words:

"*Who can find a virtuous woman? for her price is above rubies. The heart of her husband doth safely trust in her. She will do him good and not evil all the days of his life...*"

Clearly, the King did not know it was all over with Frances. And Henry was not proposing to tell him yet because, at the right moment, the end of the affair was going to serve as one more reason for getting away to Heidelberg for a while. Though, judged by this first week's observation of the Prince Palatine, it would not take much more to have Henry dispatched there for Bessy's sake. The King would want to be sure that establishing the precedence of the premier Protestant princess of Europe was in safer hands than those of young Fritz. The lad was good-natured enough and would love her well, but he was disappointingly small-timbered. What battles would he ever enter if he feared even the hazard of the tennis court? A fine brother in arms! All week, he had shied away from every challenge. Nor would he meet the Prince at the tiltyard, nor yet at the card table, offering the milksop excuse that nothing could surpass the delight of Bessy's company. They would have done better to wed her to his guardian, the young Count of Nassau, who had conducted his sister's lad here. No doubt about Uncle Harry's valour: at twenty-eight he had already proved himself a true soldier son of William of Orange and a true soldier brother of the heroic Count Maurice.

"Favour is deceitful, and beauty is vain. But a woman that feareth the Lord, she shall be praised..."

Chaplain Wilkinson preached on, but the Prince was no longer listening. He was replaying that mighty tennis match he had fought for three hours yesterday with Uncle Nassau after the poor fellow had yet again to bring his nephew's apology. This time, it was that he dare not catch the Prince's cold, lest it keep him from his sweetheart. At that, the Prince had lashed half a dozen balls out of court in anger, calming down to announce that he would proceed to sweat out not only Frederick's last remaining pretext but also Uncle Nassau's last remaining stake money. And what a game they had played: the lookers-on stamping and cheering in the dedans while the pair cut and drove and smashed off penthouse, at tambour, into gallery; their shirts soaked as they bandied back and forth, deuce upon deuce, until Uncle Nassau was five hundred crowns lighter and Jehu Webb, Master of the Tennis Play, was hoarse from marking the chases. The Prince put up a hand to mask a grin as he recalled his opponent finally going down to a brilliant backhand flick off the wall into the dedans, and the mirth from the galleries as Uncle Nassau hurled after it not only his racket but himself.

A sudden shiver ended the Prince's reverie, and questioned his wisdom in treating his body as though it were of brass. Unprompted, preacher Wilkinson was turning to the Book of Job.

"Man that is born of woman is of few days, and full of trouble. He cometh forth like a flower, and is cut down. He fleeth also as a shadow, and continueth not..."

From that stricture, the chaplain observed, princes were not exempt. "It would surely be a most fearful thing among the common sort of men if one in every three were subject to violent death. Yet from the Conquest downward, of three and twenty deceased princes, eight were slain. Oh, indeed it might be said that a king may sit when other men must stand, and may sleep when other men must wake. He may dice and card—aye, and worse—and who dares say he has done ill? Yet if men respected only quietness and worldly ease, a kingdom were not worth the asking. It is a great labour to govern man, who is so wild and untamed a beast. And besides, what perturbations are in the minds of kings more than of other men! They may fear every cup. Every bite. Every gift. They may fear their enemies and their friends—because they know not their enemies from their friends."

NOT LONG after demonstrating a healthy appetite at his father's table in Whitehall, Henry began to feel shivery again. And at three o'clock in the afternoon he left for his bed at St. James's, unsoothed by Frederick's smugness as the King pronounced upon the folly of exposing an overheated body to the cloister-cold of the tennis court on such a wintry day.

Henry did not think it necessary to summon his own Dr. Hammond from Surrey on the sabbath, but at eight o'clock Dr. Mayerne waddled in, announcing that the King had told him to call. He took the Prince's pulse, and declared it feverous. He inquired as to what the Prince had eaten at dinner, and shook his head as much at the confession of grapes as at the confession of tennis. He assessed the Prince's hot face, white tongue, dry lips and sore eyes, and concluded that it would suffice to order him a cordial potion to appease his thirst, and some broth to be swallowed when the sweating fit subsided. He would have a word with Dr. Hammond on the morrow, and prescribe a clyster if his Highness's bowels had not moved by then. Henry protested that Dr. Hammond's last clyster had worked twenty-five times, plus five more following a purging pill, and had sapped him for a fortnight. Dr. Mayerne sniffed that a clyster of his own prescription would give his Highness less cause to complain. Henry beckoned the man's fat ear close to ask if he knew whose day this was—expressing mock relief at Mayerne's unawareness that it was St. Crispin's, upon which a Frenchman might have it in mind to take revenge against the ninth Henry for the fifth's triumph at Agincourt.

Flocking about the doctor as he came from the chamber, Murray and others of the household were soon reassured. This was none other than the ordinary ague that had reigned over so much of England since the end of summer, and with ordinary treatment by his Highness's Physician-in-ordinary it would take the ordinary course. However, the extraordinary skill and learning of the First Physician would be there for Dr. Hammond should he wish to avail himself of them—or, indeed, should he not. So goodnight.

Mayerne made it easy to see how he had managed to earn the enmity of the medical faculty of Paris, to the point where they had refused to have anything to do with him. They branded him *temulentum, temerarium, indoctum, indignum*—drunken, rash, ignorant, incompetent. He was not brought down, because his successes had won the favour of the King of France, who would have made him First Physician there had not the Queen declined to put herself in the hands of any Huguenot doctor. But once his protector was assassinated, his correct prognosis was that there would be a healthier future for him at the court of King James. And now the imposition of Mayerne was to be the gentle Dr. Hammond's reward for believing that the Fourth Commandment exempted from labour on the sabbath not only "thy son, thy daughter, thy manservant, thy maidservant, thy cattle and the stranger within thy gate," but also thy Physician-in-ordinary to the Prince of Wales.

[26]

Monday the Twenty-sixth of October

IT WAS the first time Paul de Lobel had come to Paternoster Row other than on a Friday, when the College of Physicians' lecture provided his excuse to Madame. Ah, said Mrs. Turner, offering her hand, what a lovely surprise. Ah, said Monsieur, kissing each knuckle in turn, when one's brother-in-law was kind enough to entrust one (all English apothecaries being fools) with his prescription for the Prince of Wales, it was to be expected that Madame would insist that one should oneself conduct it safely into Mayerne's fat hands. But how noble of fate to arrange that one's best route to St. James's should take one's coach past this door.

Monsieur opened his satchel to draw out a green bottle, displaying it like a trophy as he held forth upon his art and mystery even as Mrs. Turner, concerned that he had not long to tarry, led him upstairs. This, declared Monsieur, was no vulgar half-crown clyster. This was a priceless quintessence fit to be piped into the royal rectum. Flowers of gold samphire to moisten and open. Leaves of acanthus to mollify the belly and make the passage slippery. Root of common marsh-mallow to void the yellow bile. Oil of peach kernel to ease the colic. Flowers of melilot and camomile to expel the wind. Ah, said Mrs. Turner, sitting on the bed to apply her own art and mystery to the breech-front buttons before her.

Furthermore, said Monsieur, physic without astrology being as a lamp without oil, one insisted that each herb be gathered when its ruler was in mid-heaven. And that no leaf be retained that was not green and juicy; nor once it lost its colour or smell, and with that its virtue. Such rubbish might be good enough to sell in Cheapside, but it would not do for Monsieur. Ah, said Mrs. Turner, and inquired whether this would do for Monsieur. Or perhaps this. Ah, gasped Monsieur, and thought how different life might be if one's wife had the appetites of one's mistress.

DR. MAYERNE gave Dr. Hammond the look that only a Frenchman who has been proved right can give an Englishman who does not seem to have noticed. Unlike Hammond's clyster, this one had worked gently, moving the choler three or four times. The Prince had found such intermission, even after another restless night, that he was now up and dressed—ready to greet Uncle Nassau and Baby Charles, who were coming to play cards. In galloping French, which he condescendingly translated into ambling English, Mayerne counseled Hammond to have patience, since agues came on horseback but departed on foot. And then he was off to earn an angel or two elsewhere, leaving the Prince's physician to order cooling juleps and tart cordials, and to be sure that they, along with some nourishing soups and jellies, were laced with such antidote powders as unicorn horn, bone of stag's heart and bezoar stone from the stomach of the wild goat of Persia.

Hammond bridled at his role of assistant to this arrogant foreigner who knew nothing of the Prince, let alone loved him. No wonder the physicians of Paris had turned their backs on the man if he behaved with them, too, as though they had not the wit to treat a common tertian. What could be simpler? Yesterday the fever, today the intermission, tomorrow the fever... until the required physic had redressed the four natural humours so that blood, phlegm, the yellow bile of choler and the black of melancholy were again in balance.

"John," said Murray, "do you think his Highness will be fit enough by Thursday for the Lord Mayor's banquet?"

"Don't ask me." Hammond rolled his eyes. "Ask *that man...*"

[27]

Tuesday the Twenty-seventh of October

THE PRINCE was having a good morning. Mayerne was not. He was breaking his brains trying to convince Hammond that bloodletting should begin forthwith. But the fellow remained quite unable to see that, should the fever become continual, they would wish they had opened a vein while the Prince was still strong and not too much oppressed by his symptoms. Hammond would only repeat that here was a textbook tertian, the third day of which was too early to incline to any dramatic course.

As though to prove his point, today's bout duly began at noon, sending the Prince back to bed with his cordials. But Mayerne was still crying for blood when the King's Surgeon, John Naesmith, conveniently put his head round the door to join the consultation on Hammond's side. Was this the way they did things in Paris? Would they treat a dauphin for a condition that had not arrived—and might never arrive? Mayerne stormed out, muttering that the judgment of the First Physician deserved more respect. He had learned no lesson from his difficulties at the French court, since he was sure that his failure to become chief there was entirely because he would not follow Henri Quatre to Rome. Hammond might not match his rank, nor his degrees from Heidelberg, Montpellier and now Oxford, but he was by far the superior courtier. Surgeon Naesmith's appearance had been no accident. And neither had been the King's consent to bring in tomorrow from Hammond's university that eccentric old tosspot, Will Butler of Cambridge, who had been licensed to practise since before Mayerne was born.

The pair were as certain to cross lancets across the Prince's sickbed as they had across the Earl of Salisbury's. Butler had given some hard tooth to Mayerne over his treatment of the great lord, and quickly wound himself out of the business. All Mayerne's attempts since to win his good opinion had been rejected. He would have done better to conceal his view that if this was the most celebrated scholar of medicine in England, then no wonder the King had had to look to France. For his part, Butler's contempt for Frenchmen was legendary.

One who journeyed to Cambridge for a consultation and had been kept waiting for hours made a bow as deep as his veneration when the old man finally came out to meet him. Butler's response was to whip a leg over the stooped head and nip back into his chambers, locking the door behind him. But he would get no homage from Mayerne. Indeed, since he had never achieved a medical degree, he would be lucky to find himself addressed as doctor.

[28]

Wednesday the Twenty-eighth of October

"Now the tongue, Highness... a bit more... uh-*huh*." Old Will Butler peered through smudged spectacles. "Thirsty all the time?"

"All the time."

"So am I, sir. So am I."

Butler had insisted on seeing the Prince alone. Had it not been for Mayerne's display of outrage, Hammond and Naesmith would have objected. Now they were relishing their reward as he paced and growled outside the Prince's doors, waiting for the man to emerge in that tattered blue gown he had worn since Bloody Mary sat on the throne. Dressing after Butler's careful examination, Henry was in no hurry for him to go. This merry old soul was the best of medicines, prattling irreverently about cases and colleagues as he extracted from the patient every last detail of his symptoms.

"Highness, it may encourage you to do as I bid, if I warn you how I treat those who do not."

"Never, never let it be said that I was averse to encouragement."

"Well then, sir, this obstinate creature was coming to see me at the Savoy hospital. He had wasted enough valuable time already, so I gave a signal and two of my men came up behind him—and threw him over the balcony into the Thames. The surprise absolutely cured his ague."

"Are you sure that is quite true, Dr. Butler?" Henry gave him a wry look.

"Is it quite true, Highness? Is it quite true? What do you mean, is it quite true?"

"I mean, doctor, is it quite true?"

"No, sir, of course not... it didn't cure his ague."

"Then we had better drink to his health, doctor. And to yours. And—especially—to mine." Henry poured a julep for himself and a muscatel for Butler, who downed it in one swallow and presented his glass for refilling.

"Sir, this tertian is running its course. You are altogether without fever today. You will be recovered in a week or so, if you are not fool enough to go on defying nature. Your only danger is those who think princes are ague-proof and may be permitted none but the grander ailments—requiring none but the grander physicians. If I had my way, French doctors would be brought in only to treat the French disease."

"Now, now, doctor. Don't go upsetting Mayerne."

"No, sir?" Butler did not conceal his disappointment.

"No, sir." Henry could not keep a straight face. "You can leave that to me."

As Butler came out, Mayerne's eighteen stone and thirty-nine years loomed over his nine stone and seventy-seven years. "Well then, Master Butler?"

"*Doctor* Butler."

"*Master!*"

"Doctor!" Butler looked to the others. "Or he does not get another word from me."

Tempted, Mayerne was silent for a moment as Hammond and Naesmith avoided his eye. But he managed to exhale the required title midway through a massive sigh employing forehead, eyebrows, nose, lips, neck, shoulders, arms and spread fingers. "Well then, doctor..."

"Well then, yourself." Butler drew his flapping gown over his arms. "I gather you gave your poor patient a clyster on the second day."

"Of course," snorted Mayerne. "Belly costive. Pulse feverous. Head aching. Tongue white. Of course."

"Oh, of course." Butler mocked the Gallic accent and gestures. "Could you not pause to consider that you might be too forward for your patient's good? Could you not allow three or four ague fits to come and go so that you might better judge the nature of the affliction before dispersing it into all parts? Dead-dear-dear-dear-dear."

"From that, I take it you have nothing to suggest."

"Oh, no, doctor. You are chief in this case. You must conduct it as you think fit."

"Bleeding is what I think fit."

"Then why did you not bleed at first? It would have made more sense than your purge."

"It makes sense now."

"Not to me. You have missed the tide. You must await the crisis."

"And meanwhile, will you oppose me over even a mild purgation?"

"How mild?"

"Just senna and rhubarb—to lighten him of bile and phlegm, yet leave him loose."

"I concur, doctor. I concur." Butler weaved airily as he moved to go. "Now, I may come in for an hour this afternoon. Or I may not. But I will give you an hour in the morning, I promise. So carry on, doctor—and I will leave you with a saying we have in this country: Agues come on horseback but depart on foot."

Hammond and Naesmith almost felt sympathy for Mayerne as he put his fingers to his great temples.

RETURNING from his seventh trip to the closestool, the Prince invited Murray to judge for himself just how fit he would be to go to the Lord Mayor's banquet tomorrow.

"The Princess will be so disappointed," said Murray.

"Oh, Bessy will not begrudge me this excuse to hold the damned marriage-brokers from my door for a day or two."

"I doubt, sir, there will be any complaint from Savoy. Rumour has it they cannot find even half the dowry they have offered, and are mustering up courage to beg four years to pay."

"Aha! My father will not welcome that. If the French think they are left on their own in the race, they will feel they do not have to run so hard. But then, neither will I."

"Quite." It took more than a tertian to blunt Stuart cunning.

"And another thing."

"Sir?"

"As discreetly as you can, go about arranging to sell off some properties in the Duchy of Cornwall. By my reckoning, we shall need the best part of four hundred thousand crowns to carry the flag to Heidelberg."

"You are set on it?"

"Can you think of a better way of making up to Bessy for missing her Guildhall dinner?"

"Indeed, I cannot." Beyond the Narrow Seas, on the mainland of Europe, waited the prospects, marital and martial, that would decide the destiny of Henry the Ninth.

[29]

Thursday the Twenty-ninth of October

AND SO, my dear, I sent my husband to find out more," said the Countess of Suffolk, just come to Mrs. Turner's from Guildhall, where the Lord Mayor had announced the Prince's apology and returned the company's wishes for a speedy recovery. "But all he could garner was that Henry is so physicked that he dare not stray far from the jakes."

"My Monsieur de Lobel will be delighted that his clysters are royally proven." Mrs. Turner smiled.

"Your Monsieur? You know the little apothecary?"

"The big apothecary." She lifted an eyebrow.

"Anne!" The Countess clasped her arm. "Tell me all."

Mrs. Turner did so, with much mirth and much detail. The Countess had but half an ear to it. Here was the opportunity Providence wished to place in her hands.

"The instant that Madame lets him slip the leash, he cannot wait to run to me! Fingers crossed, there will be more such prescriptions to deliver before the tertian is done."

"Fingers crossed," said the Countess.

IRIS A DUPLEX...wrote Mayerne in his Latin notes on the case, duly recording the portentous appearance of a rare double lunar rainbow in the mist from seven until nine this night, across the very chamber in which his Highness lay. Of what was Providence warning, so that the good might act to avert it or the wicked be deterred? He was still wondering as he switched to his red ink quill to order another of his brother-in-law's noble clysters for the morrow.

THE PACKAGE brought to Paternoster Row late that night by de Lobel's apprentice contained a medicine bottle labeled *Mrs. Turner—to be taken first thing in the morning*. She smiled at the thought. Sweet man! She removed the cork and sniffed at the bottle. Sweet man, indeed! He had filled it with perfume. Musk? Sandalwood? Damask Rose?

"Cantharides?" offered the Countess of Suffolk, impishly.

"I'll ask him first thing in the morning," said Mrs. Turner, anointing her neckline. "Well... maybe second thing."

[30]

Friday the Thirtieth of October

MRS. TURNER'S ROLE in this was to part de Lobel from the satchel containing his clyster for the Prince and keep him occupied upstairs. Ah, she said, relinquishing his hands to close the bedchamber door behind them, Monsieur was so lavish with his enchanting perfume that she had been quite unable to resist the temptation to dab it everywhere, yes, *every*where. Ah, said Monsieur, already savouring his new concoction at her warm neck, how fortunate one was to find such an opportunity to appraise just where it went best. Ah, said Mrs. Turner, arranging herself obligingly on the coverlet, and tucking her hands behind her head. Ah, said Monsieur, from time to time.

Downstairs, the Countess of Suffolk carried de Lobel's satchel from the foot of the stairs, out of the hall and along the passage to Dr. Turner's dispensary, still dusted and shined each day as though the old man were alive. Setting the bag on the table by the scales case, she went to the medicine cabinet, which occupied a whole wall and bore the Turner coat of arms on its central doors. These the Countess opened with the first of the keys Mrs. Turner had given her. With the second, she unlocked the poisons chest.

It was terraced with small, labeled drawers: vitriol, hemlock, stibium, belladonna, rosalgar, white arsenic, aqua fortis, lapis causticus, great spiders, powder of diamonds... all of which she passed by to fetch out a jar of mercury sublimate. This was the one the doctor's widow and the Lord Chamberlain's wife had selected for the task. Physicians used it to treat syphilis. Quacks called it Soliman and sold it to silly women, for whom it more than lived up to its promise to remove freckles, warts and blemishes. It was corrosive. It was colourless. It was odourless. A few grains taken internally might be expected to linger a week or more, their fatal presence indistinct among the symptoms of a simple tertian fever seeming to have taken a turn for the worse.

Catherine, Countess of Suffolk, carried her head as though it wore a halo. Like her sainted namesake martyred on the wheel, she was blessed to be chosen as a humble instrument in God's grand design: to destroy Henry, and save Catholic Europe from the Antichrist. To destroy Henry, and save England's faithful from the final tyranny. To destroy Henry, and save the Howards from oblivion. To destroy Henry, and save Frances from his curse. She opened de Lobel's satchel and unstoppered the bottle.

Upstairs, Monsieur was tidying himself at Mrs. Turner's mirror and grinning that, since one must not discompose Madame by missing a Friday lecture at the College, one would return here when one had completed one's errand to St. James's. Ah, said Mrs. Turner, inquiring as to what might then be Monsieur's pleasure, and thinking that she ought to give the Countess a little longer to be on the safe side. Ah, said Monsieur, and whispered his desire to her. Ah, said Mrs. Turner, and readied Monsieur to enjoy that service forthwith. By the time he did himself up again, his satchel was waiting at the bottom of the stairs.

AGAIN, quiet morning had followed restless night. De Lobel's clyster seemed at first to give the Prince further ease, but by three in the afternoon the doctors were distressed to find him shaking with fever when there should have been intermission. His body was afire, his pulses racing, his breath short, his head bursting, his mouth parched.

The Prince's nose began to bleed, affording some relief by the time it ceased after two ounces. Mayerne hailed nature's invitation to open a vein without further delay. The dour Naesmith was won to his side. Butler and Hammond, though, continued to cling to their insistence that conclusions ought not to be forced so soon. Hammond admitted to himself that he was not sure what to make of this sickness. Was it still no more than a tertian, common or bastard? Or was it becoming something strange? He sensed that Butler was as perplexed, but Old Will was no more going to give him the comfort of such a confession than give Mayerne the satisfaction.

[31]

Saturday the Thirty-first of October

THIS DAY was the worst yet. At times, the Prince grew delirious, his limbs twitching convulsively. His throat became so sore and his tongue so dry that it hurt him to speak, and his doctors to listen. For all that, he was driven to complain of exceeding pain in his forehead, lessened now that his nose had bled again.

"How much lower must he sink for you?" the First Physician hissed at Butler as the doctors moved from bedside to antechamber.

Butler counted fingers. "It is but the seventh day. Too soon to meddle."

Hammond sighed, and returned to open the Prince's door a crack. He could see him shielding his eyes against even the light of a far candle. He could hear him allowing himself a whimper, thinking himself alone. Hammond closed the door and remained facing it for some moments before turning to his colleagues. His gaze settled on Butler. "Dr. Mayerne is right. We must act."

"Gentlemen"—Old Will seized his chance—"since I find you all against me, what can I do but withdraw and leave you to bleed as you think fit?"

"Oh, no, sir!" Mayerne barred his path. "You shall not run away without first telling him yourself that you dared set nothing but cordials and juleps between him and the embalmer."

Naesmith offered deliverance. "Dr. Butler, might not our Prince's courage have concealed from us that his indisposition earlier this month, before you came, was the true onset of this illness?"

"In which case"—Butler sidestepped out of Mayerne's shadow—"you could have had my agreement long ago."

[32]

Sunday the First of November

THE DOCTORS came early to the Prince's bedside after an unquiet All Hallows' Eve. Naesmith lanced the median vein of the right arm, and some relief was apparent—not only on the face of the patient. The Prince encouraged them to let more, but seven to eight ounces was judged enough.

Mayerne's arrogance drew blood from his colleagues, too. Were it not for them, this corruption would have been voided days ago. The First Physician's symptoms increased as the Prince's decreased and, by afternoon, when the royal family arrived to visit, he was bowing low enough and long enough to permit his Majesty to dub each shoulder and bid him rise as *Sir* Theodore. The accolade was not yet forthcoming, but the headier were Mayerne's words to the King, the more put out were his fellows. What madness, when they were becoming uncertain they knew the disease, let alone the cure.

The King, though assured before he even set foot in St. James's that there was no contagion—not another such case in the household here or at Richmond—spent only a few fidgety moments at the bedside, waving away the proffered stool as if it were a plot to stay him. As he shuffled off, Hammond was at his ear. In humble duty, he ought to advise his Majesty that the arrival of the estimable Frenchman and the wise Old Will had given mischief-makers the excuse to put it about that, beyond Hammond, no Fellow of the College of Physicians was trusted with the case. Ever amused to fuel a conflict, the King promised to reinforce him with Dr. Henry Atkins, thrice President of the College, and more than able to take Mayerne a buttonhole lower. That accomplished, the King approached the Lord Chamberlain to complain of the havoc wrought to his best Barbary stallion because some fool stud groom had let a mare kick the stuffing out of him. And, incidentally, how were things with the fair Frances and young Rochester? The Lord Chamberlain confessed that, since the minds of women in love must needs be read backward like the sacred tongue, he was at a loss to understand his daughter. She had taken it into her head to dash off home to Audley End after the Banqueting House reception, and seemed quite unwilling to return to court. Rochester would have to get used to it. Like her dear mother, she was one on her own.

Bessy, determinedly cheerful, sat holding Henry's damp hand. Now and again she would pass his julep and implore him to rest his throat and let her do the talking. Baby Charles just stood by, keeping back tears at the sight of his glorious brother laid low. Frederick, full of his own thoughts and the burden they laid upon his conscience, took refuge in pleasantries with Mayerne across the foot of the bed. The Queen said silent prayers to the pantheon of martyrs whose day this was. To supplement their mediation, she summoned Murray and commissioned him to go to Ralegh on her behalf. She had herself taken his Great Cordial with remarkable success. Others, too, swore by it. Murray was to tell Sir Walter that it was never more needed than now.

The visitors had not long gone, soothed on their way by more optimism from Mayerne, when it became clear that the night was not going to live up to the hopes of the day.

[33]

Monday the Second of November

"HOW MANY MORE of you?" the Prince teased hoarsely as the austere Dr. Atkins did his peering and probing, observed by the others around the bed.

"Highness, you may benefit from more than one kind of good counsel."

"Is it not enough that I am already at the mercy of three kinds?" He surveyed Mayerne, Butler and Hammond. One choleric, one sanguine, one phlegmatic. Clearly, the melancholic Atkins had been needed to complete the set.

"A fourth may further speed your recovery."

"Then summon your entire College—and have me up and about by tomorrow." His throat was hurting. He took a drink.

"Agues, Highness, arrive on horseback but depart on foot."

"I must remember that," said the Prince, and Butler's ancient elbows nudged Hammond and Naesmith.

Henry closed his eyes to signal that he had had enough of them for a while. Their games were ceasing to amuse him. He lay back, his face damp and red, his shivers increasing. Hammond mopped his skin and smoothed the covers about his shoulders. All the way to the antechamber, the doctors could hear the Prince's short breath.

"I, sir," said Atkins, "should have been brought in earlier. Much earlier."

"You, sir," said Mayerne, "should not have been brought in at all. You heard his Highness—what is he to make of it but that suddenly he is in some danger?"

"Do you think he is not?"

"Do you think you would be wrong to join us in sustaining his hope that we possess the skills to cure him?" Mayerne looked for support, but Butler and Hammond were content to leave him to receive a bruising to match that which he had given them.

"In my judgment, this is a putrid fever."

"Oh, I am sure we should never have guessed that."

"I shall be obliged," said Atkins, "if you will hold your tongue until I am done." He allowed a moment to show that his point was taken. "Now, gentlemen, what can the extreme pain in the forehead signify, but that the humours have been thrown with some violence toward the brain? Nevertheless, I have no doubt that the seat of the illness is under the liver, in the first passages, where the malignity is now of such high degree that it is having the effect of poison."

"Poison, sir?" Mayerne went for him. "Poison is not a word to employ unless you mean poison—or you mean to be misunderstood."

"I did say, quite distinctly and in the King's English, *having the effect of poison.*"

"But what is heard by the layman is of more consequence than what is uttered by the physician." Mayerne's mastiff jowls loomed over the defensive Atkins. "How do you imagine the word *poison*"—he let it hang in the air—"would be heard by his Majesty?"

Atkins was down. "I am sure there are better things to occupy us than bandying over a word."

"A word!"

Hammond offered a hand to his College brother. "Perhaps none of us would argue if the malignity is simply described as being of a high degree."

"And perhaps," said Mayerne, snapping at the advantage, "none of us would argue with further bleeding."

"I would argue." Atkins was up again.

"Come, sir. Will you let such corruption linger?"

"No more than you. But I am impressed that those clysters did such good work..."

"*My* clysters," said Mayerne, disarmed.

"...such good work that it would be wise to assess the effects of another before we return to the question of letting blood."

"On that basis—agreed," said Mayerne as though no other opinion mattered.

Butler had not spoken a word. Did he alone fear to voice the possibility that the effect of poison might have been brought about by poison?

RALEGH'S BRITTLE JESTING did more to reveal than conceal his anxiety as he concocted his Great Cordial for Murray in the garden shed laboratory under the Tower walls.

"There you are, David. It should cure him of fever. I only wish I were as sure it would cure him of physicians."

He fell to his knees as soon as Murray had departed, and begged

God to preserve the Prince who seemed his only hope of ever leaving this place.

A COUPLE OF HOURS after the King had come and gone, with Mayerne's renewed assurances of recovery, the Prince became delirious again. He cast himself out of bed, calling for clothes and rapier so that he might be away. Murray took up duty at his bedside, concerned that none other should hear his master's feverish ramblings.

"Oh, Fra," the Prince sighed. "Oh, Fra..."

Murray bit his lip. Would she never leave him be?

THE MIXTURE AS BEFORE, said the label on the bottle delivered to Paternoster Row by de Lobel's apprentice. Mrs. Turner was soon sniffing blissfully at the perfume, and looking forward to entertaining her eager friend on his way to St. James's again in the morning.

"The mixture as before," she said, offering the Countess of Suffolk a turn at the bottle.

"The mixture as before," said the Countess.

[34]

Tuesday the Third of November

STILL USING the licence of his years, Butler had stayed no longer than his hour this morning before disappearing into the taverns of Westminster to distance himself from a case, and a chief, he could not master. Now, with dusk, he came none too steadily into the antechamber to join the others at the table. The day had left them fearful, though it had begun promisingly enough with de Lobel's clyster doing its work. But hour by hour since, though the cordials were redoubled to strengthen the Prince, his fever had become more alarming. As the doctors' forebodings alternately drew them together and drove them apart, their patient's shivering became quite convulsive. His sweating increased. His limbs manifested numbness. And though his tongue and throat grew more parched, he no longer called for drinks to relieve the torment.

"God in heaven!" Mayerne shook his fists at them. "Do you not see that the seat of reason is affected? His brains must be drowning in blood. What further sign do you require before you admit that I was right? We should have opened a vein this morning."

"My dear Mayerne"—Atkins lowered his voice to disdain the First Physician's thunder—"an Englishman is not so ready to take a lancet to his Prince."

"Englishmen! You are too dainty for your Prince's good. If you desire to save him, you must forget who he is. You must proceed as though he were no better than some common fellow. Else he will die because he is the Prince—when if he were any Jack or Tom he might be recovered."

Atkins sniffed. "Only a noddy would adventure to take a lancet to a weakened man."

"Very well then, let us settle for pigeons and cupping glasses."

Coming from the bedchamber, Murray paused at the door as they wrangled. He reached them in a rage. "Damn you all! He lies there—and all you can do is argue, argue, argue..."

* * *

The prince was insensible of it as his head was shaved and the warm carcasses of newly slain doves held to his scalp. To draw from the opposite direction, surgeon Naesmith took his scarificator to make shallow incisions in the flesh of each shoulder so that four-ounce cupping glasses, the air within rarefied by heat, might be applied to good effect. The activity gave the doctors some brief comfort, but it made no difference to the Prince. Soon he sank from drowsiness into delirium, singing incomprehensibly as he plucked at his sheets.

Gathering up his master's shorn hair, a Gentleman Groom of the Bedchamber tiptoed away, his cheeks running with silent tears.

[35]

Wednesday the Fourth of November

HAMMOND wondered why he had been summoned to ride across with the King from Whitehall this afternoon. Was it to obtain his private opinion of Mayerne's conduct of a case now so far out of frame, so confusedly evil and so without hope of amendment that it would soon be more in need of doctors of divinity than of medicine? Hammond's nightmare was that charge would be transferred to him. So he was hardly going to suggest that things might have taken a more fortunate course had they been in other hands. True, the doctors would have fared better, but the patient would be much the same. The King, however, showed little interest in either, and they reached the Clock Tower of St. James's before Hammond had his answer: his task was to prepare his colleagues to agree that, for all the good it could do to wait at the gates of sorrow, his Majesty might as well go hunting at Theobalds. Hammond was taken aback, though he had served long enough to experience the King's aversion to sickbed, childbed and deathbed—even to the point of staying away from his own mother's entombment in Westminster Abbey not a month ago.

This time, Mayerne bowed as low, but not as long. This time, he had no more thought of honour than a pilot expecting the vessel to run aground any moment and proclaim to the world that he knew not where he was. He reported further efforts to draw humours from the brain by applying a cloven cockerel to the soles of the Prince's feet; alas, with no more success than was gained by increasing the cordials in strength and frequency.

"Therefore, Majesty," sighed Mayerne, "there is little to do now but to await the crisis, at which time we may better judge the methods to resolve it."

The King cupped an ear to cue Hammond. "What was that you were saying?"

"Sire, the fact is that if everyone who loves his Highness may visit him, he will have no peace at all. Therefore I beg you to order that none be allowed, beyond those who must of necessity attend upon him."

"So be it."

"And, Majesty"—Hammond would despise himself for this, but what could he do?—"I pray you will permit yourself to be included in that order. His Highness's throat is yet too dry for him to speak without pain, but I fear he will not wish to distress you by remaining silent. Indeed—if I may be frank—to see him in this condition would serve no purpose but to add to your grief, and to his. Your Majesty would be well advised to retire from London for a while."

"Wait!" Mayerne jumped in before the King stopped nodding. "Once the crisis is upon us, we may need to seek his Majesty's authority for perhaps desperate and dangerous measures. We must be able to reach him quickly."

"Quite, quite." The King turned to go. "Come to me in the morning, Dr. Mayerne, and you shall be given all the authority you require before I set one foot on the road to Theobalds."

NOW CAME the Archbishop of Canterbury, with much finger-wagging in the antechamber at those who took infinite care of the mortal body but neglected the immortal soul. He did not remain with them long enough to learn that the Prince was more ill than he and the rest of the world surmised. Hence his question was on its way across the darkened chamber as he followed it to the bedside.

"Really, Highness, how could you let these eleven days go by without once having prayers in your chamber?"

"I confess, your Grace"—each syllable rasped Henry's throat—"that I was not put in mind of it until now."

Before the sentence was half done, the Archbishop had discerned in the candlelight this waxen effigy of the Prince he had not seen since that magnificent night at Woodstock. Perspiration glowed on the shaven skull into which the eyes had sunk deep. Arms and legs poked like sticks at the blankets. Contrite, the Archbishop lay benedictory fingers upon the Prince's crusted lips.

"Dear Prince, please do not try to speak. And forgive me—I am sure you have never failed to pray quietly by yourself."

The Archbishop thought it appropriate to take him through the general confession, assuring him it would suffice to nod at each verse rather than repeat it with him. He lowered his voice as though that might tax the patient's throat less, and he was sure the Prince smiled before tapping an ear to signal him to speak up.

"Almighty and most merciful Father, we have erred and strayed from thy ways like lost sheep."

Nod.

"We have followed too much the devices and desires of our own hearts. We have offended against thy holy laws."

Nod.

"We have left undone those things which we ought to have done. And we have done those things which we ought not to have done."

Nod.

"But thou, O Lord, have mercy upon us miserable offenders. Spare thou them, O God, which confess their faults. Restore thou them that are penitent."

Nod.

"And grant, O most merciful Father, for the sake of Jesus Christ our Lord, that we may hereafter live a godly, righteous and sober life. To the glory of thy holy name. Amen."

Nod.

[36]

Thursday the Fifth of November

IMPATIENT to be on the road to Theobalds, the King was already mounted and waiting when his First Physician arrived. The audience was given at the trot between the Court Gates and Charing Cross, where Mayerne turned left for St. James's, armed with absolute power to do whatever he might consider necessary, with or without the advice of his colleagues. These he called together as soon as he returned, adding his new authority to his old argument.

"Not blood again!" Butler groaned. "Have mercy upon us."

"Gentlemen." Mayerne chose for once to ignore the bait, and in that he was at least assured of the support of Hammond and Atkins. "If nothing is done by man or by nature, his Highness will not survive the week. What places him in such danger is the quantity and malign acrimony of this blood cast violently upwards into the brain. The convulsions and the rest grow worse—though the poor fellow will not let us judge them by pain, because either he is so brave or his spirits are so oppressed that he feels nothing. It is my verdict that opening a vein is the only means to save him." He looked from one to another. "Do I have your agreement?"

"Do you need it?" Atkins tested him.

"I would rather have it."

"I would rather not give it."

"Nor I." Hammond sighted along an accusing finger. "Are you set upon going down in history as the Frenchman who killed our Prince?"

"I have the King's authority to act as I judge fit."

"He has the King's authority!" Hammond secured a sniff from Atkins, and returned to the quarry. "Why do you think him so eager to part with it? He does not want to make any decision that may prove fatal. And if you are fool enough to do so, the King will swear blind he gave you no such fiat."

"I have a witness."

"Namely?"

"Rochester."

"Then, sir, you do not have a witness."

The First Physician rose, felt the invisible noose at his neck and sat down again. Atkins leaned across to pat his arm, soothing him as he might his richest patient.

"Mayerne, my friend, we must stand together in this, or we shall fall separately. The Prince is beyond physic. If the Almighty wishes him to live, then live he will. If not, then not. But should we open a vein and speed fate, the world will say we bled him to death."

Hammond kept to himself his thought that the world would more likely say he was poisoned, as always at the untimely death of princes. But in this case the world could be right. Convulsions. Delirium. Acute head pain. Raging thirst. Urine scant. Apparent remission midway. Nose bleeding. Abdomen distended. Exhaustion. Old Will had recognised the syndrome: why else was he out to provoke Mayerne into dismissing him? And now Atkins, who had so alarmed them by employing the word *poison*, was employing all his guile to stop Mayerne from pulling himself down, and the rest with him.

"You shall have the full support of Hammond and myself if you care to propose the following: One, that we attempt some revulsion from the brain not by bleeding but with a clyster—and simple senna this time, no more of your fancy French concoctions. Two, that we use your royal authority to summon a couple of high officers of the College of Physicians to share our burden."

"And three," added Hammond, "that we administer Ralegh's so-called Great Cordial to his Highness, if only to ensure that the Queen cannot scream that it might have saved him."

Mayerne drooped.

THE COUNTESS OF SUFFOLK did not send to know for whom the bells of St. Paul's tolled when they suddenly ceased pealing joy on this anniversary of the deliverance of King, Prince and Parliament from the Powder Treason and began instead to ring solemn changes. She threw open the upstairs window and put on her St. Catherine face, listening for the change of tune from other neighbourhood belfries as the Archbishop's command to pray for the Prince's life spread from church to church. It was the first the world outside the court knew that he was even in danger.

By the time Mrs. Turner came in, the Countess was in such a state of ecstasy that she could hardly take in the news that, though the Prince was despaired of, he was not yet gone.

* * *

WITH the King's blessing, Rochester had left the company at the gates of Theobalds and spurred on up the Cambridge road to spend an hour or two with his sweetheart. And now he crossed the bridge over the Cam, his canter muffled by the carpet of leaves along the linden avenue to Audley End: a proclamation in stone of the achievement, avarice and ambition of the Howard clan. As much as Rochester, it owed its existence to the favour of King James. As much as Rochester, its prospects grew better as those of the Prince grew worse.

Waiting in the Great Hall for Frances to come down, Rochester found himself beneath a head and shoulders portrait of his rival, and crossed to stand under the Howard and Audley ancestors on the fireplace side. He had been bothered by Overbury's mischievous intelligence that the Prince was still pursuing her and that they had been heard to exchange high words on the night of the Banqueting House reception. So he was looking forward to bringing her the comfort that it seemed unlikely that Henry would trouble their lives for many hours more.

Frances came down the staircase in a full-length cloak, and did not stop as she reached him but led the way out across the innermost courtyard and into the grounds. He read displeasure on her face, and supposed that he was being punished for leaving her alone these eighteen days, as though it were his neglect and not her flight from court that was to blame. He gave her the news about Henry as they passed through the gate of the walled garden to the park beyond. She said nothing. Putting her hands to her hood to pull it in closer, she walked a little faster into the east wind.

MURRAY did not rebuke the page running to say that the Prince was calling out for him. Instead, he broke the same rule of the household and ran to the chamber.

"David... David..."

"Highness, I am here."

"David..."

"I am here." He took hold of the Prince's face as he would a child's and directed its gaze. "I am here."

"I would say somewhat"—the Prince looked into his eyes, lips moving as a spasm took him and he fell back to the pillow—"but I cannot utter it."

Murray did not doubt that though the brain was confused and

the speech confounded, the heart was still full of that girl. Say Henry now asked for her, what would he do? He would go fetch her himself. Anything, *anything,* if it would bring him ease, let alone salvation.

"THEN *tell* me that you do," Rochester was demanding of her.

"I do." Frances scarcely heard a word he had been saying, scarcely felt his arm about her shoulders.

"You do what?"

"Love you," she guessed.

He drew her into the wilderness of bare-branched forest out of sight of the house and turned her for an embrace. She was numb to it all. This was not how the story was meant to end. That last time together, sweet Hally had forced himself to be cruel. What other way could he have put duty before a love such as theirs? Yes, he would have gone on to marry the French princess, and she to marry Rochester. But there would have dawned the day when an older, though not a whit less handsome, widower king would have come riding across the bridge to the side of an older, though not a whit less beautiful, widow countess—and together they would be for all eternity...

Frances declined to be aware of the reality of Rochester. It was not her under whose cloak his hands were busy. It was not her whose arms were round his neck as he palped, parted and primed without response. It was not her whose head rested open-eyed against his chest until her unreadiness became his.

"I am so cold," she said. "So cold." Oh, oh, if only God would let Hally live.

"THE NATION is on its knees for him," said the Archbishop to the First Physician.

"The nation would do well to pray that my colleagues gain the courage to bleed him," said Mayerne.

"The nation will not call it courage if it kills him," said Hammond.

"Gentlemen, *gentle*men." The Archbishop put out an open hand toward the doors to the Prince's chamber. "He may be beyond such argument. It is high time to prepare him his antidote against the fear of death."

They warned the Archbishop that all was much amiss. He set his stool by the Prince's pillow and, leaning close to that drained, pained face, spoke with the confidence that every word would be taken in, and would give comfort. He was gentle and smiling, wagging a finger here and there as he did when the Prince was well. He felt the peace he sought to bring.

"Now, dear Prince, you are not to think my little sermon means that you might not recover. You are indeed in danger, but we all hope and pray that you shall survive. Nonetheless, that will not make it less inevitable that another day will come when death will claim you, as it does all men. Be it sooner, be it later, it is the final reward of our sins." The Archbishop paused to wipe perspiration from the Prince's face and to see it replenished within moments. "But, sir, thinking on death cannot and will not bring it the sooner. Rather will it arm you the more against it. For you will be put in mind of the excellency and immortality of the soul—and, oh, the unspeakable joys awaiting God's children. Consider, sir, all that in exchange for leaving behind the baseness and misery of this earth! All that for leaving behind our vain, inconstant, momentary pleasures! And now I have to ask whether, should it so fall out, you are pleased to submit yourself to the will of God." The Archbishop looked at the half-conscious Prince. "Sir, unless you speak otherwise to me, I know your answer to be, *Yes, yes, yes! With all my heart!* Likewise, I accept your confession that you live and die a member of the true church, wherein only is there true salvation. Likewise, that you believe in the resurrection of the body, life everlasting and the raptures of heaven. And all these, dear Prince, you may look forward to enjoying with the saints. So hallelujah!" As Henry opened and closed unseeing eyes, the Archbishop rose and bowed. "Sir, I will disquiet you no more, except to counsel you to be grateful if God desires to bestow greater glory than can fall to you here below."

Taking his leave of the physicians, the Archbishop prayed that they might yet have as much success with his Highness's body as his Grace had experienced with his Highness's soul.

FLAPPING his hands, Mayerne stood with his back to the antechamber fire. Atkins had been all of six hours fetching his College reinforcements: no doubt they had hoped to delay long enough for the Prince to expire before their reputations could be hazarded in the eyes of the world. And, indeed, when Dr. Richard Palmer and Dr. John Gifford did arrive, it was with the zeal of pressed sailors. They hardly had time to put off their cloaks—with apologies for having been out visiting—before the First Physician had them in to see the Prince and out round the table to hear his renewed argument for opening a vein.

"Too late for that." Gifford's response, without even a moment's reflection, told Mayerne that Atkins had schooled his fellows.

"*Far* too late," echoed Palmer.

"And if we leave it too late for this"—Hammond displayed a vial of pale green liquid—"which of you will tell her Majesty that you let her son die rather than try such a renowned remedy, the efficacy of which she herself attests to, and against which none of us has ever heard a word?"

"Not Ralegh's Great Cordial!" Butler supposed right and five noses wrinkled in judgment.

"It could be poison." Palmer took the vial and held it to a candle, then removed the stopper and smelled the contents. "Men locked away in the Tower have been known to plot revenge."

"Better try it on a dog first," said Atkins.

"Here"—Hammond seized the vial and swallowed a mouthful—"try it on me. If I am still alive in the morning, you may safely give it to his Highness."

For the present, they decided to administer a more ancient cordial, diascordium, made from leaves of water germander. It was virtuous as a great inducer of sweat and urine, though it would generate such heat that the doctors debated yet another hour before agreeing the extent to which it ought to be tempered with cooler cordials. In the event, its operation was slight, but they did not judge it wise to go against nature by forcing a sweat with warmed blankets. The Prince sank back into delirium.

At midnight, as the doctors again gathered round his bed, the Prince reached out to catch surgeon Naesmith's hand and draw him close. He thought it was Murray—Naesmith could make out the word *David*—but the rest of his speech was quite garbled. Seeing that he was not understood, the Prince turned away with a sigh. Murray was sent for.

"Sir." Left alone with his master, he took a hand in both of his.

"Ah, David." The Prince began a smile, but was distracted by a new cough. Murray was thankful Mayerne had advised him that this catarrh was a good sign: the brain was thus voiding itself of superfluous humours.

"Highness, I beg you, tell me whatever is troubling you."

"That... secret cabinet... in my closet."

"Yes."

"Burn... everything."

"Highness, it is not necessary. You are going to live."

"Promise."

"You must believe me, sir. You must."

"Promise." The word rattled in his parched throat.

"I promise." Murray resolved that he was not going to keep his word while the Prince yet had breath in him.

[37]

Friday the Sixth of November

HIS HIGHNESS'S GUARD trod softly through the small hours as they made their rounds of the Palace. None of the household was abed. Doublets unbuttoned, hose untied, they took what rest they could where they could. Officers, greater and lesser, nodded off in chairs or slumped over tables. Grooms and pages curled against walls or napped in chimney corners, their hearts sick with deferred hope.

Cornwallis was among the many who kept vigil in the Chapel Royal, where the prophetic text of the visiting chaplain on the eve of the Prince's illness seemed still to hang in the air: *He cometh forth like a flower, and is cut down.* Oh, Death, besought Sir Charles, will you gather none but our fairest, scarce-blown rose? Like every officer in St. James's this night, he knew the grim reaper would scythe their hopes and expectations in the same sweep that claimed their master. The household would fall with him. They were his men and none other's. By the time Baby Charles was old enough to be proclaimed Prince of Wales, they would long be deprived and dispersed. The King was never going to allow about his second son spirits grown to such pride and power with his first. Money, too, would argue them from office. For until Charles came of age, Henry's revenues would revert to the King, who was sure to find better use for an annual windfall above a million crowns than maintaining officers devoted to that son who might soon have deposed him.

Three hours after midnight, a groan began in the antechamber and gathered like a wave through the Palace. Rumour that the Prince had given up the ghost was out of the gates and on its way to the city before the truth set off in vain pursuit. Coming from the chapel, Cornwallis was given a path through the silent press outside the antechamber doors. He learned from Murray that they thought the Prince gone when he fainted away after a series of violent convulsions that had racked spine, shoulders, arms and tongue. But he had come round and, bathed and lain in fresh linen, was now resting quietly in a cold sweat.

"He is loath to leave us," said Murray.

"Death is loath to take him," said Cornwallis, his eyes as damp as his throat was dry. "Death hovers... in doubt as to what to do. His hard heart is moved to pity by his Highness's young years, by the triumphs awaiting him on earth, by this great cry of his servants, and by the tears of all our land. Death hovers... as though expecting some merciful message from heaven."

"Try to get some sleep, Charles."

Murray returned to the doctors, for once united as they huddled together against the looming tempest. If the patient lived, it would be no great thing for six famous physicians to have cured him of an everyday fever. If he died, then their ignorant bungling would have lost the delight of mankind, the expectation of nations, the strength of his father, the glory of his mother and the hope of the reformed religion throughout Europe.

FRANCES leaned up on her pillow, quite certain that what had roused her in the middle of the night was Henry calling her name. She listened for it again, until she gave up for shame. Why did she hope to hear it a second time when she could no more respond than the first?

"WE MUST SPEAK with one voice," said Hammond.

"Or go hang," said Atkins.

All looked to the First Physician, who drew himself up from the table and shuffled across to warm his backside at the fire. Atkins and Hammond swung on their stools to face him. Gifford and Palmer needed only to turn their heads. Old Will, however, preferred to sink chin to chest and close his eyes.

"Gentlemen," said Mayerne, thumbs lodged under his armpits to signal that advocacy was about to take place, "we must expect, as always, to find that the easy cure we could not see while the patient lived, even the blind will discern once he is lost. But the fact will remain that we tried everything that art or experience could provide. We omitted no duty. We did nothing but by common consent. We gave his Highness no substance of which we did not know the composition and the apothecary. But if it pleases not God to give his blessing to the means, shall foolish people rail upon the poor physicians for lacking the power to alter his providence?"

"Ha!" Butler's head came up. "And shall the poor physicians lie with one voice about those several occasions upon which they spoke with four, five or six? To bleed or not to bleed? To clyster or not to clyster? To sweat or not to sweat? To give Ralegh's cordial or not to give Ralegh's cordial? Or shall we speak the truth—and say that God obtained his will by creating such confusion among us as he employed to overthrow the Tower of Babel?"

"Old man"—Mayerne swayed forward as though to advance upon him, but to visible relief swayed back again—"are you telling me you will not subscribe your name to the general opinion?" He paused to allow enough time to discern that no answer was forthcoming. "Because, if you are, be sure I shall announce that for each hour you condescended to consult with us at that table, you deserted his Highness for five—preferring to pickle your brains in some alehouse or other."

Butler muttered something about Frenchmen, and sunk his head again. Mayerne resumed the case they would present to the world, apportioning blame to everything from the heat of the sun to the phases of the moon.

"And so, gentlemen, his Highness, already of a very warm constitution, heated his blood extraordinarily by hour upon hour of violent pursuits. It made no difference to him that this was a summer excessive in degree and continuance beyond the memory of man. He continually fatigued his body, scorning rest all day long. Furthermore, he ate strangely to excess of fruit, especially melons and half-ripe grapes. And he took his fill of raw and cooked oysters beyond rule or measure. Then, in order to cool the burning heat which worked in his body, he would plunge into the river and remain there several hours." The tilt of Mayerne's head invited confirmation from the Prince's physician.

"Quite so, doctor," said Hammond, taken by the man's mastery.

"After all these irregularities, gentlemen, was it any wonder that he fell to a fever? Though heaven only knows how long he concealed it, his invincible courage forbidding him to admit that he could ever take ill like ordinary men. It is apparent that, even after we were called in, his Highness continued to hide the true extent of his malady. We could never dream of his danger until, too late, the symptoms overcame his ability to mask them—and ours to treat them."

Atkins raised a hand. "There will be evil rumour..."

"I know, I know," said Mayerne. "But I do not propose to lose sleep over it unless"—his eyes searched theirs—"unless there are any of you who do not share my confidence that when we six are appointed to open the body we shall discover nothing to oppose our judgment that he fell to the rage of a malicious and extraordinary burning fever.

When I had lost one shaft,
I shot his fellow of the self-same flight,
The self-same way to find the other.

—WILLIAM SHAKESPEARE,
The Merchant of Venice

Afterword

TEN MONTHS later came the strange death of the next great enemy of the house of Howard: Sir Thomas Overbury.

As with the Prince of Wales, it was officially at the hand of God and none other. As with the Prince of Wales, that verdict might have gone down in history. Two years on, however, an appprentice of apothecary de Lobel was moved by the fear of eternal damnation to confess having poisoned Overbury. He had been bribed by Mrs. Turner to add mercury sublimate to a clyster prescribed by the First Physician to the King.

The Lord Chief Justice and the Attorney General suspected that Henry could have fallen to "a fellow of the self-same flight." But they were commanded to let the matter drop—and the King James version prevails to this day.

ONE may find the following warrant among the State Papers preserved in her Majesty's Public Record Office:

April 21, 1613. The Council to the Lieutenant of the Tower. Order to receive and keep close prisoner Sir Thomas Overbury, against whom the King is displeased for a matter of high contempt.

James had been induced to appoint him ambassador to Muscovy, and Overbury had been induced to refuse to serve abroad. For that offence he was rowed under guard through Traitors' Gate and locked away. He was never to leave that place, alive or dead, and his bones still lie imprisoned under the Tower chapel of St. Peter ad Vincula. Overbury had no doubt as to who was at the root of it all: he declared himself to the Lieutenant as "the Countess of Suffolk's prisoner." She wanted him out of the way so that he could not give evidence to the Archbishop's commission about to be set up to grant Frances her nullity.

At first, Overbury believed Rochester would use his influence to get him out. But, after five months of misery, he realised that his friend had sacrificed him. So he wrote his last known letter, threatening that "whether I live or die, your shame shall never die but ever remain to make you the most odious man in the world." To achieve this, he was setting down "secrets of all kinds" in a document under eight seals, and smuggling it out to his friends. The letter survives. The document under eight seals does not. Suddenly, Overbury was found dead in his cell. And ten days later the nullity was delivered. The Archbishop had blocked it month after month until the King packed in two extra mitres to give Frances her majority, Rochester his bride—and Spain's principal agent her grip on England's principal minister.

Two years passed. Rochester was promoted Earl of Somerset and appointed Lord Chamberlain. His wife became pregnant. His father-in-law became Lord Treasurer. His mother-in-law had him pushing for Prince Charles to marry the Infanta who had been rejected by Henry. The Howards were at the height of their power. Then de Lobel's apprentice made his confession. At the trials that followed, Attorney General Sir Francis Bacon proclaimed Overbury a victim of "the arrow that flieth by night." The phrase was particularly apt because he was wondering whether this was the proverbial second arrow shot to find the first.

Mrs. Turner was hanged, along with the Lieutenant (a Howard placeman) and two other small fry. Frances and Rochester were also sentenced to the gallows, knowing in advance that the King would reprieve them as mere accessories. De Lobel was awhile under suspicion but did not come to trial. Neither did the Countess of Suffolk, though implicated by two of those condemned.

James liked to be regarded as the British Solomon, holding it the honour of a king to search out a matter. But not this matter.

He silenced all attempts to connect the deaths of Overbury and the Prince of Wales. He was notably angry with Lord Chief Justice Coke, who conducted the investigation into the Tower murder. The great judge had questioned Frances and others about the death of Henry, and noted such items as Sir Arthur Mainwaring's having slept at Mrs. Turner's. In public, he contained himself save for one outburst that undid him: *God knows what became of that sweet Prince, but I know somewhat...*

That can be looked at now in the light of Ambassador Foscarini's secret dispatches in the archives of Venice, reporting that Mrs. Turner "is said to have confessed in private to knowing something about the poisoning of the Prince." He also passed on that Frances had "confessed having recourse to witchcraft in order to obtain the love of the Prince, and the statue made for this purpose has been found."

Coke's rival, Attorney General Bacon—on the winding stair up, as the Lord Chief Justice came tumbling down—was cunning enough to leave to the King the question of what would be convenient if the matter of Henry's death arose. Bacon inquired thus: "Whether, if Rochester confess at any time, his Majesty shall stay trial in respect of farther examination concerning practice of treason, as the death of the Prince, or the like; for till he confess the less crime there is no likelihood of confessing the greater?" Bacon went on to list tidbits from Coke's files. A report that the late Howard Earl of Northampton had said the Prince "would be a tyrant if ever he came to reign." An overheard conversation suggesting that Henry "came to an untimely end by a mistress of his." Mrs. Turner pointing out "the man who poisoned the Prince." A letter to the Spanish Netherlands stating that "the first branch was cut from the tree, and that there should, ere long, be joyfuller news." And attempt by Rochester and others to have de Lobel appointed apothecary to the new heir to the throne.

To all this, the King wrote in the margin, "I have commanded you not to expatiate nor digress upon any other points." Bacon did as he was bid. The fact remains: He could not suppose there might be a confession by anyone, without presupposing that there might have been a murder by someone.

Clearly, the Attorney General did not regard Mayerne's autopsy report with the reverence of today's historians. Neither did James; else this King who did not suffer geniuses gladly would have dismissed out of hand Bacon's suspicions, if not Bacon himself. Yet it is that report by Mayerne (lunar rainbow and all) and the inference drawn from it by a single Victorian physician, Dr. Norman Moore, which has led historians since 1882 to record that Henry was a victim of typhoid. However, a closer look shows Moore admitting that Mayerne's meagre postmortem did not even involve opening the intestines. So he had no evidence of ulceration of the ileum, a principal distinguishing feature of this fever. Moore nevertheless announced that typhoid "is the only diagnosis consistent with an epidemic fever attacking several in one house." He ignored the fact that, neither in 1612 nor since, had there been the slightest suggestion that any member of that vast household but the Prince himself had been so attacked. Mayerne had never heard of typhoid, and would not have known that it is spread by contaminated water or food, but had there been any kind of epidemic at St. James's he could never have included in his case notes this remark: "Not one of those who drew in a thousand times the breath of his Highness and continually watched about him felt at all the worse."

Today, it is accepted that the symptoms of typhoid can resemble those of other conditions—among them, poisoning by mercury sublimate.

FRANCES AND ROCHESTER spent six years at ease within the Tower walls. He was allowed to wear his Garter ribbon, she was allowed three maids. In 1619 they were briefly joined by the Earl and Countess of Suffolk, finally brought down for defrauding the Treasury. We now know that the King's ambassador in Madrid had already discovered that the Countess had been paid "very great sums" for secret services to Spain, and that Zuñiga had said of the agent code-named Roldán, "She would sell her soul to hell." Since she was never tried for treason, it is probable that she was a double agent.

The only child of Frances and Rochester, the virtuous Lady Anne Carr, is said to have fainted away when she learned that her parents were convicted murderers. From that girl, who married the first Duke of Bedford, is descended Lady Elizabeth Bowes-Lyon, better known as the Queen Mother. She married into the royal family in 1923, and her husband became George the Sixth when his brother, Edward the Eighth, abdicated. Her grandson, Charles, is the present Prince of Wales. It is ironic that today's successor to Henry should turn out to be the descendant of his mistress and his rival.